A TWIN CROWN

CAPTAIN
⚓F
FATES

PRAISE FOR THE TWIN CROWNS SERIES

'TWIN CROWNS cast a spell on me from the very first pages with its glittering blend of harrowing adventure, charming wit, and intricate world-building. Add in delightful romance and two unforgettable narrators, and I was thoroughly bewitched by this marvelous book! Don't miss it!'
Sarah J Maas, #1 *New York Times* bestselling author of
A Court of Thorns and Roses series

'TWIN CROWNS has all the charm of THE PRINCESS BRIDE and all the stakes of GAME OF THRONES – but Wren and Rose are in a league of their own. Addictive, swoony, tender and vivid – I loved it with all my heart.'
Kiran Millwood Hargrave, bestselling author of
The Mercies and *The Girl of Ink and Stars*

'Riotously funny, fast-paced and dripping with romance, TWIN CROWNS manages to deliver a tale as familiar and nostalgic in the way of childhood blankets and fireflies in jars, while at the same time wholly refreshing with its levity, charm and quirky tale of sisterhood rediscovered. TWIN CROWNS is so joyous that days after reading, I'm still grinning.'
Roshani Chokshi, *New York Times* bestselling author of
The Gilded Wolves and the Aru Shah series

'An absolute delight from start to finish. TWIN CROWNS is a dazzling gem of a book. Magical, clever, surprising, and pure fun from its captivating start to its spectacular finish. If you love wicked kings, sexy bandits, and sister stories that are full of heart, this is a must read.'
Stephanie Garber, *New York Times* and
Sunday Times bestselling author of *Caraval*

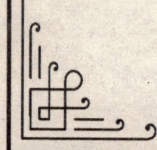

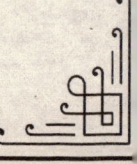

'Doyle and Webber give readers twin plots of daring deception, spectacular settings and two very appealing love interests . . . you'll root for both twins in this dangerous web of intrigue.'
Kendare Blake, #1 *New York Times* bestselling author of the *Three Dark Crowns* series

'Reading TWIN CROWNS left me giddy. Adventure, romance, TWO incredible protagonists, magic, sisterhood . . . I loved it.'
Laura Wood, author of *A Sky Painted Gold*

'Fresh, funny and exciting.'
Louise O'Neill, bestselling author of *The Surface Breaks*

'A gripping fantasy series for teens'
The Times – one of the 50 best Irish children's books to buy for Christmas.

'I haven't cried over a book in ages . . . I rarely laugh out loud and I'm also just bawling my eyes out!'
Amber Bayley, author of *The Haven Ten*

'Such a rollercoaster, a million out of five stars'
Ella likes Books

'One of my favourite reads of the last year'
Sam Falling Books

'A magnificent marvel of a book'
Becca, *Pretty Little Memoirs*

'I couldn't put it down!'
readinginwonderland.com

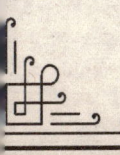

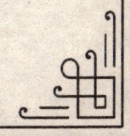

**THE BESTSELLING
TWIN CROWNS SERIES:**

Twin Crowns
Cursed Crowns
Burning Crowns

KATHERINE WEBBER

A TWIN CROWNS NOVEL

CAPTAIN OF FATES

ELECTRIC MONKEY

First published in Great Britain 2025 by Electric Monkey, part of Farshore
An imprint of HarperCollins*Publishers*
1 London Bridge Street, London SE1 9GF

farshore.co.uk

HarperCollins*Publishers*
Macken House, 39/40 Mayor Street Upper, Dublin 1, D01 C9W8, Ireland

Text copyright © Katherine Webber 2025
Map illustration copyright © Tomislav Tomic 2025

The moral rights of the author and illustrator have been asserted

PB ISBN 978 0 00 868852 3
Special edition (Land) ISBN 978 0 00 875254 5
Special edition (Sea) ISBN 978 0 00 875255 2

Printed and bound in the UK using 100% renewable electricity
at CPI Group (UK) Ltd

1

A CIP catalogue record for this title is available from the British Library

All rights reserved. No part of this publication may be reproduced, stored in a retrieval system, or transmitted, in any form or by any means, electronic, mechanical, photocopying, recording or otherwise, without the prior permission of the publisher and copyright owner.

Without limiting the author's and publisher's exclusive rights, any unauthorised use of this publication to train generative artificial intelligence (AI) technologies is expressly prohibited. HarperCollins also exercise their rights under Article 4(3) of the Digital Single Market Directive 2019/790 and expressly reserve this publication from the text and data mining exception.

Stay safe online. Any website addresses listed in this book are correct at the time of going to print. However, Farshore is not responsible for content hosted by third parties. Please be aware that online content can be subject to change and websites can contain content that is unsuitable for children. We advise that all children are supervised when using the internet.

MIX
Paper | Supporting responsible forestry
FSC™ C007454

This book contains FSC™ certified paper and other controlled sources to ensure responsible forest management.

For more information visit: www.harpercollins.co.uk/green

For Kevin, who makes me believe in true love and for our daughters, Evie and Mira, who light up my world

E
N
S
W
Gilded Palace
Goldwave Mountain
King's Beach
Lana's Bakery
King's Cove
Pearl Beach
Sugar Cove
Shipwreck Bay
SOLVORA

Solvoran Ring

Farmland

Lowlands

Cherry Cove

*Go past the horizon, across the sea
And there you'll find your destiny*

CHAPTER 1
Marino

Captain Marino Pegasi could not remember the last time he had spent so much time on land.

He was at his fourth ball in as many weeks and had been introduced to countless 'eligible young ladies', who had all started to look the same after a while.

It was not that Marino didn't love to dance. He enjoyed a party as much as anyone, maybe even more than most, but where some might become seasick after weeks bobbing above the waves, he found himself becoming waltz-sick after weeks bobbing around the dance floor.

The constant spinning round and round and round, the faces changing but the conversation ever the same. He stayed courteous, bowing to each partner at the end of the dance, even as he heard the whispers from the nobles and royals of Eana, wondering who, if anyone, Captain Marino Pegasi would dance with a second time.

He knew he made a striking figure in the ballroom, standing taller than almost all the guests in his perfectly tailored burgundy frock coat and fitted black trousers, with an embroidered waistcoat over his starched ruffled collar and rakishly tied cravat. And of course, he wore his earrings, three simple gold studs on one earlobe, and two small pearls on the other. At these events, Marino had his tightly coiled black curls tied into a knot at the nape of his neck, but a few always managed to spring free, brushing against his cheekbones as he danced.

And dance he did, with partner after partner. Until the evening came to an end, and he could collapse in a luxurious bed in his guest room at Anadawn Palace, wishing that he was in his own bed on his ship instead.

But he knew that would be rude not only to Queen Rose and King Shen, who were graciously hosting him at Anadawn until his next voyage, but also to his sister, Celeste, who expected to see him at breakfast where they could regale each other with tales of the evening before.

Marino feared he was becoming more proud by the day, increasingly unimpressed with the ladies paraded in front of him.

He would never admit as much to his sister or to Rose, who was almost a sister to him. He knew they were trying to help him. And he had learned long ago that when they teamed up they were a force to be reckoned with. They were certain that this time spent on land, away from his ship, was the perfect opportunity for him to find his match, someone to keep his bunk warm. Someone to care for him, they claimed. So, he kept smiling and laughing and made sure they only ever saw the charming Marino they knew and loved.

How could he tell them that for him love was complicated? Marino had his sights set on a life of adventure, and that meant he was always going to be at sea, looking to the horizon. He was far too much of a gentleman to make any false promises of settling down to the ladies presented to him.

In his heart, Marino dreamed of a romance greater than any he could find in a ballroom. It wasn't that he didn't want love, the opposite of it, he wanted the kind of love that inspired grand gestures and epic adventures. The kind of love those closest to him had found.

It felt like everyone around Marino was starry-eyed and love-drunk. Everyone but him.

Queen Rose and King Shen had wed several months ago, but Rose was still the blushing bride. She could not stop looking at Shen. And when he looked back at her, well, the heat in his gaze was enough to raise the temperature of the entire room. It made Marino feel oddly . . . lonely, in a way he never felt when he was on his own in the middle of the sea.

And nothing had surprised Marino as much as Celeste finding, and keeping, love herself. Celeste had always sworn off true commitment, saying there were too many fish in the sea for her to ever choose only one, and yet here she was, canoodling with Princess Anika of Gevra. Celeste shunned propriety and only danced with Anika at the balls, and the two were a liability on the dance floor – twirling and prancing around with no regard to what song was playing, only dancing to the tune in both of their hearts.

At least Rose's sister, Queen Wren, and her beau, Tor, were away, spending the summer in Ortha, where Wren had been raised. As much as Marino liked both Wren and Tor, he was relieved not to be *entirely* surrounded by loved-up couples.

Finally, it was the last ball of the summer.

It was nearly autumn, but the night air was still warm and inviting enough for the ball to be held outside in the grand Anadawn courtyard. Queen Rose had enchanted the candles to float in the air and garlands of flowers were strung overhead. The musicians played the favourite songs of the season, songs Marino had heard so often, he knew he would never forget them even if he tried.

His back was straight as he twirled Lady Sophie, a petite blonde noblewoman visiting from the northern coastal town of Norbrook. Next to them, Celeste and Anika twirled and laughed, and Marino wished he could dance with someone with as much abandon. Celeste caught his eye and nodded her head towards Lady Sophie, eyes wide with a silent question. Marino shook his head slightly. No, Lady Sophie was not destined to be the great love of his life. Celeste rolled her eyes in response and then focused her attention back to Anika.

'Are you enjoying the evening, Captain?' Lady Sophie asked, and Marino felt a quick pang of guilt for not trying harder to get to know her. It was so easy to keep things at surface level, to smile and charm and never truly let his guard down. Perhaps he should at least make a small effort. It was the last ball, after all.

He rewarded her with a warm smile. 'I am,' he said. He saw how she blushed in response to his smile, which he had to admit was pleasing, even if he had no romantic interest in her. He knew that dancing at a ball, being seen as the catch of the season, was no true hardship. He simply missed the sea, and that wasn't Lady Sophie's fault. 'It is a beautiful night. Queen Rose is, as ever, an exceptional host.'

'This is my first Anadawn ball,' Lady Sophie said, sounding a bit breathless with excitement about it all. 'I've never seen magic before, not until tonight. It's spectacular.'

The land of Eana was ruled by witches gifted with a unique magic. For all of Marino's childhood, witches had been banished and abhorred, and they had only come back into their rightful power when the twin witch queens, Rose and Wren, had been reunited just before their eighteenth birthday.

Rose had been raised in the palace, with no knowledge of her true heritage nor the existence of her twin. Meanwhile Wren had spent her whole life living with a hidden sect of witches far on the western coast of Eana, preparing for the moment when she would take Rose's place and usher in the reign of the witches. Back to their rightful place, ruling the land that had been created by, and named for, Eana the first witch. And while things had not gone exactly to plan for either twin, the result had been something even better – two queens working together for the good of their people. And with the return of the witches to power, and the strengthening of the land itself, many Eanans had discovered their own latent magic. Including Marino.

Marino hadn't known he was a witch until Rose and Wren welcomed magic back into the kingdom. He had been surprised, and then pleased, to know he had the gift. It had once been believed that witches were only able to access one of five distinct strands of magic. Enchanters could do small magic and minor spells of enchantment or manipulation. Healers were gifted with the ability to cure those who were ill or injured. Tempests could control the weather, calling down storms or shifting the wind. Warrior witches had tremendous strength and agility and were unparalleled on the battlefield. Seers could glimpse the future, usually by reading the movements of flocks of beautiful starcrest birds that were unique to Eana.

When Marino had first discovered his witch heritage, he realised he was a natural tempest. It was a joy to sail on the sea and practise his gift – catching a strand of wind in his hands and then sending it to fill his sails so his ship practically flew over the waves.

Now, since Rose and Wren had freed all five strands of magic, Marino could access *all* his gifts. Every witch still had a dominant power, but with practice, they could master all five strands. Marino's power was growing stronger all the time.

Hearing Lady Sophie's awe made Marino feel a twinge of guilt for being so immune to it all. 'There is nothing quite like an Anadawn ball,' he said, and he meant it. Then he turned his attention back to Lady Sophie. 'And what do you like to do in Norbrook?' She was a beautiful dancer, but he felt no draw towards her, nothing made her stand out from any of the many others he had danced with all summer, but he should give her a chance.

Lady Sophie held her head high. 'I am quite an accomplished pianist. And I paint as well.' She sounded unbearably smug, and Marino had a sneaking suspicion that she was exaggerating her talents.

He nodded, trying to muster more interest. 'What do you like to paint?'

'Horses, mostly. We have quite the impressive equine collection, you know. And the occasional self-portrait, of course.' She fluttered her lashes coyly, as if even she was immune to her own charms.

Marino cleared his throat. 'And do you like the sea?' Perhaps she painted seascapes. 'I've not been to Norbrook, but I've sailed past it before. The coast is quite dramatic.'

She scrunched her nose up. 'The sea! Goodness no. The salty air ruins my hair, not to mention my jewellery!' Her laugh was high and sharp. 'And the smell of fish! No, it is not for me. I prefer to stay in town. Or go riding.'

'But!' she went on, clearly seeing Marino's disappointment and seemingly remembering what he did. 'I do love to watch the sun set from my father's house. The light *is* very pretty when it dances across the waves.'

'So it is,' said Marino, with a deep sigh. Saying she liked sunsets did not endear her to him, not because he disagreed, but because he had yet to meet someone who didn't enjoy a sunset. It was akin to saying that she enjoyed breathing.

They finished the dance in silence, and Marino bowed politely before turning away and striding to the edge of the dance floor.

'Marino!' Rose swept towards him with a warm smile. 'Come, let us dance.' Rose looked radiant. She was wearing a flowing pale green gown embroidered with golden thread and her long chestnut hair was loose and hung to her waist. On her head was a delicate gold crown inlaid with emeralds, and matching jewels winked on her wrist and fingers. She beamed at Marino, green eyes sparkling, and Marino couldn't help but smile back at her.

'How did you find Lady Sophie?'

'A very fine dancer,' said Marino diplomatically.

'And? Do you want me to invite her to tea tomorrow? I've not spent much time with her, but I am happy to get to know her better if you enjoyed her company.' Rose's eyes were wide and hopeful.

Marino raised his brows. 'I do not think she is the one for me. But I appreciate the effort.'

Rose sighed. 'Marino! It is the last ball of the season. And none of the ladies in Eana have caught your eye. No noblewoman *or* any of the witches! How will we ever find you a love match?'

'Rose, with Wren away, surely you have more important things to do, like running a kingdom? Playing matchmaker for me should be at the very bottom of your to-do list.'

Rose wound her arm through his and guided them towards the drinks table, the very place he had been heading before she caught him on the dance floor. 'Marino, finding you a love match is not on my to-do list. It gives me much joy!'

'At least one of us is enjoying it.'

Rose rolled her eyes. 'Oh, Marino! You are impossible. But you know I am not one to back away from a challenge.'

'I know that all too well,' said Marino, with an affectionate grin. 'We grew up together, remember?'

'Rose, my love, my forever queen, are you badgering poor Marino again?' Shen had appeared next to them, looking debonair as always in his red and gold royal regalia. Through his marriage to Rose he was now a rightful king of Eana, but he still ruled his own land, the desert-based Sunkissed Kingdom.

The Sunkissed Kingdom had been lost in the sands long ago, hidden from the rest of Eana, but Shen and Rose had rediscovered it. When they did, they found not only an entire kingdom, but Shen's history and heritage, as well as his right to the throne. Now the pair of them ruled both lands together, allowing the Sunkissed Kingdom and Eana to prosper alongside each other.

Rose pouted. 'Shen! I'm not badgering him. I'm helping him!'

Shen raised his brows. 'Marino?'

Marino cleared his throat. 'Ah, well, she did take me to the drinks table when I sorely needed a drink. So, yes, she has been helping.'

Rose preened. 'See?' Then she swatted Marino on the arm. 'Marino! I am helping more than that!'

Shen laughed as he handed Marino a glass of wine. 'I'm sure you are missing your ship. And the freedom that comes with it. Perhaps I can join you on a voyage one day.'

'You will do no such thing,' said Rose. 'Leave me to run both of our kingdoms while you go off gallivanting with Marino? I think not!'

Marino clinked his glass to Shen's. 'Ah, as we both know, the king answers to no one but his queen.'

'Too true,' Rose said smugly. But then she leaned up to press a kiss to Shen's cheek. 'I suppose if you really wanted to join Marino on a voyage you could. But wouldn't it be more fun if I came along too? And Celeste and Anika! Why don't we plan it for when Wren and Tor are back?' She turned to Marino. 'You know, I've never been to the southern continent. And I've always wanted to go to Demarre. Is it nice in the autumn?' She clapped her hands together with glee. 'Oh! It could be an official royal visit. What a wonderful idea, Shen!'

Shen shook his head in bewilderment. 'Ah, yes. That was my *exact* idea.' But he was smiling at Rose, taking delight in her clear joy.

'Marino, what do you think? You've been missing your ship all summer, and this way you can be back at sea and we can all still be together!' Rose beamed at him.

Marino took a small step back, suddenly dizzy from more than the wine. He felt overwhelmed by all of Rose's plans. It was one thing for her and Celeste to decide what he was doing while he was in the palace, and entirely another thing to imagine them all on his ship for weeks on end. 'Autumn is a wonderful time to visit Demarre.'

'Oh, there will be so much to plan!' said Rose, sounding delighted by the prospect. 'And Marino, who knows? Perhaps you'll find someone to your liking in Demarre.'

'Perhaps,' he said with a smile. 'Perhaps. Now, if you'll both excuse me, I think I must retire for the evening. It has been, as ever, a delight.'

'Won't you stay for the fireworks?' asked Rose. 'Please? This is the last ball of the season, after all.'

Marino didn't want to disappoint Rose, so he slung an arm around her and Shen and grinned at them both. 'I wouldn't miss it for anything.'

After what Marino had to admit was a truly spectacular fireworks display, he said his goodnights and slipped back into the castle and up to his guest room. The windows were open, and he was grateful for the evening breeze. He went over to the window and gazed out at Wishbone Bay, thinking he could spy his own ship, the *Siren's Secret*. The summer Marino turned fifteen he'd joined a crew and set sail, and he knew he was meant for a life at the sea. By the time he was seventeen, he had the *Siren's Secret*. And now, at twenty-one, he had his own crew. They spent their days sailing to far-off lands and bringing back goods to trade and sell in Eana. Now that Rose and Wren were the queens of Eana, he had been given the title of Royal Captain of Eanan Sea Merchants. So, he was captain of his crew, of his ship, but apparently not of his own destiny.

For Marino, being on land this long felt more punishment than reward. He found the palace air stifling; he missed the sea winds. Most of all he missed seeing nothing between him and the horizon and feeling like adventure could be anywhere.

Well, it sounded like he would be joined on his next adventure by the whole palace.

CHAPTER 2
Marino

The next morning, Marino overslept.

His dreams had been full of the sea, which wasn't unusual. What had been different, and deeply unpleasant, was that he hadn't found himself on his ship. Rather, he had been deep beneath the waves. He'd dreamed of drowning.

He woke up in a sweat, his bed sheets tangled around him as if he'd been battling them in his sleep. Marino reached for the jug of water on his bedside table, trying to keep his hands from shaking. The dream had felt so real, unsettlingly so. But dreams were nothing more than dreams, he told himself.

Except when they are a prophecy, said a small voice in his head. Didn't he also have the seer strand of magic within him? Seer witches saw the future in the movements of the starcrests, who would spell out a hint of tomorrow in their movements, discernible only to those with the seer gift.

Seeing was the strand of magic that Marino was least comfortable with. Celeste was the seer, not him. Occasionally, out in the ocean, he would turn his gaze to the sky and try to read the movements of the starcrests, but he could rarely get a grasp on any true visions of the future.

He had never had a dream that had felt so real before, though. It unnerved him, and it made him uncharacteristically glad to be on land, and not at sea.

Marino gulped down a glass of water, and then strode to the window to fling open the curtains and look at the distant Wishbone Bay. He knew Rose had deliberately put him in this guest room so he would still be able to see the water, even glimpse his beloved ship. Perhaps his dream had been nothing more than his heart telling him what he already knew – that he needed to be back at sea.

For the first time in a long time though, he felt worried by what was waiting for him in the waves.

By the time Marino came down to breakfast, everyone else was already there.

Breakfast was always served in the morning room, a beautiful space with large windows overlooking the palace gardens. Rose sat at the head of the table, laughing with Celeste as she slathered butter on a piece of thick bread. Celeste was in a yellow silk dressing gown, with her dark brown curls piled up high on her head, and dark eyes sparkling at whatever it was Rose was saying. Shen was on the other side of Rose, pouring tea for Anika, who was demonstrating something with two knives and a napkin. Marino was certain it was some kind of battle enactment. As a princess of Gevra, a country known for its military prowess, Anika wasn't afraid to use a weapon, and as a warrior witch, Shen was a natural in combat. Anika wore a white nightgown trimmed in blue, and her long red hair was pulled back in a braid. Officially Anika was a visiting royal – but she had never been one to worry about propriety.

In the centre of the table was a platter of glistening fruit – strawberries, blackberries, cherries and pears – as well as a large basket full of fresh bread. There were bowls of jewel-coloured jams, a jug of golden honey, and plates of sliced cheese and meats. The atmosphere was relaxed and warm, and Marino stood for a moment in the doorway, watching the scene. The two couples, the close friends. He had a brief pang of feeling like an outsider, like an extra piece to a completed puzzle.

But then his sister looked up and grinned at him, and he felt silly for letting his insecurities get the better of him.

'Marino! There you are! We've been waiting. Come, come!' Celeste stood and moved one chair down, so Marino could sit between her and Rose.

He strode in, hiding his momentary feelings of inadequacy with a broad smile. 'And good morning to you all.'

'Rose has already told me that you didn't take to Lady Sophie, which is a shame.' Celeste clicked her tongue with disapproval.

Marino raised his brows. 'You wouldn't say that if you'd met her.'

'Marino!' Rose whacked him on the arm. 'That isn't very gentlemanly of you!'

Marino arced an eyebrow. 'Who said I was a gentleman?'

Celeste rolled her eyes. 'Just because you carry a sword now, you think you are some kind of rogue.'

'Excuse me, dear sister, I have always carried a sword.' Marino leaned back in his chair, affronted. 'And I would argue that I have many other rogue-like qualities.'

'He could absolutely be a rogue,' Shen agreed. 'Look at

his smirk. And his earrings.'

'What's wrong with my earrings?' Marino was even considering adding a few more. He enjoyed the occasional scandalised gasp the sight of them elicited in ladies he met in ballrooms.

'Nothing! They add to your roguishness. Perhaps I should get some earrings.' Shen tilted his head as he pondered.

'Since when are you the expert on rogues?' asked Rose, pressing a kiss to Shen's cheek.

'Well, I might wear a crown now, but I'll always be a rogue at heart.' Shen spun a knife in the air with perfect precision.

'A king of rogues,' said Marino, tipping his teacup towards Shen.

'Exactly.' Shen grinned back at him.

'You two are ridiculous.' Rose attempted a stern expression, but Marino saw her lips were quivering from trying not to laugh. 'And whether or not you are rogues –'

'I believe it has been established that we are indeed rogues,' Shen interrupted with a wink.

This time, Rose couldn't hold back her smile. 'Ahem. As I was saying, whether or not you are rogues, which is still very much up for debate, is beside the point. We were discussing my absolute failure to find Marino a match. And making a plan for what to do next.'

'We all have to admit defeat sometimes,' said Shen. 'Even you, my darling.'

'Not me,' said Anika, tossing a blackberry in her mouth and biting down with relish. Dark blackberry juice dripped down her chin.

'Is that a challenge?' Celeste said, leaning towards Anika

and wiping off the blackberry juice with her thumb.

Anika gave Celeste a wicked smile. 'Oh, this could be fun.'

Marino stared up at the ceiling. 'Not fun for all of us, I have to say.'

Anika cackled with glee, and Celeste rolled her eyes before throwing a bread roll at her brother. 'Marino, since when are you so proper?'

'I just want to keep my breakfast down,' Marino retorted. 'And that is hard to do when your sister is being wildly inappropriate at the breakfast table.'

He kept his tone light, but he didn't miss seeing Celeste's eyes flash in annoyance. He let out a long breath. 'Sorry, Lessie. I didn't sleep well last night.'

'Well, you've certainly ruined my morning mood,' sniffed Anika. She stood up and tossed her braid over her shoulder. 'Celeste, I'm going back to bed and I suggest you join me. And bring some more of those berries.' She stalked out of the room, pausing in the doorway to turn and stick her tongue out at Marino. 'We really do need to find you someone to warm your bed, clearly it has been far too long and it is making you unbearable.'

Marino felt heat rise to his face but held his tongue. He hadn't known Anika long, but he had learned that when the Gevran was in a temper, it was good to give her a wide berth. And he *had* been rude. Although, it could be argued, so had she.

He turned back to Celeste, expecting another rebuke, but instead she looked worried, her dark brows furrowed. 'It is true. You haven't been yourself recently.'

Marino shifted uncomfortably in his seat. 'I don't know what you mean.'

'You are so moody. And don't think I haven't noticed how you barely speak to your dance partners. Or any of us, really.' Celeste looked over at Rose, who was focusing very hard on putting jam on a slice of bread. 'Right, Rose?'

Rose cleared her throat. 'Oh, I couldn't speak to that. Marino, I know you miss your ship. And I know I've been meddling. But I promise, it comes from a good place. I want you to be happy. You deserve true happiness.'

Marino heard the words she didn't say. *'The kind of happiness Shen and I have.'*

'Rosie, you wouldn't be you if you weren't meddling,' Marino rarely used her childhood nickname these days, she was queen now, after all, but it felt right in this moment. He gave her a gentle smile. 'And I'm sorry if I've been rude. Truly. That is the last thing I want to do.'

Rose reached out and took his hand. 'You haven't been rude. But . . .' Her voice trailed off.

'Go on, Rose. I can take it,' said Marino wryly.

'You've been distant. That is certainly true. And I kept thinking that if we had another party, another ball, well, it would make you happy to be here at Anadawn for the summer.'

'Ah! If only I had found my true love at the first ball of the season, I could have saved you a fortune.'

'Marino! Don't be such a dunderbrain.' Celeste whacked him on the arm. 'You know what Rose means.'

'I do. And I appreciate it. Truly. I am grateful to have been here all summer.' And he was, in a way. Marino sighed. 'But I am not meant for this life. A palace life. You both know that.'

'It is more than that, though,' said Celeste. 'You can't

fool me, Marino. I know you better than anyone. And there is "Marino misses the sea so he's being a bit antsy" and there is whatever . . .' She waved her hand in the air. 'Whatever this is.'

Rose cleared her throat and stood. 'I suppose Shen and I should head up to the throne room. We've got a meeting about . . .' She trailed off. 'A meeting about trade. And the treasury! Yes. That's it.'

Shen, who had been silently watching this conversation unfold, nodded and stood as well. As he passed behind Marino, he patted him on the back, and Marino knew he was wishing him luck in the ensuing conversation with Celeste.

As the door closed behind Rose and Shen, Marino rubbed his temples. He hadn't meant for breakfast to go so sideways and wished he could start it again.

'Celeste, truly, nothing is wrong. Please don't make this into something it isn't. Can't I just be tired?'

'Something *is* wrong, Marino. I can tell! Sister's intuition. And I'm going to figure out what it is whether you tell me or not.'

Marino scowled at her. 'You know I don't like it when you try to see my future.'

It felt like an invasion of privacy, like she was peeking into his brain. It was his future, after all. And wasn't his future tied up in his wants and his wishes? He didn't like anyone knowing what might befall him before he did.

Hurt flashed across Celeste's face. 'I said sister's intuition, not seer's intuition. But I don't need to be a seer to tell you that if you keep pushing people away and rejecting offers of help, you are going to be miserable.'

Marino felt his bottled-up frustration bubble over. 'I don't need your help! Or Rose's! There isn't anyone for me here in Eana, can't you see that?' He glared at his sister. 'I think this summer we've all learned that I don't belong in Anadawn. I outgrew this place a long time ago, Celeste. And it is best that we all see that.'

'This is your home, Marino.' Celeste sounded close to tears.

Marino softened his voice and took his sister's hands in his own. 'No, it isn't. You are my sister, and I love you, but Anadawn hasn't been home to me for years. Stop trying to force me to live a life that I don't want.'

Celeste ripped her hands out of his and stormed across the room. 'Trying to help you find love isn't forcing you to do anything! You can't just sail the seas until the end of your days.'

'Of course I can,' Marino scoffed. 'Why do you take it so personally?'

Celeste turned to gaze out of the window. 'Because our mother left. She couldn't stand to be in Anadawn and she left us. I can't lose you too, Marino. I know you love the sea, but I won't lose you to it.' She turned back to him, eyes glazed with unshed tears. 'You need to put down roots at some point. Maybe not now, but one day.'

Marino stilled at her words. Their mother had left when they were young. Marino still remembered the night before she disappeared. She'd seemed tired, and sad, which was unusual because she had always been joyful and energetic. His earliest memories of his mother were of her laughing and singing. But on this night she'd been solemn. She had hugged him and Celeste close, told them how much she loved them. Told them they had to look out for each other, no matter what. She'd said Celeste needed to keep her gaze on the sky, and that Marino was meant for the sea. She'd kissed them both on the forehead and sung them to sleep, a last lullaby that Marino would never forget.

And then, in the morning, she was gone. She'd taken her cloak and her jewels. Celeste had cried for days, but Marino hadn't truly believed she wasn't coming back. He would stay up until dawn, watching out the window for her, waiting for a secret message that never came. When he was a little older, he'd begun to lurk around the docks, certain that he'd spot her. Hoping that when she said he was meant for the sea, he would find her there. Or at least meet someone who had news of her. But he never saw her or heard word.

Their father would not allow them to mention her. He was embarrassed by her disappearance, Marino could sense that even as a child. Marino wanted to blame someone for their mother leaving, and he decided it must have been his father. But still, he wondered if he could have done more to make her stay.

For a long time, Marino and Celeste used to make up wild stories about their missing mother. She'd been kidnapped. She'd turned into a bird. She had swum to Gevra. Become a pirate. Anything that meant that one day she would come back.

But she never did. And slowly, they stopped making up the stories. Stopped mentioning her at all.

Marino crossed the breakfast room and gathered his sister up into a hug. 'You'll never lose me, Lessie. You know that. I always come back.' He pulled away to grin at her.

'You know all about birds, right? I'm like one of those birds that comes home every season.'

Celeste laughed and wiped her nose. 'Just because I'm a seer doesn't make me a bird expert. I know about starcrests, and that is all.'

'Well, know that no matter what, I'll always come home to you. I promise.'

CHAPTER 3
Marino

Marino waited until Celeste had left the breakfast room to drop his head into his hands, exhausted by the exchange. He had meant everything he had said, he would always come back to her, but it didn't change the fact that he felt claustrophobic in the castle. Trapped.

Marino felt the air closing in around him and knew he had to get away, if only for a few hours. So, he slipped out of the palace unnoticed and spent the day down at Wishbone Bay. He ate at his favourite tavern – feasting on a platter of shrimp – and listened to the stories the sailors were telling. Everyone in the tavern knew him, and it was almost as good as being back out at sea. By the time the sun was setting he had cheered considerably, and decided to invite Shen to the docks with him the next day. King he might be, but a day down at the bay would do him good.

Marino whistled as he walked back to Anadawn along the Silvertongue River. He was in high spirits until he reached the golden gates of the palace, and Anika stepped out of the shadows, like she'd been waiting for his return.

'Where have you been?' she demanded, glaring at him. She was dressed in a corseted black velvet gown embroidered with tiny silver snowflakes. A regal nod to her Gevran home, Marino assumed.

He raised his brow at her question. 'And good evening to you too, Anika. I've been down at Wishbone Bay, not that it is any of your business. But I've had a lovely day and I hope you have too.'

Anika poked him in the chest, hard. 'I have not had a lovely day. Celeste has been worried sick about you. And I do not like that for her *or* for me.'

Marino frowned. 'But everything was fine when I left this morning. Perhaps you two have had a lover's tiff? Sounds like you need to work it out with her. I kindly request not to be involved.' He went to step around Anika.

Anika stepped back and poked Marino again in the chest, harder this time. 'She came to the bedroom in tears! Something about her mother telling her to always take care of you, and she was letting her down, letting you down.' Anika threw her hands up in the air, like she was tossing Celeste's words in Marino's face.

Marino flinched as the words struck their mark, and his good mood evaporated. 'I already told her I'm *not* like our mother, that I'll always come back.'

'Well, she thought you had followed in her footsteps and disappeared. You could have told someone you were going to be gone all day.' Anika wagged her finger in Marino's face and he gently but firmly moved it to the side.

'Anika, I am twenty-one years of age. I am captain of my own ship and crew. And of my own life. I do not need to tell anyone where I am going, nor ask for permission. Does your brother, Alarik, let everyone know where he is at any given moment?'

Anika let out a sharp bark of a laugh. 'Alarik is the king of Gevra. He does as he pleases. But when I am home, of course I know where he is! Even kings and captains are not exempt from sisters knowing their whereabouts and worrying about them.'

Marino took a deep breath. 'Let me speak with Celeste. Where is she?'

Anika scowled. 'Celeste is sitting on the damned roof, of all places, trying to make out a message from those birds that everyone in this country is so obsessed with. A message about you, I'm sure. We were *meant* to be having a romantic evening together, but no, she had to go and look at the birds.'

Marino frowned. 'The starcrests only come out at night.'

'Well, she's been waiting for them for ages. And for you.'

Marino ran a hand through his curls. 'I am sorry, Anika. Truly. I only want Celeste to be happy.'

'Well, she only wants the same for you. You are both incredibly stubborn. Must be genetics.' Anika wasn't quite smiling, but she had stopped scowling, which Marino took as excellent progress.

'Thank you, Anika. For coming to find me and telling me where Celeste is.'

'Don't thank me yet, I'm still furious at you. Now go! And make whatever heartfelt conversation you need to have a quick one, all right?' With this, Anika finally did smile – and it was bright and beautiful and wild – and Marino caught a glimpse of what his sister saw in her tempestuous lover.

Marino hurried up the stone steps to the room that Celeste had slept in ever since their mother left. Before that, they had lived in a small house in the nearby city of Eshlinn. But after her disappearance, their father had moved them to the castle. As the royal physician, it had been his right to have quarters there.

He knocked once, firmly, before pushing Celeste's door open and striding into the room. It was sumptuously decorated in blue and yellow, Celeste's favourite colours, and smelled of jasmine. As Anika had said, the window next to the wardrobe was open. The way the blue curtains billowed in the breeze in an otherwise empty room made Marino think of ghosts, and he gave an involuntary shudder. 'Celeste?' he called out. 'Are you truly out on the roof?'

There was a long silence and then a muffled curse. 'I almost had it! Don't distract me!'

Marino sighed and poked his head out of the window. Celeste was lying on the sloped roof directly below her window. Her head was near the window, on the highest point of the roof, with her bare feet nearly over the edge, and her eyes were glazed as she stared up at the sky above. Dozens of starcrests, small white birds with a star-shaped crest on their breasts, were soaring in intricate patterns.

Even looking at the patterns for a moment made Marino's head spin. He couldn't imagine what it would feel like to watch the birds for hours. 'Celeste, come inside. You are a gifted seer. If the starcrests aren't showing you their secrets, there must be a reason.'

Celeste ignored him.

'Anika told me you were upset.'

This got Celeste's attention. She sat up, quickly, and

turned her gaze to Marino. Her eyes were still cloudy from trying to divine the future.

'Anika shouldn't have gone to you,' Celeste muttered. 'And I'm fine now. Or I will be once the starcrests show me the future I'm looking for.'

'My future, is it?' Marino ran his hand across his jaw. 'Lessie, let it go. My future and my fate is mine and mine alone. I will decide it. There is nothing you can see in that sky that will change that.'

'But Marino . . .' Celeste's voice trailed off and then she flicked her eyes back up to the starcrests and gasped. 'Oh! I see! I see now!' She tilted her head back and began to grin. 'Marino, you must listen to me. You will find love. The starcrests are certain. The signs are strong. You will find love and you will find it soon. But it will be hard and . . .' She squinted as she tried to decipher what the starcrests were trying to tell her. 'Hard and unexpected.'

Marino snorted. 'How helpful. Finding love in an unexpected way. You don't need the starcrests to know that. *I* could have told you that. *Anyone* could have told you that.'

'Marino, just hold on! I can sense it. The starcrests are trying to tell me something that I can't quite understand. It feels like two separate visions that are somehow linked. Don't you want to know?'

'No, thank you. I've asked you to stop.'

'But . . .'

'Why don't you look up Anika's future? Or Rose's? Or anyone else's but mine? I know my future. My future is at sea. Mama told me, remember?'

Celeste twisted her body around to look right at him, and this time Marino wasn't sure if her eyes were glazed from staring for too long at the sky, or if she was going to cry again.

'She told *me* to keep my eyes on the sky. And to stay close to you. How can I stay close to you if you are always sailing off every chance you get?'

'Celeste, we'll always be close. No matter where I sail or how far I go. You know that.'

'You don't think I can see your future, do you? You don't think my seer gift is strong enough. You think your future is so special that it's hidden from even the starcrests.'

Marino sighed heavily. He was beginning to regret coming to Celeste's room. He wished he had gone straight back to his chambers and gone to sleep and left Celeste to stare up at the starcrests to her heart's content. Left Anika to deal with her. 'I think that your wish for me to find happiness, to find love, is clouding your seer ability. I think you are seeing what you want to see.'

'And I think that you are an ungrateful dunderbrain who doesn't know how lucky he is to have people who care for him!' Celeste's voice cracked, and she blinked back tears.

'I won't sit up here all night, waiting for you to find me the future that you think is suitable. I'm going to sleep. And you should too. You'll exhaust yourself trying to summon a vision that isn't there.'

'I'm not *summoning* a vision. That isn't how seeing works!' Celeste spoke through clenched teeth. '*I am trying to help you.* How many times do I have to tell you?'

'And how many times do I have to tell you I don't want your help! I don't need to see a vision of my future, Celeste. I know what my life holds. You can stay up here as long as you want, sleep under the starcrests if you must, but know that you aren't doing it for me – you're doing it for you, so you can claim some kind of control over my life. I know what will happen if you get a clear vision. You'll tell me the version you want to believe, that you want me to believe.'

Celeste turned away from him again and settled herself back on the roof, eyes back on the starcrests. 'I won't dignify that with a response. It is insulting to me as a seer and to me as your sister.'

Marino blew out a long stream of air. 'I'll tell you something – the more you try and force me into a future that you want for me, the further away I will go.'

'Just leave then, Marino.'

And so he did. He left his sister on the sloped rooftop, watching the starcrests with a furious focus. He went back to his guest room several floors down and got ready for bed, feeling like a right ass. It was fine. He'd apologise to Celeste in the morning at breakfast. Offer to take her and Rose and Anika out on his ship so she could be reminded that she too loved the sea. But right now, he knew that if he tried to talk any kind of sense into her, they would argue again. And he was tired. Bone tired. So, he went to bed and tossed and turned and tried to convince himself that he was in the right.

Marino didn't know how long Celeste sat up there, trying to see his future. Trying to solve his problems. Trying to find him a love that might not even exist.

But he knew the moment she fell.

She screamed once, high and sharp. Marino had heard her scream like that only once before, when they were young and had raced each other up the mast of one of the Anadawn ships, clambering up using their hands and feet. Celeste had been faster than him, reached the top before him, and as she had gloated her victory, she'd lost her grip. Marino would never forget the sight of his sister falling to the deck. They hadn't had healers then, the witches were still in hiding, so it had been their father who had set her broken bones. Their mother was already gone, and so it was Rose and Marino who comforted Celeste when she cried out from the pain.

The roofs of Anadawn were much higher than the mast had been. So Celeste screamed longer, until suddenly, she wasn't making a sound at all.

When he heard that terrible scream, Marino ran to the window, panic making his heart pound. And he saw his sister plummet towards the ground at a sickening speed. He lunged out of the window, grasping for her, but his fingers closed around empty air.

Then, in the garden below, there was a whisper of steel and a burst of speed, and Shen Lo was somehow there. He and Rose often walked the gardens at night, Marino remembered now. Rose was right beside Shen, running in her pink nightgown, and even though everything was happening so fast, too fast, Marino felt like he was watching it happen in slow motion.

Rose flung her hands up, snatching a wisp of wind, and flinging it up into the air towards Celeste, using her tempest magic to bend the wind to her will. The wind cradled Celeste, slowing her descent, but she was still falling. Until Shen leaped up and caught her. He did it with such ease that for a moment Marino thought he must have imagined it. Imagined the King of Eana and the Sunkissed Kingdom practically taking flight to save his sister.

Marino waited for Celeste to sit up. To laugh brazenly at her close brush with death. To demand that they get a drink to settle their nerves.

But Celeste lay limp in Shen's arms. Shen held her as Rose smoothed Celeste's hair off her forehead, held her wrist to check her pulse, put her head on her chest to listen to her heart. Marino knew that she would be using her healing strand to find the golden thread of life within Celeste, to mend it. To mend her.

Marino watched this all from above, like he himself was a starcrest flitting in the sky, with knowledge of what was to come but no way to stop it. He felt strangely frozen, unable to snap himself out of the daze he was in. After a few agonising minutes, Rose lifted her tear-stained face and locked eyes with him, and the expression on her face made his blood run cold as reality came rushing back in. And with it, a shattering realisation.

If Rose could not heal Celeste, he did not know who could.

CHAPTER 4
Marino

Marino did not remember running up the stairs to Celeste's room. He only remembered how he felt when he saw Shen carry his sister in and lay her gently on her bed. The panic that clawed its way through him, the helplessness that left him standing paralysed at the side of the room.

Celeste was still as death.

Rose was trying to stay calm, but her hands were shaking. 'Shen, please go and wake Thea. Tell her it's urgent.'

Shen nodded and strode out of the room. As he passed Marino, he squeezed his shoulder. 'She will be all right,' he said, and Marino hoped he was right, even as he felt deep in his bones that something was very, very wrong.

Rose lovingly pushed Celeste's hair out of her face, before turning to Marino, eyes shining with unshed tears. 'Do you know what she was doing on the roof?'

Marino's mouth went dry. 'She was watching the starcrests. She was looking for my future. We . . . we fought. And then I left her there, all on her own.' He found himself sliding to the ground, as if his legs could not support his weight, as if his body could not process what was happening. He put his head in his hands, unable to look Rose in the eye. 'It's my fault. Whatever happened, it is my fault.'

There was a rustle of skirts, and then Rose was next to him. 'Hush. Celeste often watched the starcrests from the rooftop. I've told her time and time again not to. I should have built her a viewing platform. With a railing.' Rose drew a shuddering breath. 'When I heard the scream, I knew it was her.'

'Me too,' said Marino. 'I went to the window but I was too slow.' He looked up now at Rose, at his sister's best friend, the person who loved Celeste as much as he did. 'What if you and Shen hadn't been in the garden?' He felt sick as he said the words, as if by even uttering them he would turn back time and make them true.

'But we were.' Rose took Marino's hand and held it between both of hers. Her hands were unusually cold, and Marino wondered if it was from the shock. Rose shook her head, as if she was trying to shake out the memory of seeing Celeste fall. 'You know, we often walk the gardens in the evening, and tonight, I had the strangest urge to take another turn. I can't explain it.' Goosebumps rose along her skin. 'We were almost directly under her roof when she fell. And Shen moved . . .' Rose's voice grew thick with emotion. 'He moved so quickly.'

'So did you, Rose. You used your tempest gift to slow her fall. Without you two . . .'

'The important thing is that we were there. And that she will be fine.' But she looked away as she spoke. 'Although, I don't know why she won't wake up. If we heard her scream, she was awake when she fell. I don't know what happened between the fall and when Shen caught her.'

'Was she conscious when Shen caught her?'

Rose shook her head. Then she took another long, deep breath. 'But Thea will know what to do. Thea will fix her.'

Thea was the Queensbreath – the person granted the most power in the kingdom after the queens. She had also been the wife of Rose and Wren's grandmother, Banba, before she died. And most importantly to Marino in this very moment, she was one of the greatest healers in all of Eana.

The door swung open and Thea hurried in, with Shen close behind. She had deep brown skin, a similar shade to Marino and Celeste's, and wore an eyepatch over one eye. Her black and grey curly hair was cut short, even shorter than Marino's. Her expression was grave.

She took Celeste's hand in her own and closed her eye. Marino held his breath. Thea would be able to heal Celeste, be able to wake her, and then he could apologise to his sister for being so bull-headed and he would gladly sit with her while she pulled whatever future she wanted for him out of the sky.

Celeste's whole body shuddered violently, and a strange white mist poured out of her mouth and nose. It was a horrifying sight that made Marino's blood run cold. The mist dissolved, and Celeste went still again.

'What is that?' Marino said in a hoarse whisper. 'Falling off a roof doesn't cause that.'

Thea's eye opened. 'I cannot cure this. We must call on my cousin. And quickly.' Thea's cousin, Willa, was the healer on high who lived in the Mishnick Mountains across the Ganyeve Desert. Marino had never been to the Mishnick Mountains but he had sailed past them. He knew it was over a day's journey, and that frightened him. He wanted Thea to cure Celeste *now*.

Shen stepped forward. 'I will leave immediately. Storm is the fastest horse in Eana. She's desert born and bred and can practically fly across the sands. We'll be back in two days' time – with Willa.'

It was at that moment that Anika strode into the room, carrying a tray piled high with chocolate biscuits. She took one look at Celeste's prone body, dropped the tray and began to wail.

Anika's screaming snapped Marino into action, as he and Shen held her back from leaping on to Celeste. Rose ran to the Gevran princess, taking her face in her hands. 'Shhh! Shhh. She'll be all right, she'll be all right.'

Tears rolled down Anika's cheeks and she suddenly went limp, as if all the fight had gone out of her. She turned to stare at Marino. 'You were supposed to be talking to her! What happened? Did you push her?'

Marino felt anger, hot and pulsing, surge through him. 'Of course not,' he said roughly. 'Do you think me a monster?'

'I think you're the last person who saw her. And you two had been bickering. Even fights between siblings can get out of hand.' Anika glared at him. 'I once pushed Alarik through a window.'

'Well, maybe that's how siblings behave in Gevra, but I would never harm Celeste. Not even in anger.'

Anika merely clenched her teeth, and turned as if she couldn't even bear to look at Marino.

'Anika.' Rose spoke sharply. 'I know you are upset to see Celeste like this, but it is entirely out of line to blame Marino. He is as upset as any of us, more so. We must do what is best for Celeste, and that is focusing on her. Not blaming each other for what happened. Especially when we do not even know the truth of how she fell or why.'

Marino felt his anger evaporate, replaced by a cold, creeping guilt. 'But I know why. It has something to do with what she saw in the sky. And . . . we did argue before I left her there on the roof. I shouldn't have gone, I should have made her come back inside. Or I should have stayed with her until she saw what she was looking for in the sky.'

'Marino, it is more complex than that.' Thea had risen from her perch on the edge of Celeste's bed. 'Willa is the one who can confirm, but I suspect Celeste has the seeing sickness.'

'What is the seeing sickness?' said Rose quickly. 'I have not heard of it. Why is it something we cannot cure her of? We are healers after all.'

'The seeing sickness is no ordinary disease. It strikes suddenly, in the brain, and then spreads throughout the body, poisoning the blood. I believe it can be reversed, but only if the cure is administered quickly.'

'And Willa knows of the cure?' said Marino, feeling a fragile thread of hope unspool within him.

Thea swallowed thickly and would not meet Marino's gaze. 'She knows more than I do of this. If there is anyone in Eana who can cure Celeste, it is Willa.'

'Speaking of Willa, I should be on my way,' said Shen. 'I don't want to waste any time. I'll be back as soon as possible.'

'Thank you, Shen,' said Marino, his voice thick with emotion.

'Celeste feels like my family now too,' said Shen. 'I'll do whatever it takes to help her.' He turned to Anika.

'Everything will be all right.'

Anika said nothing, and all Marino could do was hope Shen was right.

Marino spent the next two days in Celeste's room. His father, Rose and Anika were there too. His father dealt with medicines and broken bones, not healing magic and illnesses brought on by visions. But Hector Pegasi, a stoic and quiet man, did his best to cure his daughter in the ways he knew. He put warm compresses on her forehead, and had tinctures of bark and roots brought into the room.

'It isn't too different from a spell,' Rose murmured, watching Hector stir the concoction.

But nothing Hector did seemed to help. And Marino feared he was watching his sister die before his very eyes. Her breathing grew shallower with every passing moment, punctuated by tremors that wracked her whole body.

Rose, who with her healing gift could at least still feel the golden strand of life within Celeste, tried again and again to rouse his sister while they waited for Willa to arrive.

Marino saw the tears slip down her cheeks, heard the desperation in her voice. Marino knew that if Rose could, she would use every waking breath she had to try to heal her dearest friend.

At least there was something she could do. Anika paced the halls relentlessly, like a Gevran snow leopard. She said nothing to Marino, glaring at him when they made eye contact across Celeste's sickbed.

When Willa arrived at Anadawn, after a day of hard travel across the desert, she came straight to Celeste's room. Thea embraced her cousin, and Marino was struck by the similarity between them. They both had warm brown skin, their faces deeply wrinkled. But whereas Thea wore her greying hair cut short, Willa had long white braids that were twisted and pinned, like a crown, on the top of her head. After she hugged Thea, Willa turned to Rose.

'Queen Rose, you should know that King Shen rode faster than the wind to get us back here. I would not have believed it possible, if I myself had not been hanging on to that horse for dear life. I imagine both horse and man will need to sleep for a week.'

Rose managed a watery smile. 'Celeste is very dear to all of us.' She nodded towards Marino. 'This is Marino, Celeste's brother.'

'That much is clear from simply looking at them,' said Willa. 'Marino, Shen told me that you were the last to speak to Celeste before her fall.'

Marino cleared his throat and bowed his head, unable to look at Willa for his shame.

Then there were soft and calloused hands lifting his chin. When Marino met Willa's gaze, her eyes were kind and warm. 'I say that not to blame you. I seek to understand what Celeste was searching for in the sky before she was struck by the seeing sickness.'

Marino told her what he could, avoiding looking at Anika.

When he finished, Willa exhaled. 'The seeing sickness can come from a psychic strain, from searching too hard for something that cannot be seen.'

'But I heard her scream as she fell. It was not as if she

simply was struck with this so-called seeing sickness and then slipped off the roof. She was still awake, still conscious when she fell.'

Marino was glad for the scream. The scream had alerted Shen and Rose, had saved Celeste's life.

'I cannot say for certain what happened between Celeste and the starcrests. We will not know that until she wakes to tell us herself.'

There was a snort across the room. Anika had been surprisingly and uncharacteristically quiet when Willa had arrived, leaning against the wall with her arms crossed, watching everything unfold. 'You certainly sound confident she will wake.'

Willa drew herself up to her full height. 'I am the healer on high from the Mishnick Mountains. Celeste Pegasi is one of the finest seers in generations of witches. I will do everything in my considerable power to save her. So, yes, I am confident that she will wake.'

Anika shifted back against the wall, sulking but silent.

'As I was saying,' Willa went on pointedly, as she began to rinse her hands in a bowl of steaming water that a maid had brought up, 'while I cannot know for certain what caused Celeste to scream, it is possible that she saw something in the story the starcrests were weaving that shocked her. To the extent that it would trigger the seeing sickness. We cannot know if the scream came before the fall, or the fall caused the scream.'

What had Celeste seen? What was in his future that was so shocking, so terrible, that it broke her in this way? What tragedy had she foreseen?

Surely it had to be tragedy, because what else would have

made her scream like that, made her slip off the roof in shock? If he had only stayed with her while she tried to find his future. Marino could not help but feel like this was his fault.

'And we will not be asking seers to try and divine the vision that led to her being struck with the seeing sickness,' said Thea. 'As Willa says, Celeste either pushed herself too hard trying to read an uncertain future, or the vision she found gave her a shock that sent her into this state, leading to the seeing sickness.'

'It can spread,' said Willa grimly. 'The last time the seeing sickness struck, we lost many of our seers.'

'And now we all have the seeing strand, so we could all be at risk.' Thea's voice was grave.

'How do we stop it from spreading?' said Rose, drawing herself up, looking every bit the queen she was.

'No seers must use their gift until Celeste is healed. This is no mortal illness that can be contained with quarantine. It is a magical ailment and is as slippery as an eel. It seeps out in visions. It is a poison of the mind, of the very spirit, that spreads to the heart itself. And it is deadly.'

At the word deadly, Marino thought he felt his own heart stop. No. He would not believe it. There would be a way to save Celeste from this.

'I will declare an edict,' Rose said firmly. 'I'll send word to Amarach Towers right away.' Amarach Towers was where the seers lived and trained. 'And letters, to every home in Eana. There will be no visions. We will save Celeste and we will stop it from spreading.'

'Sometimes visions come in a dream,' said Shen gently. 'It will not be as easy as sending letters out to every witch in Eana.'

'It is better than nothing,' said Rose, her voice trembling lightly. 'And Willa will save Celeste this very moment, I am certain.' She turned to Willa, the hope and fear in her eyes mirroring Marino's own. 'You can save her, can't you?'

'I will do my best. Give me a moment with her,' said Willa. She went to Celeste and brushed her hands over her closed eyes. A moment later, Celeste's eyes flickered opened.

Anika gasped, and Marino felt his heart leap. But then he looked more closely at his sister's eyes. They were fixed on the ceiling, staring at something none of them could see. And instead of bright and shining, they were cloudy. Marino recoiled when he realised the cloudy film across her eyes was moving like a living thing.

Willa drew a shaky breath. 'The seeing sickness is more advanced than I was hoping. It has only been two days, but it is spreading quickly.'

Marino began to feel queasy as he realised that it might already be too late. If only Willa had been closer, if only Rose or Thea had known what to do . . .

'I will do my best to pull it from her without harming her,' said Willa. 'Her seer strand will be tied up in her heart and her mind, and I do not want to cause further damage.' She turned to Thea and Rose. 'I will need both of your help. Please, take her hands. And channel your healing into her.'

Willa pressed her hand against Celeste's brow, and Thea and Rose each took one of her hands. Between them all, sunk into her pillows, Celeste looked like a doll. And then her body began to tremble. She shuddered and shook until her teeth clacked and her body nearly raised up off the bed.

'Stop it!' screamed Anika. 'You're hurting her!' She lunged at the bed, red hair streaming around her face, and

Marino had to step forward to restrain her, holding her back as she kicked and shouted. She wrenched her head around and bit him on the forearm, hard enough to draw blood.

Marino swore, but he held on.

'Get her out of here!' snapped Willa. 'She will disturb the magic.'

'No!' Anika screeched. Still Celeste writhed and shook on the bed, eyes rolling.

'Now!' commanded Willa. Marino didn't want to leave the room, not even for a second, but he had to do what was best for Celeste.

With a frustrated sigh, he hauled Anika to the door, where his father stood with a grave expression. His father flung the door open, and Marino took Anika into the hall. A moment later the door slammed shut and Marino heard a lock click.

Anika wriggled free from his grasp and began to hammer the door with her fists.

'Stop it!' Marino ordered, grabbing her wrist. 'Didn't you hear the healer?

Anika turned to him, eyes wild and red-rimmed in her pale face. 'You forget, Captain, I've seen these so-called healers do more harm than good.'

Marino suddenly remembered that Anika's brother, Alarik, had forced Wren to attempt the impossible. To bring their younger brother, Ansel, back from the dead. With disastrous consequences.

His voice softened. 'Rose is a healer, Anika. Celeste is her best friend. Even before Rose's healing magic appeared, she took care of Celeste.'

All the fight seemed to drain out of Anika and she

slumped against the door. 'She looks so . . . small. Like all the life has gone out of her.' She turned to Marino, eyes shining with unshed tears. 'Do you know the first time I saw your sister? On the dance floor at that cursed welcome ball. And I had never seen someone look so vibrant, so alive. I took one look and I fell hard.' Her voice dropped to a whisper. 'And I've been falling ever since.' She shook her head. 'There is nobody like Celeste Pegasi.'

Marino hadn't realised how deep Anika's feelings went. How true.

He reached out and squeezed her hand. 'Celeste will be all right,' he said. And as he spoke the words, he willed them to be true. She had to be.

The door to the bedroom creaked open. Marino's father stood there, his face somehow even more sombre than before. He levelled a stern look at Anika. 'If I allow you back in this room, can you control yourself?'

Anika swallowed hard and nodded. Marino offered her his arm for support, and was surprised when she took it.

Hector Pegasi stepped back, opening the door to allow Marino and Celeste back in. His gaze darted to his son. 'You'll want to listen closely to what the witches have to say.'

Marino knew it must be hard for his father, who had trained to understand and heal the human body, to see his daughter in such a state and be unable to do anything to help her. It was a magical sickness coursing through her, and for all his father's skill as a physician, there was nothing he could do but stand by and watch. His father was most certainly not a witch, which sometimes made Marino wonder if his mother had been. If that is why she had fled.

But his mother, whoever or whatever she might have been, wasn't here now. And he refused to lose someone else he loved. Marino and Anika approached the bed where Celeste lay still as death. Her eyes were open, and that terrible moving cloud was still shifting across her irises.

Then Willa looked up, and Marino saw the defeat etched across her face.

'You can't save her.' It was Anika who spoke, her voice a dead thing.

'Not on my own,' said Willa.

'Then bring in all the witches of Eana! Every healer!' Anika's voice rang out, and Marino nodded. Whatever needed to be done, they would do it.

'It will take both more than that and less,' said Thea.

'Spare me your riddles,' snapped Anika. 'What do we need to do?'

'Please, Thea.' Marino's voice cracked.

Thea looked right at Marino. 'We need you to find the cure for Celeste.'

CHAPTER 5
Marino

'The cure is out there. It has been found before. But you will have to go further than you ever have.' Thea's voice was grave.

'I will go as far as I need to,' said Marino. His mind was spinning. 'But . . . what am I looking for?'

Thea and Willa exchanged a look. 'Most likely a plant,' said Willa slowly. 'But exactly where it grows . . . is unknown.'

'Time is not on your side,' added Thea. 'And it will be a dangerous journey.'

'I'll go with Marino.' But even as Rose leaped up, eyes bright with purpose, Marino knew this was something he had to do on his own.

'You and Anika stay here, by her side. If Celeste wakes up, she'll want to see you both.' He gave them a crooked smile. 'And I'll be back before you know it.'

'Please note that I did not volunteer to accompany you,' said Anika. But she offered Marino a smile. 'But I do believe in you. If only because you are Celeste's brother. Surely you must have some of her competence.'

'You must find it,' said Willa, her gravelly voice cutting

across the room. 'And not just for the sake of your sister. We are all at risk of the seeing sickness, remember. If Celeste dies –'

'Do not even say it,' hissed Anika.

'If you do not find the cure, the sickness will not die with your sister. It will spread.'

Marino scraped his hand over his jaw. 'And so, I just sail with no direction? No compass? Hope for the best?'

'The seaswifts will guide you. You are a witch, Marino Pegasi. It is time you prove yourself.'

Marino frowned. 'The *what* will guide me?'

'The seaswifts. They are the sea-sisters to the starcrests. What the starcrests do in the sky, the seaswifts do in the sea. But they do not tell of the future. They guide you to where you most want to be.'

Marino's frown deepened. 'How am I meant to follow some mythical bird-fish thing I've never seen or heard of?'

'What is the furthest place you've been?'

'The Ochre Isles.'

'Then go there, and further. If your heart is true in your purpose, the seaswifts will show themselves.'

'Just . . . like that?'

Willa's voice took on the tone of an incantation. 'When the sky is clear and the moon is high, when you can see your own face staring back at you from the depths of the sea, offer a drop of your blood to the waves. The seaswifts will come, for they are bound by the blood of the witches of Eana.'

'Why have I never heard of this before?' Marino burst out.

'Marino, Willa speaks the truth,' said Thea. 'The seaswifts

are real, and they will guide you. The witches of Eana have not often had need to leave our motherland, to leave the land that Eana, the first witch, created, but when we do, we call on the seaswifts.'

Marino remembered the legend of Eana. How she had once lived in the stars, with the sun himself as her consort, before growing curious about the land below. How she had landed her giant green-tailed hawk in the sea, and it had formed the land of Eana.

'Once Eana had turned into a woman, she sought something across the unknown seas. To guide her, she created the seaswifts. She created them with her own blood. A drop of her blood in the sea that was new to her, her blood that was made of the same stuff as the stars, and her determination. The seaswifts led her to what she desired, and then home again.

'Some say she was chasing the sun, over the horizon, missing him in her old age.' Thea smiled at Rose, who had a particular affinity for the legends of the Sunkissed Kingdom that celebrated the love between Eana and the sun himself.

'Seaswifts,' Rose murmured softly. 'There is still so much I don't know. About the witches. About magic. About my own history.'

Thea took Rose's hand in her own. 'There is time to learn, Rose. And we are here for that. To pass on what we know. And in time, you will pass it on to the next generation of witches.'

'Tell me more of the cure itself,' said Marino, starting to pace the small room. 'You say it is a plant, but how will I know when I find it?'

'Are you a witch or not, Marino Pegasi? Let your magic

guide you. You will know when you find it. You will feel it here.' Willa rose and put her hand on Marino's chest. 'But you must go off the map, Marino. Sail until you can sail no more, and there you will find the cure Celeste needs. And when you find it, the leaf or bloom or fruit or whatever it may be, you bring it back, and we will save her.'

'I remember when the seeing sickness spread,' said Thea, her one eye gazing into the distance, into her own memories. 'It was a long time ago. Before Lillith's War.' A war named for Rose and Wren's mother, the witch who had married a king without magic, who had hope that witches and those without magic could live peacefully together, a witch queen who had been murdered the night her twin daughters were born. Marino had been only a toddler in the war, but he had heard stories of it his whole life. Thea went on. 'I remember seeing a ship leave Eana, a ship full of sailors and tempests.' She blinked and her focus returned to the people in the room. 'They were gone a long time, Marino. They didn't know what they were looking for, but still they found it.'

'And why don't we have any records of it here?' Rose demanded.

'Because, Rose, my dear, everything to do with the witches was destroyed, remember?' Thea spoke gently. 'We will ask the seers at Amarach Towers if they have any record of it, anything at all that might help us. But that will take time, which we do not have. Especially as they cannot look to the sky for answers.' She turned back to Marino. 'You must leave right away. Follow the seaswifts. They will guide you. And you will find what Celeste needs. What we all may need if the seeing sickness spreads.'

'How much time do I have?' Marino asked gruffly.

He couldn't look at Celeste, couldn't see his strong sister lying there like she was already dead. 'Is there time for the seers to at least give me a hint of what I must find?'

Willa took a long, ragged breath. 'We can keep her alive for a month. But after that, if we do not have the cure, Celeste will die.'

Her words echoed like a cold vow, and sounded for all the world like it was a curse. Marino clenched his fist at his side and said nothing, not trusting himself to hold his temper, to keep back the words he wanted to say to this woman predicting Celeste's death.

'But it takes me nearly a month to go to Caro and back. And I am meant to go beyond Caro, beyond the Ochre Isles . . .' His voice trailed off. 'I must leave right away. And sail faster than I ever have.'

Then Rose was next to him, taking his hand in her own, coaxing it open so she could intertwine their fingers. She squeezed four times in quick succession, and when Marino glanced down at her it was like looking back in time, like they were twelve years old again and speaking through the secret code of handshakes and knocks they had made up with Celeste. He hadn't thought about their secret language for years. He remembered now – four fast knocks meant 'everything will be fine'.

'You will find the cure,' Rose said, eyes on his. 'You will find it and we will heal her.' Her voice broke. 'We will save her, Marino.'

Marino found he could not speak because of the sudden lump in his throat. All he could do was nod, and squeeze Rose's hand back.

Marino knew he could not take a whole crew with him. He did not know where he was even going, and he would not risk his crew like that. But he also knew he could not sail so long and so far completely on his own. He needed a skeleton crew. And so that very day, he brought his entire crew together and told them that it was their choice. He offered to pay everyone what they would make in a merchant season, regardless of whether they came with him or not.

Every single member of his crew volunteered to come with him. And when they did, Marino had to swallow the tears he felt would undermine him as a captain.

In the end, he chose three. Red-headed Emelia, who hated being on land, could scramble up the mast faster than anyone and was the best deckhand Marino had ever had. Sturdy George, who could steer the ship and sail as well as he could cook and patch up a hole in the hull, a man who seemed like he could be in three places at once. And that was without having any magic that Marino was aware of. And Dooley. His first mate, his longest-standing crew member, who had been on Marino's ship since the start.

He gave them half a day to gather their belongings and say goodbye to their loved ones. 'I can't tell you where we're going, or how long we'll be gone, but I can promise I'll do everything I can to get us back to Eana as quickly as possible.'

By sunset, the *Siren's Secret* was ready to sail.

Marino had become more familiar with magic in these past few months. He felt it tingling in his fingers, felt it bubbling up inside him. His crew had accepted his new gifts with ease, even with joy. After all, his tempest powers made the *Siren's Secret* the fastest boat on the seas.

But Marino knew that magic had its limits. It could only do so much. And that the cost was sometimes not worth it.

His mind turned once again to the mysterious seeing sickness. Why had nobody warned Celeste? Why had Thea not protected her? Anger, wild and unfamiliar, ripped through him. He gripped the ship's wheel tightly, his grip so hard he wondered if the wooden wheel would crack beneath his fingers.

The *Siren's Secret* had already passed the Ochre Isles, a collection of orange-tinted tropical islands, covered in palm trees and lush foliage. Marino had only been there once before, and it had taken weeks. He couldn't quite believe that they had come so far in only a few days. He was barely sleeping, instead staying up all day and night, exhausting himself by drawing on every wisp of wind that floated by to push the ship faster through the waves.

He remembered Thea's wrinkled hand on his own. Willa putting her hand over his heart, and the words she had said. *'The cure is out there. It has been found before. But you will have to go further than you ever have.'*

He remembered Rose's eyes shining with unshed tears, the hope and trust that she put in him, her complete faith that he would save Celeste.

He sailed with a single-mindedness that drove him onwards, further and further from Eana.

'I will find this cure,' he told himself. 'I will find it and I will bring it back and Rose will save Celeste.'

That night, the sky was clear, the sea was still and the moon was high. Marino stood at the prow of the boat and stared down into the water. His own face stared back. His eyes were wide and wild and he had stubble growing on his chin. He looked like a desperate man. It felt apt. He had travelled so far, pushed his own tempest gift more than he ever had. Now he needed the help of the seaswifts. He unsheathed his dagger and pricked his fourth finger.

A single drop of blood fell into the sea.

Marino felt like the entire ocean stilled, like the world stopped turning.

'Lead me to the cure,' he whispered. 'The cure for Celeste.'

He waited in the silence. And then silver poured up and out of the ocean, as if its own moon was rising through the waves, and then, in a flutter of silver wings and shimmering tails, the seaswifts appeared.

They sparkled beneath the waves as they rose to the surface. They looked like hummingbirds of the sea, with fins that flapped like wings and silvery tails that propelled them forward. They were iridescent in the water, shimmering like liquid starlight.

And there were hundreds of them. With one drop of blood, Marino had called on an entire flock. The seaswifts leaped and dived in joyful arcs, and to Marino they looked like hope itself. For one impossible moment he was tempted to dive in with them, to let the seaswifts carry him in their current, all the way to the cure he so desperately sought. But instead he settled for leaning over as far as he could, hands stretched out, feeling the kiss of the ocean spray. The seaswifts glowed as their shimmering scales and silver tails created a trail across the surface of the sea.

Marino was so entranced by the sight of the seaswifts he didn't notice George and Emelia had joined him at the prow until they were right next to him, both laughing and whooping in wonder.

'We found the magic fish!' cried George, turning to Emelia and picking her up by the waist and twirling her around. Emelia laughed and whacked George on the shoulder. 'Put me down, you big oaf!' But she was grinning. 'I knew we'd find them. I never doubted it, never doubted the captain once.'

Marino raised a brow. 'I certainly hope not.'

'They're beautiful,' said George reverently, staring down at the sparkling trail that stretched out ahead of the ship, towards the horizon. He was a ruddy-cheeked, sandy-haired sailor who had been on ships since he was a boy.

'They'll lead us to the cure, I just know it,' added Dooley.

Marino didn't know where the seaswifts would lead them, but he knew he would follow that trail to the end of the earth if he needed to. For the first time since Celeste had fallen off the roof, he felt hope.

'This calls for rum in the captain's quarters!' he declared. 'Come with me, all three of you. We must celebrate the victories when we can.'

※

They followed the seaswifts for two days.

Marino was terrified to close his eyes, worried that if he looked away the seaswifts would descend back into the waves, taking his chance of finding the cure with them.

He ordered a round-the-clock watch, grateful that in the end he had decided to bring along a small crew. Marino used his tempest gift to keep the winds on their side, so they moved quickly, but he was always making sure to stay behind the trail of the seaswifts, never overtaking them.

The sun shone high in the sky, beating down on the ship with an unrelenting brightness. Marino had eschewed his velvet frock coat for a billowing white shirt, tucked into his black breeches. They were alone at sea; he didn't need to worry about propriety or etiquette.

On the third morning of following the seaswifts, day seven at sea, Marino spotted an enormous white stork, larger than he'd ever seen, hovering above the mast. The stork flew alongside the ship for hours, until another one joined it. Marino grinned at the sight, knowing that land must be close.

'Captain, you don't think they will try to gobble up our seaswifts, do you?' George wiped a bead of sweat from his brow as he watched the birds.

'They better not,' muttered Marino, his joy at the sight of the birds punctured by the threat they suddenly posed.

That afternoon, to Marino's horror, the seaswifts disappeared as quickly as they had arrived. One moment they were there and then it was almost as if they had never been there at all.

Marino leaned desperately over the water, hands outstretched as if he could catch one. Where was land? Where was the cure? He fumbled for the knife at his waist. He could pierce his finger again; he could use his blood to call them again . . .

Dooley and Emelia each grabbed one of his arms and pulled him back.

'That won't work, Captain,' said Emelia gently. 'You told us what the witches said. Only at night, when the moon is high and the sky is clear.'

'And we must be close,' added Dooley. 'We saw the storks. We'll find land soon. Land and the cure.'

Marino stared forlornly at the disappearing seaswifts. 'What if the cure isn't on land? What if it is beneath the waves? What if I'm meant to follow them?' He began to unbutton his shirt and leaned further over the edge.

'Careful there, Captain,' warned George, joining them at the prow. 'Don't drown just yet. I don't think you are meant to dive down with the fish.'

'The witches said that the seaswifts *show* you the direction. They don't take you right to what you're looking for,' added Emelia. 'They must be disappearing because we're close. That's the only explanation.'

How did Marino explain to his crew that magic didn't have explanations, that it was as changeable and unpredictable as a cloud?

'Take your spyglass up to the crow's nest,' suggested George.

Marino watched the last of the seaswifts disappear into the depths. It felt like they were taking the last of his strength, his sanity, with them.

He went up to the crow's nest, spyglass in hand. His first instinct was to try to gaze into the sea below, as if he could still track the seaswifts there.

Then he turned his gaze to the horizon, and gasped. He twisted the spyglass until the image sharpened. He let out a whoop. They had made it past the edge of the map. They had made it to a part of the world he had never seen before, never even heard of before.

'Land ahoy!'

Marino left Emelia at the wheel, and George and Dooley on deck. He felt utterly wrung out and exhausted.

'Get some rest, Captain,' said George. 'We'll wake you when we're close.'

Arriving unannounced in a new territory always came with risks. White sails meant peace where Marino came from, and he had to hope that this new land would have similar customs.

'Hoist the white sales, and don't get too close,' he warned, as he headed for his captain's quarters. 'Wherever that is – we don't know how they welcome uninvited visitors.'

As he drifted off to sleep, he could have sworn he heard drumming on the hull, and the distant sound of singing.

CHAPTER 6
Kira

She had been watching him on his ship. She had been waiting for his arrival.

When his blood dropped into the sea, three days ago, Kira had sensed it. Smelled it in the water. Smelled him. From miles and miles away, she felt him and his magic – and something more. She had sensed his determination and his fear. And that made her curious.

Kira knew men felt fear. She and her sisters were often the cause of it, and the scent, the taste, was unmistakable. But she had never smelled the kind of fear mixed with determination. As if the fear brought with it a kind of strength. As if it was the fear that made him brave.

The scent of his single drop of blood had roused her from slumber. The blood and breath of man was not something she craved, not like her sisters, but she wanted to see with her own eyes the man who had blood like this. Blood that had the tang of fear, but more.

Then she had heard the wings of the seaswifts. It had been a long time since the seaswifts had visited them, longer still since they had brought someone.

Her sisters chortled with glee, the sound echoing in

the water.

Their thoughts came quick and fast, overlapping and crowding her mind. It was always hard to block them out, and almost impossible when she was still groggy from sleep.

What will the seaswifts bring us?

I hope there is treasure on that ship. I want new jewels.

The ship brings us something better than jewels. It has the smell of magic.

Start the storm.

Do not let them reach Solvora.

The last comment was louder than all the others, as if it was being prodded deeper into her brain. She shook her head, as if she could shake out the order.

But her other sisters had taken up the chant.

Do not let them reach Solvora.

Her mer-sisters told her to hate humans. All humans. Even though they only knew Solvorans.

The Solvorans want us all dead, they chorused. *The Solvorans are our enemy. The Solvorans are why we are trapped here in their sea, why we cannot swim every ocean. We are doomed and destined to swim circles around Solvora forever.*

But for all their supposed hatred of humans, of Solvorans, some took lovers. Kira had seen it, seen them entice humans into the sea and give them the kiss of air, before taking them down into the depths. One of her mer-sisters kept a man down there for three moons, until eventually she tired of him and brought him back up to the sand. Leaving him without a look back, as if he was nothing more than seaweed that had washed ashore. But the kiss of air might have been the kiss of madness, for he could not stay away from the sea after that. Kira heard him wailing, tearing at his hair and his clothes, begging her mer-sister to take him back, take him back.

Eventually, he dived off a cliff. Her mer-sister did not save him.

I had taken all his life, she'd said, with a shrug. The man was but a husk by then, dead in every way that mattered before he even hit the water.

He had been Zella's lover. Zella, the oldest of her sisters. Zella, with her silver hair that glowed like starlight in the sea. Zella, with her golden eyes that blazed with hunger, with anger, with revenge. Zella, who loved Kira with a fierceness that sometimes frightened her. It surprised Kira that Zella was the one who most often brought humans down to the depths. She wasn't sure if Zella took so many humans because of her hatred for them, or despite it.

Zella wasn't the only mer who brought humans down below. Her other sisters nearly swooned when they described what it was like.

When you breathe from their lungs, you will feel like you can do anything. Like the whole world is yours for the taking. Breath from a human's lips is the best thing you will ever taste, her sisters promised.

Kira had never stolen breath from a human. Breathed the air of life. The very idea scared her.

She was scared she would like the taste too much. That it would change her forever.

As soon as the ship had crossed the barrier, as soon as he was in the Solvoran Sea, Kira had felt it like a jolt, like lightning in the water.

Her mer-sisters felt it too.

But as they began to whisper to the waves and whistle to the wind, Kira slipped away. She wanted to *see* him. With her eyes. She wanted to see this man who smelled of bravery and desperation. Of love and hope. Of magic.

Kira did not let her curiosity cloud her judgement. She still made sure to protect herself before she surfaced. She did not know the true measure of his heart, after all. When she peered above the waves, she began to shimmer so she could not be seen. Even if he looked right at her, he would see only the sparkle of the sea – the only hint of her true self a faint, shining mist moving as she did. He would not see her midnight-blue hair, flowing out behind her. Nor the rest of her, beneath the sea. The fuchsia sea orchids tied around her breasts. Her powerful tail, a blend of shimmering lavender and deep purple scales. Not even her eyes, a glowing violet flecked with silver.

In the open air, her vision sharpened and her eyes glowed brighter. Even though the ship was still far, she could see the captain clearly. She focused her vision even more, until she could properly see his face, as if she was a mere arm's length away from him.

The sight of him sent another jolt through her.

Kira had thought she knew beauty. She had seen the human lovers her sisters cajoled beneath the waves, seen the male merfolk that swam through every season. Daily, she saw the true faces of her mer-sisters, and their beauty was so powerful that it could drive men mad, even more so than their song.

But Kira had not known that a human face could look like this. Any face. A jaw that could have been carved from stone, but with full lips, lips she knew from looking would be soft to the touch, and eyes that were warm and dark. She knew she should rejoin her sisters, but she couldn't tear her gaze away.

Oh, she whispered, the sound lost in the waves. *Oh*.

He was holding on to the ship's wheel and staring ahead with that fierce determination she had scented in his blood. She could not help noticing the strength of his arms, the broadness of his shoulders. The surety with which he steered the ship. She had the strangest urge to rest her head on his chest to listen to the beating of his human heart.

As she watched him, he saw something that changed his entire expression. His eyes lit up, and he broke into a wide grin. He threw back his head and laughed, the sound so joyful that Kira found herself rising further up out of the water to hear it better.

'Land!'

He had seen Solvora.

Two others joined him at the wheel. Kira could tell from the way they spoke to him, the way he responded, that he was respected and admired. And that he cared for his crew.

Kira had never felt anything more than a passing pang for the ships they sank. But she had never felt so drawn to anyone, human or mer, before.

She had not planned to save him.

But he was no Solvoran.

And she would not let him die.

CHAPTER 7
Marino

In Marino's dreams, he was in the sea. Far above him he could see the sun shining through the water, the light splintering and refracting in the waves. He began to swim to the surface, but seaweed wrapped around his ankles, pulling him deeper down.

Do not struggle, whispered a voice in his ear. *Embrace the sea, and we will embrace you.* Marino turned towards the voice, eyes wide even in the water, and all he saw was the flicker of a golden fin with shimmering scales. Laughter echoed all around him, strange and distorted in the sea. The laughter grew louder and louder until it echoed in his ears.

Marino woke to the sound of thunder and the smell of smoke.

He jolted out of bed and ran to the deck, his heart hammering. Raindrops pelted his face and jagged streaks of lightning kissed the sea. The sky was alight with it, and it looked as if the sky itself was about to crack open.

But Marino barely noticed the lightning. Because his ship was on fire.

Plumes of smoke billowed from the front of the ship where flames leaped and grew, despite the heavy rain.

Marino ran towards the inferno, ripping his shirt off to try to smother the flames.

But they kept growing. Even as the waves sloshed up on to the deck as they tossed the ship around like it was nothing more than a small toy. Marino tried to summon a strand of wind, something, anything to help keep the ship afloat, just long enough to steer it to safety. But it felt like his magic had been blown away by the storm. Why hadn't he brought another witch with him? Why had he been so headstrong and cocky? Now his ship was going to sink, and along with it his crew and any chance of finding his sister's cure.

'EMILIA! GEORGE! DOOLEY!' His voice rang out in the storm, but the crash of thunder was the only reply. Where *were* they? He shouted their names over and over again, searching desperately for any sign of them, but the wind swallowed his screams.

Marino watched in horror as the flames reached the sails. He knew there was no saving the ship now. His only hope would be trying to swim to the land they had seen. The land where he thought he would find the cure for Celeste.

I'm sorry, sister. He sent out the thought as if it could reach her across the waves and all the way back in Eana. *Please wake without me. Somehow. Please live.*

He fell to his knees, even as all around him his ship burned. All he wanted now was to find his crew, try to get them to safety. It was his fault they were so far from home.

Then, through the din of the storm and the roar of the fire, he heard a shout.

'CAPTAIN!'

The cry came from overboard.

Marino leaped up, higher than the flames, and through

the smoke saw Emelia, George and Dooley in a rowboat. Relief flooded through him. His crew would survive.

Marino held this close like a lifeline. He'd always instructed them to abandon ship if needed, to not wait for him. His crew would not die for him. But now, if he could make it to them, make it to the rowboat, he could live too. But as the flames grew higher all around him, and the smoke began to choke him, and he could hear his ship cracking in a hundred different places as if it was crying out in pain, he felt his strength shatter.

'CAPTAIN!' The voice of Emelia was further away now. Good. He hoped they were rowing as hard and fast as they could away from the ship, away from the danger. 'CAPTAIN! JUMP!'

The wall of flames was closing in on him, but he knew she was right. That his only chance was to charge through it and into the thrashing waves. He was a strong swimmer, he could swim to shore, he could swim to his crew, he couldn't give up hope yet, not when his heart was still beating.

With a whispered prayer to Eana, he leaped through the fire, as his ship splintered in two beneath him.

The pain was immediate, and excruciating. He must have only been in the air for a moment, but it felt like time had stopped. His whole body lit up, as if he had been doused in kerosene. Through the haze of pain, he saw that flames truly were dancing on his skin. And some small part of him recognised that this was no ordinary fire. This fire smelled of magic.

Marino plummeted, screaming, into the furious sea, and it swallowed him up like it had been waiting for him.

Blessedly, the flames went out. The seawater soothed him, took away the agonising, burning pain, but it did not release him. Instead, it pulled him deeper down. He couldn't tell which way was up, and as he tried to fight against the waves, tried to get to the surface, he began to lose consciousness.

Swim, Marino. Swim! There was a chorus of voices in his head, and it was Celeste's voice and his long-gone mother's voice and his crew and everyone he held dear. He summoned every ounce of strength he had left and kicked as hard as he could, forcing his way through the waves.

Finally, he broke the surface of the water.

Marino took a desperate breath, gasping for air. His throat burned but at least he was breathing. He was alive. And he intended to keep it that way. All around him were broken pieces of his ship, and he foggily registered that his captain's chair, his beloved crushed-velvet chair that had been bolted to the floor of his captain's quarters, the one that Celeste had gifted him on his eighteenth birthday, was sinking next to him.

There was no sign of the rowboat, or his crew. But surely something from the ship would float. He needed to find something, anything, he could grasp and then make his way to the distant shores of this unknown land. Yes, he could do that. He *would* do that. Through the haze of smoke he tried to see if there was a broken door or a piece of wood that would support his weight. He needed to focus on staying afloat, on staying alive.

Then a shimmer of light caught his eye.

Coming towards him, cutting through the water effortlessly, like a shark, was a woman. Only her head was visible, and her face was obscured by some sort of flower mask, but her eyes . . . her eyes were glowing. And the water all around her was glowing too, little flecks of silver luminescence lighting her way through the waves.

Marino stared at her, entranced. He momentarily forgot where he was, who he was. All he could do was watch her approach.

There was an ear-splintering crack from above, and he looked up just in time to see the top of the mast come crashing down.

Then darkness. Complete darkness.

CHAPTER 8
Kira

Kira knew her sisters would not understand.

They would say that the ocean had claimed him. That he belonged to the sea now. To them.

But Kira had seen the look in his eyes. She had *felt* it, as if his gaze was a physical touch, stroking her face. And she wanted to know what his true touch would be like. For the first time, Kira yearned to bring someone down to the soft seabed below.

But not like this. Not when he was dazed and stunned and near death. And not when she had felt him across the waves even before she had laid eyes on him or his ship. She had been waiting for him, and she would save him.

Kira cut through the water, faster now, and dived down to where the captain was sinking beneath the waves. He was even more beautiful up close, even in repose. His eyes were closed, and his face was relaxed. She could still hear his heart beating, and that spurred her on.

Because Kira could save a man from drowning, but she could not bring one back from the dead.

Kira looped her arms underneath his, and holding him against her body, swam him to the surface, grateful that her tail was strong enough to propel them both.

It was the most she had ever touched any human.

She felt her own skin warm as it pressed against his, even though the sea was cold.

Warmth was not something she encountered often, and it sent a thrill through her. She only knew it from the kiss of the sun on her face when they basked in their favourite coves. She had not known that another body could warm her this way.

Kira kept swimming for Solvora. The sun was just starting to rise, stretching orange and gold fingers across the sky.

She knew, if she truly meant to save this man, she needed to leave him somewhere he would be found. Somewhere safe.

And she would have to go closer to the shore than she ever had before.

What are you doing?

It was Zella's voice in her head, and then all her sisters joined in, the chorus echoing. *What are you doing what are you doing what are you doing WHAT ARE YOU DOING?*

I am saving him. She thought it loud enough to break through their words.

There was a moment of silence.

We do not save men. It was only Zella now, her disdain clear. Her disappointment in Kira. *We do not save Solvorans.*

He is no Solvoran. Did you not see his magic? What man can do magic?

Magic should not be in the hands of men. It cannot be trusted. Men cannot be trusted.

But it is more than the magic. Can't you see that he is a good man? He was looking for his crew. I saw him! His panic when he could not find them. His relief when he heard their voices.

And of the others? Will you save them too? Do you now want to save all flailing humans?

They are in a boat. Kira was less concerned about the other three. Only interested in them because he clearly cared for them. And they had left in the boat without their captain. If they drowned, perhaps they deserved it. It was only the pain it would cause him that gave her pause.

Boats can be flipped. Ships can be sunk. Do not be so naive. Do not be kind to those who would kill you in an instant.

We do not know if they would kill us. Let the waves decide.

We control the waves.

Let the true spirit of the sea decide. The sea in her purest form, waves and wind moving without the mer intervening. The mother of the sea. Her mer-sisters may have started the storm, started the sea-fire that had burned the ship – to stop it from reaching Solvora, so they could plunder it for themselves – but the mother of the sea had more power than any of them. It was she who had gifted the mer their magic, and even though Kira had never seen her, she worshipped her.

Who are you to decree such a thing? Zella's voice was a warning, danger radiating in every word. *You do not tell the spirit of the sea what to do.*

Please, Zella. All I'm asking is to let me save this man. To try. If the spirit of the sea stops me, then so be it.

Kira was the youngest of the mer, she knew they coddled her, as much as creatures of tooth and claw and fin could coddle and care. And she had never asked for anything from her sisters before.

Come, sisters, ordered Zella. *Let us find ourselves some treasure from this wreck. Kira, do not lose your head over this man. Solvoran or not, he is still a man and cannot be trusted.*

Kira knew it was the closest thing to approval she would get from Zella.

His breath had slowed. She had not noticed because she had been so focused on getting him to the surface, getting him to the shore, that she had forgotten to listen to his heart, listen to his breathing.

No. She would not defy her sisters only to have him die.

The water was shallower now. She had never been in such shallow waters. Never dared come so close to the beach itself.

But she was not afraid. Kira knew she was strong in the way that all mer were strong. She could drag herself back out to sea.

Kira called on a wave to propel them up on to the sand. Once they were out of the water, he was suddenly so heavy, and she nearly dropped him on the sand. But she had done it. They had made it to shore.

She could hear the water in his lungs, and because it was seawater, it listened to her, so when she commanded, *leave him*, it did. It trickled out of his lips, but still, he did not breathe.

Slowly, and much more gently than she'd ever seen her sisters do it, Kira pressed her lips to his.

The taste of his lips, the feel of them beneath her own, sent a shock through her, and for a moment, she wanted to breathe in his own life air. Take whatever of it was left for herself.

No. She fought the urge to take his life air, as delicious as it would be. She did not want his life air. She wanted him to open his eyes. She wanted to kiss him properly, with him awake. And, mother of the sea, she desperately wanted him to kiss her back.

But to do that, he had to live. So, with her hand on his heart, she breathed life back into him.

He opened his eyes.

CHAPTER 9
Marino

Marino was certain he had drowned.

He was dead.

He had to be.

But as he opened his eyes and sensations slowly came flooding back (sand under his skin, sun on his face, body aching everywhere a body could ache) he realised he was not dead. He was alive.

There was a shadow over him, and he realised it must be whoever had saved him from the wreck. Someone had saved him, had pulled him from the waves and up on to the shore.

The sun was directly behind them so he couldn't make out their details, couldn't see their face, and then their hair swung forward, brushing against his chest.

It felt like wet silk. And, he marvelled, it was blue. Deepest, darkest blue. His eyes must be playing tricks on him.

There was a movement above him, and the hair disappeared from his chest. He squinted because the sun was shining right in his eyes, and he had to see who it was who had rescued him. He had to thank them.

His vision was blurry but then, suddenly, came into sharp

focus, and he found himself staring into a pair of glowing violet eyes. The top half of her face was obscured by a mask made of strange purple flowers, but he could see the bottom half of her face. See her full lips that were curling up into a smile.

'You,' he breathed, because he remembered now, seeing the woman swimming towards him in the sea.

'Me,' she said. Her voice was low and melodic, and strangely sounded how he had always imagined the voice of the sea would sound. Then she whipped her head up, as if she had heard a sound in the distance. She turned her gaze back to him, and he reached up and stroked her cheek. Her skin was cold and soft, and as his fingers touched her face, a shiver of pleasure ran through him.

'Thank you.' His voice was a hoarse whisper.

'Do not die and let it be for nothing,' she said. 'Stay alive.'

And then she moved out of his eyeline again, and he heard a shuffle in the sand.

'Wait!' Marino wanted to go after her. But as he tried to rise, his body protested. His muscles felt like jelly, he was weaker than he'd ever been, but he managed to prop himself up on his elbows, just in time to see a shimmering purple tail disappear into the shallows.

Could it be? Had he been saved by a *mermaid*?

'Wait!' he cried again, but his voice was still nothing more than a hoarse croak.

Marino's head was spinning. Maybe he *was* dead. Or dreaming. Or –

A series of loud barks broke through his thoughts, and then there was a dog at his side, then two dogs, then three, all with short black fur and cold wet noses, all sniffing and licking and barking in his ear, and he lay his head back down on the sand and began to laugh. He was alive, he was sure of it. Gloriously, gloriously alive.

And, apparently, he had a blue-haired mermaid to thank for it.

An old man came after the dogs, stumbling in the sand. His flowing white hair was blowing in the wind, his mouth flapping open in awe. 'A survivor! Shark's teeth, I never thought I'd see the day!' He staggered forward, using a fishing pole as a walking stick.

As he came closer, Marino managed to sit up again, pushing one of the dogs off his chest. He held up his hands to show he was unarmed, and as he did, the old man paused and began to laugh so hard he started to wheeze, and he dropped his fishing pole in the sand.

'You think I'm afraid of you? My dogs can smell danger a mile away, and they seem fond of you. And I know you've got nothing on but those breeches.' The old man let out a whistle between his teeth. 'A survivor! I saw your ship go down. I heard the song of that storm and I thought, it has been a while since the mer sang down a storm, let me pop my head out and see what's happening, and what do I see out in the night? The most beautiful ship that has ever graced our shores, going down in flames.' He shook his head. 'Sat and watched it, I did, and it was a terrible thing to see. I went back to bed, but my dogs here they were barking down the door, so I let them out, and then I see you washed up on the shore!' He shook his head. 'I've seen too many wrecks to count, and never once have I seen a man survive.' He whistled again. 'Bones! Heart! Luck! Heel, now! Get off the poor man. He's had enough without you licking him to death.'

The dogs let out one more bark. Marino's head was whirling as he tried to take in everything the man was saying. Storm songs? Shipwrecks? No survivors?

Where *was* he?

But the first thing he said was, 'Bones?' His voice came out in a croak.

'Ah, yes, the name of one of my fool dogs climbing all over you.' The affection was clear in the old man's voice. 'Bones is the big one there. Heart is the little one, and Luck is missing an ear. Two brothers and a sister and I've had them since they were pups. Found them whimpering on the beach, near drowned themselves, brought them right in to get warm, and they never left.' The man stepped forward to offer a hand to Marino, pulling him up to his feet. His arms were lean and wiry, and his strength belied his years. 'Much like I've just found you. I've got a gift for finding strays, that's what my missus used to say to me.'

Marino blinked. He'd never had anyone describe him as a 'stray' before. The old man let go of Marino's hand. 'Where are my manners? I'm Samuel Troumaine.'

Marino nodded. 'Thank you, Samuel. It sounds like I'm lucky to have found you. Or rather, lucky that you found me! I'm Marino Pegasi, and I've come from Eana.' Samuel showed no sign of recognition at the name, and Marino realised if he had come all the way off *his* map, that Eana must be as much of a mystery to the people here. 'Where am I?'

Samuel let out a big, booming laugh that showed all his yellowed teeth. 'You don't know? Welcome, Marino, to Solvora.'

Solvora. Marino rolled the word around in his mouth. *Solvora.* He liked how it sounded, how it felt to say.

'Now I won't have been the only one who saw the wreck. And someone else will have seen you down here on Pearl Beach, and there is sure to be a commotion. Because as I said, when a ship is wrecked, there are no survivors. The mer make sure of that.' Samuel turned and spat into the sand.

Marino shielded his eyes from the glare of the now fully risen sun as he glanced back out at the sea. He could make out what was left of his ship, still slowly sinking beneath the waves. 'A mermaid saved me.'

Samuel laughed again. 'You must have hit your head. The mermaids do not save. They only sink. And if a mermaid got her claws and teeth into you, she would not have tossed you up on the sand with your wits about you. She would have dragged you down beneath the waves and driven you mad before returning you a shell of yourself. No. A mermaid did not save you.'

'But I saw her.'

'Trick of the light. A hallucination. Not a mermaid.'

'But . . .'

Samuel stepped closer to Marino and lowered his voice. 'Listen, Marino. It is a miracle you are here on our shores. And I know you've lost a lot, and you don't know our ways, so you are saying things that don't make sense. But listen here.' He gripped Marino's arm, digging in his gnarled fingers to make his point. 'Do not tell anyone here in Solvora that you think a mermaid saved you. Do you understand? The mer are our enemies, and as long as we stay away from the sea, stuff our ears to avoid their song, and don't look directly at them, we are safe. But if you start telling people a mermaid saved you . . .' Samuel let out an incredulous snort, 'you'll be thrown back in the sea faster than you can blink. *Do you understand?*'

Marino nodded. 'I understand.' Then he cleared his throat. 'My ship was the *Siren's Secret*,' his voice cracked as said his ship's name, 'and I was her captain. I had a small crew of three, and before the ship went down, they managed to escape in a rowboat. I can only hope that they survived too. Did you see them?'

Samuel released Marino's arm, and his intensity turned into something else. Into a gruff pity.

'Get your ears cleaned so I can stop repeating myself. *When there is a wreck, there are no survivors.*' Marino fell back to his knees at Samuel's words, and all that they implied. He thought he would be sick in the sand. The littlest dog, Heart, nuzzled his cheek. The dog's tail was wagging, and Marino envied the dog and its happiness and simple life. In that moment, he felt he would never be happy again.

Samuel sighed deeply. 'Shark's teeth, get back on your feet! Come on. *On your feet*. There will be a time to grieve, but it is not now. You need to get cleaned up. Word of your arrival, your survival, will spread, and they'll want you up at the palace, no doubt, and you don't want to be trekking sand in there. Oh no. No sand in the Gilded Palace.' He squinted at Marino. 'We should get you in some clean clothes too. Or at least, in any clothes.' He gestured at Marino's lack of a shirt, and torn breeches.

There was the blare of a bugle, and Samuel groaned, tilting his head up to the sky, as if he could see answers there. 'Looks like the palace has decided they want to see you now. You better come up with a better story than being saved by a mermaid, and you better do it quick.'

A strange numbness had overtaken Marino. 'It's my fault if they are dead. My crew, they only came on this mission because of me. I should be the dead one, not them. I should be the one at the bottom of the sea.'

Samuel crouched down, bones and joints creaking, so he was eye level with Marino. 'Pull yourself together. There is a reason you survived. And to throw away that chance, well, that is an insult to the memory of your crew.'

Marino drew a shaky breath. He knew the fisherman was right. He needed to live, if only to do what he had set out to do and find the cure for Celeste.

Samuel patted Marino on the shoulder. His watery-grey eyes were kind. 'And who knows? Maybe they rowed their way to safety. If they are on Solvora, we'll find them. And if not, maybe the mer took mercy on them. They didn't drown you, maybe they were feeling generous.'

'You don't believe that though, do you?'

'It doesn't matter what I believe, now, does it? What matters is the story you tell yourself. Whatever you need to survive. And if you need hope, well, I'll toss a little your way. Doesn't hurt me none.' Samuel tapped Marino's chest, right above his heart, with his finger. 'You keep them alive in there for as long as you need to.'

Marino blinked back tears. It felt like he'd had two miracles today. The mermaid – he *knew* a mermaid had saved him, he had seen her with his own eyes, had felt the silky wet of her hair, the brush of her fingers against his chest – and now this fisherman offering him wisdom and hope by the handful. He nodded and stood, and this time he was the one who helped Samuel to his feet.

'I owe you a great debt,' he said, shaking Samuel's hand.

Samuel rolled his eyes. 'Just see if you can survive the day, and then we'll go from there.' Then he grinned. 'But it's no bad thing to have a fancy foreign captain with a knack for survival in my debt.' One of the dogs, Bones, barked, as if in agreement. 'Now, time to meet the Solvoran soldiers. Prepare yourself, they are a spectacularly grumpy bunch.'

'Don't worry, Samuel. I've faced worse than grumpy soldiers.' Marino rolled his shoulders back, and for the first time since he'd washed up on its shores, turned to face Solvora.

CHAPTER 10
Marino

The white sand of the beach Marino stood on stretched up to meet a grey stone cliff face that merged into the mountain that was clearly the heart of the land. Perched along the side of the mountain were buildings covered in colourful tiles. Some tiles had intricate patterns in them, winking down to Marino like they had secrets to tell. In all his travels, Marino had never seen anything like it. And at the very top of the mountain, like icing on a cake, was a grand gold palace, glinting in the early morning light. It had dozens of towers stretching to the sky, and as Marino squinted to get a better look, he realised that the towers themselves were slowly twirling.

'She's a beauty, isn't she?' said Samuel proudly. 'I've never seen any other lands, but I know none could ever compare to Solvora.' He tilted his head towards Marino. 'Tell me, is your home as beautiful as this?'

Marino smiled as he thought of Eana. Of the grandness of Anadawn Palace, the charm of Eshlinn and Wishbone Bay, the dramatic cliffs of Ortha, the rolling sands of the Ganyeve Desert. 'Eana is indeed very beautiful. But my true home is the sea, and to me, nothing can compare to that.'

Samuel gave a dismissive humph. 'Any fool who thinks the sea is their home isn't in their right mind.'

Marino just laughed. 'There is no doubt that Solvora is a beautiful place.' He raised his chin to try to take it all in. 'Is the entirety of Solvora built on that mountain?' He could not see anything beyond it.

Samuel shook his head. 'On the southern side of Goldwave Mountain the land stretches out, like a lady's train. All the way down the mountain there are terraced farms, and then they sprawl out along the lowlands. Farmers live there, mostly.'

The Solvoran soldiers were closer now. Marino picked up a fistful of sand. It was not Eanan earth, the strongest for casting small spells, but it would be better than nothing. All strands of magic needed something in exchange, and enchantments needed earth. Marino had never fully mastered the art of enchantments, but he figured it couldn't hurt. He dropped the fine sand slowly back to the shore as he whispered a spell.

'Slow your steps
Trust my face
Forget that I'm
Not from this place.'

Samuel turned towards Marino with a frown. 'What's this, then?'

'Just want to make a good first impression on these soldiers,' said Marino.

Samuel raised his brows. 'Smells like trickery to me. But as long as it isn't directed at me, I don't mind it. Nice to see magic on the shore again and not just in the sea.'

Marino wanted to question this statement – what magic

was in the sea? Was it the magic of the mer? And the word *again* – was magic once more prominent on Solvora? But there would be time for questions later. Now he had the approaching soldiers to contend with. The spell seemed to have worked, they had certainly slowed down, and they all had a slightly stunned expression. There were three of them, two men and a woman, all wearing bright blue tunics woven with gold and white. Marino assessed their weapons. One was carrying a large net that seemed to be woven out of some sort of metal, the woman clutched a harpoon with a sharp golden point, and the third held a sword unlike any Marino had ever seen. It was curved in an S shape at the end, almost like a hook.

'Do they plan to throw that net on me?' Marino muttered to Samuel.

Samuel grunted. 'You came from the sea, so they are approaching you like a sea creature.'

The woman soldier raised her voice. 'Samuel Troumaine, step back so we can interrogate the new arrival.'

Marino sighed. So much for them forgetting that he wasn't from here. He still struggled with enchantments.

'I'll take responsibility for him,' Samuel called back. 'I found him, after all.'

The three soldiers were still several paces away. 'We need to take him to the Gilded Palace. The king will want to meet him.' The soldier who had spoken, the one with the net, eyed Marino warily. 'It has been a long time since anyone survived a wreck.'

'I can't believe they haven't thrown the net on you yet.' Samuel spoke under his breath.

Marino allowed himself a small grin. Perhaps his

enchantment had worked, at least a little. Then he cleared his throat. 'Good soldiers, it is an honour to meet you, and to be on your fine land. I come from across the sea and my ship, as you know, sank in the storm.'

'You were attacked by the mer,' said the one with the strange hook-sword. 'They call the storms. They start the sea-fires. They destroy the ships.' As he spoke, he swiped the sword in front of him, as if battling an invisible foe.

'So I hear,' said Marino. 'But the point stands – I am a captain with no ship, no coin, and no clothes. All I ask of you and your ruler is to take mercy on me, to welcome me the way I would welcome any of you to my home, and I promise I will return any kindness, any cost, ten-fold when I am able to sail again.' He put his hand to his heart, signalling the seriousness of his vow.

The soldiers paused and then burst out laughing. The woman spoke first. 'Captain, as you call yourself, do you think the mer let any ships leave? No. Just as none can arrive, none can leave. We are stuck here, on Solvora, and now you are stuck with us. So, you better come up with another way to repay any kindness that does not involve you sailing away.'

Marino's blood pounded in his ears. This could not be. He had survived only so he could find the cure for Celeste and return to Eana. To save her, and to stop the seeing sickness from spreading. He could not be stranded here on Solvora. On a land he had never heard of. On a land off the map. His face fell.

'Chin up,' said the one with the net. 'There are worse places to be stuck.'

Marino could only nod, still reeling.

'And in the meantime, we need to take you up to the palace. You can come willingly or not, but you're coming with us,' the soldier went on, taking a menacing step towards Marino.

'I will gladly come and meet your king,' said Marino quickly. 'But please, let me find something suitable to wear.'

'And let him catch his breath!' said Samuel, tsking loudly. 'The man nearly drowned. He isn't in a state to meet King Leonel. Let him get some food at least, and some rest.'

'I suppose that is sensible,' said the woman soldier slowly. 'But who will vouch for him?'

'I already said that I would!' Samuel snapped. Then he turned to the soldier with the sword. 'Abilio, you know I was friends with your father. He was a great fisherman, before the accident. One of the best. I give you my fisherman's oath that I will be responsible for this survivor, and that he will arrive at the Gilded Palace tomorrow. In time for the midday meal. Besides, isn't our good King Leonel a bit . . . peculiar about his scheduling? Surely he'll want to prepare for our visitor. I wouldn't want to be the one surprising him. He doesn't like surprises, our king.'

It was as if Samuel had cast his own enchantment spell with his words. Marino stood back and watched in amazement as the three soldiers conferred with each other and then nodded.

'We invoke our power as Solvoran soldiers and command that you, one Samuel Troumaine, take charge of this survivor named . . .' Abilio's voice trailed off.

'Marino,' supplied Samuel. 'Captain Marino.'

'Yes, the survivor *Captain* Marino – you will take charge of him and if he disappears or causes misconduct, it is you who will be responsible and take any blame and punishment. Understood?'

'Understood,' said Samuel.

'We expect you tomorrow at the Gilded Palace at midday,' said the woman soldier. Then she gave both Samuel and Marino a sharp look. 'Do not disappoint us.'

The three soldiers turned and began the trudge up the sand. Moments later, the bugle sounded again.

'Salt-brained soldiers can't go anywhere without trumpeting their arrival,' muttered Samuel.

'Thank you. Again, thank you.' Marino felt the word was a hollow offering for how he felt. How many times had he said thank you to this old fisherman in the past hour?

'Don't make a fuss of it. Now let's get you something to eat. You must be famished. Drowning will do that to a man.'

CHAPTER 11
Kira

Kira watched the man on the beach until he was led away by the old fisherman. Marino. She had a name for him now. It suited him.

She heard every word they said, her mer-ears sharper by far than human ears.

He had seen her.

And he knew what she was.

Kira wasn't sure how that made her feel. But she did know that she had to see him again. Touch him again. To find out from him what the world was like past Solvora. To know what it was that he was seeking.

But she would not tempt him back to the sea. Because she knew that if she did, if she used her voice or her face, he would be caught. And it would be a trick. And if she were to ever press her lips to his again, she would want it to be in the way that she had seen humans do together – not one breathing in the other, but a back and forth of kissing and shared sensations. She wanted him to want her because she was Kira, not because she had enticed him with her song, or any of her other mer-tricks, as she thought of them.

Kira had long wanted to be known, truly known, but had

never thought it was possible – until she had seen the kindness and warmth and light in Marino's eyes. But perhaps she was being foolish. Perhaps as a mermaid she would only ever have lovers for sport, and never for love.

Kira rolled these thoughts around in her mind as she swam further out to sea.

Not too far, never too far. Never able to go past the ring around Solvora, the ring that kept them close.

Other mer could come and go and they did, but the Solvoran mermaids were destined to stay close to Solvora. And that made them hateful and hungry.

Or so Zella told her, as she tied shells in Kira's hair and strung stolen gems on strings of seaweed to make necklaces and bracelets.

We will take what we can, we will take what is ours, Zella crowed. And it was true, they took whatever came into the ring around Solvora. And sometimes they would sing to the Solvorans, tempting them to the depths, to their deaths.

Solvoran mer used to be able to swim in the wide sea, the whole ocean, or so her sisters told her. Kira never had. Her memories were all of the Solvoran Sea.

The Solvoran mer were once the favourite of the mother of the sea, her sisters whispered. The most beloved, the most beautiful, the most trusted, the most powerful.

Until they had disappointed the sea herself.

A Solvoran mer had swapped her tail for legs, her magic for so-called love. She had married a man, and not any man, but the king who had ruled before the current king (Kira did not know his name, she did not care to know the names of kings), and the mer had given up what made her mer to live with him in the Gilded Palace.

But the mer missed the sea like a child would miss their mother, and she came down to the shore every night, until the mother of the sea allowed her to swim again with her sisters. To return to where she belonged.

And all would have been fine, if her hateful husband had not hunted her for leaving him. He had slain her with his own hands, so said Kira's sisters. And then his rage turned to grief and madness and he had thrown himself from the highest tower, begging for mercy from the sea and from Solvora. Murdering a mer, one who had given him so much – one who had wanted to join humans and mer together, had proved that men and mer could not live peacefully. And the sea herself would seek revenge.

From the day the king before the current king killed his mer-bride and himself, the mother of the sea made it known that the Solvorans would be punished.

The mother of the sea's punishment was that the Solvorans could never leave. And none could ever join them in their exile. All ships that came too close to Solvora must be sunk.

And it was her Solvoran daughters who were her soldiers. Because the sea was angry with them too. They had failed to protect their sister, who the sea had allowed back into the sea. *Prove you can protect each other, prove you can protect yourselves. And never let the Solvorans leave. Punish them for what they did to you.*

That was what the sea told them, in whispers on the waves. And the mer were left with figuring out how to live as both prisoner and guard. The oldest, and boldest, of the mer struck a strange truce with the new young king. To make all their lives easier, while still obeying the will of the sea. To show they were not completely without a heart, the mer would wear masks to hide their faces, and lessen the power of their beauty.

In return, the Solvorans would not hunt them if they stayed below.

Neither mer nor man always abided by these rules, but they were there all the same.

So, the mer were bound by the invisible ring in the sea – proving where their loyalties lay, and the Solvorans themselves were trapped by the mer and the sea – punished for what their king had done. And almost two decades had passed like this, each side getting more hateful and more hungry each day. There must be more, the Solvorans whispered to themselves. More beyond the Solvoran ring. Remember when there was more? The mer murmured. *Remember when the entire sea was ours?*

But Kira, even though this was all she'd ever known, didn't feel hateful. She felt hunger, though. Hunger and yearning and desire for what she had never known.

Now she knew.

She hungered for whatever magic it was that danced inside Marino.

She hungered for a human who she had chosen to save. She told herself she was not going against the sea's wishes, he was not Solvoran. And her sisters had sunk his ship, as the sea decreed.

But she didn't know if she would ever see Marino again or touch him or speak to him and she felt a rush of longing to take what she could, like Zella said, and if that meant singing him down to the sea than maybe she should but –

No. She had seen the light go out of their eyes, the men her sisters took.

She would not take the light from Marino's eyes.

She would watch him, though. Watch him in Solvora to see what he would do. Who he would become.

Kira found her sisters plundering the wreck.

She could hear their laughter, their joy, before she even reached them.

A portion of the ship had already sunk to the seabed. Her sisters were darting around it, in one window, out another, careful not to cut their tails on any of the sharp and broken edges.

Kira! We found you some pearls! He had a whole collection!

Kira wore pearls in her ears, and pearls on her neck and around her wrists. She liked that they grew from nothing into something. She liked that they came from the sea and went to shore and came back again.

But she didn't want to wear the pearls that Marino had carefully carried with him from where he had come from, *Eana*, to here. But perhaps she would keep them safe for him. To give to him if she ever met him again.

She felt sleep tug at her. She had overextended herself. She had not known how much it would take out of her, to save him.

She hoped he would be worth it.

She hoped she would see him again.

He is a waste of your energy. Do not think on him again.

It was Zella in her head. Her oldest sea sister swam towards Kira, silver hair streaming out behind her.

Did you at least take some of his life air?

Of course not.

Her sisters were all abandoning their treasure hunt to gather round Kira. She wished they would let her be.

Not even a taste?

No.

But. That was a lie. She had *tasted* a little of his life air, when her lips had pressed against his. It had been an accident. But still. She had known then how delicious it would be. How delicious he would be. But she had stopped herself and that was what was important. She had saved him.

She felt her eyes beginning to grow heavy. She was so tired. Her sisters saw, and they laughed, poking her with their long nails.

You need to take a lover, they teased. *That will keep you up all night and all day. Breathe in the air of life and you will feel like you can live forever.*

Weren't you tempted? It was Mei. The sister Kira felt the closest to. Mei had a pale green tail and light pink hair, and her eyes were flecked with silver like all mer. *By the man you saved. He was very handsome.*

Kira laughed. *Leave me be. I'm tired.* And she saw the glance that passed between them. The secret her sisters shared but didn't tell her. The secret of why they coddled and cuddled her, even though she was old enough to drown a man if she so liked.

Then sleep, sang Mei. *Sleep as long as you need.* They swam with her to the cave where she slept. Where they all slept. Curled up in turquoise seagrass, protected by the cave. Kira knew they took turns sleeping, but it was never her who had to keep watch. She grew more tired than her sisters. Her sisters were strong. They could swim without stopping, they could sing for days on end. But Kira could not. Sleep came for her, and when it did, she could not fight it. But she knew her sisters would protect her. The mer had learned the importance of protecting each other.

We will be here when you wake, they sang, a chorus of safety all around her, and Kira knew it would be true. They were always there when she woke. Always there when she needed them. Always there. Telling her stories, singing her songs. Answering her questions, even if she didn't like the answers. When sleep began to drag Kira into its depths, much as the mer did to the men, her mind grew fuzzy, and she asked the questions that swam in her head. She knew the answers her sisters would give her, but they never rang true. So, she kept asking. But the answers were always the same.

Why do we wreck the ships?

Because we must punish the Solvorans.

Why must we punish the Solvorans?

Because they are the reason we cannot leave. We are of Solvora and can never leave it.

Never? Kira always asked. Never was a long time to be bound. Never and forever felt like two sides of the same fin. As unfathomable as the darkest depths of the sea she loved so much.

Until the mother of the sea decrees it. Until the Solvorans have been punished to her liking.

Our fate is their punishment.

Our punishment is their fate.

Solvora, Solvora, Solvora.

Do not forget, do not forgive.

Now sleep, Kira. Sleep.

CHAPTER 12
Marino

Marino woke to the sound of the dogs barking.

He was lying in a small, unfamiliar bed and wearing strange clothes. A coarse shirt, patched breeches. His head ached something fierce, and when he reached back around to gently inspect it, he felt a lump the size of an egg on the back of his head.

Marino sat up, trying to get his bearings, and immediately hit his head on a low beam. Cursing, and now rubbing the top of his head as well, he sat up again, more carefully this time.

The small dog with matted black fur was curled up on the bed next to him. The dog looked at him with soulful black eyes and let out a small whine, as if to say, 'I'm not the one who woke you, I wanted you to keep sleeping.'

Two more dogs were barking at the back of an old man cooking over a small stove in the corner.

'Pipe down, you two, or there'll be no breakfast for anyone,' the man grumbled at them. He turned then, and when he saw Marino was awake, he beamed, showing a mouthful of crooked teeth. 'Ah, and I see the captain is awake! Just in time for breakfast too. I've got some sausages frying in the pan here. Although you'll have to fight the dogs for them. Spoilt creatures think it's all for them. Down, Bones!'

It all came back to Marino, then. The storm. The shipwreck. His crew in a rowboat. Leaping into the sea. The crack of the mast. The mermaid.

The mermaid. Her violet eyes and her silky blue hair. The spark of recognition that had lit inside him when their gazes met. How she had disappeared all too quickly.

Samuel and his dogs. The soldiers.

Solvora. He had landed on Solvora. This is where the seaswifts had brought him. Thinking of the seaswifts filled Marino with an irrational anger. They were meant to guide him to what he most wanted, the cure for Celeste, and instead they had led him to disaster.

And then, coming back with Samuel to his small hut at the base of the cliff, nestled in the sand. Samuel frying fish in the same pan he was cooking the sausages in now. A plate of pickled red peppers. Crusty bread and a jug of fresh water. Samuel opening a trunk in the corner, full of musty clothes. Shaking things out until he found something that would fit Marino. Tucking Marino into bed, like he was a child. One of the dogs, Heart, climbing up next to him, soothing Marino with her nearness.

Morning light had still been streaming in through the window when Marino had fallen asleep, just like it was now. Marino was not sure if he had slept only a minute or the whole day through.

His stomach growled, answering the question for him before he could even ask it aloud. Samuel seemed to sense what he was wondering as he brought him over a mug of tea.

'I'm pleased to see you awake. And alive, to be honest. You slept so soundly I thought you might be dead.' Samuel sounded unperturbed by this possibility. 'I've never seen a man sleep so much.'

Marino gratefully took the tea. It was lukewarm and weak, but it would do.

'Thank you.' His voice sounded hoarse. 'I promise, I will return your kindness a hundred times.'

Samuel tutted, going back to the stove to turn the sausages. 'All in good time. What I want most is to hear what the world is like outside of Solvora. And what fish you find where you come from. We don't have much variety here, I have to say. Cod. Sardines. Shrimp. Crabs. Lobster. Ah yes, shellfish aplenty. But I remember years ago when we could fish from boats, not from the shore and in the shallows. Ah, we used to catch all sorts! Ah. The joy of being on a ship! Or at least a ship not caught in the Solvoran ring.'

Marino peered at the old man quizzically over his mug. 'You speak as if you spent a lot of time on ships.'

'And so I did. I wasn't always landlocked the way I am now.' Samuel spoke with a distant look in his eyes. 'It was a long time ago, though. A tale for another time. And there are worse places to be stuck than Solvora.'

'Indeed,' said Marino, remembering the beauty of the mountain towering over the beach, standing as proudly as any lady at a ball in her finest gown. With the gold palace as a crown, and the colourful tiled buildings shining like jewels all down the mountain side.

'You'll see more of it today, when you go up to the Gilded Palace. I'd go with you, but it is a long walk, and my legs aren't quite up to it these days.' Samuel poked one of the sizzling sausages with a fork and plopped it on a wooden plate. 'Solvora is small, but what you do and where you live are closely intertwined. There are the folks who live low and close to the sea, like myself. Fishermen, mostly. And guards against the mer.'

Marino wanted to question why they would need guards against the mer, but Samuel kept speaking, ticking off the areas of Solvora on his fingers. 'Then there are those who live in the streets carved into Goldwave Mountain, mostly tradespeople and artists – your bakers and butchers and tailors and what have you. And the painters and the potters, of course.'

'Of course,' murmured Marino, as if painters and potters were always needed. He supposed that here they were needed more than most, given the painted tiles on every building.

'The palace itself. Where the soldiers and the king and what passes for nobility here on Solvora all live. And then on the north side, behind the palace, that is where the goldweavers work.'

'Goldweavers?'

'The ones who pull the gold from the sea.'

Marino stared at Samuel. 'That isn't possible. Gold comes from the ground, not the sea.'

'I've seen it with my own eyes,' Samuel said with a huff. 'There is gold in the land and gold in the sea. And our weavers have mastered the art of pulling it from the water itself. It comes out looking like fine sand. And then the weavers melt it together.'

'That is remarkable. I'd love to see how it works,' mused Marino. 'What does it look like when it comes out of the water?'

'Like I said, fine sand. The weavers either blend it with other metals and materials or melt it down to use as coins or for gilding.'

'Who gets the gold?'

'Who do you think? The king! The goldweavers keep some for themselves, of course. And the king doesn't hoard it. It is used throughout Solvora. And on Goldwave Day, all Solvorans benefit – King Leonel gives gold to all.'

'How generous of him.'

'You will see when you meet King Leonel, that he is a very generous man. But I warn you, he has a temper. Be careful with your words.'

After they'd eaten breakfast, Samuel sent Marino out of the door. 'Go all the way up the mountain path. You can't miss the castle, even if you tried.'

Marino thanked him yet again, and stepped out into the sun, shielding his eyes as he gazed up at the land he had found himself in.

Solvora looked like a jewel box.

Every building was covered in those colourful tiles that shone and beckoned.

Walking through the winding hills felt like stepping into a painting. Flowers bloomed along the stone paths, and citrus trees grew on vertical orchards up the side of the mountain. And high in the centre, at the very top of the hill, was the Gilded Palace. The golden spires twirled up towards the sky, their sharp points glinting in the sun.

As Marino watched the golden castle shimmer and shift and spin, he let out a slightly hysterical laugh. The Gilded Palace looked like it was spun from golden sugar. Like something out of a dream.

It *all* felt like a dream. Marino walked on unsteady feet, swaying slightly. He turned up unfamiliar streets, trying not to get lost. He had found himself on Sugar Street. What a ridiculous name for a street, he thought. But he made a note of it, so he would know how to get back down the mountain.

He had given himself plenty of time to reach the Gilded Palace – the soldiers had told him he needed to arrive by midday, and it was still early morning. He didn't need to rush. He didn't want to show up sweaty and unkempt. Marino knew how important it was that he made a good impression on the king. His very life depended on it.

***

The thunderstorm came without warning.

Marino had been in many storms in his life, but he had never experienced a storm like this. Buckets of rain poured from the sky. Even stranger was how the sun was still shining through the clouds, making the raindrops glimmer like diamonds.

In seconds, Marino was soaked to the skin.

He groaned. He couldn't go to the palace like this. He needed to make a good impression after the disastrous scene on the beach. After all, what would it look like if every time he met someone from the Solvoran royal guard he was half drowned or drenched?

He strode across the cobblestone road and into the first shop he saw without taking note of what wares it was selling. As he walked in, he was welcomed by the delicious smell of freshly baked bread and the sweet scent of caramelised sugar. There was a glass counter lined with dozens of pastries, tarts and cakes.

And behind the counter stood a young woman, staring at him in surprise. He could only imagine how he appeared to her, blown in by the storm, dripping wet. He found himself unable to tear his gaze away, and for a long moment, they simply drank each other in.

She had long black hair that tumbled to her waist and was pulled out of her face with a red ribbon tied back in a bow. She wore a sky-blue apron, tight around her slender waist, and she was tall, only a few inches shorter than he was, and held herself with a quiet confidence. Her eyes were night-dark with flecks of gold, and it felt like he was staring into pieces of the midnight sky. She had rosy cheeks, as if she'd been laughing right before he came in, and flour smudged on her nose and forehead. Her lips were pursed in concentration, as if she was trying to recognise who he was. As his gaze lingered on her rosebud mouth, he felt longing stir deep inside him.

Mother of Eana, what was he thinking? He needed to get to the palace. *Pull yourself together*, he told himself, with a quick shake of his head. It must be the heady smell of the sugared cakes and the warm bakery air making everything seem more tantalising. But . . . he could not stop looking at her and, he realised with a slow unfurling delight, she could not stop looking at him either.

CHAPTER 13
Lana

Lana stared at the man who had appeared in her bakery. He was sopping wet, water pouring off him in rivulets, raindrops glistening in his short, curly hair. His shirt was plastered to his skin, and she felt a flush rise in her cheeks as she quickly averted her eyes back to his face.

He looked like how she imagined the god of the sea might appear, rising up out of the waves. Or perhaps a god of fire, because she could not deny the heat rolling off him, even as he stood there soaking. Or maybe it was her own temperature rising.

He stared back at her with dark brown eyes framed by thick black lashes, his full lips pursed in concentration. She knew everyone on Goldwave Mountain by name and trade, and she couldn't place this man. And she was certain she would remember his face if she'd seen him before. But how unusual, how peculiar, for there to be someone new.

He kept looking at her with an intense focus, like he was trying to remember if he had seen her before as well. It wasn't an unpleasant expression, but it made her feel like he could see to her very core. Then he smiled, and it was like the sun breaking through the clouds.

'Sorry about the mess,' he said, his voice low and warm. It sent a delicious shiver down her spine. 'I don't suppose you have a towel?'

Lana raised her eyebrows. 'Sir, this is a bakery.'

He laughed and the sound rumbled through her. 'I'd deduced as much.'

'Well, I think you might be better off at the tailor down the road. Or the fabric shop,' she went on. 'I do not have an abundance of spare linens here. Tarts, yes. Sugar, of course. But unless you want to dry yourself off with a sponge cake, I don't think there is much I can do for you.'

'If you don't mind, I might wait out the worst of the storm here.' He nodded towards the window, where the rain was still lashing down.

'I certainly hope you plan to buy something while you wait,' she said, crossing her arms. He might be handsome, but he was making a mess in her bakery, and she would be the one who would have to mop up the puddles.

'I, ah, well, this is awkward.' He hooked his thumbs in the pockets of his trousers. 'I don't have any coin. Not on my person. You see, my ship sank.' He paused and cleared his throat. 'And everything on it is in the sea. Including my towels. Or any coins. I'm hoping to go out later to try to salvage something but until then . . .' He pulled his pockets inside out, showing how empty they were.

Lana's eyes widened. '*You* are the survivor from the shipwreck! The one they found on the beach!' Goodness. She wiped her hands on her apron and dipped into a clumsy curtsy. 'Welcome to Solvora. You must forgive me; it is rare that we have any visitors.'

'So I have gathered,' he said. He glanced around the

bakery, eyes landing on a caramelised egg tart she had made that morning. His stomach growled, loud enough for them both to hear. Lana bit back a smile. The least she could do was offer the poor man some baked goods.

'Here,' she said, reaching for the tart. 'I insist.'

'It looks delicious, but I truly have no way to pay.'

'This one is on the house.' Lana sighed. 'But I suppose I should find you something so you can dry your hands before you eat.' She put the tart back on the counter.

'Oh, it's fine,' he said, holding his hands up in protest. 'Honestly, the tart is more than enough.'

'Absolutely not. This is the first time you are trying one of my tarts. I refuse to let you make it all soggy before you've even had a bite.'

The man laughed, and Lana found herself leaning towards the sound. Leaning towards him. Even though Lana had not been trying to be funny, she'd meant what she'd said, she was very glad she'd amused him. She wanted to make him laugh again, just for the pleasure of hearing the sound.

'So, for your pastries, you can procure towels. I see how it is.' He grinned at her, pushing a wayward curl out of his eyes.

Lana raised her brows. 'Sir, for my pastries, I can procure anything.' Without breaking their eye contact, she untied her blue apron and tossed it to him over the counter. 'Here. Use that. When your hands are dry, then you can have the tart.'

'I chose the right shop to stumble into,' said the man, wiping his hands on the apron. 'But I'm sorry for getting your floors all wet.'

'They'll dry,' she said. 'And so will my apron.' He was still standing with the apron in his hands. 'Here, give me that.' She stepped out from around the counter and took the apron from him. As she did, their hands brushed, just for a moment, sending a jolt through her.

'Thank you.'

'Don't thank me yet, you haven't tried the tart. You might not like it.' She turned back towards the counter, not only to pick up the tart but to hide the flush she could feel rising in her cheeks. He was only a man, she saw men every day. Yes, he was an exceptionally handsome man. An exceptionally handsome, dripping-wet man. Nothing for her to get all giggly over. After all, she had her pride.

'I meant thank you for the apron. But I'm sure the tart will be delicious.' He grinned at her and again she felt a buzz of yearning flicker through her.

Of course, the tart will be delicious, Lana thought. Her tarts were always delicious. They were her speciality. Everyone on Solvora knew that the Rising Moon Bakery on Sugar Street made the best tarts.

She composed herself and turned back to the mysterious man who had arrived on Solvora and held out the custard tart.

As he took it, their fingers brushed again, and Lana felt that buzz of yearning spark into something like a crackle between their skin.

'Oh!'

She let go of the tart so quickly he nearly dropped it.

'Sorry,' she said.

'You've done nothing to apologise for,' he said. 'You've let me drip all over your bakery, and you are feeding me free baked goods.' He inhaled deeply. 'This smells incredible.'

'Wait until you taste it,' said Lana, leaning ever so slightly towards him. She couldn't help herself. She loved to watch people eat what she had made.

He raised the tart to his lips, and her eyes followed the movement. He paused, just for a moment, before biting into it. His eyes closed in pleasure, and he made an appreciative sound that made Lana break into a wide grin.

'Told you,' she said.

'That is perhaps the singularly most delicious thing I have ever put in my mouth,' he said, opening his eyes before taking another bite. 'I need to find a way to make money immediately so I can come back and buy a dozen of these tarts.' He craned his neck to look over her and see what else was on the counter. 'And at least two of those apple crumble cakes.'

'I'd offer you more, but then I'd be out of my bakes for the day with no money to show for it,' said Lana.

The man dropped into a polite bow. 'My lady, you have done more than enough. I did not feel lucky when the sky unexpectedly opened up on my way to the palace, but now that I have had one of your tarts, I feel I could take on any storm.'

Lana let out a decidedly unladylike snort. 'I think the rain must have seeped into your head and addled your brain. Because you are speaking nonsense.'

'I am speaking the truth.' But his lips were twitching into a smile.

'The power of sugar and buttery pastry,' said Lana. 'And, by the way, that storm wasn't unexpected. It is the summer rain season. It will rain at least once a day until autumn. True storms, not ones that the mer sing down.'

'How long do the storms usually last? True storms, as you call them.'

'An hour. Maybe a little less.'

'Ah.' He turned his attention to the rain still pounding on the windows.

Lana sighed. 'I suppose it would be terribly rude of me to send you back outside, wouldn't it?'

'I'm sure I can find a way to make myself useful for the next hour. I often cook on my ship.'

Lana snorted again. 'Are you offering to be a baker's assistant for the next hour?'

He rolled up his sleeves and held out his hands. 'I could knead some bread. Whatever you need.'

Lana's gaze snagged on his hands – his broad palms and long fingers. She swallowed.

'I'll find something for you to do. But don't expect me to pay you in coin. Cake is the only currency I can offer you.'

His smile lit up the bakery. 'That'll do.'

'And . . .' Lana smoothed down her apron, 'I should probably know your name before I hire you as my assistant.'

'Marino. Marino Pegasi.'

'Marino,' she repeated. 'Marino.'

'And what should I call you?'

'Lana. I'm Lana.'

'Lana.'

Oh. She liked the sound of her name on his lips. She cleared her throat and brushed a strand of hair behind her ears. 'Well, Marino Pegasi. Let's see how good you are at making bread.'

CHAPTER 14
Marino

Marino had never been so glad of a storm.

Lana beckoned him behind the glass counter where she sold her wares, and through the arched doorway that led to the small kitchen nestled at the back of the building. Marino realised that the kitchen was carved into the mountain face itself, almost like a cave. From Sugar Street, he hadn't been able to tell, but once they were in the back of the kitchen, he saw that some of the walls were exposed, showing the grey rock glimmering with golden flecks that he recognised as the same rock that made up Goldwave Mountain.

'Here,' she said, pointing through another small door. 'There's a washroom there. The water is clean, it comes from the heart of the mountain itself. Careful though, it's hot.'

'Fascinating,' he murmured. 'Even the palaces in Eana do not have the ability to have instant hot water.'

'Eana?' Lana tilted her head. 'Is that where you are from?'

Marino nodded. 'Yes. The capital city is called Eshlinn, and I grew up there and in Anadawn Palace.'

Lana burst out laughing, and the sound floated in the air, mixing with the delicious smells of sugar and fresh bread. 'Anadawn?'

Marino frowned. 'What is so funny about that?'

'Go wash your hands, and then I'll tell you.' Lana turned from him and began to take out ingredients from the cupboards and shelves lining the walls of the kitchen. Marino watched her for a moment, the sureness of her movements, the way she hummed to herself as she went up on her toes to reach a jar on a higher shelf. It was like watching someone dance.

He tore his gaze away and went into the small washroom. As Lana had said, hot water came almost instantly from the ceramic pipe over the basin. Marino washed his hands, as instructed, and then grinned when he saw a small linen rag hanging on the back of the door.

He came back out into the kitchen, still drying his hands on the linen. 'I see you *did* have a towel.'

Lana looked up from where she had started mixing dough and raised her brows. 'Isn't that a little small to dry . . . all of you?'

Marino laughed fully, for what felt like the first time since he had left Eana. His clothes were still damp, but at least he was no longer dripping all over the floor. 'A fair point. Now that I'm clean, and mostly dry, I think I'm ready to make some cakes.'

'Oh no. Cakes are far too advanced. You, Captain, will be kneading bread.' Lana nodded at the lump of dough on her counter. Marino stood next to her and began to prod at the dough, aware of Lana watching his progress.

'I could be an expert cake maker, you know.'

Lana snickered. 'I can tell by how you are handling that dough that you most certainly are not a baker. Here, like this.'

She took the dough from him and began to push the heel of her hand into it in a rhythmic movement. 'And then stretch it like this.' She pressed the dough out. 'Then fold it back and do it again.'

'Like this?' Marino leaned slightly closer to her, so their shoulders were touching, and began to mimic how she had been kneading the dough.

She stilled at his nearness, and then cleared her throat. 'Yes, exactly like that. But be careful not to overwork it!' She didn't move away from him, instead kept watching how he pressed and pulled on the dough.

'How do I know when it is done?' asked Marino. He found the process surprisingly soothing. He couldn't remember a time when he'd ever made bread.

'You'll be able to feel it. It has this kind of springy, bouncy feel.'

'You are putting a lot of trust in me.' Marino folded the dough back on itself and stole a glance at Lana. He had thought she'd be monitoring his bread-making progress, but instead he caught her looking at his face. As their eyes met, a blush rose in her cheeks, but she didn't drop her gaze. From this close, Marino could see the golden flecks in her brown eyes.

Then she nodded down at his hands. 'You seem fairly capable. You survived a Solvoran shipwreck, I think you can handle making bread.' She stepped back from his side, where they'd been standing closer than Marino had realised. 'And while you do that, I'm going to make lemon cake.'

Lana hummed as she moved around the kitchen, gathering everything she needed.

'So, are you going to tell me why you laughed at

Anadawn?' Marino asked, keeping his focus on the dough.

Lana laughed again, softer this time. 'Because my name is Lana Dawn.' The pronunciation was slightly different, but it was undoubtedly similar. She grinned. 'Perhaps I'm related to your royals. Did one of your queens name the castle after her?'

Marino chuckled. 'The royals of Eana have a complicated history. My understanding is Anadawn is named for Eana, the first witch. And she was known to travel everywhere, not just in her own land, so perhaps you are linked to her.' He looked over at Lana, noting her high cheekbones and dark eyes with corners that crinkled when she smiled. 'But you resemble more the people of the Sunkissed Kingdom, a separate land that resides within our borders.'

'A witch queen? The Sunkissed Kingdom? You must be making up stories,' Lana scoffed.

'You are the one who lives on a land that pulls gold from the sea and is at the mercy of mermaids. When I return home, nobody will believe me about Solvora.'

His words hung in the air for a moment, because Marino knew the Solvorans believed it impossible to leave.

'Tell me more, of the witch queens. Of Anadawn and this Sunkissed Kingdom.' Marino heard the hunger in her voice, the yearning to hear of places new and unknown. He recognised it, because it was the same feeling in him that drove him to the sea. The feeling that the world was bigger, that there was more out there, if he only dared to go.

Marino knew he should leave the bakery. He should hurry up the hill to the Gilded Palace to meet the king who would be waiting for him. It was nearly midday. He knew it would be rude to be late.

But something tugged at him. He wanted to stay a little longer here in the warmth. Stay a little longer with Lana.

And for a moment he was tempted to tell her the truth about why he had come to Solvora, tell her about Celeste and what he was looking for. But he didn't want to invite sorrow into her bakery, or show too much of himself. So, instead he pushed thoughts of his sister and his stress to the back of his mind, just for a moment, and he told her what she asked for. He told her some of his favourite legends and tales of Eana.

After a while, he felt the dough change in consistency, just as Lana said it would.

'Lana,' he said, and it felt strange to say her name so casually, as if he had known her for more than the morning. 'I think the dough is done.'

Lana walked over to him and pressed gently on the dough. 'Well done, Captain.'

Marino couldn't hold back his grin. 'Well, do we bake it now?'

Lana grinned, and Marino fought the urge to wipe off the flour on her cheek. 'You truly know nothing about bread making. Now it rises. And then I'll shape it, and bake it.'

'I don't even get to eat the bread I made?'

Lana leaned back on her heels and crossed her arms. 'Not unless you want to stay here all day.' Her cheeks flushed pink. 'I didn't mean that as an invitation.'

'That's a shame,' said Marino, and to his surprise he found he meant it. He could have stayed all day in the bakery kitchen, kneading and shaping bread with Lana.

'And weren't you on your way to the Gilded Palace? King Leonel doesn't like to be kept waiting.'

Marino glanced out of the bakery, where the rain had finally stopped. He knew Lana was right. He had to face whatever fate was waiting for him in the Gilded Palace.

'Well, thank you for letting me wait out the storm. And teaching me how to knead bread.'

'Perhaps . . .' Lana's voice trailed off.

'Yes?'

'Perhaps tomorrow you could come back. And try the bread. And in the meantime . . .' Lana went to the front of the bakery and came back a moment later carrying a small cake wrapped in parchment. 'Take this with you. I did promise you cake as payment.'

'I feel like I've not done enough work to merit payment.'

'You did a little,' said Lana, grinning up at him. 'Take the cake, Captain.'

Marino's hands closed around the cake. 'If you insist.' They stood a moment more, the cake between them, before Lana stepped back. She adjusted her blue apron, eyes still on his.

'Until tomorrow then, Captain. Try not to get caught in any more storms.'

He smiled at her and bowed. 'I'll do my best.'

CHAPTER 15
Marino

When Marino stepped back out on to Sugar Street, the cobblestones were shining from the rain, but the sky was clear. And stretching out across the sky, like a beacon of hope, was a rainbow.

Marino walked up the winding streets, vaguely aware of the stir he was causing by his arrival. He heard whispers and saw pointing, and at one point a little boy even jogged along next to him.

'You're the survivor!' he called out. 'Where'd you come from?'

'Far from here,' said Marino. He was tempted to do a little magic, really give them something to stare at, but he thought perhaps he should save that particular skill for a time when it would be more useful. But he smiled at everyone, glad that they were happy to have an unexpected visitor instead of being wary of him.

From what he could see, the people of Solvora were as varied as in Eana. Some had brown skin like his, some had similar features to Lana with dark hair and eyes, and others had pale skin and light hair. There were children laughing in the streets, neighbours calling out to one another, covered markets selling fruit and flowers that all smelled incredible.

It seemed like a joyful place. Marino wondered how King Leonel kept his people so content. What were the secrets of the Solvoran people? What stenches were hiding beneath the sweet smells of the flowers? Because Marino knew that no place could be as idyllic as Solvora seemed.

When he finally arrived at the Gilded Palace he was sweating slightly from the walk up the hill, but as he turned to gaze back down to see how far he had walked, the view nearly took his breath away. From up here, he could see the sea all around the island and how its colours changed as it kissed the shore. Along the white beaches, the water was a sparkling turquoise, and further out to sea the colour shifted to the darker ocean blue that he was more familiar with. All of it shimmered more than any seawater he had ever seen. He remembered Samuel telling him that the Solvorans could pull gold out of the sea itself; perhaps that was why the water shimmered so brightly.

Marino watched as the waves came in, and then squinted, confused as they seemed to almost leap over an invisible line in the sea, before crashing on the shore below. It was as if there was a perimeter drawn around the island. As he looked more closely, he saw that the water itself seemed to change there, almost like it had a current of power vibrating through it. From here, Marino could see what was left of the wreckage of his beloved ship. Most of it had sunk beneath the waves already, but the mast still jutted through the water's surface, a reminder of all he had lost. Marino closed his eyes a moment, hoping against hope that his small crew were safe somewhere, and not in a watery grave alongside his ship. When he opened his eyes again, his gaze slid to a nearby darker patch of water. There were dozens of dark spots, all dotted around the island. And the water that slammed against the rocky cliff face was a dark grey blue. Stormy water, Marino liked to call it.

Clear, shallow water often looked lighter in the sun, and more turquoise. Darker water usually meant it was deeper. He wondered what was in those dark pockets of water, if that was where the mer chose to hide. Waiting for ships to sink, waiting to tempt Solvorans who tried to leave.

But, try as he might, Marino couldn't match the mermaid he had seen, the one who had saved him, with the stories that Samuel had told him. He had never heard of murderous mermaids. He had heard of how sirens could tempt sailors to their deaths, of course, but never of mermaids that stayed in one spot purely to punish people. Something was amiss in the Solvoran Sea, he was sure of that.

Marino turned his attention from the beauty of his surroundings to the grandeur of the palace in front of him.

He was used to decadence, he had grown up in a palace after all, but never had he seen anything quite like the Gilded Palace.

It glistened and shone in the midday light – its dozens of spiked turrets slowly twisting, like gilded flowers moving their faces to follow the sun. The gates were open and appeared to be made of giant sheets of transparent turquoise glass, but Marino knew that couldn't be possible. It was some other material; one he had never seen before. If the Solvorans truly could pull gold out of the sea, who knew what other metals and materials they could mould and make?

Two guards, dressed like the soldiers he had met the day

before, stood on either side of the open gates. They seemed prepared for him as they merely nodded and waved him through as he approached.

Once through the gates, he strode down the tree-lined entryway. The trees were all orange blossom trees, and as he breathed in their sweet, citrusy scent he noted a strange crunch beneath his borrowed boots and glanced down. The path was made of crushed shells that crunched with every step he took.

Finally, he stood before the palace doors. They were enormous; inlaid with thousands of pearls and shells. Here was another guard, this one wearing a more formal gold and blue uniform. The guard assessed Marino with frank interest and curiosity.

'You must be the survivor. I didn't believe it, when I heard. Nobody has survived a Solvoran storm in years. It is a miracle.' As he spoke the man moved his hands inwards, towards his heart, and then twisted them out again in a gesture that seemed practised and familiar. 'You must thank your gods, wherever they are. In the air or in the sea.'

'I thank the fisherman that fed and clothed me,' said Marino, with a wry grin. He knew it would not be wise to share with the Solvoran guard that he also thanked the mysterious mermaid who had dragged him onto the beach.

The guard guffawed. 'Fair enough. Now come with me. King Leonel has been waiting, and he is not known for his patience.'

King Leonel was well named. He reminded Marino of a lion. He had tawny light brown skin, bright brown eyes, and dark golden hair that hung far past his shoulders.

He sat on a large golden throne encrusted with shells and pearls. The top of the throne was carved with crashing waves and mountains, and the legs were in the shape of fish tails. The king was lounging back, as if relaxed, but Marino noted that his eyes were sharp and focused. He wore a thin crown that came to one sharp point in the centre, echoing the mountain and wave symbolism around the throne room.

Marino was glad that he had spent enough time among royals all over the world to know how to win them over. He paused midway through the room and gave a deep bow, his back straight and his arms at his side. And when he straightened back up, he waited for the king's permission to proceed further.

'Come closer,' said King Leonel, his voice a low rumble. 'I want to see the man who survived a Solvoran storm.'

Marino walked with his head tall. It was a fine balance, being confident but also respectful. One that he hoped he had mastered.

King Leonel stayed seated, and his throne was tall enough that he was at eye level with Marino when Marino reached the dais.

'Tell me your name, survivor. And what you were doing when you were shipwrecked on Solvora.'

'My name is Marino Pegasi. I am the captain of my own ship, the *Siren's Secret*.'

Marino paused, because the king's countenance had changed from one of curiosity to one of rage.

'Siren you say?' King Leonel sat up straight and spat on the gold floor. 'Tell me, Marino Pegasi, do you have any allegiance to those with slippery fins and fickle hearts?

Those who would drown and damn a man without a second thought?'

Marino faltered for a moment, stunned by the hatred in the king's words.

'No, Your Majesty. I named the ship when I was a young man of only sixteen. Before I had ever laid eyes on a true mermaid. And in all my travels, I only glimpsed them in the distance. At least until I arrived upon your shores.'

King Leonel relaxed, the fire going out of his eyes, and his smile returned. It was like looking at a different man. 'Ah yes. The follies of youth. That, I understand. A youthful mistake! But I must say, you were asking for trouble with a ship name like that.'

'Or perhaps the name is what saved me,' said Marino before he could think better of it.

King Leonel scoffed. 'Are you saying the *mer* saved you? Took pity on you? That is impossible. They do no such thing. Murderous, meddlesome creatures.' He took a knife from his belt and shook it in the air. 'I would kill them all if I could, but it is forbidden.'

'Forbidden by who?' Marino knew he was being bold in his question. After all, the king was the one who wanted to interrogate him, not the other way around.

But the king was angry enough to answer. 'By the sea itself. The sea protects them and punishes us. It is our penance for an event that happened long ago. One I will not bore you with now. But know this, the mer are no friends of ours. Every year, dozens of men and women are tempted by them into the sea. Most never come back, and those who do are never the same.'

Marino thought of how he had felt when he had locked

eyes with the blue-haired mermaid, and he knew that he too would never be the same.

'Not only can we not go in the sea, we do no trade. It is a miracle you were able to make your way through the reef. You see, the sea has decreed that we shall be isolated here, on our own. Only a lucky few have made it here. Such as yourself.' His voice rose. 'The Solvoran waves are hungry ones. And they devour ships. It is why we are unable to sail for other lands. We have built ships, but the storm rises as soon as we try to sail away. The mer sing down the storms, and they sing us to our death.'

The fire in the king's eyes faded, and his good temper seemed to return as quickly as it had left. 'But soon, *soon* we will control the seas again.' It sounded like a promise.

Marino let out a light laugh. 'Nobody controls the seas, Your Majesty.' Not even the witches of Eana would claim to do that. He felt unsettled by Leonel's rapid shifts in mood. He supposed he must grow accustomed to the king's temperament, if he were to convince the king to give him a ship to leave. Because Marino was determined he would leave, no matter what the Solvorans said was possible. No matter what the mer did. He had defied death to reach Solvora, and he would do it again to return to Eana. He had to save his sister. He would do whatever it took.

'The Solvoran Sea is different,' King Leonel said curtly. 'It can and *is* controlled.'

Marino tried to keep his voice light. 'Who controls it, if not you? Are you not king?'

He tensed slightly, unsure if the king would respond with rage but King Leonel's laugh boomed. 'King of Solvora. Not king of the Solvoran Sea.' His eyes hardened. 'Not yet.' And in his words, Marino heard what could have been a promise . . . or a threat. 'Now, tell me, Marino, where you come from.' He leaned forward hungrily. 'Tell me of land not held captive.'

King Leonel wanted to hear everything of Eana. Of the water and lands surrounding it. Of everything far from Solvora. Before Marino knew it, it was early evening, and the sun was starting to set outside the windows of the throne room. He had been talking to the king for hours. Answering all his questions, about Eana and all the other places he had been. But he was careful not to share with the king a key element of Eana . . .

At some point, King Leonel had snapped his fingers and demanded a chair be brought forward so Marino could sit. And then cups of wine and a plate of cheese arrived. The king stayed in his throne throughout, shifting his position occasionally. Marino could not help but think that the throne looked uncomfortable, but Leonel seemed determined to stay in it. If he had any other obligations that day, he did not seem to care. He only wanted to devour all the tales Marino had to tell.

It made Marino feel strangely claustrophobic, the way the sea was all around him. He had never felt that way on his ship, because at sea he was always moving. He could go in any direction he pleased. And no matter how long he sailed with only the horizon in his sight, no matter how the water might look the same, day after day, he knew what direction he was heading in. But here in Solvora, the waves below moved but the people stayed in the same spot. Trapped. Prisoners.

'What a wonder – for you to sail the open seas and trade

with whoever you like,' sighed King Leonel.

Marino nodded in agreement. He had still not shared with the king the true wonder of Eana. The magic that ran through the country; the magic running through Marino's veins. The power he had at his disposal. He was not sure what the king would make of magic. What he would think of witches. A man who hated the mer with such venom might have the same feelings for those with the gift of magic. Marino had been planning on showing him, using it to his advantage, but now he thought he would wait until the time was right. And in the meantime, he would keep his magic close and quiet.

His stomach growled loudly, and King Leonel laughed.

'You must think me a beast of a host. I have kept you in here for hours without a proper meal.'

'Not at all,' said Marino. 'You have allowed me, a stranger, to enter your home, and have made me feel very welcome.'

'I have not only been questioning you for my own entertainment,' said Leonel. He nodded towards a tall mirror that was at the edge of the throne room, and to Marino's surprise, a blonde woman with pale white skin stepped out from behind it. As if she'd been hiding. She was dressed entirely in white and had golden bracelets going all the way up her arms. 'My soothsayer, Talia, has been watching you. Listening to you. If she heard you speak an untruth, she would know.'

Marino whipped his head around. That sounded almost like magic. Was Talia a witch, like the ones in Eana?

'What a useful gift,' he said. 'How did you come to have such a skill?'

'Through practice,' said Talia tartly. 'And watching many

men lie to the king.' Then she smiled at Marino. 'And I have heard and seen enough to decide that you are a friend to Solvora.'

Marino exhaled. He was not certain that she was speaking the truth about her skill. It sounded like a kind of magic to him. 'I certainly want to be.'

'If Talia says you are a friend of Solvora, then it is true.' King Leonel opened his hands expansively. 'You will be my guest at the palace.'

Marino paused. He did not want to stay here in the Gilded Palace. He wanted to go back to Samuel's hut by the sea. Where he could sleep peacefully, where his every move would not be watched. Where he could hear the soothing sounds of the sea around him. Where he could easily go to the shore and search for the blue-haired mermaid who had saved him. 'The fisherman who fed me, he is awaiting my return.'

King Leonel waved his hand. 'I will send him a bag of gold to thank him. He will be glad not to have another mouth to feed, I am certain.'

Marino knew he could not refuse the king. And he did not want to deny Samuel the bag of gold.

He stood and bowed. 'Thank you for your generosity,' he said. 'It will be an honour to be a guest at the Gilded Palace.'

CHAPTER 16
Lana

That night, Lana couldn't sleep.

She tossed and turned in her small bed above the bakery, and it creaked beneath her.

Benedita, who she thought of as her aunt despite there being no blood shared between them, used to live above the bakery too, in the even smaller room across the hall. But that was before Benedita died, leaving Lana alone. Benedita had been the one who had taught Lana how to bake, how to grow her own ingredients, how to make sure her bread was the best on the island. 'The bread must be good enough that they want it every day but that they forgive you if they must wait for it, do you understand?' Even then Benedita had known that one day Lana would be on her own, and when she had one of her blinding headaches – the ones so bad that she would sleep for days, lost in a haze of pain – she wouldn't be able to bake and the bakery would be closed.

Benedita had done more than teach Lana how to bake. She had raised her. Brushing her hair out every night before tucking her in. Rubbing her temples when Lana was taken to bed with a headache. And then, Benedita watched over her. When Lana had her walking dreams, Benedita would find her out on the balcony and guide her back to her bed. And when she woke, Lana would rub her eyes in confusion, her dreams still heavy in her head. It almost felt like she'd been dead, and now she was coming back to life. And as her head cleared, Benedita would point to the stars in the sky, showing her constellations and whispering the legends that the people weren't allowed to speak aloud any more.

Lana had been embarrassed of her headaches as a child, because they marked her as different and, worse, they made her vulnerable. But Benedita tutted and said everyone had a burden to carry, and at least all Lana had to do was go to bed.

Benedita was the one who told her that the small pearl earrings she wore were from her mother, and that she must never take them off because they were all she had from her mother who had drowned. She told Lana that her mother had wanted a better life for her, it was why she had tried to leave Solvora. But she had promised that she would be there for Lana as long as she could.

And then Benedita left her too.

And now Lana wondered what else was here for her in Solvora. It had been six months now, and Lana missed the old woman with an ache so deep it felt as if it was carved into her bones. Lana did not remember her parents, gone before she could walk, drowned in a storm when they tried to leave Solvora, with Lana in tow. Lana had been found alone in a rowboat, knocking against the cliff beneath Benedita's bakery. And so Benedita had brought her in, the child she had always longed for but never had. Lana sometimes thought she could remember it, the waves tossing her in the sea. She'd never been properly in the sea since, not daring to go any further than ankle-deep. King Leonel said those who swam in the sea were asking for the mer to take them. Better to be safe and stay out of the water.

And yet, Lana dreamed of the sea. Had slippery memories of the waves tossing her, carrying her. Could almost feel the sensation of bursting through the water's surface, breathing in blessed air.

But Lana had not been found in the waves, she had been found in the boat, Benedita would reiterate with a tsk. *The sea brought you to me*, she often said, making the gesture for sea-blessed. Two hands moving in towards her heart, and then out again, almost like a wave.

It was a dangerous thing, these days, to openly thank the sea for anything. King Leonel had declared the sea and all who lived in it the sworn enemies of Solvora. But still, the Solvorans fished, and still they wove the gold from the sea, but King Leonel said these were not gifts. They were the bounty that Solvorans deserved. It was their right to take the fish and the gold. '*If the sea felt differently, it would drown us all,*' Solvorans were fond of saying, as they dumped their nets of fish and the weavers pulled strand after strand of shining gold from the sea itself.

Sometimes Lana felt like the sea tried to swallow Solvora. She had woken up on more than one occasion to see waves splashing over her balcony, battering against the windows, as if it was begging to be let in. Lana's room faced out to sea and even though her window was shut, she could hear the waves crashing on the rocks far below her bedroom window. The sea was angry tonight. And Lana thought she knew why. The sea had a taste for Marino Pegasi, and it would rage until he returned to it again. She sometimes wondered if it felt the same way about her, since she was also one who had got away. She had almost told him that she too had been in a shipwreck, and lived to tell the tale, but what was there to say when she could not remember it? That her dreams were flooded with false memories of crashing waves?

And yet, the sound of the sea at night didn't scare Lana the way it would have scared so many Solvorans. Rather, she found the sound soothing. She always had. Even those nights when she had woken on the balcony, sure that she could feel the spray of a wave way up the cliff. And maybe she had. After all, she'd seen the water slosh over her balcony, drenching her little cliffside garden. Who was to say that it didn't drench her in her sleep, disappearing before she fully woke?

She felt disloyal to Solvora, for how much she loved the sea. How she flung her windows open whenever she could so she could breathe in sea air, feel the sting of the sea breeze on her face.

Maybe that was what she needed tonight. The smell of the sea, the feel of the wind in her face. Anything to make her feel like she was somewhere other than Solvora.

For this was what Lana dreamed of most of all. Leaving one day. Finding a life somewhere else. She loved the bakery and Sugar Street and all of Solvora, but she was so sure there was more waiting for her. She felt it under her skin, like the very beating of her heart was telling her to be brave and set off on an adventure.

She would have done it too, if it wasn't for the mer that kept them trapped here.

Lana still didn't know if the storm that had made her an orphan was mer-made or sea-brewed, but it didn't matter. The mer were the reason she couldn't leave Solvora. And even if the sea itself wasn't her enemy, if she secretly found it soothing, if she truly did feel sea-blessed, she knew the mer were no friend to her. She was not that much of a fool.

But she still liked to watch for them. In a strange, twisted way, she felt like glimpsing a mermaid was good luck. She would stare out to sea, hoping for a glimpse of their tail. Occasionally she'd seen a flash of their hair when they dared to pop their head above water. And it was daring for them to do so. Because showing any part of themselves above the surface was dangerous.

Beneath the water, they could not be harmed, that was the deal the Solvoran king before Leonel had made to keep the sea from rising so high it would swallow all of Solvora. Or so the stories went. Lana didn't think anyone could make a bargain with the sea itself. But Solvorans were suspicious, so the mer stayed safe beneath the waves. And the Solvorans took their fish and their gold and muttered about how the mer kept them trapped. But it didn't matter that the mer kept them trapped and kept anyone from arriving.

It was only when they showed their faces they could be hunted.

They got around this too, by wearing the masks of seaflowers and scales. Hiding their true faces from the humans, Benedita had said.

'Because they are so monstrous?' Lana had once asked. What was the difference between a sea monster and the mer, anyway?

Benedita had laughed. 'No, child. Because their beauty is terrifying to behold. One glimpse would drive a human mad! And in return for keeping their faces hidden, they are allowed to roam the Solvoran Sea. But once any human goes into the sea, they are at the mercy of the mer.'

It was only the foolish men who became prey of the mer. The ones who were transfixed by their song, the ones who wanted to see their true faces. Lana had seen them, walking the shore for hours. The truly desperate ones dived from the cliffs. Sometimes they disappeared for days before returning with glazed eyes and babbling tongues.

Sometimes they never came back at all.

Occasionally, a woman would give in to the call, but they too rarely came back.

And this is how it would go, day in, day out. All of them trapped, mer and Solvorans alike. The sun would shine and the storms would come and the mer would sing some to their doom and the smart Solvorans would stay out of the sea and Lana would sleep and wake and bake and nothing would change. At least that was what she had thought before Marino Pegasi had walked into her bakery.

Marino Pegasi with his wide smile and his kind eyes and his stories of magic. Lana hadn't believed half of what he'd told her, tales of witches and legends of hidden kingdoms.

But was Solvora itself not a hidden kingdom?

And were the mer not a kind of magic?

Lana gazed down at her hands, the ones that had worked all day in the kitchen, making and shaping bread, before she had been just as busy in her cliffside garden full of plants that could do miraculous things in the right hands. In her hands.

Perhaps magic was not so hard to find as she had always thought.

But if Marino had the kind of magic he had hinted at, perhaps that was why he had survived the storm. And if that magic had been how he had made it here, maybe it would be how he would leave.

Because Lana knew he had come here seeking something. Why else would he have come so far from home? What was he looking for?

Well, she would find out. And she would help him find it. And then, if he used that magic he spoke of to do the impossible, to leave Solvora, well, she would be on that ship with him. She would make sure of it. Marino would be her salvation, one way or another.

Holding that thought close to her heart, Lana finally gave in to sleep.

Lana did not dream of being beneath the waves. No, she dreamed of ships and sails and clear blue skies. Lana knew almost nothing about ships, she had not been on one since the fateful time with her parents, but her mind conjured a ship all the same, and it felt tantalisingly real to her – the deck solid beneath her feet, the sun warm on her skin.

In the dream, a figure stood on the prow of the ship, and Lana knew who it was even before he turned around.

And as she smiled in her sleep, the waves below her bedroom rose higher, climbing the cliffs and coming ever closer to where Lana lay dreaming.

CHAPTER 17
Marino

Growing up in Anadawn Palace, Marino was used to decadence, and he had seen dozens of palaces and castles in his travels, but the Gilded Palace bordered on the obscene. Every inch was covered in gold or pearl. He realised that the spiralling towers turned, as the day went on, to reflect the sun as much as possible, always glowing and always golden. And when the sun went down, the winding halls were lit with hundreds of small sconce lights, the candles flickering and casting strange shadows. There were mirrors and reflective surfaces all around, and Marino had twice walked down empty halls convinced someone else was there, only to realise it was his own reflection.

The room that the servant had escorted him to was as opulent as the rest of the palace. A sumptuous four-poster bed hung with billowing white curtains. A private washroom, with hot water from a tap, like at Lana's bakery. Thinking of Lana made him grin to himself. Lana Dawn, who baked bread and made him laugh – even at a time like this. He knew he would seek her out again.

He assessed the rest of the room and was pleased to see that a trunk of clothes had been sent up. And while the clothes were not a perfect fit, everything slightly too snug, Marino was grateful.

But, for all the decadence and comfort of the room, Marino found himself wishing he was back in Samuel's small hut on the beach. He somehow knew the king would make demands of him sooner or later. He had kept his magic hidden so far but the way Talia had looked at him made him wonder if she suspected. Even if the Solvorans did not wield magic, magic clearly danced around them. The cure he sought was here, after all.

He *must* find someone to help him find what he was looking for. His thoughts drifted back to the blue-haired mermaid. He wondered if she would help him, *could* help him.

Marino stretched out in the large bed, his mind reeling from the past few days. He knew he was lucky to be alive, but he couldn't stop thinking about his crew. About his sister, far away in Eana and waiting for him to return with a cure he didn't have the first idea how to find. The seaswifts had led him here, but where was the guidance on where to find the cure? And what was the good of finding the cure if he couldn't get back to Eana?

He closed his eyes and tried to steady his breathing. He had known the journey would be dangerous, but he had never thought he'd lose his ship and his crew. He hadn't yet had a moment to process his grief. But he wouldn't allow himself to call it grief, not yet. He had to hold on to the hope that his crew had survived, somehow. Perhaps they were on the other side of the mountain. Anything was better than imagining them drowned and dead.

Hope was his only driving force. Hope that he would find

the cure for Celeste. Hope that his crew was alive. Hope that he could leave Solvora. He knew if he lost hope, he would lose everything.

When Marino fell into sleep, he dreamed as he often did, of the sea. And in his dream it was not the blue-haired mermaid swimming towards him, but Lana Dawn. In his dream, she was still in her white dress and blue apron, and both billowed out around her as she swam beneath the waves with him, hand in hand, with no fear of drowning, no need of air. As if they were mer themselves and they had the whole sea to explore.

Lana danced through his dreams all night, leading Marino deeper into the sea of sleep, and when the bells clanged in the morning, he woke with a start.

He half expected to find Lana next to him – she had felt so real in his dreams. But he was alone. Sun was streaming in through the open windows, he must have forgotten to close them last night.

Marino knew that King Leonel would want to see him, but after spending so many hours with the king yesterday, effectively trapped in the gilded throne room, he was not keen to repeat the experience. He dressed, grateful for the borrowed clothes that Leonel had sent. The black breeches were snug but the white collared shirt was of a fine material. It was warm enough that he wouldn't need a coat.

There was parchment and a quill on the desk, so he quickly wrote out a message to the king, letting him know that he was going into town, and passed it to a servant to deliver. He knew King Leonel had called him his guest, but there was a thin line between royal guest and royal prisoner.

Marino did not have time to entertain King Leonel today.

Marino planned to scour Solvora for any hint of a cure. He'd seek out the apothecary. Find the healers of Solvora. Someone, somewhere on this island must know something about this mysterious cure he sought. The cure that would save his sister.

But first he needed breakfast. And he was craving freshly baked bread.

It seemed as if the sun was shining even more brightly today and all Solvora sparkled and shone beneath its rays.

From the top of Goldwave Mountain, where the Gilded Palace glittered, there were six winding paths that led down the mountain in different directions.

Marino asked the doorman which path was fastest to Sugar Street. The doorman had frowned at him in confusion. 'With respect, sir, all roads lead down to the sea, and all roads lead back up to the palace.' He twirled his two index fingers around in a loop. 'Solvora and the sea are always connected, can never be sundered.'

Marino sighed heavily. Everyone here seemed destined to speak in riddles. 'Yes, yes, I know. But I am not trying to get to the sea, I am trying to get to Sugar Street.'

'Take the path on the west side of the mountain, that will take you through the trade district.' The doorman pointed out the turquoise gates. 'The western path will guide you to Sugar Street. And if you keep going all the way down the mountain, you'll end up at Shipwreck Bay, where you were found.' The doorman gave him a crooked smile. 'And do not worry, you won't get lost coming back up to the Gilded Palace, all roads go from the sea to the palace.' Again, the twirling loop of his fingers.

There was something strange and unsettling about the movement. Marino nodded his thanks and hurried down the path the doorman had indicated.

When he arrived outside Lana's bakery, he paused. He felt unexpectedly foolish – an entirely unfamiliar feeling for him.

What if Lana hadn't meant it when she had asked him to come back? What if she thought it odd that he had returned so swiftly?

Never mind, he told himself. He wasn't a caller, after all. He was a customer buying bread. And then he would be on his way.

He flung the door open and strode in – and immediately bumped into Lana, who was carrying a tray of blueberry muffins.

The tray flew up into the air, and Lana cried out in dismay as the muffins tumbled towards the ground.

Marino called on his warrior witch strand – the gift that offered agility and speed – and caught as many muffins as he could. He saved all but one.

With an armful of blueberry muffins, he looked up at Lana, who was staring at him agape. She wore the same blue apron around her waist and red ribbon in her hair that she had yesterday. The same ones that he'd seen in his dream. Her small pearl earrings winked in the morning light.

They stared at each other for a moment in shocked silence, before Marino cleared his throat and glanced down at the muffins now cradled against his chest. 'I suppose I should ask you to add these to my tab?'

Lana burst out laughing. 'You caught them, they are yours.' She gathered up the muffin that he had not managed to catch, and looked up at Marino with a quizzical expression. 'But how did you move so swiftly?'

'You remember how I told you Eana is home to witches? I am one of those witches.'

It felt good to share this with Lana, and Marino felt instinctively that he could trust her. He put down the muffins on a nearby platter and took an elaborate bow, sneaking a look at her and grinning to see her delighted smile. He straightened back up. 'I channelled the warrior strand of magic to catch the muffins.' Marino shook his head, chuckling to himself. 'I am friends with some of the greatest warrior witches Eana has ever known; they would laugh me out of town if they had seen me stumble into you like that. The least I could do was catch some of these delicious-smelling muffins so they didn't go to waste.' There it was again – the ease Marino felt about sharing who he truly was with Lana. He felt so drawn to her, and that he could trust her already. 'I am sorry, though – you must think me an oaf.'

Lana raised a brow. 'Far from it.'

Marino felt his mouth go dry as Lana boldly gazed back at him. Then she grinned, lightening the unexpectedly charged moment. 'But my neighbours might call you worse when they find out you've robbed them of their morning muffins.'

Marino chuckled. 'I've only been here two days and I'm already making enemies.'

Lana fondly shook her head. 'What are your plans today? Other than making enemies of the locals.'

Marino let out a long breath. 'I'm hoping to see more of Solvora. Actually, you might be able to help me. I came here seeking something specific, without knowing what it looks like. You see my sister, Celeste, has a mysterious illness that our healers call the seeing sickness. It strikes seers who strain their gift too hard, and she was looking . . .' Marino cleared his throat. 'She was looking into my future, trying to help *me*.' The guilt struck him hard, almost a physical blow that he felt in his chest. 'Our healers told me the cure was off the map, and to follow the seaswifts, who would guide me to it. They led me here.' He ran a hand over his stubbly jaw. 'But now I don't even know where to start.'

Lana gently reached out and laid a hand on his arm. 'I'm sorry your sister is ill. She is lucky to have you as a brother.'

Marino gave her a small smile. 'I feel it is my fault that she pushed herself too far. And now that she has the seeing sickness, it can spread to the other seers in Eana. I must find the cure as soon as I can, and then I need to leave Solvora.'

'Nobody leaves Solvora. Surely the king has told you.'

'Everyone has told me. But I will find a way to leave. Once I've found the cure I need.'

'How will you know when you've found the cure?'

Marino tilted his head to stare at the ceiling. 'The healers told me I would know it. That I'd be drawn to it. I have to trust them. I have to trust myself, I suppose. But I don't know the first place to start looking here.'

'Are you asking for a tour guide, Captain?'

Marino cleared his throat. 'I would never be so bold to assume that you had the time, or the inclination, but if you are offering . . .' His voice trailed off. 'I would be a fool not to accept.'

Lana assessed him, and then her face broke into a smile. 'I suppose I could close the bakery today. The perk of running your own business is that nobody has to tell you when to be open.'

Marino felt a warm glow within at the thought that Lana wanted to spend the day with him. 'I promise when I have my ship back, when I have my resources, I will pay you back for your time and kindness ten-fold.'

Lana waved her hand in the air. 'A kindness is not something done in hope that it is returned one day. I may have never left my own shores, but I too one day want to leave Solvora.' Her eyes grew bright. 'I know there is so much more of the world to see.' She turned her attention back to Marino, dark brown eyes shining. 'So, promise me a place on your ship. That's all I want. And in return, I'll show you around Solvora, and I'll help you find what you are looking for.' She nudged him gently with her elbow, the movement so familiar that it made Marino feel he'd known Lana for years. 'And surely a baker would be useful on a ship, no?'

'I'm sure we can find a use for you.'

Lana's grin spread. 'That's the spirit.'

After she had locked up the bakery, Lana took a basket of bread and muffins across the road to the butcher's. Through the window, Marino saw two men hanging huge pieces of meat to dry, their heads close together. Their eyes widened when Lana strode into their shop, Marino in tow.

'*This* is the survivor,' she said with a flourish, her voice dripping with scandal and satisfaction. She pushed Marino in front of her, and the two men stared, agape.

'And this is Jonah.' Lana nodded at the shorter one, who had light brown skin and wavy dark hair. 'And that's Carlos.' Carlos was burlier, with his hair shorn and a black beard.

Marino cleared his throat. 'Good morning.'

'Oooh, let's get a look at him,' said Jonah, tipping his head back to do just that as he wiped his hands on his apron. 'Oh, he's a fine catch, that's for certain.'

Marino cleared his throat again and Lana let out a loud laugh at his clear embarrassment.

Carlos swatted Jonah on the arm. 'Please excuse my husband. It has been so long since we've had anyone new to Solvora. We're all starved for fresh faces around here.' He turned to Lana. 'Speaking of starved, what have you brought us this morning, love?'

'A loaf of walnut bread, and some blueberry muffins. I would have had more but Marino dropped one on the floor.' Lana handed over the basket.

Jonah leaned forward with a smirk. 'What were you doing that made her muffins topple over, eh?'

Now it was Lana's turn to flush. 'He opened the door into me, that's all. By the grace of the sea gods, don't make me regret introducing him to you two.' She glanced at Marino. 'Ignore them.'

'Oh, Lana, let us have a bit of fun! This is the most you've smiled since Benedita died, may her soul fly free in the sky and sea.' Carlos did that same move that Marino had seen several Solvorans do, turning his hands towards his heart and back out again.

Marino wanted to ask who Benedita was, but Lana spoke before he could. Almost as if she wanted to stop him from asking, stop him from prying.

'I am showing Marino around Solvora today. I've locked the bakery, but if anyone asks where I am . . .' Her voice trailed off.

'We'll tell them it will be open soon. Like we always do,' said Carlos, his voice warm. 'Just bring us more muffins tomorrow, all right?'

'Thank you,' said Lana. And Marino sensed that Lana was thanking her butcher neighbours for more than keeping an eye on her bakery for an afternoon. He nodded to Jonah and Carlos.

'A pleasure to meet you both. Perhaps another time I can sample some of your wares. Eana, where I'm from, has particularly excellent lamb and beef.'

Carlos puffed up his chest. 'I guarantee you that you'll find Solvoran beef better than any you've ever had. Something to do with the grass that grows here. And, of course, the excellent butchery.'

'Well, I look forward to trying it.'

'Don't forget, he can't pay for anything,' said Lana, with a bright laugh that seemed to light up the shop. 'He doesn't have any coin to spend. Only flattery.'

'I'd take some flattery from the handsome captain,' said Carlos, with another wink.

Jonah tsked. 'Shameless, shameless. And in front of your husband too!'

'I offer more than flattery,' said Marino, affronted. He turned his full attention to Lana. 'I will pay you back one day. I am a man of my word.' They stared at each other for a moment, the air between them charged, and Marino wondered what exactly he was promising to the baker he had only just met. Then she smiled, broadly, and let out another laugh.

'So you say.'

Carlos leaned forward. 'Don't worry, Captain. We'll take your word for it. Come back and we'll have a feast.'

Still laughing, Lana wound her arm through Marino's and dragged him from the butcher's and back out on to Sugar Street.

As they stepped on to the steep narrow street the sun shone down on them. Flowers grew on vines that danced across the shop fronts in riotous colour and burst through the cobblestones and up along the mountain itself. The colours were so vibrant, so bright, it almost made Marino dizzy, and the air was heavy and sweetly scented. His head was already spinning when he glanced down at Lana, her arm still linked through his.

Marino had never thought of the different shades of black, but he was transfixed by the glossy sheen of Lana's hair, how it shone in the light – it looked like it would feel like silk.

'What is it?' said Lana, gazing back up at him.

Marino coughed, suddenly aware that he'd been standing in the middle of Sugar Street, staring at Lana like a fool. 'Nothing. Nothing at all. My eyes were just adjusting to the light.'

That was it, he told himself. The light here was so bright, it made everything shine in a way that was hard to look away from. It wasn't *Lana* that he couldn't look away from. It was the Solvoran sun playing tricks on his eyes.

Lana's lips curved into a small smile, like she knew he was lying. 'Well, if your eyes are ready – shall we carry on with the tour?'

'Certainly. I'm eager to see as much of Solvora as I can.'

Lana and Marino wound down and around the Solvoran streets. Marino was aware of the stares they were drawing, and he wasn't sure if it was because he was new to the land, or if it was because he was walking arm in arm with Lana.

As they walked, he told Lana his predicament. How it felt an impossible task, to find a cure when he did not know what he was looking for. They walked past the fruit stalls, the fishmonger's, the goldsmith and the glassblower. Lana explained that King Leonel loved beautiful things, all Solvorans did, and that there was such an abundance of gold on the land that it was used in jewellery and art, and even on the tiles that covered so many of the shops.

'Could the gold be the cure?' mused Lana. They stood at the edge of one of the winding streets, the steep cliffs of Goldwave Mountain beneath them, the sea beyond.

'I do not know why the gold here could do what gold in Eana could not,' said Marino. 'And the healers at home, they said it was most likely a plant. But it is possible. Maybe the sea imbues it with something different.' He sighed heavily. 'But what would Celeste do with gold? It cannot be swallowed. Maybe it can be placed on her, like some sort of poultice.' But that sounded silly, even as he said it. How would he know for certain when he had found the cure? Going back with a 'maybe' cure was almost as bad as going back empty-handed. Almost as bad as not going back at all.

He heard Willa in his head. *You will know when you find it. Let your magic guide you.*

'Then, next we will take you to the goldweavers. You can see the sea-gold for yourself.' Lana spoke with a surety and a determination that made Marino smile. 'You said you suspect it is some sort of plant. Perhaps it is a ground herb of some kind.' Lana tilted her head to the side. Marino had noticed she did that when she was thinking, like she was shaking her thoughts from one side of her mind to the other. He found it hard not to notice all her movements, hard to take his eyes off her at all. 'We will go to the apothecary after the goldweavers, they might have something. Or at the very least, they might be able to advise.'

Marino sighed again. 'I fear it will not be a cure that I can find in an apothecary. It is a magical illness, which means it will need a magical cure.' He looked out to sea. 'The mer have magic, do they not?'

Lana scoffed. 'The mer will not help you. And if they think you are trying to take something from them, they will tear you limb from limb.'

'Are they so strong?'

Lana nodded emphatically. 'Don't be deceived by their lithe limbs and pretty faces. They are as fierce as any monster in the sea.'

Marino remembered how the blue-haired one, the one who had saved him, must have dragged him to shore. That would have taken strength, most certainly.

He looked at Lana quizzically. 'Do you truly think them monsters?'

The wind had picked up, and Lana's hair was blowing all around her. So, he couldn't see her face when she replied.

'Solvora says they are, and so they must be. But sometimes . . .'

'Sometimes?' Marino leaned closer, curious to hear what

she had to say about the mer.

'Sometimes I think that they must be *more* than monsters. They are ancient, like the land itself. And I think that to them, we must be the monstrous ones. I've seen the tools that the soldiers use, if the mer dare to show themselves or come to shore. If I was a mermaid, I would never surface.' She shuddered.

'Why do you think they do? When it is safer for them to stay below?' Marino himself was curious why the mer would ever bother with the Solvorans.

Lana shrugged. 'I think perhaps we have more in common with them than we realise. They can't leave the Solvoran ring. And we can't leave the land. We are trapped together, endlessly. I imagine they come to the surface because they want to see more. Because they want more.'

Marino caught a piece of Lana's hair that was blowing across her face and pushed it back behind her ears, so he could see her eyes.

'And you? What do you want?'

The gold flecks in her brown eyes shone in the sunlight. 'I want more too.'

The goldweavers worked on the shore, directly below the Gilded Palace. Dozens of Solvorans lined the beach, casting what looked like ropes into the sea. But when they hauled the ropes back in, they were covered with a fine gold silt. They took this and poured it into buckets before hauling it up to the Gilded Palace.

'Can anyone do it?' Marino asked, fascinated. It smelled like magic to him, this gift of pulling gold from the sea.

Lana shook her head. 'It has to be learned, and it doesn't come naturally to everyone. If I tossed a rope into the sea, even a goldweaving rope, it would sink right to the bottom. But the goldweavers know how to flick it through the water, how to call the gold from the water itself.' She gestured towards the shore. 'And they can only do their work here, on King's Beach. It is part of the bargain with the mer. If anyone tried to goldweave from another part of Solvora, they'd be at the mercy of the mer.'

'And you never run out of gold?' Marino was fascinated. It seemed impossible – an endless supply of gold from the sea. If Solvora were ever able to trade again, they would have much to offer.

'The waves come in and out every day – refreshing the supply. I suppose eventually the sea might run out of gold, but there is so much sea, I cannot imagine it. It would be like the sky losing all its stars.' She picked up a handful of fine sand and let it run through her fingers and into Marino's hand. Their fingers were almost touching, but not quite. 'Sea-gold is even finer than sand. It is impossible to see or hold by hand, only the dance of the rope can draw it from the water.'

Lana took Marino closer to where the goldweavers were doing their work. Hauling in what looked to be nets of shimmering melted gold.

Marino took a closer step, dazzled by all the glimmering gold. An ocean breeze tickled his neck and blew a fine smattering of sea-gold from the nearest rope and on to his skin, where it settled like a dusting of sugar.

Could this be it? Did Celeste need to be coated in this sea-gold? Or perhaps breathe it in, let it settle in her lungs?

'Excuse me,' Marino called out. The nearest goldweaver, a short woman with light brown skin and a long black braid, glanced up, frowning at the interruption.

'This is the survivor,' Lana explained, and the goldweaver's expression changed to one of curiosity. 'I wanted to show him how goldweaving worked. Show him what makes Solvora special.'

'May I?' asked Marino, nodding towards the gold-covered rope.

'Certainly.' The goldweaver held the rope out, grunting slightly under the effort of moving it.

Marino touched his finger to the wet gold on the rope. It felt like melted butter with sugar drizzled through it. It reminded him of the gold flecks in Lana's eyes.

Then he felt a jolt. Heat flared beneath his fingertips, and for a moment his veins seemed to light up from within. The goldweaver let out a sharp cry and dropped the rope.

The shimmering silt was *moving*, as if it had come to life, pouring off the rope and making puddles in the sand, swirling into strange shapes.

'Get back!' cried Lana, pulling on Marino's arm, tugging him away from the goldweaver's rope.

'Wait.' Marino crouched next to the swirling gold and put his whole hand in it. This time the result was immediate. He felt a blast of heat go through his body, and the magic within him responded, unfurling and stretching. His magic felt heightened – sharper and more agile than it had mere moments ago.

In response, the gold beneath his fingertips seemed to leap up in the air, hardening as it did into the shape of an arrow, and then falling back down to the sand.

And then all was still. All Marino could hear was the sound of the waves. He was aware of every eye on the beach staring at him. He cleared his throat and turned to Lana, who was staring at him, dumbfounded.

'Does that usually happen?'

Lana's smile lit up the beach as much as the sea-gold. 'No, Captain. It doesn't.'

Marino did not touch any more of the sea-gold, wary of what might happen. As they left the beach he noted a small group of soldiers coming down from the Gilded Palace to see what the commotion was about. He knew they would report back to King Leonel. Marino wasn't quite ready to talk to the king and his sly-eyed soothsayer about his magic, let alone the fact that it had responded to the sea-gold.

With permission from one of the goldweavers, Marino had taken the now-hardened golden arrow with him. Could this be the cure? It had woken something in him, certainly.

With the piece of sea-gold tucked into his pocket he strode from King's Beach with Lana. They walked in companionable silence until they were nearly back at the bakery.

'Do you think the gold is the cure you are seeking?' Lana asked. The light was softer now, spilling over the buildings and reflecting off both the mountain and the sea.

'The healer on high told me I would feel it, with my healing gift.' Marino let out a puzzled laugh. 'Before this afternoon, before I touched the sea-gold, I could barely feel my healing strand within me. But now . . . it's like all the strands of my magic have been awakened.' He took the small arrow out of his hands and turned it over. Hardened, it felt like any other metal he'd handled. But he could see the slight print of his fingertips on it, the mark he'd left on the gold. 'On the beach, I felt something from the sea-gold. But now, it feels like a lump of metal and only that.' He sighed. 'There is something about this gold, that is certain, but I don't believe it is the cure.' He shook his head. 'I admit, I've never felt so out of my depth. And that includes when I nearly drowned.'

'Marino. You have sailed to the ends of the world to find this cure.' Lana touched his arm briefly, so gently that it might have been a butterfly landing on him. 'I always longed for a sibling, a sister or a brother, someone to keep me company.'

Marino glanced away, guilt gnawing at him. 'I feel like I've failed her already. Even if the Solvoran sea-gold is linked to the cure, how will I get back to Eana?' He thought longingly of his ship, long gone beneath the waves.

He found himself filled with a desire to swim out to the wreckage, to say goodbye one final time to his beloved ship. His ship that had taken him all over the world. His ship that had carried him to Solvora. An old captain had once told him that you never know what a ship's final voyage will be, and he had not believed him. Marino had thought that he would be the one to decide the *Siren's Secret*'s last sail. He had been wrong.

Perhaps if he went and said a final goodbye. He glanced up at the sky, where the half-moon was already rising. It would be a clear night. A perfect night to slip into the sea unseen.

He knew what the Solvorans said, that to go into the sea

was a death sentence. But he was not Solvoran. And the mer had protected him once. Surely they wouldn't save him only to drown him upon his return?

The thought of seeing his beloved ship, and the possibility of seeing the blue-haired mermaid again, filled Marino with a sense of purpose, and he began to stride more quickly down the street towards Lana's bakery.

'You've perked up,' Lana remarked as they approached the door of the bakery. Her voice brought him back to where he was. With Lana. Who had spent all day showing him Solvora. Trying to help him. And here he was, already thinking of where he was going next.

Marino slowed down and smiled at her. 'Apologies. I know it is late, and I feel bad for keeping you out all day.'

'I'm glad that we found something at least.' Lana held her hand out. 'May I see the gold?' Marino handed it to her, enjoying the sight of her furrowed brow as she studied it. 'Look! The inside is still swirling.' She held it up and Marino leaned close to her to see what she was talking about.

'It didn't do that when I held it. How strange.'

'It reminds me of something I've seen in my aunt's plant journals. Not the gold, but the way it was swirling. She was a brilliant botanist. I'll try and find her journals tonight, to see if it can give us more of a clue.' Lana looked more closely at the swirling patterns. 'I wonder . . . there is a plant that grows deep in the Solvoran Sea. I've never seen it in person, only drawings of it, and whispers of what it could do. But it is called the liffen bloom and it is said that when it blossoms under the full moon, it shimmers like melted gold.'

'Maybe that plant holds the key to the cure. Can you show me what it looks like?' Marino wondered suddenly, frantically, if that was why his ship had sunk where it had. Could this plant grow where his ship had sunk? Maybe it was not a coincidence.

Lana let out a small snort. 'You'd have to dive deep into the sea to find it, and the mer would never allow that.'

Marino gave her a crooked smile. 'I can be very persuasive.'

'I'd like to see it.'

They were at the bakery door now, and as Lana unlocked it, she looked up at him from under her long lashes. In the early evening light, she seemed to glow from within. She smiled at him, and then she suddenly winced, and seemed to sway on her feet. Marino reached out to steady her, holding her beneath her elbows.

'Are you all right?'

She blinked rapidly. 'I'm so sorry, I need to get inside.'

'Are you hurt? Do you need someone to stay with you?'

Me, he meant. Do you need *me* to stay with you.

She shook her head. 'I'll be fine. It's only a headache.' She managed a thin smile. 'There isn't anything anyone can do. Usually there are signs, but this one is unexpected.' She winced again, and Marino knew it was more than 'only a headache'.

Celeste was often plagued by headaches. Especially after she had become a seer. Sometimes they would confine her to her bed for days. She told Marino that it felt like a storm was erupting inside her skull, complete with lightning strikes and thunder.

Luckily Rose or Thea were always nearby to help soothe her and take away some of the pain with their healer strand.

Perhaps he could help Lana? His healer strand had to be strong enough to help ease a headache. Especially after the sea-gold had, seemingly, strengthened his magic.

'Let me help you up the stairs at least,' Marino said. 'You look like you might collapse at any moment.'

Lana nodded and Marino helped her inside.

'I'm so sorry that you are seeing me like this,' she murmured, and slumped back against his chest. Marino wrapped his arm around her waist, supporting her.

'I'm sorry that I kept you out all day in the sun.'

Lana's eyes fluttered open. 'I'm Solvoran. I can stay out all day in the sun. That isn't it. This . . . this is an affliction.' She said the word with a sharp bitterness. 'I've suffered from these headaches my whole life. It feels like someone is putting a rock to my skull over and over again. All I can do is sleep until it subsides.'

'I might be able to help,' said Marino. 'Here.' He gently turned her around so she was leaning against the bakery counter. He carefully put his fingers to her temple and summoned his healing strand.

He focused on Lana's breathing, closed his own eyes and, using his magic, reached for where her pain was.

It felt like being in a storm at sea. Thrashing and crashing, with sharp shocks of light slicing through the haze of her pain.

Quiet the storm, he thought. *Soothe the sea.*

Lana drew a sharp breath, and Marino's eyes flew open. What if he was hurting her? What if he was making it worse?

'Are you all right?' His voice was hoarse.

'You . . . you made it stop.' She sounded breathless. 'Not completely but it is more muffled now. As if I have a pillow to protect me from the rocks raining down on my head.'

They gazed at each other, Marino's hands still on her face, before he came to his senses and dropped them to his side.

'Good,' he said, more brusquely than he meant. 'I'm glad to have helped. You should get to bed while you have the energy.'

Lana was still staring at him in a state of amazement. 'Will it last?'

'I'm not sure. I'm not an expert healer by any means. But the pain should ease slightly, at least enough for you to sleep comfortably.'

Lana slowly raised her own hand to his cheek, and the touch of her fingers on his skin made his breath catch. 'Thank you,' she whispered.

Marino cleared his throat and took a step back, widening the space between them. Which was the last thing he wanted. What he wanted was to be even closer to her, to close the small distance that had been between them, to press her up against the bakery counter and feel her hands on him . . . but she was unwell and he was a gentleman. Or a captain, at least.

'Goodnight,' he said, tipping his head to her as he took a step towards the door. 'Make sure you lock up behind me.'

'Will you be back tomorrow? For more bread, of course,' said Lana, her eyes on him. She had more colour in her cheeks now. 'And I can show you my aunt's botany journals. Perhaps we can find something in them that is useful.'

'I would like nothing more than to return. For the bread, and the journals, but also to make sure you are all right.' Marino let out a long sigh. 'But I admit I am not being a good guest to King Leonel. I left this morning before he could summon me, and I know he wants me to tell him more of my home country. The man is starved for stories of the world beyond Solvora.'

'We all are,' said Lana with a wry smile. 'But I suppose you can't deny a king's wishes. Not even for the best bread in Solvora.'

'I'll come back as soon as I can. For the bread. And the journals.' He gently pushed her hair behind her ears, his thumb lingering on her jaw. 'And to see that you are all right.' He reached into his pocket and pulled out the sea-gold arrow that had responded to his touch. 'And just so you know I will come back, can you keep this safe for me?'

'Of course.'

He dropped the golden arrow into her hand and closed her fingers around it, and then lifted her hand to his lips. He wanted to kiss her on the delicate skin of her wrist, trail kisses all the way up her arm, across her collar bone, along her neck and . . . he realised he was staring and still holding her hand. She was unwell and needed rest and he needed to get a hold of himself.

But then she opened her hand, frowning at the golden arrow there. 'Odd,' she said. 'The sea-gold, it is stinging my skin.'

Marino saw a red welt on her palm where the arrow had been. He knocked it to the ground, eager to get it away from her. 'I promise I really am trying to ease your pain, not add to it.'

Lana let out a light laugh. 'Don't blame yourself. I must have burnt my hand baking and the salt on the sea-gold probably irritated it.'

'Well, we can't have that happening,' said Marino. He

very carefully pressed another kiss to the burn on the inside of her palm. A soft sigh escaped her lips.

'That helps,' she breathed. 'Thank you.'

He let go of her hand, even though it was the last thing he wanted to do.

'I'm glad. Goodnight, Lana. Sleep well.'

'Goodnight, Marino.' His name in her mouth stirred something inside him. He had never felt like this before, what was it about Lana that made him lose all sense?

He waited outside the door until he heard her slide the lock into place.

The sun had fully set while he'd been in the bakery with Lana, and the stars shone brightly in the dark sky above.

Marino glanced up at the Gilded Palace, with every intention of walking up to it.

But then he heard the crash of the waves on the cliffs below. And he could have sworn they were calling to him.

And Marino Pegasi never could resist the call of the sea.

CHAPTER 8
Kira

The moon was high when Kira woke in her sea-cave.

She woke hungry, which was not unusual.

What was unusual was how close Mei was to her, as if she was waiting for her to wake.

Good moonrise, said Kira. *Do you have any seaweed? Sea snails?*

Sea snails were Kira's favourite delicacy. She could eat them by the dozen.

Sometimes, she had the strangest craving for food that was *hot*. She knew this was how humans ate, and she knew it was an impossible thing for her, there was nothing hot beneath the sea, only the occasional blasts of hot water that came up from the very bottom of the sea, the ones that all the mer, even Zella, stayed far from. The closest thing to warmth Kira felt was when she lifted her face to the sun.

She had told Mei once, that she wanted to try food that was cooked over a fire, and Mei's eyes had widened and she had said that Kira must never even think such a thing, in case Zella sensed it.

It would upset her, to know you were yearning for human things. You already have a soft spot for them. I know you do. I know that is why you never take any down beneath. You never breathe their life air.

It was true. She didn't. It didn't seem fair, when they had so much more power than the humans. Even the ones who tried to kill them weren't very good at it.

But the humans were the reason the mer were bound to the Solvoran ring.

And for that, they must be punished.

Zella is angry, Mei said to her, drawing her back to the moment. Her voice was an urgent whisper, even inside Kira's head. It was risky to think such a thing, because they could all speak to each other, and Kira still sometimes believed that she couldn't shut Zella out, that Zella, as the eldest and most powerful of their small mermaid clan, could hear all her thoughts.

Zella was almost always angry.

But there was something different in the way that Mei was behaving. There was a fear in her eyes that made Kira pay attention.

Why is Zella angry this time?

The man you saved, he has been in the Gilded Palace. We saw him go all the way up. He slept there, in that poisoned place. That magic you sensed in him, what if he uses it to help the Solvorans?

Kira scoffed. *How can one man's magic help all the Solvorans? His magic is small. It is a drop compared to the whole sea.*

I don't know. I'm not the one who is angry. But Zella thinks he should have drowned. More than that, she thinks you should have drowned him. Taken his life air.

Frustration began to mount in Kira. She felt drowsy – and hungry – and did not want to have to think about Zella and her moods.

Well, there is not much I can do about that now.

Mei's eyes suddenly flashed in a mix of fear and excitement.

You are wrong. He is in the sea right this minute.

That snapped Kira fully awake. *He cannot be.*

He is swimming to the wreck. To his ship. And Zella is waiting there for him.

A fool. The man is a fool, Kira thought to herself as she swam swiftly through the night, leaving Mei behind in the sea-cave.

The human was a fool.

But so was she.

Kira could almost laugh at herself. Swimming as fast as she could to the wreck so she could arrive before he did. So she could stop her mer-sister from drowning him.

From taking his life air for herself.

If anyone was to take his life air, it would be her. Kira saved him, so by rights he should be her human. She had never interfered with any human that Zella dragged down to the sea. This was no different. Kira had claimed him.

Kira swam faster, letting the current guide her. She knew exactly where to find the wreck, but she also knew exactly where he was. The scent of him was almost overwhelming.

The moonlight filtered through the water, but she didn't need the moonlight to see. Like her sisters, Kira could see in the dark and did not need the light.

So, she saw Marino long before he saw her.

He was beautiful, underwater.

He moved with a grace rare for humans. He'd swum out

further than she'd ever seen any human swim of their own volition.

And he kept diving down, as if he thought he could reach the depths where his wreck was.

Of course, he went back up, breaking the surface noisily and gulping in air before going back down again with a forceful kick. And there was something else in the water, something that Kira recognised as magic, and then suddenly he was close enough to touch the broken shell of his ship.

But as he reached for it, Zella emerged from within. The top of Zella's face was covered in star-blossoms, but her silver eyes glowed and she wore a wicked grin. A grin that Kira had seen many times before.

Kira knew what that grin meant. It was the grin of someone who was about to take something that didn't belong to them but that they were determined to have.

Kira did not save Marino for her older mer-sister to take him for her own.

Zella reached her hand out towards Marino, who suddenly stopped swimming and hung in the water, as if in a trance.

STOP!

Kira's sea voice echoed in the water. Not only in her sisters' heads but distorted through the sea itself. Her voice was loud enough to make Zella look up and then she began to laugh. A laugh loud enough to be heard beneath the waves.

It was loud enough to break Marino's trance, to make him realise he had lost the air he thought he had.

Kira summoned her energy, her own magic, and pulled Marino towards her on a current of her own making.

What are you doing?

Kira sent the question towards Marino without thought, forgetting in the moment that she could not speak to him the way she could with her mersisters.

Marino's eyes grew wide, and she sensed that his lungs must be screaming for air. But he wouldn't have time to get above. He had come too far down.

Keep him below.

From Zella. An order.

If he is so desperate to be reunited with his ship, then let him. Take his life air. Give him the sea-kiss. He can stay down here as long as you want him to. A fine first kiss of air for you.

No.

No?

NO!

If you will not keep him here, I will. He has come back on his own. We did not lure him. We did not sing for him. He wants to be here, so give the man what he wants.

Marino turned from them and started kicking towards the surface. As if he had heard their conversation and was trying to show that he did not want this.

He wanted to live. Kira felt that in the thrum of his blood, in the defiant beating of his heart. But it didn't matter how much he wanted to live. He was too far down now. It was too late. He would not make it back to the surface.

Unless she helped him.

Again.

Kira, twice saved is twice fooled.

Zella's voice was sharp in her head.

Kira did not want to go against her sisters or displease them. It felt unnatural to her. But as she felt her own beating heart within her, she knew she would save this human again.

He is mine to kiss. Kira imagined Zella's sigh of relief. To kiss is to kill, after all.

And he is mine to save.

Deep down Kira knew that she was fast, powerful, but she had always kept it leashed, fearful of what would happen if it spilled out of her. Fearful that she wouldn't be able to control it. Fearful of what would happen if Zella realised that Kira was stronger, faster than all her sisters. She had always felt it thrumming within her, aching to be released. So, it was a relief to let her power burst out of her, propelling her towards Marino and carrying them both up to the surface.

They burst through into the night air and suddenly he was gasping, his eyes wide and wild.

Kira was grateful that she was wearing her flower mask, because she wanted this man, this man gifted with magic, to *know* her. And if he saw her true face he would be dazed and dazzled and would believe himself in love with her and Kira realised long ago that she wanted the kind of love that they said it was impossible for mer to ever have.

Her breasts too, were covered by the same pale blue starflowers. And she would have no shame in showing them, for she was not a human girl who felt shame or embarrassment or even fear, but she was still glad, because she thought the starflowers were beautiful, and they adorned her body like living jewels.

'You saved me,' said Marino, breathlessly. 'Again.'

'You came back.' Kira heard her own voice in the air, low and hoarse and like the sound of waves crashing against the shore. 'Why?'

'I wanted to say goodbye to my ship.' His eyes narrowed. 'My ship that you sank.'

'I did not sink your ship. There was a storm.'

'It was like no storm I have ever seen. It was not a natural storm. My ship . . . my crew . . .' His voice faltered. 'Gone.'

'Do not blame the mer,' Kira said sharply. 'Blame Solvora. Blame the king who has invited you into his poisoned palace.'

'The king did not wreck my ship.'

Kira began to wonder if she should have kept the captain below after all. But then she remembered the scent of his blood in the sea. The smell of his magic. His determination that had brought him all this way. 'Why are you here?'

'I told you. To say goodbye to my ship. And to see if there was anything there I could salvage.'

'I do not mean here in the sea. I mean here in Solvora.'

Marino's eyes lit up. 'I am looking for a cure for my sister. She is a seer and very ill; the seaswifts guided me here.'

'I have never heard of the seaswifts helping a human.'

'I am different from the Solvorans,' he said slowly.

'Yes, that is clear. You have a magic in you.'

Marino startled. 'How . . . how did you know?'

Kira gave him a sharp smile. 'I can smell it on you.' She tilted her head. 'Your scent is different now, though. Stronger.'

Marino cleared his throat. 'Are you implying that I smell?'

'It is a delicious smell.' Kira spoke plainly, and then enjoyed the way he responded to her words. His throat bobbing and his eyes darkening.

'But I am curious why the humans do not kill you. Humans hate magic. They hate what they cannot understand.'

Marino gave her a crooked smile. 'It is a long story.

Perhaps one for another time, when I am not treading water in the middle of the sea.' His gaze sharpened. 'I told you how the seaswifts guided me, how they helped me. Will you help me? Do you know of a cure for the seeing sickness?'

Kira shook her head. 'I have never heard of such a sickness. I know nothing of the so-called seers.'

'I have recently learned of a plant that grows in the sea. The liffen bloom. I think this might be what I'm looking for. Can you bring it to me?'

Kira reared back from him. 'How do you know of the liffen bloom? It is not for humans.' She would not bring him something so sacred to her and her mersisters. Not even if his need for it was noble.

'So, it is real. Well. We've established that I am not like the other humans.'

'You are greedy like them. I've helped you more than enough. And you still want more.'

'Why?' He swam closer to her, so close that they were nearly touching. 'Why have you helped me?'

Kira wondered if her sisters were down below, watching. Laughing. Waiting to see if she would change her mind and take his life air.

Instead of pulling away from him, Kira leaned into her yearning, leaned into *him*. 'Can the waves explain why they crash? I am drawn to you in a way that I cannot explain, in a way that terrifies me. Perhaps it is your magic. Perhaps it is calling to me.'

'I understand,' said Marino, his voice was low. 'Perhaps *your* magic is calling back to me.'

He took a long breath, as if he was breathing in her scent. 'The ship is not the only reason I returned to the sea.'

This filled Kira with such a strange giddiness, she felt like she might float up and out of the sea and into the night sky.

'Have you enchanted me?' His voice was low and searching, and his breath was warm on her skin.

Kira almost wished that she had. Because then she would understand what was happening between her and the man who had come from beyond. The man with magic in his blood.

Their lips were nearly touching. All Kira needed to do was lean forward, let the waves push them together . . .

'What is your name?' he asked suddenly. He let out a low laugh. 'When I think of you, which is more often than I would like to admit, I think of you as the blue-haired mermaid, and I would like to know your name.'

A mer's name was sacred. Armed with it, he could call her in the sea, and she would hear it, no matter where she was. She would not have to go to him, but she would hear him. From anywhere.

But she already knew that she would sense Marino in the sea whether he knew her name or not. And she wanted him to know her name. She wanted to hear it on his lips.

'My name is Kira.'

'Kira. Kira, Kira, Kira.' He said it like an incantation, like he would never forget it.

It was enough for her, that he knew her name. That she could haunt his dreams until the end of his days. She leaned closer to him, lips brushing against his ear.

'You are a beautiful fool, Marino Pegasi. Do not come back in the sea. You will not survive again.'

And with that, she summoned a wave that pushed him to shore before she let temptation get the better of her.

CHAPTER 19
Marino

As Marino lay gasping on the sand once more, he felt every bit the fool that Kira had said he was.

He had nothing to show for his ill-advised dive down to the wreck. He hadn't found the liffen bloom, hadn't found anything that might give him a clue to where the cure was, and he didn't even feel at peace after seeing the remains of the *Siren's Secret* lying broken on the ocean floor. All he'd found was . . . Kira.

Who had saved him. Again. Because the silver-haired one had nearly dragged him to his doom. He had seen it in her eyes, the hunger and the violence.

The fact that he lived was only thanks to Kira.

The one who had saved him not once, but twice.

Kira. She had a name now. Kira. Kira. Kira. He heard her name in his head in time with the beating of his heart.

He could not forget how her eyes had stared into his own, how they had darkened from violet to indigo and the silver in them had shone like pieces of starlight.

He could still hear her voice, the whisper in his ear.

You are a beautiful fool. And then, harsher. *Do not come back into the sea. You will not survive again.*

It sounded like a promise, it sounded like a threat. And yet . . .

He knew he'd go back. If only to see Kira again. She would not let him drown, would she? Not after she had saved him twice.

Not after she had told him that she was drawn to him like the waves were to the shore.

He needed to see her again. If only to convince her to help him find the liffen bloom. Her reaction to it had convinced him that this mysterious plant that was linked to the sea-gold was what his sister needed. What all of Eana needed. Tonight he had used his magic to propel him deeper, to help his lungs hold more air, but the enchantment had worn off too quickly. He would perfect it and then he would return to the sea and find the cure for his sister, no matter what it took. No matter how many mermaids he had to face to get it.

But Marino knew that his desire to see Kira again was about more than the liffen bloom. There was a connection between them that he could not deny.

Marino dragged himself to his feet and pulled on the shirt he had left on the beach. His breeches were still wet, but they would dry on the long walk back up to the palace. The night air was warm.

Despite returning empty-handed from his dive, he felt a strange sense of satisfaction having seen his ship again. And better yet, he had not seen any sign of his small crew or their rowboat. And that might mean that they were still alive. Marino chose to believe that. It gave him strength and hope – and he knew he needed both.

At the Gilded Palace, the night guards recognised him and nodded as he passed.

It was strange to be so known somewhere that he had been for such a short time. It reminded him a little of being in Anadawn, where everyone knew him

Anadawn. Home, even if it didn't feel like it. Home because Celeste was there.

He would leave Solvora. He would make it back to Celeste, and he would save her and save all of Eana, too.

Marino made it back up to his room and collapsed into bed. He dreamed of the sea, again.

He saw Kira first, laughing as she swam just ahead of him, just out of reach. As he swam after her, he saw Lana waving to him from the cliffs. He felt torn, wanting to follow Kira, but also to swim to where Lana was.

Make a choice, Marino.

But before he could make up his mind, the dream darkened. A storm came in and both Lana and Kira disappeared. He was floating in inky darkness. And then he heard Celeste's voice. Crying and begging him to come home with the cure. A chorus of wails joined her, Rose and Thea and everyone he had left in Eana.

The next day, Marino was awakened by a sharp knock at his door. He stumbled across the room and swung it open to reveal a young page dressed in the blue, white and gold of Solvora. He nodded at Marino.

'Good morning, sir. The king has requested your presence at breakfast.' The page paused and lowered his voice. 'And sir? It is not a request. If you catch my meaning.'

Marino did indeed. This was an order.

'Thank you,' he said. 'Let me dress, and then would you take me to breakfast?' He offered the page a kind smile. 'I don't know my way around the palace quite yet.'

The page nodded. 'Certainly. I'll be right here.'

Marino closed the door and glanced out of the window. For a moment, he was overcome by the desire to leap out into the sea below. Surely Kira would save him again? And then she could help him find the cure and together they would swim back to Eana . . . But no. He was being the fool that she accused him of. He could no more swim all the way back to Eana than he could fly. Even with an enchantment. And Kira could not leave the Solvoran ring. And he didn't have the cure for Celeste. And she had made it clear she would not help him any further. These were the desperate thoughts of a desperate man.

Pull yourself together, Marino.

He would be of no use to anyone if he completely lost his senses.

He had to tackle this morning first. Breakfast with King Leonel. He needed the king on side, because even if he managed to convince the mer to let him leave the Solvoran ring, he needed a ship to do so and the only way to get a ship was to convince the king to give him one. One step at a time, he told himself, as he sorted through the trunk of clothes that Leonel had provided. He chose a pale blue shirt, and it was only when he had buttoned it up that he realised it reminded him of the colour of the flower mask that Kira wore. Thinking about Kira in the sea, wearing only the pale blue seaflowers, made him feel dazed with desire, and he quickly turned his focus to the day ahead.

Breakfast with King Leonel and then he would visit the bakery on Sugar Street. He wanted to see those journals that Lana had mentioned, and to see how she was feeling.

Thinking of Lana, when he had just been daydreaming about Kira, made Marino feel vaguely unsettled. As if he were being unfaithful, which was ridiculous. He was not promised to either of them. He needed their help, that was all.

But he could not deny the connection he felt to them both.

After Marino had dressed he strode out into the hall, where the page was still waiting patiently.

'This way,' the boy said, leading Marino up a winding staircase. 'The king likes to start his day close to the sun. The breakfast room is in the tallest tower of the east side of the palace.'

'A fine custom,' said Marino. King Leonel seemed slightly fixated on the sun, obsessed with being as close to it as he could be. And perhaps as far from the sea as possible.

Like the throne room, the breakfast room was airy and bright. Floor-to-ceiling windows showed views of the sea and sky, and the sun illuminated the entire room.

Leonel was sitting at the head of a long wooden table. Today he wore no crown and was dressed all in white. When he saw Marino he stood, opening his arms in welcome.

'Good morning, good man! Come, come. Your seat is here. Next to me,' he said, with a wide smile that showed his gleaming white teeth.

Marino knew it was an honour to be invited to sit at his side. He bowed and quickened his pace. When Marino reached him, Leonel clapped the captain on the back, a hand heavy on his shoulder. 'Tell me, what did you get up to yesterday?' He waggled his eyebrows and winked. 'Did you devour any of our delicacies? Dance with any of our lovely local ladies at a tavern or two?'

Marino laughed politely. 'Your Majesty, you are as much a matchmaker as my queen back home. No, I did not dance with anyone nor visit a tavern, but today is a new day after all!' Marino waited for Leonel to sit, knowing the etiquette was that he must not sit before the king.

'Hmmm.' Leonel assessed Marino the way a hawk looks at a rabbit. 'There were reports that you were seen all over town with a raven-haired beauty. I try to keep track of my subjects, of course, but it's impossible to know them all. Especially the tradespeople.' He waved his hand dismissively. 'Tell me, who was it who kept you so captivated all day?' He leaned in closer, eyes gleaming with interest.

Marino felt suddenly strangely protective of Lana. He did not want the king to know her name, to know that he had become fond of her. And he didn't like that the king had kept eyes on him. Did he know that he'd gone into the sea?

Marino shrugged casually. 'I fear your reports are misleading, Your Majesty. I walked with many townspeople yesterday. All were eager to show me the beauty of Solvora. One was dark-haired, but I couldn't tell you her name.' It was dangerous, to tell such a bald-faced lie, but surely the king couldn't have seen his every move.

Leonel glanced to his left, where Talia sat quietly. Marino felt her gaze on him, and remembered that she was the king's soothsayer, that she was trained to catch a lie.

He slowed his breathing, calmed his heart, and gave her

his most charming smile.

She blinked, as if flustered, and then nodded back at the king. This seemed to assuage any worries Leonel had.

Marino carried on speaking, as if he hadn't noticed the exchange between the king and his soothsayer. 'I was very impressed with everything I saw, and dare I say, everyone I met. Solvora is a very special place.'

Leonel practically preened. 'It is. I have worked hard to make it so. It was not always this way. The king before me, my uncle, had gone mad. And that made the people afraid . . .' His voice trailed off. 'When I first became king there was a terrible storm – the streets were flooded. Almost all of Solvora climbed to the top of Goldwave Mountain, to my palace, seeking safety. We didn't know then that we would be unable to leave the kingdom again. But with time, and with a firm and steady hand, I have made Solvora the place it is now.' He sat and nodded at Marino to sit as well. He helped himself to a slice of potato omelette and passed the platter to Marino. 'Be sure to have some of the sausage as well.'

'On my wander yesterday, I met some butchers.' Marino said. 'They spoke very highly of Solvoran meat.'

'As they should. Our farms are blessed with abundance, and our livestock are lucky to eat grass grown in the Solvoran sun and rain.'

'I also saw the remarkable feat of goldweaving. It is a shame that a country with so many resources is so cut off from the rest of the world. You would make an excellent trading partner.'

'We will one day,' said King Leonel. 'I will do whatever it takes. The fact that you made it here gives me hope that

Solvorans will sail again.'

Marino nodded and took a bite of his omelette. There was a platter of rolls on the table as well, and he wondered if they were as delicious as the ones that Lana baked.

'You never told us how you found Solvora,' said Talia in her breathy voice. Today she wore pale green, her long hair tied back in a braid wrapped round her head like a crown. Marino could not deny that she was very beautiful. He idly wondered if she was romantically involved with the king. 'We are so far from anywhere. Was it luck?'

'In a way.' Marino took a large gulp of water to buy himself some time. He had not yet disclosed his magic to the king, and he couldn't explain the seaswifts without admitting his own magical heritage. 'I'm seeking a cure for a mysterious illness. The healers in Eana said the last time this illness struck our land, many years ago, a cure was found on this side of the world. So, I set my course for the Ochre Isles, and once I passed those, I found my way to Solvora. And here I hope to find the cure my sister needs.'

'What is the illness?' asked Talia, her pale eyes boring into Marino. He rubbed the back of his neck. 'Could you be carrying it? You must excuse my directness, but we must protect our people.'

Leonel snapped his head around, fear flickering in his eyes. 'A good point, Talia. Wise as ever. An outside disease could ruin us all.'

'Oh, you have nothing to fear from me,' Marino said quickly. How to explain the seeing sickness? 'I am in fine health.'

'And you said it is your sister who is sick?' said Talia, watching him closely, like a bird of prey.

'Yes. She had a fit that triggered her sickness.' Marino rubbed his own temples, trying to push back his rising stress. 'I am desperate to find a cure for her. I'd do anything.' When he opened his eyes again, both the king and Talia were staring hard at him.

'So, your voyage was no royal decree,' said Leonel.

'It was in a way. My sister is very close to the queen of Eana. She is as desperate as me to find a cure. I hope that I will find it here in Solvora.'

He knew that he couldn't say he suspected it was in the sea, and that he would be enlisting the help of the mer.

'I see,' said Leonel. 'Well, of course, we hope you find what you are looking for. And you have my full support. But I must ask something of you in return. Which, I'm sure you'll agree, is only fair.'

'Of course,' said Marino.

'But first answer us this. Why did the mer let you live?' Talia's gaze sharpened.

'I . . . I do not know,' stammered Marino. 'I was lucky.'

'He's lying,' said Talia quickly, and Marino did not miss the sound of a blade being drawn somewhere in the room.

'There is something about you I cannot place,' Talia went on. 'It is not only that you are a stranger, there is also something strange about you.' Marino met her stare, and as he did he noticed his own magic responding within him, rising in defence.

He knew he had a moment only to decide what to do, and hoping it was the right choice, he raised both his hands in a motion of surrender. 'I will admit, I have not been entirely truthful with you.'

King Leonel's face was like thunder. 'You have thirty

seconds to explain yourself, and if I do not find your answer to my liking, we will throw you out of that window.'

Marino spoke quickly and thought even faster. 'You often say that Solvora is blessed. The land I come from is blessed as well, but so are the people. I am a man, I am a sea captain, but I am also a witch. Many of the people in Eana are. Our gifts range from seeing,' he nodded towards Talia, 'healing, small enchantments, battle, and my personal favourite – tempest magic. Bending the wind to your will, calling a storm.'

'The way the mer do?' Leonel was watching Marino very carefully, like he was a powder keg about to explode.

'The mer's magic feels very different to mine. That storm that I experienced, that was nothing like tempest magic.'

'And you use your so-called magic for good?' said Talia, eyes narrowed. Again, Marino felt his magic recognise something in her, something strange. Perhaps she was wearing some of the sea-gold. Or perhaps he was being paranoid.

'Indeed,' said Marino. 'And you are not at risk of the sickness my sister has as it is unique to witches. And you must understand that what I seek is magical in itself. There is magic here, on Solvora. In the Solvoran Sea. And I will find it.'

King Leonel leaned back, folding his arms across his broad chest. 'I have never heard of such a thing. Humans with magic.' All the air seemed to disappear out of the room while Leonel deliberated. 'Well, Marino. I applaud you for being truthful with us. We prize truth here in Solvora. I wish you had been more forthright on your arrival, but I understand why you were not. But this proves we trust each other, does it not?'

'Yes, I suppose it does,' said Marino slowly. He felt like he was being caught in a trap but he wasn't sure what it was.

'And you grow more fascinating by the day. Are you saying that it is your magic that kept you alive? The reason the mer did not drown you?'

'It is possible,' said Marino. 'I do not know the thoughts of the mer.' An image of Kira, with her shining purple and silver eyes, appeared in his mind. 'It is more possible that it was luck. A kind of magic in itself.' He summoned a grin. 'And I have always been luckier than most.'

'Indeed,' murmured King Leonel. 'You say you can bend the wind. Can your magic stop a storm? Take back control of our seas?'

Marino shook his head. 'I can call a wind, perhaps slow a storm, but I cannot control the seas.'

King Leonel stroked his beard. 'Fascinating,' he murmured. 'Perhaps with enough practice, you will be able to slow the waves that keep us trapped here, enough for us to get back out to the open ocean.'

'Once I find the cure for my sister, nothing, not even the sea, will be able to stop me from leaving,' said Marino firmly.

'We will be sorry to see you go,' said Leonel. Then he clapped. His eyes were hungry. 'Let us go on the terrace and you can show me some of this magic you speak of.'

CHAPTER 20
Lana

Lana was tidying up the kitchen when there was a knock at the door of the bakery.

The day had been long. She'd woken early – before dawn. It had taken her a moment to realise how long she had been sleeping. Before Benedita had died, she would be the one to tell Lana how much time had passed.

Once, not long after Benedita had taken her last breath, Lana had woken from one of her headache-induced sleeps. Her stomach had cramped in hunger, and her mouth was dry. She had staggered down the stairs, unlocking the door and stumbled out into the sun, blinking like a newborn baby.

She'd seen Jonah – cheerful, curly-haired Jonah, and in response to her faltering questions, he'd told her it was market day. She had slept for three days. Lana had nothing to sell at the market; her bread and cakes had gone stale.

Jonah knew of her ailment – he had often brought over bone broth for her. When Lana explained, with a lump in her throat, that with Benedita gone she lost track of how long she'd been confined to her bed, his eyes had softened with concern, and he and his husband Carlos came up with a plan.

Market day was every fifth day. In the window of their shop were various animal skulls, cleaned and bleached by the sun, all familiar to Lana. She had seen the skulls every day that she walked down Sugar Street, and they did not frighten her any more than a loaf of bread or a ripe tomato would. On the day that Lana had come to them to find out what day it was, Carlos rearranged the skulls. He placed a cow skull, followed by four rabbit skulls. He plucked a sprig of lavender growing in a pot in their cliffside garden and put it in the eye of the cow's skull.

'This is market day. Every day, Jonah or I will move the lavender to mark the days. That way, all you need to do is look across the street, and you will see what day it is.'

Lana found she could not speak, but threw her arms around her neighbours, hugging them tightly.

Carlos patted her on the back. 'It is nothing, Lana. It is what neighbours do.'

'But we wouldn't say no to a few of your tarts,' added Jonah, with a smile.

Carlos and Jonah had kept their word – moving the sprig of lavender from one skull to the next, so all Lana had to do was count from market day to know what day it was.

This morning, she'd woken with a strange metallic taste in her mouth and was afraid that this time she'd slept longer than she ever had before. Her headache was gone, leaving only the faint ringing in her ears that lingered hours after she woke.

She could not forget how it had felt to be healed by Marino. How he had taken so much of the pain away, but not the urge to lie down that came with her headaches, her body demanding that she sleep it away.

She had been worried about how much time had passed and possessed with such a sudden and strange fear that Marino had somehow managed to leave, and it had happened while she was sleeping, that she'd lit a torch and crept out in the pre-dawn dark to see what day it was.

The skulls looked eerie in the torch light, but she'd seen with a deep sense of relief that the lavender sprig was only one skull over from the one before. Only a day had passed.

She'd spent the day selling bread and cake to the Solvorans who had missed her the last two days, who were patient enough to come back day after day until the bakery was open again. It was a long but satisfying day. And now that it was over, she was tired. Not fatigued like she felt in the onslaught of her headaches, but tired in a pleasing way. She was looking forward to drawing herself a bath. So, when she heard the knock at the door, she assumed it was someone hoping to buy the last of the day's bread. But when she pulled open the door, Marino stood there. He filled the doorway, and she found that in the time it had been since she'd seen him, she had somehow forgotten just what the mere sight of him did to her. How had she forgotten that his warm brown eyes gazing into her own made her tingle all over? Or how his smile sent her heart racing? Nobody had ever made her feel like this before. She had not known she *could* feel like this, without a single touch, only the heat of his gaze.

'Oh!' she said, still holding her broom in one hand.

Marino's gaze roamed over her. 'I didn't mean to interrupt you,' he said. 'I wanted to check on you, see how you are doing. I came by yesterday, but the shop was shut.'

'You aren't interrupting.' Lana smiled and stepped back,

opening the door more so he could come in. 'I'm just cleaning up for the night.'

'Let me help.' Marino deftly took the broom out of her hands and began to sweep. He glanced up at her with a grin. 'I've had to swab the deck once or twice, you know. A bakery and kitchen is easy.'

Lana's laugh bubbled out of her. 'Consider me impressed, Captain. And thank you. For helping ease my headache the other night.'

Marino paused and looked at her more closely. 'I'm glad to see you up and about. I was worried about you, Lana.'

His words were like a balm, as soothing as his hands had been the other day. 'I'm much better now. And I'm used to it, truly.' She laughed again, feeling slightly self-conscious. 'I've suffered from headaches like that my whole life. When my aunt Benedita was here, it was easier . . .' She realised she'd still not told Marino about Benedita, and let her voice trail off.

Marino was still sweeping and had moved into the kitchen. Lana followed him in, enjoying watching his progress. She couldn't help but notice the surety of his movements, the confidence with which he did everything, even something as mundane as sweeping the floors. She cleared her throat and hoped that he hadn't noticed her staring. 'And how have you been? How is life going up in the Gilded Palace?'

Marino paused and leaned back against the counter. 'It's complicated.'

Lana said nothing, waiting for him to elaborate. He put the broom to the side. 'I told the king about my magic. And now he wants me to use it against the mer. He says that because I am not Solvoran, I'm not bound by the same rules, bound by the same agreement that was made between the men and the mer years ago. Do you know what started the war between Solvorans and mer?'

Lana crossed the kitchen, so she was closer to Marino. 'I was young, when it happened. Only a baby. But the story I've always been told is that the king before Leonel, King Ferdinand, fell in love with a mermaid. Which of course is common. What was different was that this mermaid fell in love with him too, and she gave up her tail and her mer-magic and her sea-life to be with him. But she missed the sea and spent all her days on the shore, begging the sea to take her back. King Ferdinand grew mad with jealousy, especially when it became clear that his new wife was expecting a child.'

'How can a man be jealous of the sea?' asked Marino.

'Shh! I'm still telling you the story. King Ferdinand overheard his wife offering the sea anything to go back. And this is where the story varies, depending on who tells it. Some say he drowned her in a fit of rage, some say the sea relented and she turned back into a mermaid and then the king hunted her down, but the result is the same: he murdered his wife, and their unborn child too. But he did not know that she was one of the sea's most favoured daughters, and so the sea bound the mer here with the sole purpose of never allowing us to leave, nor anyone to come.'

Marino frowned. 'That doesn't sound very fair to the mer, I must say. One of their own is killed by a king, and then they are stuck here forever punishing his own people?'

Lana swatted him on the arm. 'Oh you! Don't side with the mer! Do you know that they try to drown us all because if there are no Solvorans, they are free to leave? There wouldn't be anyone left for them to punish. It is why they sing so many Solvorans into the sea.'

'But you are allowed to fish from the shore? And goldweave as well. That seems an unnecessary kindness, does it not? Why do they not send waves to drown you all instead? It would be much more efficient.'

'After King Ferdinand killed his queen, he fell into despair and he offered his own blood to the land, to Solvora, as a sacrifice to atone for what he had done. They say the earth drank up his blood and Goldwave Mountain stretched higher to the sky. And now as long as we are on Solvoran soil we are safe. The sea has become our enemy. But . . .' Lana's voice trailed off and she lowered her voice, as if the walls were listening. 'Benedita was of the old believers, those who worshipped the sea. She told me once that Solvora itself was born from the union of the sea and the earth, deep below the waves.'

Marino raised his eyebrows. 'That is quite the origin story.'

Lana grinned at his reaction. 'She used to say that the mer too were the original children of the sea and her human lovers. Until the sea learned humans cannot be trusted.'

Marino shrugged. 'The witches of Eana have similar beliefs about where our land comes from. But I still don't understand – who brokered the truce? Yes, the mer are your enemy but you manage to live in some harmony.'

'With his dying breath, King Ferdinand appointed his nephew, Leonel, to be the new king. Supposedly Leonel and the eldest of the Solvoran mer came up with the terms of the truce. It is bound by salt, unbreakable for both. But there are ways around the rules, and in recent years there has been more hatred for the mer than there ever was in my childhood. And those who loved the sea, like my aunt, are growing old and dying, leaving only Solvorans who view the sea as a threat.'

'Which is why I am such an appealing prospect to Leonel, because I have no part in the truce.'

'Exactly.' Lana gazed up at Marino. 'You must take care. He would sacrifice you in an instant if he thought it would help Solvora.'

'I'd like to see him try,' said Marino and Lana laughed, shaking her head.

'Have you always been so infuriatingly confident?'

Marino's lips twitched into a smile. 'Only when I want to make a good impression. Am I?'

Lana stilled, letting her gaze roam over him. 'I'm still deciding.'

Marino held her gaze until she felt her cheeks flush, and then she was the one to look away.

'Now that I know the whole history of Solvora, I want to know more about you. How did you come to live in the bakery?'

'Oh. My history is linked to Solvora's. When the old king died, many people tried to leave. They didn't believe that the sea, that the mer, would stop them. My parents were among them. Their boat sank, of course. But I survived. I don't remember it, I was far too young, but I still dream of waves.'

'I'm sorry,' said Marino, his voice thick with emotion. He took her hand in his for a moment.

Lana shrugged. 'I am sad to have never known them, but

I have lived a good life. I was found floating in a rowboat, the boat was knocking against the cliff right below here. Benedita said it was a sign she was meant to raise me. And she did.'

'Your aunt Benedita who loved the sea and was a botanist.' Marino had dropped her hand, and Lana found herself hoping he'd take it again.

'Yes. She loved to forage for ingredients to make her cakes taste better. She taught me so much. Oh! I need to show you her journals. I found the one with a sketch of a liffen bloom.'

'Thank you.' Marino's voice was warm. 'I'm lucky the storm sent me in here. I don't think I could do this without you, Lana. Find the cure. Survive Solvora.'

'Where is that confidence?' teased Lana.

But when Marino spoke again his tone was sincere. 'I only hope I've not been too much of an imposition.'

'Marino, you've given me a glimpse of the world outside of Solvora.' Lana shook her head. 'More than a glimpse. You've given me hope that there is so much more to explore, and that maybe I'll be able to leave one day. For as long as I can remember I've lived above the bakery. I've never known anything else but here.' She laughed lightly. 'My world must seem quite small to you, someone who spends all their time at sea, seeking adventure. But I can see the sea from my room. The sound of the waves soothes me to sleep at night.'

They had somehow edged towards the doorway of the stairwell that led up from the bakery and into Lana's living quarters. Lana paused. This was the moment where she should say goodnight. Lead him back through the bakery, nudge him out of the door into the early evening, lock up, and prep the bread for tomorrow morning.

But she didn't want to do that. She wanted to invite him up, to show him more of her small world. Show him the view from the window. The thought of being alone with Marino in her bedroom sent shivers of desire running through her.

'Our worlds are not too different,' Marino said. He leaned forward, placing his arm on the doorway, and locked eyes with her. Her breath hitched, her limbs felt loose, she felt like she was slowly melting from the heat of his gaze. 'The sound of the waves often soothes me to sleep, when I'm on my ship. It is one of my favourite sounds.' His voice turned wistful. 'I miss it.'

Her mouth felt dry and she swallowed. 'Do . . . you want to come and listen to the waves with me?' Then she broke their eye contact and looked away, suddenly embarrassed for being so bold.

Marino gently ran his thumb under her jaw and tilted her face up so she could see his face again. He slowly moved his thumb across her bottom lip, and as he did, she leaned back against the door frame. The air felt deliciously heavy, and she was aware of every part of her body.

'I'd like that, very much,' said Marino. He nodded up towards the stairs. 'I'll follow you.' He dropped his hand from her face and interlaced his fingers with hers.

Lana was filled with a sudden giddiness and anticipation, and she squeezed his hand before turning to make her way up the stairs.

'This way,' she said, sounding a little bit breathless before they had even started the ascent up the stairs.

She took him up the winding, spindly staircase that

creaked with each step. There were small windows carved into the walls, and their shadows flickered in the fading light. 'Mind your head,' she said, as they reached the small landing outside her bedroom.

Lana's room was small but it was her haven. Standing in the doorway with Marino, she tried to see it as he might.

One wall was filled with bookshelves, lined with tattered old books. And then there was a small wooden desk, with a crooked chair tucked underneath it. She realised her diary was out, and she quickly moved into the room to slam it shut and tuck it under another book. The last thing she needed was Marino reading the words she'd written – most recently detailing the dreams she'd had of him! She turned back to Marino, watching him assess the rest of her room.

Her bed had never looked quite so small. At least she had remembered to make it this morning, the colourful quilt that Benedita had made her tucked in and folded in the corners. She felt her cheeks flame from simply looking at the bed and turned her attention to the other side of the room, where the curtains were.

With a flourish she flung the curtains open to show the glass doors that went all the way from the ceiling to the scuffed wooden floor of the room. As promised, there was an uninterrupted view of the sea. The sun had nearly set and was sinking down beneath the horizon, bathing the room in golden light.

Marino stepped closer to take a better look and let out a low whistle. 'That *is* a nice view,' he said.

'That's not all,' said Lana, and she carefully unlatched the doors and led him out to the small balcony built directly into the cliffside. 'This is my favourite part.'

She remembered Benedita telling her when she was small to always be careful when she went out on the balcony, but she had never been afraid of the sheer drop below. She had spent almost her whole life sleeping in this room, listening to the crash of the waves against the cliff. Sometimes, she even slept on the balcony. Under the stars, letting the sea sing her to sleep.

She leaned out over the balcony banister, breathing in the familiar, wonderful ocean air.

'Careful,' said Marino, putting a hand on her waist to steady her. 'I don't want you to blow away.'

Lana laughed and tossed her hair in the wind. 'This balcony has stood through worse storms than this.' Then she smirked. 'But it has never had more than one person standing on it.'

Marino raised a brow. 'You've never . . . brought anyone else here?'

She heard the unspoken words. *You've never brought anyone up to your room.* And all that it implied.

Lana wished she had a witty retort, something clever, but instead she told him the truth, in a rushed, slightly embarrassed way. There was something about Marino that made her want to tell him everything about herself, even the parts she hid from others. 'Oh, my aunt Benedita used to come up here, of course,' she said. She feared the mention of her dead aunt was like dousing the flame of the moment. Lana hurried on, words tumbling out as she tried to go back to that breathless moment in the stairwell. But although she very much wanted to be beguiling and bewitching, she found herself being entirely honest. 'And my best friend, Florence. Well, Florence has never been out on the balcony, she's afraid of heights, and the sea, which is quite the feat when we live in a tall town overlooking the sea.' Lana laughed, and as she did, Marino's smile widened, and he leaned closer to her, eager to hear more. It was all the encouragement Lana needed to keep talking, to tell him more. To show him more of her world, show him it wasn't as small as she had claimed it was.

'Benedita was the one who showed me the balcony, took me out here when I was only little, and even better, showed me these.' She pointed out over the banister. Winking in the sunset light, almost like stars growing on vines, were blue and white flowers growing on a shallow stone ledge jutting out beneath the balcony. They stretched up along the cliffside on twisting vines, bursting into bloom on other ledges like the one below them, all the way down to the sea. Lana turned back to Marino, and her voice dropped to a whisper as she waggled her eyebrows like she was about to tell him something scandalous. 'Those flowers are my secret ingredient.'

CHAPTER 21
Marino

Marino realised that he could listen to Lana talk for hours. He loved hearing her voice, he wanted to know every thought she had. He wanted to know everything about her and find out what made her happy. He wanted to bask in her smile, revel in her laughter.

The realisation startled him. He'd never felt so interested in one person before. He liked people in the broader sense, the way some people liked books. He thought everyone had a story to tell, and he enjoyed meeting new people and hearing their stories, but then moving on. Never letting anyone too close.

Marino didn't want to move on from Lana. And that complicated things significantly.

He had no business falling for someone in a land off the map entirely. He had no business falling for anyone at all. He had to find the cure for Celeste and then get back home.

But, right now, in this moment, all he wanted to do was stand on this balcony with Lana's body close to his and watch how the golden rays from the setting sun danced across her face.

'What is it?' she said, tucking a piece of hair behind her

ear. The balcony creaked beneath them as the wind whipped by again. 'Scared of heights?'

Her hair blew out of place again, and this time he was the one to smooth it back, lingering for a moment with his fingers in her hair.

Lana closed her eyes briefly and drew in a quick breath of surprised pleasure. Her lashes fluttered open, and Marino found himself caught in her gaze again, feeling like he could gladly drown in it.

'I was enjoying the view,' he said, his eyes still locked on her face. 'But I want to hear more about this secret ingredient of yours.'

'Aunt Benedita called them ria blossoms. Here, I'll show you.' In one smooth move, like she'd done it hundreds of times, Lana turned, hitched up her skirt, and swung a leg up over the balcony banister. She glanced back at him with a mischievous grin. 'Watch your step. It's a long way down.'

'I'm not afraid of falling.' Marino held her gaze.

Lana stilled for a moment at his words, with one leg on either side of the banister, as if she were astride a horse. The wind whipped around them, as if it was nudging Marino closer to her, closer to the edge.

'Well, come on, then.' Lana swung her other leg over the balcony banister, and carefully edged her way over to a small ledge covered in the blue and white flowers.

Marino took off his jacket and draped it over the banister before following Lana off the balcony to the cliff ledge jutting out next to the balcony. The ledge felt even more unsteady than the balcony, like it could tumble off into the sea at any moment, but Lana seemed completely comfortable. Blue and white ria flowers grew all along their feet, and along the walls of the cliff. It felt, suddenly, like they were completely isolated, even though he knew that on the other side of the building was Sugar Street.

Then he realised that the shoreline on this side of the island was a series of small coves, almost as if the shore was undulating. Lana's bakery, and her little attic room, were tucked inside the top of one, providing her almost complete privacy all the way down to the crashing waves below. And dotted along the cliffside were little ledges, all covered with the ria flower. It was a vertical garden from the sky to the sea.

Marino's back was up against the cliffside, and he found himself stilling when Lana came so close to him they were nearly chest to chest. 'Hold on,' she said. 'There's a beautiful blossom right behind you.' She leaned forward, going up on her tiptoes, and reached over his shoulder. There was only a sliver of space between them, and Marino yearned to close that gap, to wrap his arms around her waist and pull her towards him. 'Almost got it.' Her breath was warm against his neck. Then she rocked back on her heels, beaming up at him. 'This one is perfect.'

'Indeed.' He wasn't looking at the flower. He cleared his throat and dropped his gaze to the blue and white flower she was holding out to him. This one was bigger than those blanketing the ledge they stood on. It was about the size of a plum, and it looked like a stack of interlocking star-shaped blossoms, white on blue on white on blue. Up close, the white petals were almost iridescent.

'They grow all year, but it's best to pluck them when they have fully bloomed. See?' Lana held it closer to him. 'Breathe in.'

Marino did as she asked – and as he inhaled he felt a

sense of calm descend on him. Then he smelled it again and was struck by how familiar the smell was.

'It smells like *you*,' he said, baffled. Because it was the same smell he'd come to associate with her – one that reminded him of the sea before a storm, but if the air was laced with sugar, and a hint of citrus. As he breathed in again, he was filled with a strangely familiar sense of deep contentment. The same feeling, he realised, that he had whenever he was around Lana.

Lana's laugh rang out, the sound dancing in his ears.

'Well, that is because I use it in my cakes and tarts. And sometimes I press the flowers to my wrists.' She winked. 'Should I bottle it up? I can call it baker's perfume. See what the Solvorans think of it.'

Marino turned to her and took her hand in his own, raising it to just under his nose, and inhaled, breathing in her scent. 'Ah. Well, no offence to your special ria flower, I think that you smell even better.'

He held her wrist a moment more, wanting to press a kiss on the delicate skin there, to feel her skin beneath his lips, but instead he slowly ran his thumb along the inside of her wrist, and then let go. He wondered if he imagined the brief disappointment that flickered across her face when he dropped her hand. 'Tell me, then. What makes the ria blossom so special? Other than their rather intoxicating scent.'

Lana's cheeks flushed pink at his words. Then she slowly lifted one of the blue flowers so it was hovering right between them, and pressed her nose into it. 'Aunt Benedita told me that a sprinkle of ground-up ria blossom brings a burst of joy in every bite. Like tasting sunshine.'

'Solvorans keep telling me they don't have magic.' Marino's brow furrowed as he spoke. 'That sounds like magic to me.'

Lana gestured to the waves below. 'The mermaids have magic, remember?'

Marino knew for a fact they did. 'But what do these flowers have to do with the mer?'

Lana let out a long breath. 'Well, that I don't know, exactly. You asked about the magic in Solvora. The mermaids have it all.' She grew more animated, gesturing as she spoke. 'Supposedly, before I was born, there used to be pockets of magic all over Solvora. The land blessed those who lived here, and we gave back to the land.' She knelt in a carpet of ria blossoms. 'My ria flowers don't need fresh water to grow – they only need seawater. And something specific with this soil here on the cliffs. I've searched all over Solvora, and they only grow here.'

'Could that something specific be you?' said Marino, crouching down next to her.

Lana's laugh rang out. 'If only I had the kind of magic to make flowers bloom. No. The ria blossoms were here before me. But nobody else on Solvora knows the small power that they have, how they can bring joy.'

'I feel honoured that you've trusted me with such a secret.' Marino nudged her with his shoulder. They were close now, their shoulders and hips touching, and Marino found he wanted to be closer still.

'Well, you've trusted me with your secrets. It is only fair that I tell you some of mine.' Marino wanted to know all of Lana's secrets. He wanted to know everything about her.

'So, the ria blossoms grow here on the cliffs, and the

liffen bloom is in the sea. In Eana the land is one of the most powerful sources of our magic, but we have never drawn power from the sea.'

'You said everyone on Eana has magic?' Lana's dark eyes shone with longing. The sun had almost completely disappeared behind the horizon, but the last rays were setting the sea alight. Above, the sky was darkening to violet and indigo as the first stars began to come out. Marino couldn't help but think that the gold flecks in her eyes mirrored the way the stars danced in the night sky.

He shook his head. 'Not everyone. Only the witches. But those without magic still benefit.'

Lana gave him a shy, hopeful smile. 'Would you show me a little bit more magic?'

Marino rubbed the back of his neck, suddenly self-conscious. It was an unfamiliar feeling for him. But he wanted to use it to show her a part of himself that he was proud of, a part of himself that he was still getting to know.

'Do you remember how I told you that witches in Eana have five strands of magic but one always comes more naturally to them? Tempest magic is my dominant strand of magic. It used to be my favourite too, because it helps when I'm at sea, but now that I'm landlocked, I'm not sure how useful it is.' He chuckled. 'It would appear that Solvora has enough storms already.'

Lana tilted her head to the side. 'Tempest magic sounds a little bit like the mermaids' sea magic.'

'I suppose I can see that,' Marino acknowledged. 'But my magic doesn't come from the sea. I can't cause waves. Or stop a true storm. What the mermaids here can do, feels like a magic I've never encountered before.' He frowned, remembering what it had felt like when he tried to force back the storm that had sunk his ship.

'Well, why don't you show me more of what your magic can do?' Lana nudged him with her shoulder. 'I'd love to see. You've tasted my baking, at least you can show me what other tricks you have up your sleeve.'

'Excuse me, Lady Lana, but magic isn't trickery,' said Marino with mock outrage.

Lana's laugh pealed out. 'You should know by now, I'm no lady.'

'Says who?'

Lana rolled her eyes. 'Oh, anyone in the palace. Any of the Solvoran nobility. I inherited this bakery, and a baker is what I was destined to be. Not that I mind. I like baking. I'd rather be a baker than a lady. Nobody tells me what to do, I spend my days doing what I want.'

'Well, perhaps you are destined to be a Lady Baker.'

Lana snorted. 'Don't let anyone in the palace hear you say that. For such a small island, it is shocking how obsessed with hierarchy everyone is here. Probably because everyone knows we can never leave. So, we must know our place and stay within it until we die.'

'That's a rather grim way to look at it.'

'Don't blame me. It's just the way it is.'

'Well,' said Marino. 'Maybe some things should change.'

'You've already changed things, just by arriving,' said Lana. 'I still can't believe you survived the wreck.'

'I wish I could say the same about my crew,' said Marino, feeling the ache of guilt that went through him every time he thought about Dooley, George and Emelia. He closed his eyes, opening them only when he felt the soft touch of

Lana's hand on his face.

'Marino. It isn't your fault that they were lost.' Lana's voice was gentle, but firm. 'You can't blame yourself.'

Marino let out a long breath. 'I wish that was the case. But it is my fault. It is all my fault.' His voice dropped into a whisper as he turned his face away from Lana's touch, away from the comfort she offered him that he didn't deserve. 'Celeste was looking into the sky for *my* future, looking for *my* happiness, and she pushed herself too hard. It brought on the seeing sickness. And that drove me here, and ultimately caused my crew to be lost.'

'You are here because you care for your sister. Don't give up hope. We'll find the cure you are looking for.'

Marino looked up into Lana's hopeful, determined face. He desperately wanted to believe her.

'Thank you.' His voice was thick with emotion. 'I wish there was something I could do for you in return.'

Lana gave him a soft smile and held his hand in her own. 'Promise me one day, after you find the cure and figure out a way to leave Solvora, you'll take me with you. Promise me you'll show me that there is more to the world than Solvora.'

Marino remembered how she had asked the other day, seemingly in jest, if he would save her a spot on his ship. But now there was no teasing in her tone. Only longing. Marino was not so foolish as to mistake the longing in her voice for desire for him. He knew it was for a wider world. And that feeling, he understood. So, he swallowed his disappointment and raised her hand to his lips and pressed a chaste kiss to the back of her hand. 'I promise.' Then he cleared his throat. 'And for now, I suppose I could show you some more magic.'

CHAPTER 22
Marino

The Solvoran earth was not as potent as the earth from Eana, but it was enough for Marino to create small spells.

He picked up some of the dirt and let it run through his fingers. 'All our magic has a balance, a cost. To cast enchantments, we need earth. Warrior magic is powered by the sun itself. Healers use their own life force; they can only heal so much before becoming drained. Tempests need the wind to be able to control it, they cannot summon it from nothing. Seers can see the future in the dance of the starcrests, birds native to Eana, but also can receive visions in dreams.'

'Do you know, I had a dream about you the other night,' Lana said, her voice a little breathless. 'Maybe it was a vision.'

'What a coincidence, you've been in my dreams as well,' said Marino, locking eyes with her. He wanted to ask her what he'd been doing in her dreams. If it had felt as real as his dreams of her had.

'We were on a boat,' she said softly. 'So, I hope mine was a vision, one where we leave these seas! Where were we in your dream?'

'We were in the sea. Beneath the waves.' Marino didn't tell her that in his dreams he'd kissed her in the water, kissed her like he was drowning and she was his salvation.

Lana let out a nervous laugh. 'Well, I certainly hope your dream was only a dream. I would much rather be on a boat above the waves than under them.' She tilted her head to the side. 'Tell me more of this so-called enchantment magic.'

Marino picked a few of the ria blossoms and closed his hand around them. In his other hand, he held a fistful of dirt. He whispered a spell, and when he opened the hand with the blossoms, four blue butterflies flew out.

Lana clapped her hands in delight. 'Oh! Are they real?'

'They are still only flowers, but flowers with wings. Even witches cannot create life itself, though healers can save it.' They watched the four ria-butterflies fly into the sunset, dipping and soaring.

'What else?' said Lana, eyes hungry. 'What else can you do?'

It was getting darker now, the sun nearly set. 'I am not nearly as talented an enchanter as those I know at home. But . . . all it takes is a spell and I could silence my footsteps, or make my voice loud enough to be heard across Solvora. I could make the trees dance, and the flowers glow.' He plucked another ria blossom, and with another spell, it lit up as if it had a tiny flame within it. Marino passed it to Lana, who held it in her cupped hands. The light from it spilled out, illuminating her face.

'Oh!' she breathed. 'Can I keep it? I'll put it on my nightstand.'

'Of course,' said Marino. 'It is yours. It won't glow forever but I can always enchant you another one.'

'So, you'll still be here when the glow goes away?' Lana looked up at him, hope shimmering in her eyes.

'Or maybe we'll both be far from here.'

Marino wanted to lean in to kiss her, surely this was the moment, but then something in the sea caught his eye.

'Lana,' he said, and his voice was urgent. 'Do you see that? Is that a *boat*?' It was hard to see in the moonlight, but he could just about make out a small vessel bobbing in the waves. It was closer to shore and he realised with no small amount of shock, the boat must have come *from* Solvora.

'Who does it belong to?' he asked, fighting back the urge to dive from the balcony and swim to the boat. 'Leonel told me there are no ships on Solvora.'

'You'll see the reason there are no ships,' said Lana. 'None make it past the ring.' She turned away. 'I don't want to watch.'

Marino was unable to tear his gaze away from the small boat. It looked like possibility. It looked like hope. He didn't know who was on that boat, but he was rooting for them.

'Whoever is in that boat must be desperate. They must have heard of your arrival and thought that if the mer allowed one man to live, they might allow a boat to cross.' Lana sighed. 'It used to happen all the time. Solvorans would try and tempt the mer to one side of the island, and others would attempt to sneak out in a boat. But the mer know everything and anything that enters their waters. They can sense it.'

Marino thought about how Kira had found him when he swam down to the wreck of the *Siren's Secret*. How she had known exactly where to find him. How the silver-haired mermaid, the one that he was certain would have drowned him if Kira hadn't arrived, had known where he was too.

'Is Solvora such a terrible place that people would risk their lives?' Marino thought about how happy everyone seemed, how prosperous the people were, how beautiful it all was.

Lana took a sharp intake of breath. 'King Leonel likes things to be a certain way,' she said slowly. 'And that requires certain . . . sacrifices of the Solvoran people. Ones that not everyone is willing to make.'

A chill went through Marino at her words. He had thought the only enemy to the Solvorans was the mer, but perhaps some threats were landlocked.

He started to ask what Lana meant but then the waves began to rise, tossing the small boat like it was no bigger than a toy. An eerie sound filled the air, one that took Marino a moment to realise was the whistling of the wind, the song of a storm coming. A storm summoned by the mer.

A flash of shimmering scales and a bright streak of silver caught Marino's eye. He knew it was the silver-haired mer. The one who had wanted to drown him.

'They don't even need the storm,' said Lana bitterly. 'They can sing Solvorans to their doom without any help from the wind.'

'They aren't the only ones who can summon storms,' muttered Marino, rolling up his shirtsleeves. This wind felt wild, slippery, hard to catch a strand of it, but he was determined. He wouldn't let another boat sink if he could help it.

When the storm had wrecked the *Siren's Secret*, Marino had been caught unawares. But this time he was prepared. And he was on higher ground. 'We should get back on the balcony. I don't want to risk slipping off if I misjudge the wind.' They quickly clambered back on to the balcony, and Marino raised his hands. 'Stay behind me,' he warned. 'I don't know how my magic will mix with the mer's magic.'

'I will do no such thing,' said Lana, and when Marino glanced over at her in some surprise, he saw that she had tied her hair back and wore a fierce expression, as if she were about to go into battle. It reminded him for a moment of his sister, how she was always ready to face anything. And he felt a pang in his heart. 'I am not going to miss this.'

He finally caught a strand of wind, and it felt crackly and charged, almost like handling lightning. But once he had it caught, he was able to use it to act almost as a buffer against the wild wind coming up from the sea and direct the wind away from the small boat. The surface waves calmed, and he could have sworn he heard a cheer rise up from the boat.

And then six pairs of glowing eyes appeared from the water. Mermaids, all wearing their masks of seaflowers, and all glaring up at Marino and Lana. He took an instinctive step closer to Lana, as if he could protect her from the mermaids' gaze.

He suddenly wondered if Kira was there in the water below him. But he thought that if Kira was there, he would sense it. That he would recognise her, even from this distance. But he knew the one with silver hair was there. And anger rolled off her, so strong he could almost taste it on the wind.

Good. He was glad she was angry. She had tried to kill him, and he would not forget it.

The boat moved through the waves, the mer glared, and Marino waited for their next move.

And then, as one, they turned and circled the small boat, their tails smacking the water in a strange rhythm.

'What are they doing?' Marino said to Lana.

'They are going to sing,' said Lana. She was gripping the balcony banister so tightly that her knuckles had turned white. 'We should go inside. I don't know what will happen if you hear it. I've never seen so many of them gather.'

There was a shout from the boat, and then a splash as one of the people aboard leaped into the sea.

Then Marino heard it. It started as a hum but it rose into an aria, and then the full power of the song hit him with so much force, it nearly knocked him over.

Come to us. Come to us. Come to us and be free.

Marino leaned over the banister, as if an invisible string was pulling him. He was dimly aware of what he was doing, but it felt like he was watching from above, like he was in a dream. He had to get to the mermaids. That was the most important thing. Nothing else mattered.

Lana moved quickly, grabbing his wrist and pulling him back. 'Hurry!' Marino was aware of her tugging on his arm, but he was more aware of the mer singing, the mer in the sea, he was leaning towards the sea, a little further and he'd be with them. 'COME! ON!' Lana had both her arms around his waist trying to haul him inside. But he wouldn't budge. He felt rooted to the spot.

'Oh, for stars' sake.' Before Marino realised what she was doing, Lana went up on her toes and bit him on the earlobe, hard.

'Ow!' Marino blinked and turned towards her, and that was all she needed. 'HURRY!' This time she was able to yank him inside, slamming the balcony door shut with shaking hands. It muffled the song of the mer, but Marino could still hear it. The sound made him dizzy, but he felt in control of himself at least. Not like he had a moment ago on the balcony.

Lana was staring at him. 'Are you all right?'

'Did you . . . *bite* me?'

Lana's cheeks flushed pink. 'You wouldn't move! I had to get your attention somehow.'

Marino raised his fingers to his earlobe, wishing that he remembered how her lips had felt on his ear. He'd been so entranced by the mer, he'd only noticed the sharp prick of her teeth.

It had probably saved him from leaping into the sea. 'I suppose I should be thanking you. It all happened so quickly.'

'You're welcome,' Lana said primly. Then she glanced at the window, where rain was lashing down on the glass. 'I've never seen them sing like that. As a group, like they were hunting together.'

The wind began to pick up again, Marino could hear it howling in the air, blending in with the distant song of the mer.

'I should go back out there and try to help,' he said. 'The people on the boat . . .'

'Absolutely not.' Lana stood in front of the balcony doors with her arms crossed. 'I saw what their song did to you. I thought that maybe, because one had saved you, because of your own magic, that you would be immune. But you were about to dive off the balcony. You even had that look in your eyes, the look that comes when their song sinks into you.'

'Were *you* affected? Or is it only men?'

'No. It isn't only men. The mer have power over us all. I told you, I've spent my whole life listening to the sound of the sea. Well, I've also heard their songs.' She gave Marino a rueful smile. 'Over the years, I learned to resist their call. I find it distracting now, but nothing more. But tonight, tonight was something different.' She shuddered slightly. 'I wouldn't be surprised to hear that many Solvorans leaped to their deaths. The song was stronger than it has ever been.'

'And it is my fault,' said Marino, suddenly horrified by what he had accidentally done. 'If I hadn't intervened, only the boat would have gone down. No others would have been harmed. They are punishing me by punishing innocents.'

'You were trying to help.' Marino didn't want to be comforted by her. Not right now. He didn't deserve her comfort. It was his fault more lives had been lost. He should have listened to the Solvorans when they told him that the mer were dangerous. They were stopping ships from sailing, and they were stopping him from seeking the cure that he needed. He would not stand for it, not one moment more.

'Lana, I must go to the palace. I've changed my mind. I will help the king fight the mer. I won't let them sink another ship.' He took her hands. 'Thank you. For saving me. Without you, I'd be at the mercy of the mer.'

'You still will be if you leave right now! Their song lingers. You may not be Solvoran, but you are not immune to the mer.'

Marino stilled. There had to be a way for him to get to the palace.

And then it was as if he heard Celeste speaking to him.

Are you a witch or not, Marino? Don't be such a dunderbrain! Use your magic!

'What are you smiling about?' asked Lana, confusion etched across her face.

Marino's grin widened. 'I have an idea.'

CHAPTER 23
Marino

The streets of Solvora were in a panic but Marino couldn't hear a sound.

Before he'd left Lana, he'd asked her for a few of the ria blossoms that he could crumble and use for an enchantment to block his ears. The enchantment had worked almost immediately, and now he could walk through Solvora with no fear of the mer's song.

It was strange, it felt as if ever since he had arrived in Solvora his magic had been growing stronger by the day.

No, that wasn't quite right.

It was from the morning he had met Lana. When they had visited the goldweavers. Something in the sea-gold had lit his magic ablaze. Thea had explained many times that there were no shortcuts in magic, that there had to be a balance, and a small part of him worried what might be the secret cost of his rapidly increasing power.

But a larger part of him was glad that he had so much control over his magic. He was the only witch here on Solvora, he needed the power of many.

Right now, he was especially glad that he could block out the song of the mer. It was clear from the pandemonium in the streets that the Solvorans could still hear them. And they were struggling to resist their call.

He saw two women holding back a man who had a frenzied look in his eyes as he tried to get to the water. Locks were slid into place but still, dozens ran down the cobblestone streets. One woman leaped from her window, landing in a crumpled heap, before dragging herself closer to the sea.

Marino wanted to save all of them but he knew to do that, he had to stop the mer. He would not stand by while innocents drowned.

By the time Marino reached the gates of the Gilded Palace, he dared to take off the enchantment protecting his ears. He heard wailing from the people of the city, but no song. The mer had stopped.

He turned and squinted into the darkness of the sea. There was no sign that a boat had ever been there. The water was still. Marino felt a fury rise in him. The mer had drowned dozens of innocents tonight, they were keeping the Solvorans trapped, and they were keeping him from what he needed most: the cure for Celeste.

'I must see the king,' he said to the guards. 'Immediately.'

The guard nodded and bowed, and then led Marino into the throne room. Leonel was pacing by the window like an angry lion. Marino could feel the rage radiating off him in waves. Talia was there too, standing still as a statue, eyes closed and hands to her temple. Like she was trying to picture something that was not in this room.

Talia had magic in her, of this much Marino was certain.

Her eyes flew open, like she had sensed him staring at her.

'There you are! So, now you have seen what the mer do

to us.' Leonel's voice was ragged. 'We are their prisoners. They claim we keep them bound here, but it is them who bind us! My uncle angered the sea so much that it nearly swallowed Solvora whole. I did what I had to do to keep it safe, to keep us safe, but there was a cost.' He turned to Marino, eyes wild. 'There is always a cost.'

'I know now that I must help you stop the mer,' said Marino. 'I saw them target that boat, and I heard them sing men to their doom. If it wasn't for –' He paused. He had been about to mention how Lana had saved him, but he found he still did not want King Leonel to know about Lana. He might be on the same side as the king against the mer, but he did not trust him.

The sacrifices that the king mentioned. What was being sacrificed for the supposed greater good?

King Leonel's eyes narrowed. 'If it wasn't for what?'

'My magic,' said Marino. 'I was able to block out their song using my magic.'

'If only you could use your magic on all of Solvora.'

'I do not think such a thing is possible, but I will do what I can to help the Solvorans. I came here for the cure for my sister but perhaps I was also guided here to help the Solvorans.' As Marino said it, he knew that helping the Solvorans meant helping Eana too. After all, Solvora would make a fine trading partner, with all their natural resources.

'I sensed the goodness in you when you arrived,' said Talia. She had moved closer to him without him noticing, and now she brazenly reached out and rested her hand on his chest, directly above his rapidly beating heart. 'It is why we knew you were no enemy to us, Marino Pegasi. *You* are what we have been waiting for.'

Marino cleared his throat and gently moved her hand. Talia was certainly beautiful, but his only interest in her was figuring out what magic she was hiding. 'I will do my best to help you,' he agreed. 'But remember, my priority is to find the cure, and to return home to my sister.'

He did not miss the glance between Talia and Leonel. They clearly had different priorities for him.

'Yes,' said King Leonel smoothly. 'We understand. But even by doing that, by finding a way to leave Solvora, well, that will be helping us. We will support each other however we can, you and I.'

Then he clapped. 'We shall make it official. You are an emissary for your country, are you not?'

'I suppose so,' said Marino slowly.

'And we have a shared goal. We are now allies, are we not? Eana and Solvora.'

'I do not know if I can speak on behalf of my country.' Marino felt that the conversation was rapidly spinning out of control. 'I am a mere merchant sailor, not a king.'

'You represent Eana. You may be a merchant now, but when you return home, you will be hailed a hero. I am sure your queens will reward you for your loyalty – for making the right choice.'

'I cannot commit Eana to anything.'

'All I ask is you commit yourself to my cause. To Solvora.'

'You know my aim is . . .'

'Yes, yes. To help your sister! But don't you see, by helping me, by helping Solvora, you will be helping your sister. Let us help each other, Marino. As allies. As friends.' Leonel smiled at Marino. His smile felt too wide, Marino thought.

It was a deal dipped in poison, and Marino knew it. But tonight the mermaids had proved that they were the ones keeping him and the Solvorans trapped. They had pushed him towards the king. And besides, King Leonel could provide him with the ship that he needed.

'To helping each other,' said Marino. In his mind's eye, he saw Kira's glowing violet eyes gazing reproachfully at him, because to help King Leonel was to harm the mer, and he felt a stab of guilt. She had saved him, time and time again. And this is how he would repay her. Aligning with her enemy.

Impossibly, Leonel's smile widened even more.

'Now Marino. As we are allies, I can tell you that Talia and I know you've been keeping something from us.' Marino went very still. Did the king know about Lana? About Kira? He cleared his throat.

'Your Majesty, I don't know what you are referring to. Could you enlighten me?'

Leonel clucked his tongue in reproach. 'Oh, naughty naughty naughty! Did you not think that every ounce of gold pulled from the sea is accounted for? I heard about what happened when you went down to the goldweavers. That the gold practically came alive for you! That it danced for you! Marino, I have known for many years that the true power of the sea-gold was hidden from me. My people may think me vain, with an eye for beautiful things, which may be true, but my reason for harvesting the sea-gold has always been to unlock its true potential. And you, Marino, you seem to be the key.'

Marino thought of how his magic had responded to the gold. Could it be that the sea-gold was responding to him as well? Instead of a balance, as he had thought magic always sought to find, was it that he and the sea-gold were feeding off each other?

'Your Majesty, I cannot explain what happened with the sea-gold. It was very strange. I do not know if I could make it happen again.'

Leonel's smile sharpened. 'One way to find out.' Then he snapped his fingers and Talia scurried to the closed doors of the throne room. She flung them open. 'Bring the gold!' she cried out, and a moment later two servants came in, each heaving a bucket filled with shimmering sea-gold.

Marino watched warily as the servants put the buckets directly in front of him.

'Now! Do whatever you did on the beach.' King Leonel was watching the gold – and Marino – with a fierce hunger.

Marino wondered if he should resist. There was a dark mania glittering in the king's eyes that put him on edge. But he also could not deny that he wanted to see what would happen if he made contact with the sea-gold again. If it would unlock greater strength in his magic. If the sea-gold and his magic could work in tandem.

'Go on,' urged Talia. 'Don't be afraid.'

'I'm not afraid,' scoffed Marino, and this was all he needed to plunge his hand into the liquid gold.

He felt it immediately. The heat of it. The power in the swirling sea-gold. It called to his magic and his magic answered. It felt as if his magic had grown wings inside of him and was soaring through his veins.

The sea-gold soared in response. Just like on the beach, the gold leaped up out of the bucket, as if it were alive.

King Leonel began to clap. 'Yes! Yes! Tell me, Marino. Are

you controlling it? Are you making it move like that?'

Marino shook his head. While he might have awoken something in the gold, he had no control over its movements.

The sea-gold pooled on the floor, swirling as it had on the beach, almost creating its own current, and then rose up, like a wave. Like Goldwave Mountain itself. It crested and sharpened, hardening into spikes. Aimed towards the window, towards the sea that it had come from.

'Perfect,' breathed Talia, reaching out to press a finger to the sharpened point. She pressed, not hard enough to break the skin, and shuddered in apparent delight. 'This is what we need.'

'We must show the people!' cried King Leonel. 'We must show my people what I can do.' He coughed. 'I mean what *you* can do, Marino. What the gold can do!'

'A ball, my king. This calls for a celebratory ball,' said Talia. 'We will host a ball to show the strength of Solvora. The magic of Marino. The power that together we wield! And at the ball we will announce that now is time for us to conquer the mer.'

'I don't want to harm them,' Marino said quickly. 'I want to stop them from sinking ships, but I mean them no harm.'

'You have such a good heart,' Talia said, and it sounded like she was taunting him. 'Your goodness, your magic, why it practically shines out of you.'

Marino cleared his throat. 'And a ball seems unnecessary, does it not? I can help you awaken the gold, or whatever it is that I'm doing, without a ball.' He had been to enough balls to last him a lifetime. It seemed like a dream now, dancing at Anadawn, where his only worry was who Rose and Celeste were going to try to set him up with next. The thought of Celeste sent a pang through him. How could he attend a ball when he had to find the cure for her? And he was running out of time.

Marino knew that he still needed the mer to find the liffen bloom. But if conquering the mer meant that they had to help him, well, it would be worth it. He would rather them help him by choice, but if he had to use his magic to force them to give him the liffen bloom, so be it. He'd do anything to find the cure.

'There is no time for balls.' He didn't realise he'd spoken aloud until Talia laughed.

'Oh, Marino. This ball will mark the beginning of a new chapter for Solvora!'

'A chapter where we are no longer beholden to the mer. A chapter where we return to our rightful place as rulers, not prisoners!' King Leonel's eyes were wide and wild, and he shouted as though he were speaking to the masses, instead of yelling in an almost-empty throne room.

'It will be perfect,' said Talia, laying a gentle hand on the king's arm. 'The Solvorans need a moment to come together, to mourn the lives lost tonight . . .' she bowed her head respectfully, '*and* to celebrate our imminent victory.'

'I cannot lose sight of what I came here for. I must find the cure.' Marino had not shared with the king that the cure he sought was in the sea. That he needed the mer's help to find it.

'And we will. But won't it be so much easier when the mer are being more . . . peaceable?' Talia said in her breathy voice that Marino found so strange.

'And the sea-gold will bring this peace?' he pressed.

'It will indeed,' said Talia. 'As long as you have awoken it.'

Marino's head was spinning and his frown deepened. 'But how?'

'Oh Marino, we will show you. But let us save it as a little surprise for you. We will show you when we show the Solvorans.' Talia clapped her hands in glee.

'And if I help you with this, if I awaken the sea-gold, and ensure that the mer allows ships to sail again, you will give me a boat so I can return home?'

'Marino, if you do all of that, I'd be tempted to give you my throne.' Leonel's laugh boomed all around them. 'And I can certainly give you a boat.'

'My king, one thought. We do not want the Solvorans to fear that this is a sacrifice year,' said Talia, examining the rings on her fingers.

Marino felt a chill come over him. 'I'll need you to expand on that. Why would they fear such a thing?'

'Do not judge a king for doing what he must to care for his people.' Leonel's eyes were sharp. 'I told you my uncle sacrificed his wife, child and himself, all in honour of Solvora. The child and the mer he had married were lost to the waves, a sacrifice to the sea, and my uncle, he let his blood feed the Solvoran soil. And since then, I have made sure Solvora is never hungry. Not the people, nor the land. They feed each other, you see?'

Marino felt queasy at the implication that the land devoured its own people. How would blood not freely given strengthen a land? This kind of sacrifice could only lead to rot. This was a magic he wanted no part in.

'Oh, do not look so forlorn, Captain!' Talia gave him a wide smile. 'It is an honour to be a sacrifice. And they come so willingly. Solvora gives us so much, it is only fair that we give back. And usually we have a ball to celebrate the sacrifice. But once we can leave Solvora, we will no longer need sacrifices. You will be saving us in so many ways.'

'There will be no sacrifice at this ball,' Leonel went on. 'This ball will be a Goldwave ball. And every Solvoran will be invited. The fishermen, the goldweavers, even the bakers and the butchers. It is imperative that all Solvorans feel united in this, in our new destiny. We cannot falter.'

'It sounds like it will be wonderful,' said Marino, careful to keep his voice light. He was reeling from everything Talia and King Leonel had told him. What kind of ruler sacrificed his own people? Why did they need to feed the land? But he could not let himself get more tangled in it than he already was. He would attend this ball if he needed to, learn how his magic could work with the sea-gold to help their cause, but in the meantime he would keep searching for the liffen bloom.

'I do hope you'll save me a dance,' added Talia.

Marino bowed at the waist. 'I would be honoured.' But he knew there was only one person he would dance with if he had any say in the matter.

Lana Dawn.

For the first time that he could remember, Marino was looking forward to escorting someone to a ball.

Marino did not think he would be able to sleep, but as soon as he lay down he fell into a deep sleep. In his dreams, he heard Willa calling out to him, telling him to remember why he had come to Solvora. He heard Anika wailing as she watched over Celeste's prone body. He saw his crew floating in a rowboat in the middle of the ocean, calling out to him, begging him not to forget them. And as he had every night since he had arrived on Solvora, he dreamed of Kira. She was laughing at him in his dream, and try as he might, no matter how fast he swam, he could not catch her.

When he woke, it was nearly midday and preparations were already under way for the Goldwave ball. Marino nearly bumped into palace staff carrying flower garlands into the great hall, and he overheard from one of the maids how every household had received an invitation to the forthcoming celebration. Marino pitied whoever in the king's command had been made to stay up all night stencilling the invitations.

He hurried down the mountain. The panic of last night had been replaced with a palpable excitement. He had to admit that planning a ball was a wise distraction. Instead of focusing on their fear of the mer and the trauma of what had happened the previous night, the Solvorans were instead looking forward to the ball.

When he reached Sugar Street, he stopped short.

There was a queue of almost two dozen people waiting outside the bakery. For a moment, Marino thought something was wrong, that something had happened to Lana. But then someone came out of the bakery beaming, carrying a basket piled high with fresh bread, and Marino let out a long breath. Of course. Everyone was here for cake and bread.

Feeling a strange sense of pride, Marino took his place at the back of the queue. The person in front of him, a man with light brown skin and black hair, turned around and his eyes widened when he realised who was standing behind him. He gave Marino a wide grin. 'Even the survivor knows where to find the best bread on Solvora! You are lucky, you know. The bakery is sometimes closed for days. But it is worth the wait, let me tell you.'

Marino grinned back. 'So I have heard.'

Everyone in the queue was chatting about the upcoming ball and wondering at the short notice. One young woman with curly red hair exclaimed that it was going to be nearly impossible to put together a suitable outfit in time.

And then Marino was at the front of the queue, and when he met Lana's gaze, it felt like everyone around them melted away.

'Good day, sir,' said Lana, the corners of her lips twitching. 'What can I get for you?'

'Baker's choice,' said Marino.

'And how will you be paying?' Lana raised her brows.

Marino leaned down so his lips were close to her ear. 'Baker's choice.'

Lana's cheeks flushed pink. 'Well, in that case, I'll have to give you the best that I have to offer.' She turned to the counter behind her and selected a strawberry tart. 'Baked fresh this morning.'

'Did you manage to get any rest last night?' said Marino in a low voice, taking the tart from her. When he had left her, it had already been so late. He felt a stab of guilt.

Lana shrugged lightly. 'I couldn't sleep so I worked through the night.' She gazed up at Marino. 'I was worried about you.'

'I'm sorry I rushed off like that . . . but it was good that I did. The king and I have come to a kind of agreement.'

'And was it your idea to throw a ball?'

Marino let out a short laugh. 'No. But now that you mention the ball . . .'

'Yes?'

'I was hoping you would allow me to escort you.'

Lana stared at him for a long moment, her lips pursed. Marino cleared his throat, suddenly nervous.

Then she smiled, and Marino could have sworn it lit up the whole bakery. 'Yes. One hundred times yes.'

CHAPTER 24
Marino

Two days later, Marino knocked on the door of the bakery, and there was no answer.

He knocked again, adjusting his coat slightly. Had Lana forgotten that tonight was the ball? He had not seen her since he had come to the bakery to ask if he could escort her. He knew she'd been busy with work and preparing for the ball, and Marino had barely had a moment to himself. King Leonel and Talia had been demanding his presence what felt like every other minute, asking his opinion on all manner of things from the type of wine being served to the musicians. Marino had never been so involved in the planning of a ball before, and it gave him a new sense of appreciation for all the ones Rose had hosted at Anadawn.

But now his focus was on why Lana wasn't answering the door. Or perhaps she was suffering another headache? He knocked again, a little louder this time. There was a creaking sound above his head, and he looked up. A black-gloved hand waved down at him and then Lana's voice spilled out into the night. 'Let yourself in! The door should be open. I'm almost ready.'

Marino chuckled. Lana had once told him she was

perpetually late, and as a seafaring man he was punctual as a matter of principle. 'Take your time,' he called back.

'It's this damn corset! Flo is almost done lacing me into it.'

Marino's mouth went dry at the thought of Lana in a corset. 'Truly – take your time.' If they were a little bit late to the ball, so be it. He wasn't the one hosting.

A moment later, a girl with chin-length blonde hair leaned her head out of the window and grinned down at him. 'Oh, Lana, you were right! He *is* handsome!'

Marino grinned back at her. 'Um, good evening?'

'Flo!' Lana's voice rang out from somewhere behind the blonde girl.

'Ow! Don't pinch me!' Florence's head disappeared and then popped back out. 'Come inside! Wait in the kitchen. We'll be right down.'

Marino was still chuckling to himself as he pushed the door to the bakery open. It was dimly lit, the sconce lights flickering on the walls. He walked behind the counter and into the kitchen, where Lana did all her baking.

The cakes for the next day were already made, lined up and waiting to be decorated. He inhaled, and smelled the intoxicating mix of fresh bread, sugar and the smell of ria blossoms that he now knew was unique to Lana.

He heard footsteps coming down the wooden stairs and looked up towards the arched doorway that led to the stairwell.

For a moment, he forgot to breathe.

Lana stood at the bottom of the stairs, directly under the doorway, the sconce light illuminating her from above and behind. Her long black hair was pinned up, with a few tendrils falling around her face. She wore a red satin dress with delicate straps that hung off her shoulders. The red dress hugged the top of her body before flowing out from her hips. Her lips were painted scarlet, and she'd lined her eyes in black kohl. She gave Marino a shy smile and took a step towards him.

'Thank you for coming down from the palace simply to turn around and go right back up again,' she said.

'It is my pleasure.' Marino still could not tear his eyes off her. 'You look . . .' He paused, trying to find the right word. Beautiful didn't seem like enough.

'I know. I look ridiculous,' Lana said, laughing. Her cheeks were flushed. 'Like one of my cakes come to life. But aren't all balls a little ridiculous?'

'That certainly is not what I was going to say.' Marino closed the distance between them, and carefully, as if she might break, placed his hands on her hips. 'You are beautiful.' He wanted to kiss her, to show her just how beautiful he thought she was. She tilted her head up to him and parted her lips and he could feel his own heart hammering in his chest as he leaned closer to her and . . .

There was a light cough from behind Lana, and Marino dropped his hands as if he'd been scalded. 'Sorry to interrupt. But we are already running late, are we not?'

It was Florence, in a fitted green gown. Marino had completely forgotten that she had been upstairs with Lana. Her green eyes were sparkling, and Marino had a feeling she was delighted with the timing of her interruption.

'My Solvoran soldier is on duty tonight at the ball and so you have the lucky job of escorting both me and Lana up the hill. But don't worry, I'll leave you at the door to find my

Edward.'

'I was not worried in the slightest,' said Marino smoothly. As if he had not been moments away from kissing Lana. 'Quite the contrary. I am very pleased to meet someone who Lana has spoken so highly of.'

Florence preened. 'Oh, he's handsome *and* charming.'

'FLO!' Lana swatted her friend on the arm, and Florence merely cackled. Lana sighed heavily. 'Marino, please ignore her.'

'How could I ignore someone who clearly has excellent taste?' Marino winked at Florence, who winked back. He offered his arm to both girls, and they made their way out of the bakery. The evening air was warm and smelled of jasmine and citrus. They began the slow walk up the winding streets to the Gilded Palace. Even from here, they could hear the music that drifted down from the palace. It made him miss Anadawn. It made him miss Celeste. When he had found the cure, when he was home again, he would tell Celeste of Solvora, and how she would laugh when he told her that he had had to attend yet another ball.

When Marino had imagined escorting Lana to the ball, he had not imagined the walk up the cobblestone steps, or that there would be another person with them. He had envisioned them sitting close together in the privacy of a carriage . . . but he found he did not mind the walk nor Florence's company. She reminded Marino of Celeste – in her confidence and charm, and how clear it was that she was the type of person who would say what was on their mind. 'I have never arrived at a ball by foot,' he said now. 'Are there no carriages in Solvora? I would have liked to escort you both in a grander style.'

'King Leonel has a chariot that is pulled by his personal guard. Small carts with goods are pulled by goats, but I don't think we could all fit in a goat cart,' said Lana, with a light laugh.

'Plus, it would be monstrously unfair to the goats,' Marino agreed. 'So you must be used to walking to balls.'

'I've actually never been to a ball before. Benedita forbade me from going.'

Marino found he did not blame her aunt, if the balls were often linked to the sacrifice that Leonel demanded.

'She was a strict old cow,' Florence said with affection. 'It was impossible for me to convince her to allow Lana to do anything.'

'She was protective, that's all,' said Lana. 'She felt a deep responsibility for me after my parents died, and she couldn't allow any harm to ever come to me.'

Florence snorted. 'Benedita's idea of danger included anything from balls to going down to the shore. She barely let Lana out of that bakery! And now that Benedita is gone, rest her soul, well, Lana is discovering the whole world.'

'Not the whole world. Only Solvora,' Lana corrected. 'And it is small enough that even within the past six months I feel I have seen it all a hundred times over. But I will admit that this is my first ball.'

Marino smiled. 'What fortuitous timing that I am here for it. It is an honour to escort you to your first ball.'

Florence snorted. 'Fortuitous timing? Captain Marino, the whispers in town say that the ball is *because* of you.'

Marino tugged on his cravat, keen to change the subject. 'Tell me, Florence. How do you find living surrounded by water when you fear the sea?'

Florence leaned forward and stuck her tongue out at Lana. 'Lana! Have you been telling the captain lies?' She sighed dramatically. 'I do not *fear* the sea. I am *sensible* about it. Entirely different. The sea around Solvora does not behave as the sea should. The waves sometimes pound on our windows, as if they were demanding to be let in. I have no need to go to the sea when it so frequently comes to me.'

Marino nodded. 'That does sound sensible. I myself have spent my life chasing the sea, which is perhaps a foolish endeavour.'

'It led you to Solvora,' said Lana, looking up at him under her lashes.

'And so it did.' Marino felt a curious tightness in his chest. He had lost so much – his ship, his crew, but he did not regret coming to Solvora. He couldn't – because if it had led him to Lana.

Kira's violet gaze appeared unbidden in his mind's eye. The sea had led him to Kira too. But he couldn't tell Lana that. Couldn't tell her that he felt as drawn to a mermaid, the enemy of all Solvora, as he did to her.

'Lana has been very helpful,' he said now to Florence. 'I came to Solvora seeking a cure for my sister, and Lana has a great knowledge of the plants here. There is a sea plant she has told me of that sounds like it might be what I am looking for. The liffen bloom.'

Florence raised her eyebrows. 'It is easier to pull gold out of the sea than harvest the liffen plant. It grows on the seabed, and the mer fiercely protect it. We can cast our nets and any fish we catch are ours. But a sea plant, you'd have to dive down to find that. And do it when they can't catch you.'

'Then I will do that. I will do whatever I must do. I am

a strong swimmer.' Marino kept his voice light, but he felt more determined than ever. He would swim wherever he needed to if it meant he could find the liffen bloom.

Florence snorted. 'Lana, are you certain you haven't found yourself a merman in disguise? I have never met anyone so confident he can survive the sea.'

Lana laughed, the sound floating out into the night. 'One would think after nearly drowning twice, he would be less confident, but if anything he seems more convinced that he can take on the entire ocean and win.'

They were nearly at the Gilded Palace now. The entryway had been lined with candles, their flames flickering in the light evening breeze. 'There's Edward,' said Florence. 'At the door. Doesn't he look handsome?'

Without waiting for a reply, Florence dropped Marino's arm and hurried up to her guard, who lit up at the sight of her.

And then it was only Marino and Lana, standing at the entrance of the Gilded Palace. Lana took a deep breath. 'I've never been here, you know.' Marino heard the nerves in her voice. 'The palace, I mean.'

He put a reassuring hand on her arm. 'It is only a ball. King Leonel is only a man. There is nothing to be afraid of through those doors.' But as he spoke, the words tasted like a lie.

CHAPTER 25
Lana

The great hall of the Gilded Palace was the grandest room Lana had ever seen.

A dozen chandeliers hung from the ceiling. There were floor-to-ceiling glass windows all around them and the ocean sparkled under the moonlight. The walls that weren't made of glass were covered in mirrors and the floors themselves were gold-plated. Musicians played on raised platforms, and servers deftly moved around the room offering wine and water to the guests.

And in the centre of it all stood King Leonel. He was frowning and staring at the entryway as if he was looking for someone. Lana had a sinking feeling she knew who.

Lana had never met the king before. She had seen him from afar, of course, at Solvoran festivals and official gatherings. She had heard he was erratic and prone to anger, irrational and irritable as much as he was charming and generous. She had hoped not to meet him tonight, but as soon as his eyes landed on Marino, she knew that she could not avoid it.

The king wore his golden hair loose and flowing, and on his head was the jagged gold crown of Solvora. While most of the men in attendance wore fitted jackets and trousers, the king was in a loose white tunic edged in gold.

'Captain Marino! There you are!' The king's voice boomed across the room, and for a moment it seemed as if every dancer paused, the whole room frozen, all eyes on Marino and Lana.

Lana wanted to shrink behind Marino's broad shoulders. But no. She would be brave. The king was merely a man. And she had every right to be here at the ball. All Solvorans had been invited.

The crowd parted for Marino and Lana, and she heard a few gasps as guests who patronised the bakery recognised her. She held her head high. She may not be royalty, but she was proud to be here. Proud to be on Marino's arm.

'Marino, Marino, Marino! We've been waiting for you,' crooned Leonel once they had reached him. Next to him was the woman Marino had told Lana about. Talia, the supposed soothsayer. She assessed Lana silently. 'We need you to show the Solvorans what you can do!'

'Good evening, Your Majesty,' said Marino, with a stiff bow. 'Your ball seems to be a great success.'

'Our ball,' King Leonel corrected. 'It is partly in your honour, you know.'

Marino gave the king a tight smile. 'An honour I do not deserve, Your Majesty. Truly, I am pleased to be here as a guest. And I will admit that I hope before any kind of announcement and demonstration, there is time for dancing. It is a ball, after all.'

Leonel sighed. 'Ah yes. I suppose you are right. You should dance. It will look bad if you don't. Now tell me, who is this lucky young lady on your arm?'

Leonel peered at Lana with sharp eyes. She dipped into a curtsy, her heart fluttering in her chest. It was not the way that Marino made her heart race, the delicious rush of joy and sweet anticipation that came when their eyes met. No. Something in Leonel's gaze made her blood sing a song of danger. *Run, run, run*, was the command of her rapidly beating heart.

She had never been so close to the king before, and he was an imposing presence. That must be it. Why else would she be so suddenly afraid?

King Leonel inhaled deeply. 'Your scent is familiar to me, yet your face is not. I would certainly recall if we had met.' He dipped his searching gaze down her body, and she wished she had a cloak to wrap around herself.

Marino stiffened slightly next to Lana and moved imperceptibly closer to her.

'My name is Lana Dawn,' she said, keeping her own eyes respectfully downcast. 'I work in the bakery on Sugar Street.'

'I thought that bakery was run by an old witch,' Leonel said, with a frown. His eyes darted towards Marino, and he playfully elbowed him in the side. 'No offence to any who identify as a witch, of course.' He scoffed. 'Male witches, what a strange place the world is beyond the Solvoran Sea.'

'None taken,' said Marino, with a tight smile.

'I take offence,' said Lana, bristling. 'Benedita was kind and beloved by everyone who knew her.' She spoke without thinking, overcome by anger. 'You may not have meant Marino offence, but you certainly meant to offend Benedita.'

Leonel guffawed. 'Now I know we haven't met. I would remember the face of any subject who dared,' his gaze sharpened, 'to speak to me so boldly.' And then he let out his big, booming laugh. 'What spirit you have. I must come by the bakery more often. Especially as now that I think of it, the one on Sugar Street has my favourite custard tarts and sugared buns.' He leaned even closer, tilting his head to the side, close enough that he could have kissed her collarbones if he wanted, and sniffed. 'Yes, that's it. You smell like the sugar buns. Delicious.' He licked his lips and it took every ounce of self-control Lana had not to shudder. Then he straightened up and laughed again, spittle flying from his mouth and on to her skin. 'A baker at the ball! Delightful! Marino, you sly fox, what a tasty morsel you've brought.' King Leonel snapped his fingers and an aide rushed to his side. 'Tomorrow – go to the bakery on Sugar Street and buy two dozen sugar buns.'

Lana faltered. 'There won't be any fresh buns tomorrow, Your Majesty.'

The king's face contorted, and Lana wondered how many moods the man would go through by the evening. 'And why not, little baker?'

Marino put his hand on the small of her back, and Lana knew he was silently telling her that he was there for her, as she faced the storm that was King Leonel.

'Because I'm here at the ball,' Lana said slowly, as if speaking to a young child. 'So, I cannot make them.'

King Leonel let out a derisive snort. 'Ah. This is why bakers don't go to balls. Because then there are no sugar buns! Well, I suppose I can wait an extra day for those delectable buns.' His gaze raked over her again and then flicked back up to her face. 'There is something else familiar about you. But I cannot place it. Strange. Strange. Strange.'

He turned towards Marino and thwacked him on the back. 'An interesting choice of a guest. You are full of surprises.' Then someone else caught his eye, and he strode away with Talia on his heels. 'Enjoy your dancing, Captain,' he called over his shoulder.

Marino let out a long breath as the king disappeared into the crowd. 'I intend to do just that,' he said to Lana. 'Are you all right?'

'I'm fine,' said Lana, trying to calm her racing heart. 'I'm glad I'm here with you.'

'I'm glad you're here too,' said Marino. 'And now, may I have this dance?' Marino took her gloved hand and raised it to his lips. Lana wanted nothing more than to rip the gloves off so she could feel Marino's lips on her skin.

'I would be delighted,' she said, wondering if he could see the want in her eyes. If he could hear her heart pounding in her chest.

Marino deftly took her other hand and placed it on his shoulder, and still holding the hand that he had kissed, began to guide them around the dance floor. Lana trod on his foot, and felt her cheeks go hot.

'I . . . I never learned how to dance,' she blurted out. 'It isn't something that a baker needs to know. Especially not on Solvora.'

'You are doing beautifully.'

Lana threw back her head and laughed, attracting the attention of some couples dancing more sedately nearby. 'That is blatantly untrue, but I appreciate it all the same.'

Marino leaned down closer, his breath warm on her cheek. 'You must see you are by far the most beautiful person in this room.'

His words sent a delicious tingle through her. But she refused to let him see how much he affected her. How much his mere words melted her. How his nearness – his hand on her waist, their bodies almost touching at every spin – made her dizzy with longing. So, she merely smirked. 'Don't let King Leonel hear you say that.'

Now it was Marino's turn to laugh, and the sound filled Lana with delight. She wanted to make him laugh again.

'I've never seen two people laugh so much while dancing,' said a familiar voice next to her. Lana glanced up and grinned. It was Flo and Edward. Flo was waggling her eyebrows and even Edward, usually so serious, was chuckling.

The two pairs danced alongside each other for the next few songs, until Flo pulled away from Edward. 'I'm parched. Lana, come with me to find some wine.'

Lana wanted to stay dancing with Marino. She had not anticipated how much she would enjoy it, how pleasurable she would find it to be spun by him around a crowded room, gazing at each other as if there was nobody else there.

But she too was thirsty.

And she saw that King Leonel was striding towards them. A good time indeed to make herself scarce and seek out a drink. As Leonel approached, Edward stood up straighter, and saluted.

Both Lana and Florence curtsied, but the king ignored them all. Talia was there too, as she was never far from the king's side, and she was gazing at Marino in a way that Lana decidedly didn't like.

'Marino. It is time. I want to show everyone what you can do, what *we* can do, before my subjects are too drunk on wine. You are key to the success of my plan, after all. My people will want to know why we have never tried to defeat the mer before this, and we can tell them it is your arrival that has emboldened us. Even the sight of you will give them strength and inspire courage.'

'You do look very dashing, it must be said,' added Talia. 'But you know what would make an even bigger statement? If we put you in Solvoran colours.' She nodded at Edward. 'Give him your sash, soldier.'

Lana snorted and turned it into a cough when Talia glared at her.

Marino smiled politely. 'That is a very kind offer, but I must decline. I am representing Eana, after all.'

'Yes. It is being from Eana, being from somewhere else, proof of your survival, proof of the world past our waters, that will make you so convincing. Come with me, Marino. There are a few things we must discuss before I present you to my people. This conversation is one to be had in private, but do not worry, all will be revealed soon.' King Leonel grinned widely, showing too many teeth, and Lana forced herself to smile back politely.

She felt a strange warring of protectiveness and vulnerability. She did not want Marino to leave her in this ballroom, and she did not want to leave him with the king. It felt like danger was all around, creeping in closer and closer every moment.

We need to leave, she thought suddenly, a terrible foreboding coming over her. She had felt it from the moment they had stepped inside the Gilded Palace, it had felt like those gates could close at any moment and lock her in.

But, of course, she could not demand that Marino reject

the king. She was being foolish, she told herself. Marino could handle himself. He could handle King Leonel.

And when Marino turned to her, a question in his eyes, asking if she was all right, she felt a rush of affection for him. She smiled at him, a real smile this time, and nodded before curtsying again to the king.

'Of course, Your Majesty. And I look forward to this grand proclamation.' Which was true. She looked forward to it because after it was said and done, she and Marino could leave.

King Leonel and Marino walked to the far side of the ballroom, near the glass doors that opened up to the terrace. Lana watched them for a moment, and then forced herself to turn to Flo. She couldn't stand and stare at Marino the whole time he conversed with the king, after all.

'Well,' she said brightly, 'shall we have some wine?'

CHAPTER 26
Marino

'Now, before you awaken the sea-gold, I want you to show my people some of your magic. I was thinking you could blow the windows open. Not hard enough to shatter them.' King Leonel chuckled. 'But so they see the power you have at your fingertips. The power that *I* now have.'

Leonel's eyes bored into Marino – as if he could siphon Marino's magic by stare alone.

Marino shifted on his feet and clenched his fists at his side. He wondered if he had made a mistake in aligning himself with Leonel. 'I don't think that is necessary, Your Majesty. After all, we are still discussing exactly what my role will be in breaking the mer's hold on Solvora.'

Leonel let out another loud laugh, but his eyes stayed hard. 'Isn't it obvious? We hunt the mermaids. Because now we can. Using the sea-gold. Didn't you see how it sharpened towards the sea? You have awakened the sea-gold, and now it can be used against the mer.'

'I sensed it,' Talia whispered, suddenly close. 'I sensed your magic the moment you walked into the throne room, Marino of Eana. You asked what gift I have, and it is that. I can smell magic, and your magic has changed the sea-gold. It used to smell of mer, and now it smells of man. And what is more deadly to the mer than a man?' She smiled, like a shark.

Marino stared at Talia as if she had sprouted a second head. 'How is it that you have such a gift?'

'My family has long been on Solvora. It is a shame to me, but my great-great grandmother fell prey to a passing merman's song. This was before the ring of Solvora, when the mer could come and go, but they still used their song. Well, she had a baby. A human baby, no tail or gills, but the blood. The blood links my family to the sea. And that baby had a baby and so on, until there was me. I am not a mer, nor a witch like you, but I have heightened senses. I can hear a heartbeat, smell a lie, or even, in your case, magic.'

'But Talia has proven herself,' said King Leonel, placing a hand behind her neck. 'Her family has long shown their loyalty, and Talia especially.'

'I am no mer,' said Talia firmly, 'but I know how to destroy them. And destroy them we will.'

'With the sea-gold?' Marino's mind was still spinning from Talia's confession. And how could gold cause so much harm?'

'Oh yes, Marino. With the sea-gold that you have imbued with your magic. One cut of a knife dipped in awakened sea-gold is enough to make them bleed to death.' King Leonel grinned, baring his teeth. 'We will show the sea who has the power. We will kill the fish women once and for all and feed them to Solvora. An offering. Their magic and their blood will feed our great land. We will no longer need to sacrifice our people! We will offer the tails of the mer back to the sea, back to where they came from. And the sea will recognise our strength, and it will not fight us. Then we will be free from the mer, and we will sail once more.'

Marino's head was spinning. Even though the mer had wrecked his ship, even though they kept the Solvorans trapped and sung them to their doom, they should not – could not – be murdered in such a brutal way. How had he not seen that this was what the king would want?

He cleared his throat and lowered his voice. 'That is not what I was suggesting. Far from it.'

King Leonel's grin disappeared. 'I am not asking for your permission. You have agreed to be my ally, have you not?' Leonel's eyes were so wide that he looked like a man possessed. 'Perhaps I will drink the mer blood too. It will grant me strength above all.' He grabbed Marino by the shoulders. 'Have you seen them, Marino? Have you seen them swim? Have you seen their strength? Men are no match for them. We will never be free with them circling Solvora, keeping us trapped here. This is the only way. And you will join me. You will join Solvora. You will use your magic to fight their storms, and I will use the sea-gold weapons to cut out their hearts.'

Marino carefully stepped out of King Leonel's grip and adjusted his frock coat. He would not help this man. He would not awaken the gold for him. He would do nothing for Leonel. Marino was many things, but he was not a murderer. He would find another way to get a ship. 'Your Majesty, the mer magic is a far different, far wilder magic to what I know. I have told you I will help you, but I did not mean this.'

Leonel let out a snort of disbelief. 'If we kill the mer, you can leave. You can go home. We want the same thing, just for different reasons.'

'I am not sure if we do.' Marino gave the king a tight smile. 'With all due respect, I will take no part in any such thing. I do not want blood on my hands – that of man or mer.'

'If you are not my ally, then you must be my enemy.' Leonel's eyes narrowed. 'Make your choice, Marino.'

'Your Majesty, that begs the question, am I here as a guest, or as a prisoner?'

Leonel clicked his tongue. 'Marino, Marino, Marino. Be sensible. I allow you to come and go as you please, do I not? Do not insult my hospitality. I take that personally. I try very hard to be a good host. A good king. And it is not me keeping you prisoner, but the sea. I am giving you a way out. Take it. Join me. I will be waging war on the mer whether you help me or not. But I would rather us be on the same side.'

Marino's eyes darted to the other side of the grand ballroom, where Lana stood laughing and drinking wine with Florence. He wanted to keep her safe. And that meant not starting a battle with King Leonel here in the ballroom.

So, he simply nodded. 'I have been welcomed in Solvora, and I thank you for it. And I will help you how I can, but *I will not harm the mer.*'

'Marino, my good man. I am not asking you to personally skewer the creatures. All I want from you is a little help protecting my people. Surely that isn't too much to ask?'

Marino's mouth flattened into a thin line. 'I will always use my magic for good, if possible.'

'Then we are in agreement!' Leonel thwacked Marino on the back. 'I am, it must be said, a most magnanimous king.

And my people will love me even more when I announce the hunt. I will mark it with a new festival. When I let them take revenge on the monsters that have kept us trapped for so long. It will be better than the Goldwave Festival. It will be . . .' Leonel's eyes flashed, 'a blood wave.'

Marino meant to tell Lana he was leaving, meant to tell her that he would be back, but his mind was fuzzy and all he could think of was Kira. Of Kira being sliced apart using a knife made from some twisted form of Marino's magic. He knew that the king wouldn't wait long before waging his war on the mer. And King Leonel knew how to win, because he had Talia on his side. Talia, traitor to the mer. Talia, with magic hiding in her blood.

Marino had to warn the mer. They would never expect that the sea-gold could turn on them, that one with their own blood would be their undoing.

Marino took the crumbling steps three at a time. He had never gone down these steps, the ones that led from the palace directly to the sea. To the King's Beach.

He knew that the mer were strong, he knew that they had magic at their call, but he knew too that the fury and the might of men sometimes was enough to even defeat magic. It had happened in Eana, when power-hungry men had hunted the witches and almost succeeded. It could happen again. When he had told the king he would help him defeat the mer, he had not meant this. He had not meant their annihilation.

The King's Cove was small, a sliver of silver sand kissed by a gentle tide. Marino wondered if the mer ever came here. Well, tonight they would. He would make sure of it.

He remembered Kira telling him about how she had smelled his blood in the water. How she had known him by scent alone. With steady hands, he sliced his palm with the dagger he always kept on his person and let his blood drip into the surf. *Kira. Kira. Kira. Please, come.*

The moon shone above, its reflection refracting on the dark mirror of the sea at night.

Where was she? 'Kira!' he whispered urgently. 'Kira!' Marino took a few more steps into the sea, until it was up to his waist. His blood was flowing faster now into the water, but he didn't feel the sting.

There was a splash in the water and a flash of silver.

It wasn't Kira. The silver-haired mermaid rose out of the water and bared her teeth at him. 'You must be entranced,' she hissed. 'Why else would you come back?'

Marino stumbled back out of the surf. The mer's teeth glinted in the night.

'Where is Kira?'

The mermaid's mouth dropped open for a moment in complete shock. 'She told you her true name? She is more foolish than I realised.'

'I came here to warn her, to warn all of you. King Leonel has ordered a hunt. A mermaid hunt. You all must stay far from the shore. He is breaking the truce that you have. No mer will be safe.' Marino spoke quickly. 'I do not agree with what you do, with how you sink ships and drown men, but I do not want you to die. I do not want Kira to die.'

The silver mermaid laughed, the sound like shattered glass. 'Where would we go, human? You know we are tethered here to Solvora, against our will.' She spat in the water with disdain.

There were more mermaids now, appearing out of the water and watching the exchange between Marino and the mermaid. He saw them but kept his focus on the silver one. He picked up a fistful of sand, ready to cast a spell if he needed to. *If she starts to sing, if they start to sing, I can block it*, he thought. But where was Kira? She was the one he had come to warn, she was the one he had tried to summon with his own blood.

'But surely you can stay away from the shore.' Like Kira was now, he realised.

'Men cannot kill us. If they could, they would have done it long ago. They can try, but they will drown and die. I look forward to this so-called hunt.' The silver mermaid's teeth flashed in the moonlight. 'Because *I* will be the one doing the hunting.'

'Will you not listen at all? Do not be so proud! I came to warn you, not because I care for you, but because I care for Kira! Kira saved me and so I will do the same for her. And it is my fault that the king can now hunt you. Something about my magic, it changes the sea-gold.'

The silver mermaid's eyes began to glow with anger, and Marino realised he needed to leave. He had made a mistake, coming down to the shore. Dripping his blood in the water like the fool Kira said he was. Summoning something he did not understand.

'The magic of man should not mix with the magic of mer,' she hissed. 'What have you done to the sea-gold?'

'It was an accident. I touched it, and it awoke my own magic, and now –'

'And now the sea-gold can be used to kill us. Because of

your foolishness. The sea-gold that comes from the very place that is our home. I will show you, Marino Pegasi, just how weak men are compared to us. You may have magic, you may have poisoned the sea-gold, but to us you are nothing.' The silver mermaid began to take off her mask. 'Join me, sisters,' she cried. 'We will show this man how foolish he is. We will unleash our true power. We will show our faces and we will sing and all of Solvora will fall to their knees and crawl into the sea. We will teach Solvora a lesson it will never forget.'

As the silver mermaid and the others began to take off their masks, showing their full beauty, and started to sing, Marino felt himself entranced, trapped like a fly in a web. He closed his eyes and fell to the sand on his hands and knees, forcing himself to crawl away from the sea, even though all he wanted was to lie down and let the waves take him. Let the mer take him.

'Marino?' A voice, clear and sharp, cut through his haze. He lifted his head up, his vision blurry. But he would recognise that voice anywhere. The voice was a lifeline and with the last crumbling bits of his sanity, of knowing who he was, he reached for it and held on. His gaze snagged on a figure in red running towards him through the sand.

Lana.

CHAPTER 27
Lana

Lana had never run so fast.

She'd seen Marino speaking to King Leonel, seen how Marino had stilled when the king had turned away, as if preparing himself.

She'd seen Marino slip out of the ballroom. And she'd carried on dancing, all the while waiting for him to come back in. He'll be back, she'd told herself. But minute after minute passed. And Lana knew that something was wrong.

She'd left Florence dancing with Edward. Told them both she didn't feel well, and Marino was going to escort her home. Edward and Florence had drunk so much wine they hadn't noticed that Marino had already left. Instead, Florence had winked at her. 'Make sure he takes good care of you,' she'd said, and even in her haste, Lana had blushed at her friend's insinuations.

Lana had never been to the palace before, but she told a guard she needed some fresh air, and he pointed her towards the sprawling terrace through the glass doors.

From there, she saw Marino. Saw him on the silver sliver of beach tucked far beneath the palace, the glint of a knife in his hand.

At first, she thought he was there to take on the mer with his bare hands. That the king had made him some kind of offer, and he couldn't wait another moment before he pierced the heart of a mermaid.

But as she hurried down the steps, cursing her corset, her skirts gathered up in her hands, and saw the mer appear one by one, she realised Marino's heart was the one at risk.

They started singing right as her feet hit the sand. Their song hit Lana like a wave, but she did not falter. The mer had taken so much from her. They would not take him.

'Marino!' she cried, not caring if the mermaids targeted her next. She would break him out of their spell. She would do whatever it took.

And then, when he looked up at her, when their gazes met, it felt like he was the stone and she was the flint, and they were a fire that would never go out.

Not even in the sea.

'Marino!' Lana ran to him. Running into the sound blast of the mer felt like running into a lightning storm, but one by one they fell quiet, until only the faint echo of their song remained.

Lana was certain that it was a trick, a trap, that they'd deafened her somehow, until she heard her name on Marino's lips. She pulled him to his feet, pulled him up and out of the surf and away from the mermaids, who were all staring at her.

The silver-haired one in the front had removed her mask, and Lana knew immediately why it was decreed they could not come above water without covering their face.

Looking at the mermaid was like looking directly at the sun or a moon during a solar eclipse. The pain was exquisite and it made the air all around her go fuzzy and blurry, like the silver-haired mer was the only clear thing in the world.

Lana forced herself to look away from the shimmering air, from the silver eyes tracking her like prey, and back to Marino. And as she did, she felt the lingering echo of the hold the mer had on her float away. He took her in his arms, both of them trembling, and Lana leaned her head on his chest, listening to the thunder of his heart.

She could have sworn she heard the mermaid laugh. Then there was a splash and, inexplicably, they were gone.

There was a shout above them. The guards and guests must have heard the song, and someone was coming down the stone steps. Marino pulled Lana into the shadows, into a crevice in the cliff, their feet still in the wet sand.

'No sign of the mermaids,' said a gruff voice.

'But I heard their song,' insisted another.

'Maybe they were taunting us.'

Lana didn't want to face the Solvoran guard and explain what she'd seen. So, she stayed silent and still, pressed up against Marino, his arms still tight around her waist.

'Mermaids and their mind games. Did you hear that the king is going to let us hunt them?'

'I can't wait. It's about time.'

'But what about their song?'

'The survivor – he can protect us. He has magic that can stop them. That's what I heard.'

Another guard snorted. 'I'll believe that when I see it.'

The sound of their voices trailed off as they went back up the steps. Lana knew that the king would be wondering where Marino had gone. Where *she* had gone. She hoped the king would ask Flo, that Flo would tell the king that Lana and Marino had slipped away back to her bakery, that they were too infatuated with each other to stay at the ball.

Even though the guards were gone, and the mermaids had disappeared, Lana and Marino stood still in the silence – his arms around her waist, her chest pressed against his body, their hearts beating in time.

Lana could have stayed there all night, close to Marino in the dark. But she knew they didn't have all night, that eventually the tide would come in. It was already rising, the water kissing Lana's ankles.

And Marino, she had so many questions for Marino. Lana stepped back, and as his arms fell away, she wanted nothing more than to close the gap between them again. In the moonlight, he looked as if he had been carved from onyx.

'Thank you,' he said, his voice hoarse. 'I don't know what would have happened if you hadn't arrived. If you hadn't . . . saved me.' He took her hands in his, squeezing them.

'What happened?' Lana asked.

'I don't want to harm them,' he said, like it was simple. 'I wanted to warn them.'

Lana drew a sharp breath. 'But . . . Leonel will kill you if he finds out you want to help the mer.'

Marino ran his hand over his jaw. 'I know. I wasn't thinking straight.'

'Do you think you are entranced?'

Marino let out a strange laugh she didn't understand. 'No. Or, not now. When they first began to sing, of course I wanted to go into water, but it is something else. It is more than their song that calls to me.'

There was something slippery in his answer that Lana tried to catch but couldn't. 'I don't understand.'

'I told you a mer saved me. She is the reason why I made it to Solvora.'

Lana scoffed. 'The mer are the reason your ship sank.'

'That may be, but the one who saved me . . . I couldn't bear for her to die at his hands. For her to die at all.' He shook his head. 'But she wasn't here tonight. Only the mer who hate Solvorans, who hate me. Even they do not deserve the death that King Leonel is planning for them.'

Lana took Marino's hands. 'You have a good heart.'

Marino let out a derisive snort. 'Do not think me so kind-hearted. I want something from them too, you know. I need the mer to find the cure for my sister. I worry that without them, I'll never find the liffen plant, wherever it may be in the ocean, and it will have all been for nothing.'

'We will find it,' Lana swore. 'With or without the mer.'

Marino nodded, and then he stood back, his eyes roaming over her.

'I felt the pull of the mer, when they started to sing, and when they removed their masks. Stronger than it had been before. But you, when I saw you, when I heard you, it cut through it all.' He stared at her like she was the one who was magical, not him. The tide came in again, brushing against Lana's legs. She was tingling from the tips of her toes to the top of her head and she felt *delicious* and powerful and almost as if she had a magic of her very own.

'I'm glad you heard me,' said Lana softly. 'When I saw you – on your knees, in the surf, I thought I had lost you.'

He ran a thumb along her jaw and down her neck, and his touch lit a fire within her. 'You will not lose me, Lana.'

She put her hands on his chest and slid them up over his shoulders and around his neck. She could feel the strength of him, his muscles taut and tight beneath her fingers. She leaned up until her mouth was a breath away from his.

'What now?' she whispered.

'This,' he said, and then his arms were around her waist and when his lips met her own she gasped at the sheer pleasure of it. He pulled back, to gaze down at her, eyes dark. 'Is this all right?'

She nodded. 'Yes. A thousand times yes.' And then she was up on her toes, kissing him again, harder now, delighting in the sensation of her mouth against his, his tongue brushing against her own, the closeness of him.

Marino's hand went around the back of her neck, his fingers tangling in her hair. Lana let out a small moan, leaning more into him, wanting to be closer. His hand slid down her back, holding her tightly against him.

Lana lost track of time as she kissed Marino. She was so aware of every sensation in her body – the feel of his arms around her, the softness of his lips and firmness of his touch, the deeply pleasurable warmth that was spreading within her, the way her skin tingled beneath his fingers, the sea lapping against her legs and soaking her gown . . .

The water. The tide. She gasped into Marino's mouth and pulled back.

'The water is rising,' she said. 'We can't stay out here all night.'

'A shame,' said Marino, his voice low. He seemed unbothered by the rising tide, his eyes dark and only on her. 'You are so beautiful. Have I told you that?'

Lana laughed lightly. 'I am certain I am very dishevelled.'

'And all the more beautiful for it.' Marino pushed a lock of hair behind her ears, fingers lingering on her jaw, her neck, her collarbones. 'When I first saw you in the bakery, I couldn't take my eyes off you, but it is more than that. Every moment I've spent with you, somehow you grow more beautiful, and more radiant.' His voice grew hoarse. 'I cannot regret what brought me here to Solvora. Here to you. And I admit I cannot imagine leaving here without you.'

Lana's breath caught in her throat. 'Then bring me with you. There is nothing for me here in Solvora. I want to see the world.' And then, feeling bold, she leaned up again towards him. 'And I want to be with you.'

CHAPTER 28
Marino

Marino knew that King Leonel would be furious that he had left the ball so abruptly, that he had not showed his magic or touched more gold, but that was tomorrow's trouble.

Tonight, tonight was for Lana. They took the steps back up to the palace hand in hand, her now soaked red satin dress dragging behind them as they hurried up the rocky steps, all the way to the great, sprawling terrace. Marino saw that the base of the palace had been carved directly into Goldwave Mountain, and then the gold and glass and stone had been built on top of it.

And below, the waves crashed and rose and slowly changed the shape of the shore itself. There was no outrunning the sea, not on Solvora.

There were half a dozen soldiers milling around the marble terrace. They hadn't spotted Marino and Lana yet. Marino paused at the edge of the stairs, assessing.

'We need a distraction,' whispered Lana. Her fingers were still intertwined with his.

Marino grinned. 'That's my speciality.' He squeezed Lana's hand. 'Stay close, and don't let go of me.'

With his other hand, he picked up a few grains of Solvoran

sand before dropping them again, while he whispered a spell for darkness.

Marino was never sure how his magic would manifest when it was a spell he'd never attempted before. Tonight, the darkness he summoned came in as a rolling black mist.

He heard Lana's gasp as the terrace was plunged into dark, and shrieks as the candles and sconce lights went out in the ballroom. The soldiers shouted, and Marino heard their footsteps as they tried to find the cause of the darkness.

Marino squeezed Lana's hand again and strode forward, confident in the dark. He did not know how long the enchantment would last, but he was pleased with the effect.

Marino led Lana across the terrace, into the ballroom, and out into the halls of the palace, which were still lit with flickering sconce lights. His enchantment had only gone so far, but it had been enough to let them slip past the soldiers and, most importantly, the king.

Lana's eyes widened as she saw the edges of the dark mist floating out from the ballroom and spilling out into the hall, like ink spilled on paper.

Marino winked at her, and with several more well-chosen words, whispered a spell for the black mist to dissipate.

'Wouldn't want to completely ruin their evening,' he said. 'Or for anyone to get the bright idea to bar the doors to keep anyone from entering or exiting in the dark.'

Lana let out a soft laugh. 'They probably should have done that straight away.'

'I imagine the soldiers, and even King Leonel himself, have grown complacent in guarding the palace when the only threat you have comes from the sea,' Marino said quietly as they moved swiftly through the corridors until they were back out in the courtyard.

The guards at the door bowed as Marino and Lana passed, clearly with no knowledge of what had occurred in the ballroom.

There was a shout from somewhere inside the palace, and the guard looked over his shoulder, his frown deepening.

'Right, then,' said Marino, slowly backing away. 'Sounds like you should go and see what that is all about. Goodnight.'

Still hand in hand, they ran down the entryway, the shell-lined path crunching under their feet and the orange blossoms waving in the breeze overhead.

They ran all the way down the streets of Goldwave Mountain, laughing as they did. The sky above them was velvet dark and studded with stars that seemed close enough to touch. Soon they were on Sugar Street, which already felt so familiar to Marino, even after such a short time, and they paused outside the door.

Marino glanced down at Lana, a question in his eyes.

She gave him a sly grin as she stepped past him, pushing open the door and pulling him in after her.

They closed the door to the bakery, breathless with laughter, and then as Marino gazed down at Lana, he suddenly felt breathless for another reason entirely.

Still grinning at him, Lana led him back past the counter and into the kitchen. Moonlight spilled in through the window, bathing the room in a pearly glow.

Far below them, Marino could hear the waves crashing against the base of the mountain. The sound merged with the beating of his own heart.

Lana leaned back against one of the tables, her hands on her hips. 'Well, Captain. Are you going to kiss me again or not?' Her dark eyes shone in the night.

In one movement, Marino hoisted Lana up on to the table, nudging her knees apart so he stood between her legs. She wrapped her arms around his neck, her fingers in the curls at the nape of his neck. They were so close that he could feel every breath she took, the rise and fall of her breasts against the hardness of his own chest.

'Only if you want me to.' His voice was a low rumble.

Lana tightened her grip on him. 'Kiss me, Captain.'

It was all the encouragement he needed. Marino kissed her open mouth, revelling in the feel of her lips against his, and when she slipped her tongue in his mouth, letting out a small whimper of pleasure as she did, it nearly undid him. He deepened the kiss, slanting his mouth over her own, and wrapped his arms around her, feeling all her dips and curves.

Lana's hands explored his body as well, grappling with his shirt buttons until he was exposed to his navel, his frock coat still on. Lana pulled back from the kiss to gaze at him appreciatively, eyes darkening with want, and then she pushed his coat and shirtsleeves down his arms and to the floor, leaving him shirtless and only in his breeches.

'Well, this hardly seems fair,' murmured Marino, tilting his head back as Lana leaned forward to press kisses in the curve where his neck met his shoulder. He felt heady with desire, like he was dreaming.

Lana glanced up at him through her long dark lashes. 'My corset is feeling rather tight . . .'

'Lucky for you, I'm rather an expert when it comes to knots and rigging.'

Lana laughed, the sound sending another shiver of satisfied pleasure through Marino. 'Since when are corsets considered rigging?'

Marino arched a brow. 'Well, they do hold things together, do they not? Provide support?'

This time Lana's laugh was even louder. 'I suppose you are right.'

Marino ran a hand down her back, where a row of small pearl buttons secured the satin dress. Beneath that he could feel the boning and ribbons of her corset.

Lana's breath hitched. 'And how are you with buttons?'

'I think I can safely say I am very good with my hands in most scenarios.' Marino didn't miss the flush that spread over Lana's cheeks at his words. To demonstrate, he began to unbutton her dress with one hand, keeping his eyes locked on to Lana's as he did. When he had unbuttoned the gown to the bottom of her back, his hand hovered near the base of the corset, where it was tied.

In the dark kitchen, Lana's eyes twinkled like trapped stars, the gold flecks seeming to shine even brighter. 'Wait.' Her voice was breathy and soft. Marino immediately dropped his hands, cursing himself for letting his desire get the best of him, but then Lana pushed herself off the table, knocking off a bowl as she did, and stood before him. Without breaking their eye contact, she slipped her dress off her shoulders, and it fell in a pool of silk and satin at her feet. Underneath she wore the corset, still laced, and her undergarments. Marino let his gaze sweep all the way down her body and back up again. A slow smile spread across her face as their eyes met again.

'Corset is still too tight.' Lana slowly spun, the dress still at her feet, until her back was to him.

This was not the first time Marino had ever unlaced

a corset. But it felt like it was. He drew a long, shuddering breath as he slowly, slowly loosened the laces, pressing kisses to her shoulder as he did. Lana sighed with pleasure, arching her back and tilting her head to the side.

Finally, it was the last loop of the corset. Lana turned again so she was facing him, her corset held on by one loop of fabric. His hands rested on her hips, as he waited for her to guide him towards what she wanted. Whatever happened between them, he wanted her to feel in control.

'I think,' Lana's words came out slow, as if they were drenched in honey. 'I think perhaps we should go upstairs.' She flushed at her own words and all they implied.

Marino swallowed thickly. 'I think that is a very good idea. But Lana, I cannot say what will come tomorrow. I will not make you promises I cannot keep. You know I cannot stay on Solvora. But tonight, tonight, Lana, I am yours.'

Lana tilted her head back and gazed at him. 'And when you leave, you will take me with you? So I can see the world beyond Solvora?'

'I will try,' said Marino. 'But I must leave here and return to Eana by any means necessary. I can't promise you that it will be possible. But once I have found the cure, and brought it home to Celeste, I will return to Solvora. For you.'

Lana leaned up to press her lips against his, like she could seal his promise with a kiss.

He kissed her back, gently at first, and then with a fire and a hunger. She kissed him back just as passionately, her hands scrabbling over his back and shoulders, fingers twisting in the curls at the nape of his neck.

Marino did not remember the climb up the rickety stairs to Lana's small bedroom. Only that they did it without parting – as if they were dancing up the stairs – kissing and climbing until suddenly they were in her room, the windows open and the wind blowing the curtains and the smell of the sea mixing with the sweet, floury aroma of the bakery and the scent that was Lana, only Lana.

Her corset was still on when they collapsed into her small bed, limbs entwined. The bed groaned under their combined weight, and Lana laughed as she pulled Marino on top of her.

'Oh, you *are* handsome,' Lana said, trailing a finger along his neck down his collarbone. Her hair was dishevelled and loose around her shoulders. Lana's legs were bare except for her underthings and her loosened corset and while Marino ached to kiss every part of her, he held back. It was enough, more than enough, to kiss her lips and neck and shoulders, to feel her pressed up against him. It was a promise for more, for a future they both hoped for.

'Kiss me again, Captain,' Lana breathed. 'Kiss me like you've never kissed anyone before.'

Marino smiled against her lips. 'With pleasure.'

Hours later, though time lost all meaning as they lost themselves in each other, Marino fell asleep with Lana in his arms.

The familiar sound of the waves outside lulled him to sleep, and as he nuzzled Lana's neck, his last thought before sleep claimed him was what a strange twist of fate had led him here to her.

CHAPTER 29
Marino

Marino slept more soundly than he had in years.

His dreams were of Lana, of Lana in the sea and Lana on the sand and then suddenly the dream shifted and he was drowning. The mer were pulling him down, deeper and deeper, and he could hear their laughter and their song even in the water, and then he woke, gasping for air and reaching for Lana.

He was alone in her small bed. The window was still open, and a shaft of golden sunlight shone through the gap in the curtains. But there was no breeze, and the curtains hung still.

'Lana?' he called out. 'Lana?' He stood, quickly pulling on his shirt. He flung open the curtains, as if impossibly he might find Lana on the balcony.

She wasn't there. The sun was high, it looked to be nearly noon – he had slept through the whole morning.

Lana must be downstairs, he told himself, even as he heard no sign of her, no sound of customers or clatters in the kitchen.

He felt a fool for sleeping so long while she had woken to work. Well, he would make it up to her. He hurried down the stairs, calling her name again. 'Lana! You should have woken me!'

There was no reply.

The kitchen was empty, as was the bakery in the front. The heavy door still closed and locked.

Marino stilled, an uneasiness creeping over him. Where had she gone? Why had she left without a word? Did she regret kissing him? Regret the words she had said?

He tried to calm his panicked thoughts. She must be at the market, fetching ingredients. She must have locked the door without thinking, out of habit. A girl did not disappear into thin air.

Marino knew he needed to get back to the Gilded Palace before King Leonel sent out a search party, or worse, soldiers to the bakery. The king would have questions about where he had gone, about the dark that had descended on them.

It would be easy to blame the mer, and for that he felt a twinge of guilt, but they had tried to drown him. Some thanks for trying to help them, to warn them.

Not trying to warn them. Trying to warn *Kira*.

The thought of Kira was like a wave breaking over him.

He still had to tell her. He didn't trust her mersisters to tell her, they had laughed at him, laughed at the very idea that King Leonel could ever pose a threat.

Even without Marino's help, which he was loathe to give, he sensed a change in the king. There was a wild ruthlessness in him now. A mad desperation. The king was willing to do whatever it took to free them from the grasp of the Solvoran Sea. And a desperate man might be a match for even a mer's magic.

Marino did not want to leave the bakery unlocked and

unattended, so he instead went back up the stairs into Lana's room and out on to her small balcony.

The stone steps that were carved into the cliffs were worn, and slick from sea spray, but he could make his way down most of the way and then swim around the cove and back to shore.

He thought of the mer, the silver one, telling him never to come back into the sea.

He thought of Kira telling him the same.

He would not let them dictate his comings and goings, and if he was going to get the liffen plant from the seabed, he would have to return to the sea. And he would need Kira to help him again. But it was more than that. Even with everything that had happened between him and Lana he felt a curious tie to Kira that he could not break, not yet. Once he warned her of the King's plans, and once he had found the liffen bloom, then he would never think of her again.

Or at least he would try his hardest not to. Kira had awoken something in him that he was not sure he would ever be able to put back to sleep. But for now, he had to find her. For both of their sakes.

Marino scrawled a hasty note to Lana, telling her that he had gone to the palace but that he would be back soon. He left it on her pillow.

Then he carefully folded his frock coat and left it on the edge of her bed, and his boots by the door. A promise that he would return. And more practically – it was easier to swim without his coat and boots.

As he stepped back on to the balcony, he gazed out at the sea. The sea, the sea. His friend, his foe, his future, his freedom, his fate. Marino knew in his heart he was even more bound to the sea than the Solvorans were. He would never escape it, nor did he want to.

But he would not be foolish this time. He would take precautions.

It was a risky spell, but it was worth trying. He had seen it done before but had never attempted it on himself. It was a long swim from here back to the nearest beach. He couldn't scrabble his way around the cliffs.

The cove that Lana's bakery was carved into was remarkably private and protected. It was just large enough to house her bakery. The neighbouring buildings on Sugar Street that had sea views could not see her balcony, nor the stairs that went down to the sea. The only way to see it would be from the water itself.

And as Marino had learned, only the mer would have that view.

So, he was not worried about being spotted by any Solvorans as he made his way down the slippery steps, stopping only to pluck a ria blossom growing along the cliff.

The steps stopped two thirds of the way down the cliff, eroded by the waves into smooth sandstone.

Marino paused at the bottom of the steps. He crushed the ria blossom in his fist and dropped it into the water as he whispered a spell, desperately hoping it would work.

A moment later, he felt a strange scratching sensation on his neck. He put his hand to his neck and grinned.

The spell had worked.

He had given himself gills.

With a whoop, he dived head first into the sea.

As with any spell, Marino didn't know how long this one would last. But it was more than the gills. While he still had the legs of a man, and for this he was grateful, his whispered words had given him more strength in the water, and he slipped through the waves like a fish.

His vision too was clearer than it had ever been in the sea. Was this what it was like for Kira and the other mer all the time? And his lungs never burned for air.

Marino swam through a school of blue and silver fish, who scattered at the sight of him. Rainbow-hued coral reefs sprouted from the seabed, and seaflowers and seaweed waved in the water as if they were dancing.

He truly was in the world of the mer now.

He wondered if the mer could sense him in the water. If they would know him as a man or something else.

As glorious as it was to swim in the sea, deeper than he had ever gone before, he knew he had to stay close to the cliffs, in case the spell wore off before he was ready.

Marino swam on.

He sensed her before he saw her. There was a change in the water and when he looked over his shoulder there she was.

Kira.

If there had been any air in his lungs, the sight of her would have taken it away. She floated effortlessly in the water, her dark blue hair flowing all around her. It was the first time he'd truly seen the strength and beauty of her in all her glory.

She wore her usual mask of seaflowers, but behind it her violet eyes were faintly glowing, and her full lips were curved in a soft smile.

Kira tilted her head in a question, as she assessed him,

eyes lingering on the new marks on his neck. His gills. Her smile widened, and when she laughed, he heard it even in the sea.

He wanted to speak to her, but he knew even if he could breathe underwater, he could not speak. He pointed to the surface, and she nodded, reaching her hand out to him.

When they burst through the water, Marino had the disorienting feeling of breathing air from his lungs as the gills on his neck closed. The spell had been more successful than he had hoped.

'I have never seen a man turn mer,' said Kira, splashing him with her tail.

Marino grinned at her. 'I wouldn't go that far.'

'It is impressive magic.' Kira came closer to him, trailing her fingers along his neck, sending a shiver through him.

Then he remembered. She had not been there last night when he had called her. He took her hand off his neck and didn't miss the way her eyes flashed as he did.

'Where were you last night? I was nearly drowned, nearly killed. I was looking for you. To warn you and your sisters about what is coming.'

Behind her mask, Kira narrowed her eyes.

'I told you to stay out of the sea. And what do you do? You come and call for me. You step into the waves, let the water taste you. Your scent is unmistakable to me and my kind. I was sleeping in my sea-cave. I did not know my sisters were singing storms. I did not know they were coming for you. But they told me. They woke me up, gleeful. They said that you nearly followed them into the sea, nearly let them take you down to the depths. You didn't have your gills then, did you? No, nor your senses!'

Her anger surprised Marino. He should be the one who was angry, not her. But then he realised that she had been scared *for* him. Scared that her mersisters would have truly drowned him and then gloated about it. She had been worried about him.

Kira cared for him.

He reached a hand out to her, and she batted it away.

'I cannot protect you. Not any more.' Kira let out a long breath. Marino had the sudden thought that the way that he could breathe above and below with his magic gills must be similar to how the mer could as well.

Kira raised her violet eyes to his. The silver flecks seemed to twinkle in the noon-day sun. 'But unlike my sisters, I appreciate you coming to warn us. My sisters, they are proud. They think they are invincible. I know we are not. And at least now we have a warning. We can prepare.'

'Good,' said Marino, his voice gruffer than he meant. 'That is all I wanted.'

Kira let out a short, sharp laugh. 'Far from it. I know what you want.'

She swam close to him, so close that the seaflowers she wore on her breasts were pressed against him. She inhaled deeply, like she was breathing him in. Marino went very still, as if a wild animal were approaching and any movement would startle it into attack.

'You want to save your sister.'

Marino nodded, finding himself unable to speak. He was stunned by her nearness, to the point that it felt as if she had stolen his voice. This was no siren call, he knew that, but without even trying, she was truly dazzling by the sheer fact of existing.

Marino knew magic, and he knew beauty, but Kira *was* magic, she *was* beauty.

She was not human and she shone all the more for it.

Was all the more dangerous for it.

He needed to take hold of his senses. Especially because Kira was offering him what he needed most. So, he nodded again, more adamantly. 'Yes,' he choked out. 'That is what I want.'

Kira took his hand, lacing her fingers through his. She was so close he could have kissed her, and oh, how he wanted to.

'I know your magic has poisoned the sea-gold against us. But I know you did not do it out of malice. And I know that you will stop at nothing until you find what you are looking for. And so, because I have found myself caring for you,' Kira made a face of disgust, 'and because I think this will keep my sisters safe, I will show you where to find the liffen bloom.'

Marino let out a sigh of pure relief. Kira's words, her promise, had shocked him out of his dazed stupor, piercing through his yearning for her.

'Thank you, Kira. If you do this, I will do whatever I can to keep you and your mersisters safe. But . . .' His voice trailed off.

Kira snatched her hand back as if she'd been burned. 'But what? I offer you what you most want, what you sailed around the world for, and you make demands?'

'No, of course not. All I was going to say is that it will be much easier for me to protect the mer if you, I mean if they, stop drowning the Solvorans.'

'We are bound to stop ships from leaving Solvora. We must punish the Solvorans for what they did to us. If they stay away from the sea, we do not bother them.'

Marino tilted his head to the side. 'And when your sisters sing their siren songs?'

Kira rolled her eyes. 'You said nothing of singing. You spoke of ships. And the men who come when they are called, they die in ecstasy.' She drew close to him again and ran a nail down his neck. 'I can promise you that.'

Marino swallowed thickly. 'Thank you for helping me. I will return here and I will bring witches more powerful than me, and I will help break whatever curse this is that keeps the mer trapped within the Solvoran ring.'

Kira assessed him. 'There is more. Something else you should know about Solvora.'

'Surely there is nothing you could tell me that would surprise me now.'

Kira's teeth flashed in a wicked smile, and a heartbeat before she spoke, Marino knew that he was wrong, that whatever she was going to say was going to change his destiny once more. 'My sister tells me of someone on Solvora who is like you. Someone we let survive, many years ago. And she says this woman smells of you.'

Marino stilled in the water. 'What do you mean?'

'Your magic, I assume. This woman who smells like you hides away at the far end of Solvora, in the lowlands, where the tide rises all the way to the doorways. She keeps to herself. And she makes potions, so my sisters say. The liffen bloom alone will not cure your sister. And it would not survive a journey across the sea. It is a very fragile plant.'

'So, this woman who smells like me –'

'Well, she does not smell exactly like you because you smell delicious and she smells like an old woman.'

'You think she will know what to do with the liffen bloom.'

'More than anyone else on Solvora.'

'How certain are your sisters about this woman? Why are you only telling me this now?'

Kira splashed her fin out of the water in frustration and scowled at him. 'Where is your thanks? You are lucky I told you at all. It is your choice, Captain.' Her voice dripped with disdain as she said his title, nothing like how Lana had whispered it last night. 'You can decide if you want to seek out this woman. I do not care what you do.' She turned as if to dive back down.

'Kira! Wait!' Marino reached for her arm. 'Please. I'm sorry. Of course, I meant to show my thanks. You must understand, I am overwhelmed. Your offer to help find the liffen bloom, this new information, the very fact that we are here conversing in the sea as casually as if in a sitting room. As if we speak to each other all the time.' Marino swallowed again. 'As if I too belonged to the sea.'

He expected her to throw his hand off her, he knew she was strong, stronger than him, but instead she used his arm as leverage to pull herself close to him, even closer than before, so her lips were nearly brushing against his.

Marino's arm slid around her waist on instinct.

'You do.' Kira's voice was low. 'You may live on land, you may walk on legs, but the sea always claims what belongs to her eventually. All you have now is a reprieve. So, enjoy it.'

She ran a hand from his shoulder down his arm to his hand, and then pressed her thumb into his palm. Marino felt the pressure of her thumb through his whole body, not just his hand.

'I will tell you where to meet me. Pay attention. Here is the palace and so-called King's Cove,' she said, pinching the skin between his forefinger and his thumb. Then she traced up his finger and down again, pausing between his index and his middle fingers. 'Here is where I left you after I saved you.' Then she trailed her nails up again, going all the way around his middle finger, the sensation sending chills over his whole body.

How could someone be so beautiful even behind a mask? She did not blink, her violet eyes shimmering, and he watched as her pupils changed from round to vertical, like a serpent. Her small pearl earrings, glistening in the light, seemed to wink at him. He felt dizzy with want.

Danger, warned his body, warring with the other part, the stronger part, that cried out with desire.

'And here,' she paused between his ring finger and middle, and stroked the sensitive skin there, 'here is where you'll find me. Tomorrow. At midnight, when the full moon is high. That is when the liffen will bloom, and when I can help you.'

She released him, and put her lips close to his ear. Her voice, low and melodic, like the rush of waves.

'Don't be late.'

CHAPTER 30
Kira

As Kira watched Marino swim to shore and step up on the beach, she was filled with an unfamiliar sense of longing.

She wanted to walk on the sand. More than that. She wanted to walk with him. Hand in hand, like how they had swum. She wanted to dance, not in the sea where she was weightless and free, but dance until her body was slick with sweat and her steps were in time with his and when he put his hands on her hips there would be a friction and delicious heaviness that they never had in the water. She closed her eyes for a moment, and she could almost feel him spinning her, holding her close.

In the water when they swam next to each other and she could not see his legs, only the top of him, it had felt almost as if he too were mer. The gills on his neck were a clever trick.

Maybe he could survive below. At least for a time.

But she could never survive on land. Could never follow him into whatever life he led out of the water.

Zella and Mei and all the others had always told her that this was the gift of being a mer. After all, they had each other. And if they craved more than friendship, they could take a lover for as long as they liked (unless the lovers drowned too early, which happened more often than her sisters ever admitted) or to dally with the mermen when they came through in the season. Or mer from other parts of the ocean, the ones who were not tied and trapped to Solvora. Even mermaids were not immune to each other's beauty.

We have all we want, claimed Zella.

But Kira wanted more. This wanting – sometimes it felt like it was the thing that kept her heart beating.

She knew she was supposed to be grateful for her life beneath the sea, but she felt trapped.

And Marino Pegasi, the man who seemed more than a man but not quite mer, the man who she could not get out of her head, he tasted like freedom.

When she was with him, she saw glimpses of another life. A life she desperately, desperately wanted.

A life she could never have.

Sometimes though, the way he looked at her, she felt like he was truly seeing her. Seeing beneath her mask and beyond her magic. Like he could see the very shape and shimmer of her soul.

She was being foolish. She knew that he gazed at her like that because she was mer and he was man and even without using a glamour or her song, he would be bewitched by her very existence.

What she could not explain was why she felt the same for him.

Kira floated on her back a moment, letting the sun kiss her bare stomach and warm her face, and imagined what it would be like to live a life with Marino. He was adventurous, that was certain. Brave and bold and loyal.

Her sisters told her that Solvoran mer didn't mate for life. That the pairings were for pleasure. It was impossible to ask a mer not bound to stay forever in the Solvoran ring.

And equally impossible for a human to survive underwater for a lifetime.

So, Kira kept her longings to herself. They had been hidden and tucked away inside her heart until Marino Pegasi had dripped his blood into the water and she had caught his scent – and made the decision to save him.

Whatever there was between them was different from when her mersisters took humans below, that she knew.

He cared for her, truly. He had to – why else would he risk coming back into the sea again and again? Marino must care for her.

She held on to that thought like a pearl in her hands. Why else would he have risked so much to warn her of King Leonel's impending attack?

For as long as Kira could remember, she had respected humans more than her sisters ever did. They might have been the reason they were bound within the Solvoran ring, but the humans were not their keepers.

Kira felt in her bones a knowledge that humans could harm. She'd asked Zella once, about why she could picture with such startling clarity the sharp flash of metal and the bright crimson of blood when a sword pierced through skin. *You think too much about the humans*, Zella had retorted. *Stop going above and spying on them. It is putting ideas in your head.*

Kira had seen the Solvoran soldiers catch mer before, with their hooks and their spears, but the mer were so much stronger, it rarely happened. And when it did, they made sure the islanders regretted it. The last time a mer had been caught and killed, Zella had retaliated with storms that lasted days, battering the beaches and the walls of Solvora, sending the waves as high as they would go. The others had sung song after song, enticing dozens of Solvorans to leap from the cliffs and into the angry sea.

Her sisters had not taken any of those humans as lovers. They had let them all drown as soon as they hit the water. And if any humans had seemed like they would surface, the mer had grabbed them by the ankles and pulled them under until they belonged to the sea forever.

The last mer killed had been Vero – crimson-haired, emerald-eyed Vero. The only mer who had ever talked back to Zella. Vero played pranks on her sisters and goaded them into going close to the shore. She was fearless.

Until she was dead.

After that day, after the storms Zella called down, after so many Solvorans drowned – the soldiers did not come for the mer again. No, they stayed out of the water and watched carefully from above. Biding their time and sharpening their hooks.

King Leonel thrummed with a barely contained rage behind his wide smile, and Kira could feel the vibrations from the palace all the way down the mountain to under the waves.

King Leonel had always frightened her more than the other mer. Mer didn't show fear, and Kira could put on a brave face as well as the rest of them, but she had to convince her sisters to take the Solvoran king's threat seriously.

There was a sharp tug on the edge of her tail, on the fin where the scales were sensitive, and Kira let out a yelp.

Mei was beneath her, laughing as she pulled on Kira's tail again.

Where have you been? Zella is looking for you.

With a last look at the Solvoran shore, where Marino was now scrambling up on to the sand, Kira dived down beneath the waves after her sister.

Zella and the others were waiting for her in the sea-cave. Zella looked angry, which wasn't a surprise as she was frequently angry. What was a surprise was how angry all the others looked.

Kira paused at the mouth of the cave, suddenly wary.

Mei, who wasn't laughing now, gently pushed her in towards her sisters, who began to circle her, swimming just fast enough to create a gentle current.

A deceivingly gentle current. Kira knew she couldn't swim out of it if she wanted. Zella led the swim, her eyes never leaving Kira's face.

You promised him the liffen bloom.

Her voice was loud in Kira's mind.

That is not for you to give. It belongs to us, it belongs to the sea.

But he needs it. For his sister. I can tell his want for it is pure, he doesn't want it for himself. Kira felt strangely desperate. She had promised him she'd help him, told him to meet her. *He risked his own safety coming to warn us about the king.*

He is the reason the king is now a threat to us. Before that the fool was nothing to fear.

Why is the sea-gold that Marino touches toxic to us anyway?

Because he has man magic and we are mer. The two are not meant to mix. As if we needed more proof. And as the sea-gold feeds on his magic, he feeds on it. He cannot be trusted, Kira. You should have let him drown. You should have drowned him yourself.

But I am mer, and he is man, and I want us to mix.

Kira locked her thought away before her sisters could hear it. The thought that she was glad he could call for her, that this way he could always find her in the sea, in the same way she could find him. But from the disgust that crossed Zella's face, she wondered if her sister had heard her thought after all.

You are being foolish, and you are endangering us all. Zella bared her teeth and for a moment, true fear skittered across Kira's skin. Zella wouldn't turn on her, would she? She was her sister! And Kira hadn't betrayed her sisters, not truly.

Not yet.

No! It isn't like that. He isn't like that!

You know nothing! There was a sharpness in Zella's voice, a pain that Kira had never heard before. *We have done all we can to protect you but now you leave us no choice. You are forbidden to leave this cave unless one of us is with you. You cannot be trusted around human men! You have completely lost your senses. I do not want you to lose your life as well.*

Her sisters left her then, all of them. In their wake, the current they had made still spun, keeping Kira trapped. Only Mei looked over her shoulder as they all swam out of the sea-cave.

I'm sorry. Her voice was soft in Kira's mind. *It is for the best.*

Kira fought to stay awake, wanting to swim after her sisters, wanting to say sorry, wanting them to forgive her, but her eyes were heavy, and she found herself curling up in the kelp and seaflowers, and the current, gentler now, rocked her to sleep in its watery embrace.

CHAPTER 31
Marino

Marino found himself back on the beach Kira had left him on when she'd first saved him. He lay on the sand, looking at the sky, trying to figure out what to do next.

He knew one thing. He didn't want to go back to the Gilded Palace.

He needed his own plan before he saw the king again. He would not help Leonel murder the mer.

Exhaustion made his vision blur and his mind go to mush. He would not be much use to anyone right now, not the king nor Kira. He'd closed his eyes and was about to sink into sleep right there on the sand, when a familiar voice startled him back to alertness.

'Is that Captain Marino Pegasi I see? Famed hero of Solvora? Maker of magic to defeat the mer? You've certainly been busy!' It was Samuel, and he was exactly who Marino wanted to see.

'Samuel! You have a knack for finding me when I'm in dire straits.'

The fisherman held his hand out and helped haul Marino up. 'You look like a fish left out to dry. Why aren't you up at the Gilded Palace? Whispers in the town are that you can craft gold with your mind, fly from the clifftops, swim with the mer and live to tell the tale.' Samuel squinted at Marino. 'And right now you don't look much better than when we first met.'

Marino let out a hoarse laugh. 'I can't claim truth to any of that, except swimming with the mer. And I've barely survived that, if I'm being honest.'

'Come in and have something to eat. And tell me what has happened.'

Samuel pottered around his small beach shack. The dogs barked at his feet as he ladled out a bowl of clam soup from a large bowl hanging over the fire. 'Hush, you three. This isn't for you.'

Marino accepted the bowl of soup with gratitude. The clams were fresh and floated in a clear fish broth. It tasted better than anything he'd had to eat at the Gilded Palace.

Over four bowls of the soup, he told Samuel everything. All he left out was Kira's name, because it was not his to share.

When he finished, he felt a weight lifted, and like he could sleep for a month.

Samuel let out a low whistle and stroked his long white beard. 'You've made some fine enemies here. It's an impressive feat, in such a short time.'

'How do I stop the king from attacking the mer?'

'I don't know if you can. Any more than you can stop the mer from sinking the ships. You may have magic, Marino, but you are merely one man.' He got up and patted Marino on the shoulder. 'One tired man. You should get some rest here before you do anything.'

'I need to find Lana. I don't know where she's gone. It is

odd that she disappeared without saying anything.'

Samuel shrugged, seemingly unperturbed. 'She probably saw how exhausted you were and wanted to do you a favour by letting you get some sleep. Which you need more of! How can you save Solvora and your sister if you are draining yourself dry?'

'I don't want to let anyone down,' Marino admitted.

'You won't,' said Samuel with such conviction that Marino believed it.

'Why are you so kind to me?' he asked.

Samuel offered a sad smile. 'I had a son. He was lost to the sea a long time ago. You remind me of him.'

'I am honoured,' said Marino. And he was. So much so that he was almost overwhelmed by it. He thought of his own father, the royal physician who had distanced himself from his children after his wife disappeared. How sometimes he felt like his father didn't know him. How he wanted to mend their relationship when he made it back to Eana. 'Thank you, Samuel.'

'I'm just an old man doing what I can.'

Marino stifled a yawn.

'Sailor, get some sleep. You can stay here as long as you need. And then go fight your battles.'

'I might rest here, just for a moment,' said Marino, yawning now in earnest. Samuel chuckled and Marino closed his eyes, not caring that the wooden chair he sat in was deeply uncomfortable, only glad to be able to sleep.

Marino slept through what was left of the day, and deep into the night.

He woke just after dawn with a crick in his neck from sleeping sitting up. Samuel was already up, sitting in the corner and mending one of his fishing nets.

'Good morning,' he said. 'You slept like the dead. At one point I thought you *had* gone and died on me.'

Marino stretched. 'I did not mean to sleep so long.'

'I'm glad you did,' said Samuel, giving him a smile that crinkled his entire face. 'And while you dreamed of baked goods and mermaids, I remembered something. You said the mer mentioned a woman here on Solvora, who might have magic like you. I know who it is. She lives in the lowlands, keeps to herself, except when Solvorans seek her out in the night.'

'What do they go to her for?'

'She knows how to brew potions for all kinds of things. But more than that, supposedly she can tell your future,' said Samuel. 'Lovesick girls go to her to find out who their true love is. Couples who want to have a baby. Farmers, curious about their crops for the year. I myself went once.'

'What did you ask?'

Samuel looked down at his fishing net. 'If my boy would ever come back to me.'

Marino went to the old man and covered his wrinkled, gnarled hand with his own, knowing the answer before Samuel continued to speak.

'She told me what I already knew but didn't want to believe.' Samuel let out a long sigh. 'That was the last time I saw her. But I remember her name. Her name is Dove.'

Marino felt strangely disappointed. He knew nobody named Dove, had never heard of anyone with the name. No mention from Thea of a person named Dove. But then, it was impossible for him to have heard the name of every witch who had ever left Eana.

'I'm surprised King Leonel allows someone with some sort of seeing ability to live such a quiet life,' he said aloud to cover his disappointment.

'Oh, I doubt the king has any idea who she is. I think she keeps it that way on purpose. Wise of her, if you ask me. The king always wants to use people for his own gain.'

'And you know where to find her?'

'Let me draw you a map. I'd go with you, but as you know, these old knees aren't what they used to be, and if I went to the lowlands, I don't think I'd ever make it back here.' Samuel turned to Bones, who was sleeping at his feet, and rubbed him behind his ears. 'And who would feed my dogs then?'

After Samuel had drawn Marino a map of where he could find Dove, Marino went to Sugar Street.

He was hoping Lana could come with him to meet her. To find out if Dove would know what to do with the liffen bloom.

And more than that, he was worried about Lana. What if she still wasn't there?

By the time he had made it back to Sugar Street, the sun had fully risen. And when he arrived at Lana's bakery and pushed on the door, it swung open with ease.

Feeling a slight trepidation, Marino stepped inside. 'Hello?' he called. 'Lana?'

There was a scuffle from the direction of the kitchen, and Lana appeared in her blue apron, hair tied back and a wide grin on her face.

'There you are!' She stepped towards him, almost as if she was going to wrap her arms around him, but then stopped right before she did, as if she had realised how forward that would be.

Marino had no such qualms, and closed the distance between them, taking her in his arms. She let out a contented sigh and closed her eyes as she lay her head on his shoulder. He could feel her breath on his neck, and it took a great deal of willpower to not pick up where they had left off the other night.

'Where did you go?' he asked, still relishing in the feeling of holding her close. 'Yesterday morning?'

Lana looked up at him, her brow furrowing with confusion. 'I should be asking you the same thing. I didn't go anywhere. I woke up and you were gone.' She poked him on his chest.

Marino let go of her and stepped back. 'Lana, you weren't there. I was alone. And the bakery door was locked . . .' His voice trailed off.

'Because I was still here.' She shrugged, seemingly unbothered by his claims. 'Perhaps I was relieving myself.' She flushed. 'In which case I am certainly glad you didn't look too hard for me! But how did you get out? The door was locked when I came downstairs. Did you leap out of a window?'

Marino ran a hand over his jaw. 'Ah. Well, you aren't going to like the answer to this.'

Haltingly, he told her about how he had made the decision to swim back to the shore and told her how he had found Kira.

He left out the part about how he had called for Kira, how he had sought her out. He didn't want to think about the feelings that Kira stirred in him, not when he was here basking in Lana's warmth.

'Marino, how could you?' Lana sounded horrified, and Marino didn't blame her. 'I saw those other mer trying to enchant you. You are lucky this one hadn't come to finish the job the others had started!'

'This one, she's the one who saved me.' Marino watched Lana's face carefully, to see how she responded to this. 'I don't think she'd drown me. She's helped me before, and she's helping me again. She's promised to take me to where the liffen bloom is.'

'And you believe her?' Lana scoffed. 'Don't be a fool, Marino.'

'It's the best chance I have of finding the plant.' Marino took Lana's hands in his own. 'She told me something else. Something about a woman who smells like magic, who smells like me, who lives at the far end of Solvora. In the lowlands.'

Lana wrinkled her nose. 'Strange. And how does she know what you smell like?'

Marino chuckled. 'The mer have heightened senses. It's what makes them such good hunters.'

'Hmph. Odd for her to note your scent all the same. Although I will admit you do smell nice.'

Marino put his hand on the small of Lana's back, pulling her closer to him. 'Do I?'

She laughed and swatted his chest. 'I said it once and I won't say it again. But back to this woman she told you of. I don't understand. Even if she supposedly smells like you, which seems impossible and strange, why is this mer sending you after her?'

'She said that the liffen bloom alone, though seemingly key to the cure, isn't enough. The plant needs to be prepared in some kind of potion, and this woman knows how to do that.'

'Sounds like a trick or a trap.'

'But Lana, I asked Samuel, the old fisherman who took me in when I first washed up in Solvora, and he knew of her as well.'

'I have never heard of such a person.'

'A woman who lives in the lowlands, who sometimes is a kind of healer, or so Samuel says.'

'Oh!' Lana's hand flew to her mouth. 'I *do* know who she is! Benedita visited her once, when I was very ill as a child. But Marino, I don't know where to find her.'

'Samuel does. He's drawn me a map.' Marino pulled the folded-up map out of his pocket, carefully opening it.

'I wouldn't call this a map.' Lana wrinkled her brow as she studied the paper.

'He's a fisherman not a cartographer,' said Marino, with a fond chuckle. 'But look. We're here, and Samuel thinks that this woman, Dove is her name, is here.'

'Well then, what are we waiting for?'

Marino glanced up at Lana. Her eyes were bright and shining, and she was grinning at him. 'You want to come with me?'

'Of course! Marino, you must know I'm in with you now on this quest.' She slipped her hand into his. 'I'm part of your crew whether you like it or not. If finding this woman is as key as finding the liffen bloom, well, then we'll do it together.'

Marino basked in the warmth of her smile. Having Lana by his side made him feel like he could face anything, do anything.

He never wanted to lose that feeling.

He never wanted to lose *her*.

CHAPTER 32
Marino

The Solvoran lowlands stretched out like the train of a gown.

Marino and Lana walked through fields of towering sunflowers and sweet-smelling lavender. Past orange groves and cherry orchards, wheat fields and vegetable patches.

'This is what sustains Solvora,' Lana said, stopping to pull a few cherries off a nearby branch. 'Since we cannot trade, we must grow everything ourselves.' She tossed a cherry to Marino, before biting into the one in her hand.

Marino watched, unable to look away, as a trickle of red cherry juice spilled down her lips, and all he wanted was to kiss it all off her. She caught his gaze and laughed. 'What?'

'You've got a little bit of cherry juice, right here.' He leaned closer and swept his thumb across her lower lip. 'Got it.' They stared at each other a long moment, her chest rising with every breath, and then he remembered they were in a hurry, they had to find the so-called Solvoran witch in time for him to return to the cove to meet Kira tonight.

The thought of meeting Kira while standing so close to Lana made Marino's head spin, and he took a step back to get a breath of air that didn't smell so strongly of Lana's sugared scent.

He cleared his throat. 'And the dairy? And the meat? Where does that come from?'

Lana too took a step back, and Marino felt an idiot for bringing up cows when he could have been kissing her, but if he stopped to kiss her every time he wanted to, they would never make it through the lowlands.

She pointed past the fields where there were dozens of squat, square buildings. Unlike the colourful buildings on Goldwave Mountain, these were plain, made of wood. 'The cows and chickens and pigs are all reared on the eastern side of the lowlands. I can show you another day, if you like? Jonah and Carlos used to take me as a child.' She laughed. 'Until I kept naming the animals meant for slaughter and crying when I found out their fate. I think that is the reason I still don't eat much meat, even now. I prefer my cakes.'

'Fair enough,' said Marino. 'So, you were always a kind-hearted soul, it sounds.'

'I did spend a lot of my childhood trying to heal every injured animal I came across,' Lana admitted with a laugh. As they walked, she told him of the gull with the broken wing she'd kept on her balcony, the one-eyed cat she'd nursed back to health and the turtle she had guided back into the sea. With every story she told, every word she said, Marino found himself falling more and more for her.

It frightened him, how much he cared for her. He'd never felt like this before, about anyone.

Finally, they were on the far edge of the lowlands, right where Samuel's map said they could find Dove's cottage.

And sure enough, there was one lone dwelling close to the cliffside, overlooking the sea. It was painted green, and the colour reminded Marino of the Eanan flag.

He paused at the door.

'Go on,' urged Lana, but before Marino could knock the door swung open.

A woman stood before him. She had dark brown skin, and curly black hair shot through with white. She was much older than Marino, her face wrinkled and kind.

The last time Marino had seen her face, it had been smooth. But her eyes were the same – brown and bright. He had never forgotten what her eyes looked like.

He stared at her, unable to believe what he was seeing.

It was his mother.

Marino stood in the doorway to the cottage, feeling like all the wind had been knocked out of him. He felt like he was in a dream.

His mother stared back at him, her expression mirroring his own shock. He had never imagined being taller than his mother, and now he towered over her.

Lana let out a small polite cough. 'Hello!' she said brightly, clearly unaware of Marino's inner turmoil. How was his mother here? How was this possible? Lana continued to speak, stepping forward to put her hand on Marino's arm. She gave it a supportive squeeze that he barely felt. 'We're so sorry to bother you, but we were hoping you could help us. We were told you have a gift with potions.'

But the woman in the door wasn't looking at Lana. She

was staring at Marino. She raised a shaking hand to his face.

'Marino? Can it be?' Her voice was exactly as Marino remembered. Low and musical.

'It's Celeste,' Marino blurted out. 'Mama, Celeste is dying.'

His mother swayed on her feet, and Marino caught her before she fell.

'Mama! Are you all right?' He steadied her, helping her stand.

His mother had her hand to her chest. 'My heart. I need to quiet my heart. Come in, both of you.' She glanced at Lana. 'You are Solvoran, are you not?'

Lana's eyes were wide with shock. 'Yes. Yes, I am.'

His mother looked back to Marino. 'And you trust her, this Solvoran girl?'

'With my life,' Marinos said solemnly. And he meant it.

His mother raised a warning finger towards Lana. 'Tell no one what you see or hear today.'

'Of course,' said Lana, as they stepped into the small cottage behind Marino's mother. Marino closed the door behind them, and for a moment they all stared at each other. Marino's heart was in his throat.

'Sit down,' said his mother, pointing to the worn sofa in the corner of the cottage. She sat and patted the spot next to her. Marino sat beside her in a daze.

'Is it true? Is it really you?' Marino still felt as if he was standing in a dream, or a memory, or a wish that he'd had as a child. 'Mama?'

A tear slid down his mother's cheek. 'I could ask you the same thing. How did you end up on Solvora?'

'You've been here, all this time?'

His mother nodded, her tears coming faster now. 'I never meant to be gone so long. I was always going to come back, but then . . .' Her voice trailed off.

'Nobody can leave Solvora,' Lana chimed in. She was still standing, and when Marino's mother looked up at her, Lana dropped into a slightly awkward curtsy, holding her apron. 'Sorry to interrupt. I can leave. I should leave.'

But Marino wanted her there. More than that, he needed her there. 'Please stay,' he said.

'If my son wants you to stay –' at the word son, Marino felt a wave of nostalgia and loss roll over him – 'I want you to stay too. But tell me, who are you?'

'My name is Lana. Lana Dawn.'

Marino's mother smiled. 'Like Anadawn?'

'That's what I said.' Marino chuckled, grateful to have a moment of brevity.

'A strange coincidence, certainly,' Lana said, smiling back. 'I work in the bakery on Sugar Street.'

'With Benedita? She helped me once when I needed it.'

Lana's smile faltered, just slightly. 'Benedita died last spring.'

'May her spirit go to the stars,' said Marino's mother, lifting her eyes, even though there was a ceiling above them.

'I think she'd rather it go to the sea,' Lana said in a quiet voice.

'Ah, like my Marino then.' Her mother turned to him. 'You loved the sea, even as a boy. I knew one day you'd take to the seas. I knew it before you were born.'

'Because you are a seer.' Marino said it plainly, like the fact he now knew it to be.

His mother's eyes widened. 'You know about that?'

Marino took his mother's hands in his own. 'Mama, the witches are free now in Eana. Nobody has to hide. There are twin queen witches on the throne.'

A small sound of shock escaped his mother. 'I saw it . . . but I did not know when it would happen.'

'Celeste is a seer too. That's why . . .' Marino had a sudden lump in his throat that was hard to speak around. 'That's why I've come to Solvora.'

His mother raised her hand to her mouth in horror. 'She has the seeing sickness, doesn't she?'

'Did you foresee that too?' asked Marino.

His mother shook his head. 'No. Because I too had it, a long time ago. It is why I left. And why I came to Solvora.'

Understanding dawned on Marino. 'You were looking for the cure. And you found it.' His heart began to pound. 'Do you have it still?' Perhaps he didn't even need the help of the mer.

'Oh, Marino, I wish I did. More than anything. But that was years ago. Something like that doesn't last. The potion that cures the seeing sickness must be made using the ingredients right away, and then administered as soon as possible.'

Disappointment landed, heavy on Marino's shoulders. But at least he could confirm one thing. 'And was it the liffen bloom?'

'Yes! How did you know?'

'Lana helped me,' said Marino. 'But you must have had the mer help you?'

His mother shook her head. 'The seaswifts guided me to it. When my ship sank, I dived down, following them. I nearly drowned.'

'I knew I should have followed them!' Marino stood and paced, unable to contain his frustration. 'They dived down deep and I wanted to follow them but my crew said it was too dangerous.' He cursed. 'If I had swum after them that day, we might have found the cure and never even needed to come to Solvora.'

'Marino,' said his mother suddenly. 'Your crew. I think I have seen them.'

'What? Where?' Marino looked out of the window, as if his crew was hiding in the bushes.

'No. I've seen them. In a vision. I saw your ship go down. And it terrified me. I thought I'd seen you drown. But I never imagined it would have been here, in Solvora.'

'Tell me of my crew,' said Marino. 'Please.'

His mother closed her eyes, and Marino knew she was trying to recall the vision.

'They are trapped. In a stone dungeon.' She held out a hand, turning invisible pages, as if she was sifting through scenes. 'A red-haired girl, a man with freckles, and a big man, blonde. They are dirty, and hungry, but together.' Her eyes opened. 'I don't know when it is. My visions, they come in pieces.'

'It must be the Gilded Palace dungeons,' said Lana. 'I've never been to them, but I've heard of them.'

'If my crew is there, I will find them,' Marino said, and he meant it. 'But Mama, tonight I need to find the liffen bloom. A mer has promised to help me.'

His mother raised her brows. 'And you believe her? Marino, I've lived on Solvora long enough to know that the mer are not to be trusted. I've seen them drown men, I've seen them take a human down below for weeks on end and bring them back up and that person is never the same. You think a mer will help you?'

'Mama, you survived, didn't you? The mer could have drowned you, and they didn't. Maybe they sensed your magic, maybe it was something else. They don't drown everyone. A mer saved me. My ship went down, my crew made it into a rowboat, but I was alone in the sea, and I would have drowned, but a mer took me to shore.'

Lana took his hand and squeezed it, and when Marino looked down at their intertwined fingers, for a moment he saw Kira's hand in his. He shook his head, trying to shake Kira from his mind. 'I don't trust all the mer, but I trust one. The one who saved me. And she has promised to bring me to the liffen plant. It will blossom tonight, under the full moon.'

His mother gave him a wobbly smile. 'I don't want to lose you just after I've found you.' She let out a creaky laugh. 'Or, I suppose, after you've found me.'

'Mama, we thought you were dead.' Marino spoke plainly, the pain of having a missing mother making his words sharp.

His mother closed her eyes again. 'I don't blame you. I should have told you.' Her eyes fluttered open and she locked eyes with Marino. 'But I thought it would be quick. I thought I'd be gone a week at most. I saw the seeing sickness coming, and at the first sign of it, I left. I knew I wouldn't have much time before I succumbed to it, before I was too weak. And I couldn't tell your father that I was a witch. You remember what it was like for anyone who showed any kind of magical gift.'

'Father didn't know?' How could his mother have been

married to someone who wasn't aware of such a fundamental part of herself?

She shook her head. 'He worked so closely with the Kingsbreath. And you know how he hated the witches. My greatest fear was that the gift would show in you or Celeste.' His mother rubbed her temples. 'That was the future I was scrying for, to see when your gift would manifest. I knew, Marino, my Marino, I knew you were destined for the sea, just as I knew Celeste would want to look to the stars. I didn't need a vision to tell me that. Imagine my surprise, when instead of seeing your future, I saw my own. I saw the seeing sickness, I saw Solvora. And I knew it was a fate I could not escape. I remembered when the seeing sickness had struck, when I was your age. I could not be the one to bring that to my people, and I could not risk bringing it to you. So I waited as long as I could, until I began to feel the first signs of it. And then I left.'

'It happened so fast for Celeste.' Marino closed his own eyes now, remembering. 'She was on the roof, watching the starcrests. She was looking for my future. It's my fault.'

'Marino.'

At his mother's voice, he opened his eyes. 'It is not your fault. Do not blame yourself. Look how far you have come for your sister.' Her voice broke. 'I am proud to know that I raised a son who would look after his sister with so much devotion. I am proud that my daughter is such an accomplished seer.'

'And not just a seer,' said Marino. 'Mama, the witch queens broke the hold on our magic. Now every witch can access all five strands. Tempest magic is my core power, what came first to me and most naturally, but I can heal and

I can fight and enchant, and even see.'

'It cannot be!' His mother held out her hands and studied them. 'For years, I've dabbled as a healer, but are you saying I now have the healing strand?'

'You do indeed. It might take practice, but you do.'

'Marino. If you find the liffen bloom, and I prepare it for you, how will you leave Solvora? How will *we* leave?'

Marino's mind was whirling. 'I can stop the mer. I can stop them with the sea-gold. My magic, it turns the sea-gold against them. And with you, we will be able to coat a whole ship in sea-gold and then the mer won't be able to touch us.'

His mother let out a sharp laugh. 'And where will we get a ship? And all the sea-gold you need for your grand plan?'

Marino's gaze sharpened. 'King Leonel will give me what I need.'

'Will he now? All my years here, and the king has never seemed a good man.'

'Because he isn't,' Lana said. She'd been quiet, listening to Marino and his mother. Taking it all in. But now she spoke. 'Pardon my curiosity, but why do the Solvorans call you Dove?'

Marino's mother smiled. 'I chose that name for myself when I arrived. When I realised the truth of Solvora, when I knew I was trapped, I chose Dove. Doves always fly back, you see. And that was my promise to myself. I'd always fly back. And after a time, Salome died inside of me, and I became only Dove.'

'Dove Salome,' said Lana. 'That is who you are. Of Eana and Solvora.'

'So I am,' said Dove. She patted Marino on the knee.

'You've found a good one here, son.'

Then she grew serious. 'If tonight is your chance to get the liffen bloom, you must go. Once you have it, bring it to me. I remember how to turn it into the cure Celeste will need. And then we must leave as soon as possible.' She squinted at her son. 'What makes you so confident that the king will help you?'

'Oh, he will,' said Marino, and his voice was strong. 'King Leonel needs me and my magic. He will not deny me.'

CHAPTER 33
Marino

Marino had not wanted to leave his mother so soon after finding her, but she had insisted he return to the Gilded Palace to speak to King Leonel, to secure a ship and, most importantly, not to miss meeting Kira.

Marino spent the walk back to Sugar Street in a daze. He was glad Lana was by his side, that she was leading them through the fields and back up Goldwave Mountain. She was quiet, occasionally glancing at him as if making sure he was still there, still breathing, and squeezing his hand to pull him back into the present.

His mother was alive.

His mother was alive.

She'd been alive – and trapped – all this time.

Marino's head spun with the impossibility of it – the dream he and Celeste had shared as children coming true.

Now, more than ever, he needed to save his sister, so they could all be reunited.

The seaswifts had led him here, to Solvora, to his mother, to Lana and to Kira and the cure. Marino understood that he had always been fated to find Solvora, that the threads of his destiny would have pulled him here, one way or another.

He only needed to make sure those same threads had not tied him here too tightly, that he could leave Solvora and take what he had found, and who he had found, back home with him.

He felt a pang for Kira, because she couldn't leave the Solvoran ring. She would be here long after he left. He wondered if she'd ever think about him when he was gone.

He shouldn't be thinking about Kira though, not when Lana was there next to him, and had been there for him when the shock of seeing his mother had nearly laid him flat. Not when she was looking at him with such care and radiating with kindness.

But he knew that Kira had pierced his heart, as if she'd done it with her sharp nails, that he couldn't dislodge her even if he wanted to. And he didn't want to.

When Marino and Lana reached Lana's bakery, he paused, shaking Kira out of his head and focusing on the girl in front of him. The girl who was right for him. The girl who he couldn't imagine being without. Marino kissed her on the mouth, just once and swiftly.

'Sleep well, Lana. I must visit the king. If my mother's vision is correct, if my crew are truly prisoners in the Gilded Palace, I must demand their release. Immediately.' He looked up at the sky, where the sun was just starting to set. 'And then I must return to the sea, to find the mer who promised to help me.'

'I wish I could go with you. What if it is a trap?'

'I have to try. This is my only chance to get the liffen bloom in time.'

'Be careful.' Lana squeezed his arm. 'And when it is done, when you have the flower, come as soon as you can. It doesn't matter how late. I want to know that you are all right.'

'I will be fine.' Marino smiled down at Lana. 'Do not worry about me.' Then his smile faded. She looked wan, her golden-tanned skin paler than usual, and there was a sheen of sweat on her forehead. 'I should be worried about *you*. Are you feeling all right?'

Lana nodded and let out a long breath. 'I'm just a little dizzy. I think a headache might be coming on.'

'I'm sorry. It is my fault. I made you trek across the whole island with me.'

'Marino. I am not some weakling. It is the weather that triggers the headaches, or something I've eaten. Do not blame yourself.'

Marino cupped her face with his palm. 'Well, at the very least, I can try to help.' He sent her a burst of healing magic, and she closed her eyes with a blissful sigh. A little bit of colour came back into her face.

'Thank you,' she breathed, her eyes fluttering open. 'I must say, you are very useful to have around.'

Marino doffed an imaginary hat towards her. 'I aim to please.' He was glad though, that he was able to ease some of her pain. He pressed a last kiss to her temple and then watched her go inside the bakery, hearing the lock sliding into place behind the sturdy door.

Then he strode up Goldwave Mountain, determined not to leave the palace until he had answers from King Leonel.

'I must speak to the king. Immediately.'

The Solvoran guards standing in front of the throne room door exchanged a look.

'The king is not to be disturbed,' said one. There was a loud crash from behind the door, followed by an angry bellow, but the guards did not seem alarmed.

'He will want to see me,' Marino insisted. 'Were you not at the ball? He *needs* me to defeat the mer. Me and my magic.' Marino's hands twitched at his side at the mere mention of his magic. He knew he could call on his warrior strand if he needed to, and could take on these two guards, but he didn't know if he could fight every soldier in the palace if it came to it.

But, whatever it took, he was getting into that throne room.

Then the door opened from the inside, and there stood Talia, wearing a flowing orange gown. Her eyes were bright with a strange, glittering mania that put Marino on edge.

She reached out between the guards and took Marino's hand in her own.

'I thought I heard you,' she said, her voice breathy. 'We've been waiting for you.'

Marino fought the urge to drop her hand and run out of the palace, back to Lana, back to his mother, away from this place that suddenly smelled so rotten.

But he needed to save his crew. If what his mother had seen was true.

So, he stepped in after Talia, readying himself for anything.

King Leonel was standing in front of a shattered window, glass shining on the marble floors, the last of the sunset streaming in. He was staring down to the sea with a fury that Marino could almost feel in the air. Next to him, a solider he didn't recognise was holding what appeared to be a giant harpoon, coated in sea-gold.

Marino assessed the situation quickly. It seemed as if the soldier had shot the harpoon accidentally, and the weapon had shattered the glass.

As if Marino needed any further proof that the sea-gold weapons should not fall into King Leonel's hands.

'Careful with that,' he said dryly, getting the king's attention.

'Where have you been?' snapped Leonel, stalking towards Marino. 'You disappeared at my ball. I thought the mer had snared you!'

'You thought wrong,' Marino said, as he took in the mess in the throne room. Buckets of sea-gold and piles of weapons, swords and hooks and spears. Weapons to slay the mer.

'We are preparing for the hunt,' Talia explained. She was close to him suddenly, too close. Marino stifled the urge to shove her away. 'You have arrived at the perfect time. We need you to help awaken the rest of the sea-gold.'

'I will do no such thing,' growled Marino.

Leonel stared at him and began to laugh his booming laugh. 'Marino. Marino. Marino! Do you fancy yourself my new court jester? I will coat my weapons in sea-gold or in the blood of that girl you brought to the ball. I know where she lives, remember? Your choice.' The king shrugged.

In one movement, Marino had called on his warrior strand of magic and he hoisted the king up by his collar. 'Do not threaten her. Do not even think of her.'

'Unhand me!' shouted King Leonel. But Marino made no move to do so, overwhelmed with hatred for the man who had threatened Lana, was trying to control Marino and had imprisoned his crew.

'Where are my crew?' he growled. 'I know you found them.'

King Leonel let out a wheeze of a laugh. 'Oh, well done, Captain. It took you long enough. Now put me down and I'll tell you of your ragtag crew.'

Marino threw the king to the floor.

Leonel merely cackled. 'We found them in a rowboat. A boat without you. How is that for loyalty?'

Talia stepped forward to help Leonel up. 'The boat of your little crew crashed on the shore. Our soldiers found them before they even found you and hauled them in for questioning. Oh, I could tell right away they were not the ones we were waiting for, that they had survived but that they were not *survivors*. No. They stank of sweat and fear and they had nothing special about them. Nothing like you, Marino. But still, still I told King Leonel. Don't kill them yet. Keep them, just in case.'

Marino held back his rising rage. 'And where, exactly, have you been keeping them?'

'They've been here all along. In the Gilded Palace. They aren't in as nice quarters as you, of course, but they are given daily meals. There is a roof over their heads. A bit of a damp roof, but a roof all the same. I could have killed them, but I didn't. So, they are in the dungeons,' Leonel flashed his teeth in a horrible imitation of a smile, 'where they will stay if you don't do as I say.'

Marino felt his magic bubbling up inside of him, and he wanted nothing more than to call on his tempest strand and use the wind to throw this pitiful excuse of a man straight into the sea. But he stayed still, he stayed calm.

'I suppose I should be thanking you for saving my crew. For keeping them alive. And for that I do thank you. As I thank you for your generosity towards me.' Marino gestured down at the fine clothes he was wearing. 'You have clothed and fed me. Have welcomed me with open arms. And again, for that I give you thanks.'

Now Marino called on the wind, and it rushed in the broken window as if it had been waiting, and it howled through the throne room.

Leonel's eyes widened and he tried to stand, but the wind was too strong, it kept him hunched in his chair, pushing harder on him until he was practically bent double, until he might have been bowing to Marino.

Talia sat very still, did not fight the wind, did not push back against it as it kept her in her chair. She merely shuddered once, as she had when she'd pricked her finger on the sea-gold. The soldier at the table, who Marino did not need nor care to know the name of, had sat in a stunned silence the whole time, and might have been made of stone.

With a whisk of his wrist, another strong wind came through the shattered window and this time it came towards Marino and lifted him up. Marino rose in the air effortlessly, as if he was flying, and he looked down on the king. 'But I do not bend to your whims and wishes. I am not Solvoran. And I owe you nothing.'

The wind was moving so fast now in the room that the paintings were shaking on the walls, and the windows that had not been broken, now shattered all at once, raining broken glass down upon the king.

Marino's voice boomed amid the howling wind. 'You will not harm my crew, you will give me a ship. And in return,

I will spare you my wrath. And I will find a way to free both the Solvorans and the mer from the hold the Solvoran ring has on you all. That, I promise you. And I have never broken a vow.'

Marino summoned a final strand of wind, and flew out of the window, leaving the king, his soldier and his soothsayer gaping in awe.

CHAPTER 34
Marino

As Marino made his way down the cliff, he found himself wishing yet again that the Gilded Palace was not *quite* so high up. The wind he had summoned had been enough to assist in his dramatic exit but it had quickly abated when he was out hovering over the cliffs themselves. Even a witch could only control the wind so much.

So he had landed, less gracefully than he would have hoped, and then took the worn steps two at a time, hurrying just in case the king sent someone out after him.

Marino could not forget the awed fury in the king's eyes when he had turned on him. Or forgive the fact that his crew were currently Leonel's prisoners.

At least they were alive. He held that fact close and it spurred him on, and he picked up his pace going down the cobblestone streets. He would find the liffen bloom, he would find a ship, he would save his crew, and he would return to Eana. With his mother. He would return home. And save his sister.

He repeated the mantra to himself until he reached the King's Cove.

A part of him wanted to go back to the Gilded Palace and

break into the dungeons by whatever means necessary and rescue his crew there and then . . . but tonight was his only chance to get the liffen bloom.

Hold tight, he thought to his crew as he looked over his shoulder at the Gilded Palace. *I'll come and find you soon. I'll get you out. I'll get you home.*

Then Marino turned back to the sea and prepared himself for whatever was waiting for him beneath the waves. He was in snug breeches, good for swimming, and he stripped off his shirt, leaving it on the sand, before diving into the waves. The water was cold and bracing, and he felt like it was pushing him back, back, back to shore, but he pressed on, swimming hard until he was past the break. He was already fatigued from using so much magic in the throne room. It had perhaps been a bit over the top, but he needed to make it clear to King Leonel that he was master of his own fate, his own destiny, and that he would no longer bow to him or be told what he could or could not do with his own magic.

He swam around the bend, until he couldn't see the Gilded Palace any more, when its shadow no longer stretched out across the sea. He remembered how Kira had taken his hand in her own, how her nails had been long and sharp but her fingers gentle, as she had outlined his hand, stopping between his ring and middle finger, showing him where to meet her.

He only hoped she would be the only mer he would find tonight.

Not the first cove, he thought as he kept going, swimming parallel to the shore, far enough out not to be pushed against the rocky cliffs. As he moved through the water, it began to glow.

His shoulders and his arms began to ache from the effort of swimming so far, but he was determined.

Then he saw the second cove, the one where Kira had promised to meet him.

What if it was a trap? The thought briefly crossed his mind. But the truth was, he trusted Kira. Perhaps that meant he was losing his grip on reality, but he couldn't shake his faith in her.

Or perhaps he was confusing trust and lust and he was swimming to his death.

But she could have drowned him time and time again, and yet every time she had saved him.

And if it was a trap? Well, he was no ordinary man. He was Marino Pegasi. Captain of his own ship, of his own destiny. He had saltwater in his veins sure as any mer. He was a witch from Eana gifted with the five strands of magic. He would not be so easy to kill.

So, with one wary look back at the shore, he took a deep breath, and dived down deep.

Hours later, Marino burst out of the water, gasping. He'd been diving, going deeper and deeper each time, using his magic to propel him and help his lungs hold air for longer, and there had been no sign of Kira, nor any mer.

Where was she? Why couldn't he find her? She had promised him she'd be here. Had he mixed up the time? Confused the coves? Feeling desperate, he swam back out to sea, and into the next cove. Was this the one she meant?

He had to find her. Without her he would never find the

liffen plant, and she'd said that it only bloomed by the light of the full moon. It was a cloudy night, but he was sure it was a full moon.

Don't forget who you are, he heard Willa's voice in his head. *You are a witch, Marino Pegasi, and it is time you prove yourself.*

Still treading water, he lifted one of his hands out of the sea and focused. He grabbed at a wisp of wind and, using his tempest magic, started to direct the wind towards the clouds. He'd make the moon appear, if that's what he needed to find the liffen bloom.

At least he knew what the plant looked like, thanks to Lana and her books.

Lana. At the thought of her he was filled with longing, and he glanced up towards the direction of her window, hoping for a glimpse of her. How could he yearn for her, and her kindness and her laughter and her light, all while burning for Kira, who was wild and dark and awoke something in him he had never felt before?

How could he tell Lana that perhaps a mermaid did have a hold on him, and maybe it was magic and maybe it wasn't, but that Lana had a hold on him too?

Both were helping him in their own ways. Lana, who had identified the liffen plant was what he sought. Kira, who could find it. He needed them both.

He *wanted* them both.

He was a fool and he needed to focus. If Kira did not come, then he would have to find the liffen plant himself. Lana had said that it grew deep along the seabed and shone under the light of a full moon. 'Impossible to miss,' she'd read from one of the plant journals.

Marino let out another frustrated breath and glanced

back at the cliff behind him, as if he could draw strength from merely seeing Lana's window, where she slept and dreamed.

Then he frowned and squinted, trying to see more clearly in the dark. For what he saw didn't make any sense.

There was a floating white shape moving down the cliffside, that hadn't been there before. Marino's frown deepened, and he swam closer to get a better look. For a moment, he thought he was looking at a ghost. A ghost in a billowing white dress. But then the wind changed direction, pressing the dress against the figure and blowing her long black hair back. The figure stepped fully into the golden moonlight, and then he was sure. It was Lana. And she was halfway down the cliff in the middle of the night. She walked with a strange gait, appearing almost weightless. He knew from the time he'd spent on her balcony that the steps were steep and slippery, carved into the cliff itself.

'Lana!' he cried, but she showed no sign of hearing him. She kept walking, and now that she was closer to the sea, closer to him, he could see that her eyes were closed.

He remembered her saying she sometimes walked in her sleep. Was this what was happening? He called out to her again and again, and when she didn't respond in any way, a cold that had nothing to do with the night air or the ocean water began to seep into him.

Was she possessed? Were the mer calling her with a song only she could hear?

He began to swim in earnest, desperate to get to her. She was nearly at the bottom of the cliffs. Then she paused, and swayed on her feet, before tumbling head first into the water below.

With an anguished cry, Marino swam faster, slicing through the water. But by the time he reached where the water slammed against the cliffs, there was no sign of her.

She had to be somewhere. He had to be able to see that white nightgown, even in the dark water. She couldn't have sunk so quickly. He would find her, he would heal her, he would save her.

Lana!

Time lost meaning as he dived down again and again. He tried to do the same spell he had done the day before, to enchant himself gills so he could swim deep, but he had no earth, only seawater that slipped through his frantic hands. Marino knew that if she did not resurface soon, it would be too late. Even with his healing magic, he could not bring someone back from the dead. And someone could only stay underwater for so long.

Then, there was a movement next to him and he thought he would weep with relief.

But it was not Lana.

Kira was rising out of the water, lips quirked in amusement. 'What are you shouting about? You'll wake the whole ocean.' She wore her usual seaflower mask – behind it her eyes were twinkling. She nudged him with her shoulder, still smirking.

'Kira! Thank the stars you are here.' Marino gripped her by the shoulders, forgetting himself, forgetting decorum in his panic, in his hope that Kira could find Lana beneath the waves.

Kira let out an incredulous snort, shrugging her way out of his grip. 'And where else would I be? You are the one not at our arranged meeting place.'

'Kira. Kira. I need you to listen. There is a girl, she was walking down the cliffs, and she fell. She fell into the sea. I think she was sleepwalking. We have to find her. We have to save her.'

Kira scrunched her face up in distaste. 'I do not make a habit of saving humans, Captain.'

'You saved me. And I'm asking you to save her too. I'm begging you.' Marino's voice broke. Kira had never looked so unhuman as she did in that moment, staring back at him with no sympathy, no kindness.

'If she walked into the sea on her own accord, then she belongs to the sea. Those are the rules.'

'Then break the damned rules!' Marino roared. 'She is somewhere in this sea and I must find her!'

Kira's eyes narrowed behind her mask. 'You think that you can command me? That you can make demands of me? Your fate is in my hands, human. It is only by my grace that you have survived this long on Solvora.'

Marino had the sudden and sickening realisation that Kira was not going to help him. That every moment they spent arguing was another moment that Lana was underwater without air, another moment closer to her death. He let out a long breath. Anger was not going to get him anywhere.

'Please, Kira. Please. I will give you anything.'

'You have already promised me this,' Kira hissed. 'Told me you will give me anything. You begged me to help you find the liffen plant, to save your beloved sister. And I have angered my sisters, gone against them to help you. I have met you here under the full moon, have I not? I am here to take you to find the thing you said you needed most in the world. And now you claim you want me to find something else?'

'Not something. Someone. Where is your heart?'

'How sure are you that I have one? I am mer, after all.'

'I know you do. I know you, Kira.' Marino locked eyes with her. And, for a moment, he thought that she had relented and would help him. Her gaze softened and he exhaled. He had convinced her. And then she spoke, and her words shattered any hope he had.

'You can choose,' she said. 'You can choose between the girl and the liffen plant. Which would you rather find? Who would you rather save?'

CHAPTER 35
Kira

Kira was pleased with the choice she had given Marino.

He needed a reminder of who had the power here. He could not make demands of her. He was lucky to even be in her presence. And she did not care about some human girl who was foolish enough to fall off the cliff.

Marino appeared less pleased. His mouth moved but no sound came out.

'Your sister or the girl?'

'But . . . but we can find the liffen plant after you save Lana?'

Oh, so she had a name. Lana. Lana with her legs and her human heart. She probably pined after Marino.

Kira had never experienced true jealously, and it swept through her veins like a poison. She could not imagine Marino wailing like this for her. She would never be anyone real to him. Only a mer who he thought was at his beck and call. A mer who he would use to find the liffen plant.

Her sisters were right. She never should have saved him. She never should have helped him. But she would give him one more chance. One more chance to choose. It didn't even need to be her that he chose, but surely he would choose the liffen plant over some stupid human girl. He couldn't care for her more than his own sister. But Kira knew one thing – she would not risk the wrath of her sisters and of the sea for a human who had lost his heart to another.

'No. You must choose. We only have a small window to find the liffen plant. It will not bloom for another month.'

'But she is drowning!' Marino shouted.

'And your sister is dying, is she not? Did you not come all this way to find a cure?'

'Ask your own sisters to help us! To help me! They can find the liffen or they can find Lana. Do not ask me to send an innocent girl to her death.' He sounded desperate.

'And what of me, Captain? Would you weep for me? Would you save me if I was found floundering on the shore?' Kira came closer and ran her finger down his chiselled jaw. Marino drew a deep, shuddering breath. Kira wanted to kiss him until he forgot about this human girl. Until the only thought in his brain was her. She wanted to take him under the waves and keep him forever.

But she wanted him to want her truly, not because she had entranced him.

'If you choose the human girl, you lose the liffen, and you lose me too,' she whispered in his ear, her lips close enough to brush against his skin.

It should be an easy choice.

But he hesitated, for only a second, and in that moment, Kira felt the jealousy coursing through her bubble into rage. She dragged her nails down his neck, leaving marks, and reared back in the water, splashing him with her tail. 'You claim you want to save your sister but when you have a chance you falter? For some human girl you barely know?'

'No, that isn't it!' cried Marino. 'But I shouldn't have to choose. We can find the liffen *after* we save Lana. One is more urgent than the other and every second we debate it is a second lost.'

'And what of me? You save the girl, you find the cure, you forget me and leave me flopping around the sea?'

'Kira, you saved me. You are the reason I am breathing. I would never, could never forget you.'

'But you cannot love me.'

'I never said such a thing. But we are wasting time. Please help me save Lana and help me find the liffen plant. Please, Kira.'

'You made your choice when you chose nothing. You must not be the brother you are pretending to be. Nor the lover that Lana thinks you are. You chose nothing so you will have nothing.'

Marino's dark eyes widened in panic. 'Kira, I chose both! I choose both! And I choose you too! Please. Please. Please.'

'You cannot have everything you want, Marino. You had your chance to choose, and you lost it. You lost everything. I will not help such a fickle man.' Kira felt her heart shrinking as she desperately tried to sweep away any ties that had been there between her and Marino. Her sisters were right. Humans were worthless. She was a fool for saving him. A fool for helping him. She would not make that mistake again.

'You must help me.' Marino's voice was desperate. 'I choose the liffen plant! Kira, please.'

'I must do no such thing. You are lucky I do not drown you right here, right now, so you can join your lady love. But you do not deserve even that. You deserve to live knowing you had the chance to find the cure for your sister, and you lost it. You had the chance to save that human girl, and you squandered it. You have no convictions, no loyalty. You are fickle and foolish, and I will not waste my time on you. Leave the sea and do not come back.'

'Kira! Please!'

'Get back to shore, Marino. Get back to shore before I change my mind and drown you as you deserve.'

With that, Kira dived back down to the depths. As she swam, she thought about trying to find this human girl in the water. She wanted to see this girl that had snared Marino better than she had. And perhaps, now that her pride wasn't on the line, she would maybe even save her. Not for Marino. But because an unfamiliar feeling of guilt was pricking at her.

But to save her, she would have to find her, and the only human heartbeat she could sense in the sea was Marino's.

Perhaps she was too late, after all.

The prickling of guilt grew stronger, slicing through her.

Swallowing her pride, Kira reached out to her sisters in the sea, asking if they had seen a human girl. She had not seen them since they'd argued, and she had woken alone for the first time ever in the sea-cave, but surely they would answer her. They had made their point.

But their only reply was silence.

She could not even sense where they were in the Solvoran Sea. As she was punishing Marino for his choice, her sisters were punishing her. For the first time ever that she could remember, the sea felt empty.

Kira gazed back up through the water, where the moon still shone down, and she found she had never felt so monstrous, or so alone.

CHAPTER 36
Marino

Marino stared for a long moment at the spot where Kira had been floating, as if he could summon her back simply by strength of will.

He knew she could sense him still in the water.

Just like he knew she would be able to sense Lana.

Lana.

He had failed her. And he was failing Celeste. And even though Kira had given him an impossible choice, he felt he had failed her too.

He had come into the water hoping to gain everything he had been looking for, and instead he had lost even more.

The Solvorans had tried to warn him about the mer, had said that they could not be trusted, but he had let his feelings for Kira make a fool of him. And now he was paying the price.

How could he have lived with himself if he had said 'liffen' knowing it meant that Lana would drown? And how could he have lived with himself if he had said 'Lana' knowing it meant that he would lose the chance to find the liffen? The chance to find the cure? The chance to save Celeste?

There had to be another way.

Marino had found his mother at least. He held that thought

close to him as he made the long swim back to the shore. He half expected the mer to try to drown him, but the water was calm. And for that he was grateful, because he was exhausted.

Perhaps he had imagined the girl in white slipping down the steps and into the sea. Perhaps it had been a ghost. A hallucination. Perhaps Lana was sleeping safely in her bed. Marino told himself this was possible, even as he felt the cold truth clutch him by the heart.

Still. He would not lose hope, not yet. He used the last of his strength to hurry up the beach and to Sugar Street. The sun was just starting to rise, bathing the streets in golden light. Lana would be in the bakery, probably already up and preparing bread. He imagined her standing in the kitchen, laughing at him for dripping water all over her floor, again. He would take her in his arms and kiss her and then he would tell her how he felt about her. And then they would go together to his mother's, and they would find the cure without the mer's help.

But the bakery was dark. And when Marino banged on the door, there was no answer. But he did not stop his knocking, if anything, he grew more fervent, more urgent. And he began to call for Lana, as he had in the sea.

His knuckles were starting to bleed when Jonah came out from across the road, still in his night clothes. He grabbed Marino's arm to stop him from rapping on the door once more. 'What is this, then? Have you lost your senses completely? Do you wish to make an enemy of all of Sugar Street?'

Marino whirled on him. 'I need to see Lana. I need to know she is all right.'

Jonah took stock of Marino's wild eyes and sopping

clothes and drew a deep breath. 'What has happened? Surely Lana is sleeping, as you should be.'

'I saw her. I saw her fall into the sea. She walked as though in a trance, down the cliff, and into the waves. I could not save her.'

Jonah frowned. 'You speak nonsense. Have you been drinking tonight?'

'Why has she not answered if she is safe in her bed? You said yourself I was knocking loud enough to wake the whole street.'

'You know she suffers from headaches. She must have one now. I am sure your banging will not help. Go back to the Gilded Palace, Marino. And come back when you can speak sense. Lana will be here. All will be well.' Jonah yawned and turned to go back to his home across the road.

Marino took Jonah by the shoulders. 'Did you not hear me? I saw her fall into the sea!' He was dimly aware of windows opening, of other neighbours peering out to see what the commotion was. But he didn't care. He only cared about seeing Lana. Holding her. Knowing that she was safe.

'I will fix the door,' he said to Jonah, who frowned back at him in confusion. 'But stand back.'

Summoning his warrior magic, Marino kicked down the bakery door. Jonah gave a shout of dismay, but Marino could barely hear him. He ran into the bakery, through the kitchen, and up the stairs, taking them three at a time.

Lana, Lana, Lana. He heard her name with every beat of his heart.

He burst into her room and felt like time had stopped.

Her bed was empty, and the balcony door was wide open, the curtains blowing in the morning breeze.

CHAPTER 37
Marino

Marino was on the balcony when Jonah found him, hands clutching the banister, staring into the sea as if it would tell him where Lana was.

Jonah had seen the empty room, the empty bed. 'Well, you were right,' he said, scratching his head in clear bafflement. 'Lana *isn't* here.'

'Because she drowned,' said Marino in a flat voice. He had seen it happen, after all.

'So you keep saying,' said Jonah. 'Come on, Captain. Lana would want to make sure you had a cup of tea and something sweet to eat, to ward off the shock. Come with me.'

Marino didn't want to leave the balcony. But then Jonah was guiding him down the stairs, and Marino found he didn't have the energy to fight it. They crossed the road and went into Jonah's home, behind the shop floor of the butcher's. Carlos was making tea when Jonah brought Marino in.

They would not believe Marino's story.

'Lana would never do that,' scoffed Jonah. 'She is a sensible girl. She would never heed the song of the mer.'

'I saw her, Jonah, with my own eyes. And I tried to save her, but I was too late, too foolish.' He had still not told the butchers about Kira's part in Lana's death. How Kira could have saved her. But didn't. Marino didn't blame her, he only blamed himself. He hung his head. 'I know she's gone.'

Carlos and Jonah exchanged a look. 'We will believe that when we see her body. A mer might have taken her down below, and while some say that is a fate worse than death, I would choose it every day for myself or any that I love,' said Carlos. 'Don't give up hope yet, Captain.' He passed Marino a cup of tea.

'How long?' said Marino. 'How long can the mer keep someone down there before they are gone for good?'

Jonah shrugged. 'Days, if you want them to come back like themselves. Months if you want them to come back with a heartbeat and nothing else.'

Carlos leaned down so he was face to face with Marino. 'You might have seen her go under, but that doesn't mean she's drowned, you hear me?'

'But her fate is with the mer now,' said Jonah, and he brought his hands towards his chest and out again. 'May she be sea-blessed.'

Hope lit within Marino, hot and bright. He stood up abruptly, the hot tea sloshing out of his cup. 'Thank you for the tea.'

He needed to get back to the sea.

He needed to see Kira.

He hadn't been able to convince her before, but he would now.

Marino took his dagger with him, and as he waded into the waves, he pressed the blade into his palm, letting the blood drip into the sea.

'Kira!' he shouted, his voice hoarse. 'Kira! I know you can hear me. I know you can smell me!'

The waves were coming in higher and faster now, and Marino wondered if he would have better luck finding Kira if he went further out to sea, where the water was deeper. Where he had less power, and the mer had more.

So be it. He felt reckless, desperate, willing to do whatever it took to find Kira. To find Kira and beg her to help him find Lana. If Lana was in the water, if she was beneath the waves, Kira would know it. Surely.

Still clutching his dagger, he swam deeper into the water.

It was still early, the sun rising slowly in the sky, illuminating the waves. The moon was still faintly visible, full and round. Would the fading moonlight be enough to see the liffen bloom?

The liffen bloom. Had he wasted his one opportunity to find it? Would he have to wait another month here on Solvora, here on this land where the king probably wanted to kill him, where the girl he was falling for had slipped into the sea, where the mer were murderous?

Marino closed his eyes and tipped his head back, lifting it to the sky to let the rising sun caress his face.

He was so tired. He hadn't slept in so long.

'Back again? You truly have a death wish.'

The voice was close, a familiar rough whisper in his ear, and he snapped his eyes open and turned to find himself face to face with Kira. Her mask was made of blue flowers, pressed tight against her skin, almost like scales. She shimmered in the morning light.

'You came,' he said, his voice still hoarse. 'I called for you and you came.' He let out a broken laugh, holding out his bleeding palm. 'I bled for you.'

Kira reached out and trailed her fingers down his jaw. 'I cannot resist your call, Marino Pegasi. Try as I might.'

Marino pressed his bleeding hand against her own, holding it closer to his face, close enough that her wrist was near his lips. He could feel her heartbeat fluttering in her wrist. Felt it speed up as he pressed his lips to it. She had a heart, after all. Despite what she claimed. Despite her actions.

'She's not in the water, is she?' His voice broke as he said aloud what he feared.

Kira pulled her hand away from his face and met his gaze. Beneath her mask, her eyes were beautiful, swirls of silver and violet. She stared unblinking at him for a long moment. 'If she is, her heart no longer beats. Your human heart is the only one I can sense in these waters.'

Marino felt as though the sea was tightening its grip on him, like the water was solidifying, and it was crushing him. He was certain his chest was caving in from the pressure, that the sea was going to bore a hole right through him, taking his heart as a keepsake.

'Marino, I am sorry. Truly.' Kira's voice was gentle. 'I should have helped you.'

Marino's blood was roaring in his ears, Kira's voice sounded far away, even though she was right next to him. Even though their heads were above water, he felt as though he could not breathe.

'Marino?' Kira was closer now, eyes wide and unblinking beneath her mask and so close and so familiar in a way he could not understand. Oh, he hated her in that moment, he hated that she had been the one who he needed, the one who had saved him but not Lana, not Celeste, he hated that he still yearned for her, still burned for her, even after everything. And with that realisation, Marino could breathe again. He was alive, he was here, he was with her. He took Kira's face in his hands, her achingly beautiful face that he had still never seen unmasked. With one hand he reached around to the nape of her neck, tangling his fingers in her thick, wet hair. When he spoke, his voice was low and rough.

'Kiss me, Kira.'

She did not hesitate.

When Kira's lips met his, it was not careful and it was not kind.

It was ravenous.

She ran her hands up his arms and over his shoulders and around his neck, clawing at his skin with her long nails. Kira kissed him like she was the one drowning, and he was the one who could save her. She kissed him with a wild abandon, with a fierceness that he welcomed.

Marino kissed her back just as hungrily.

Kissing Lana had felt like a homecoming. Like a long-held dream coming true. Kissing Kira felt like a revelation. He hadn't been able to imagine it because it was completely different than any kiss he'd ever had. He felt like he had fallen off a cliff and was still falling, waiting to hit the water. It was an exploration of something entirely new and unexpected and dangerous and he didn't want it to ever end.

The sensation of the waves gently rocking them as they held each other in the sea and her lips on his and her strong body pressed against his own, the bare skin of their stomachs touching and then the strangeness of her skin melding into scales and the unknown of her powerful tail.

He ran his hands down her body, stopping at her hips, and held her against him and it was unclear who was holding who up in the water. He knew she could drown him and he did not care. He only wanted to be in this moment and let the whole world around him burn.

Marino poured all his grief and anger over losing Lana into the kiss, and he let the kiss consume him. Let Kira bite his lip, hard enough to draw blood, and he slipped his tongue into her mouth to taste more of her, to feel more of her. And her tongue met his boldly back, not letting him take charge of the kiss but making it a dance between two equally matched. He could feel her magic, her power, thrumming through her and it awoke his own magic deep within him, along with his desire.

Kira tasted like the sea.

He could drown in her, he thought, his mind fuzzy. Lose himself entirely.

And that thought was enough for him to pull back, just for a moment, to come up for air.

Kira was breathless, her chest heaving and her eyes shimmering like the sea itself in the rising sun. He wanted her to take off her mask, he wanted to see her true face, all of it, but he knew once he did, if the myths of the mer were true, he might not ever be able to come back to himself. A mer's beauty is their weapon, a mer's beauty can destroy you.

Marino wondered if he was already destroyed, if he was irrevocably changed forever. He wondered if a man could kiss a mer and move on from it. He did not think so.

He knew he would remember this kiss for the rest of his life.

It was not only because kissing Kira was like nothing he had ever experienced before, it was also because right now she was the thing that was keeping him afloat after the loss of Lana.

His sorrow and his guilt were the things threatening to drag him under, and Kira was holding him up. Saving him yet again.

Before Marino had come to Solvora, he had never needed to be saved. He had been the one sailing into stormy waters to rescue others, the one who dived in after drowning men, he had protected and fought for those he cared for and even those he didn't know but who deserved better.

He had never known what it was like to be completely and entirely at the mercy of someone who held your life in their hands, who could kill you and kissed you instead.

And it made him want to show her just how glad he was to still be alive, and just how appreciative he was.

Marino pushed Kira's heavy hair to the side, kissing along her shoulders and up her neck, tugging at her earlobe with his teeth, careful of the small pearl earring there. She let out a small moan and the sound nearly undid him. He swam behind her, kissing the back of her neck, and then again down her other shoulder, until he was in front of her once more.

He leaned forward to kiss her on the lips again, to lose himself in kissing her, to save himself, but she put a hand on his chest, right over his heart, to stop him.

'Marino, I could kiss you until nightfall and straight on until dawn. But there is something I must tell you.'

CHAPTER 38
Kira

Kissing Marino made Kira feel like she was on fire.

A heat she had never known had spread within her and she had welcomed it.

It was as if she had never known warmth before. It made her feel like she was melting from the inside out and it was delicious.

Is this what her sisters had spoken of? Is this why they took men beneath the waves?

And what was it like for him? Did he feel what she was feeling? Is this why Solvorans leaped from the cliffs and into the mer's embrace?

How did anyone get anything done when they could be kissing?

She had not seen her sisters since she had left Marino the night before. They were punishing her, that much was clear. She had not even known they could hide from her like this in the sea. And so, she decided she would do something to truly merit their treatment of her. They were the ones who had always told her to take a lover, and now, now that she had found someone . . .

'I have never kissed a man, nor woman, nor mer. The first

time my lips touched another's was when I breathed the air of life into your lungs, the day your ship sank.' Kira looked up at the sky, at the sun rising ever higher. Its warmth felt good on her face, almost as good as Marino's embrace. 'I sensed you coming to Solvora, and I was drawn to you. And I have let you kiss me here in this water, knowing your heart is broken over another, and I have kissed you because I wanted to know what it was like to kiss someone without tempting them by song or spell. So, I was selfish, and I do not regret it. I could keep you, you know. I could sing you down and make you forget her, make you forget your own name. But I won't do that. Not to you.'

She took a long breath. 'I can feel the magic within you, and I know that you hold your power leashed tightly, and that even you do not know the full extent of it. Because it frightens you, this magic you still do not understand.' Kira met his gaze again, and Marino felt a jolt go through him. 'I recognise that feeling, because I have it too. I am the youngest of the mer and yet sometimes I feel as if my link to the sea is stronger than my sisters'. And when I am with you, I feel more powerful. You have awoken something in me, Marino Pegasi. For that, I should have saved the girl when you asked.' She smiled sadly. 'I am not used to being kind. It is not the mer way. It makes me feel weak.'

Marino took her hands in his own. 'Kira, Lana drowning isn't your fault.' The way he said their names together chimed in her mind like a bell. *Kira Lana*. 'I don't know what happened last night. But I do not blame you. I blame myself.'

'She was lucky. To be loved by you.'

'Love? Lana? I don't . . .' Marino sputtered as he spoke and then paused. And when he spoke again, his voice shook.

'I never told her. I should have told her.' He ran his hand over his face. 'Oh, by the stars, I should have told her.'

'She must have known it. Even I knew it and I do not think the mer can feel love.'

Marino gave her a sharp look. 'You must not truly believe that, Kira. You are clearly capable of love.'

Kira laughed lightly. 'We mer love each other. But I imagine the love you felt, still feel for Lana, is different from the love I feel for my sisters. I am tied to them, but glad for it. I want to protect them, and they me, but it is a feeling we have always had for each other.'

'I understand,' said Marino. 'After all, it was my attempt to save my own sister that brought me to Solvora. But I have failed her as much as I failed Lana.'

'You have not failed your sister.'

Marino closed his eyes. 'I missed the chance to get the liffen bloom.'

'No, Marino. You did not.'

Marino's eyes flew open and he looked at Kira with a knife-sharp focus. 'Kira. Tell me what you mean.'

'Last night, after I ordered you out of the sea, I looked for the girl. And I couldn't find her anywhere. And my sisters, they hid from me. Punishing me for even considering helping you. And I realised that I still wanted to help you. Desperately. I didn't find your Lana. But I did find the liffen bloom.'

'And you are going to give it to me?' Marino spoke in a calm, slow voice, but Kira could hear how his heart rate had picked up. He was nervous.

Does he think me such a monster that I would taunt him with what he most wants? Kira wondered. Was she such a monster?

For a moment, she wondered if she could be like Zella, if she could laugh in his face and call him a fool and disappear down deep. Her sisters would like that, they would applaud that.

But Kira knew what she wanted to do.

'Stay here.' She dived down swiftly, down to her sea-cave where she slept, where the rocks held what few things she thought of as her own, where she had hidden blossoms of the liffen bloom that she had harvested last night, in the silvery light of the full moon. The plant itself was a glistening silver, almost emitting its own light. Each of its eight petals was long and wavy, and as Kira swam back to the surface with it in her hand, she thought it looked like the liffen bloom was dancing. Or perhaps waving goodbye. Kira knew that the mer used it for their own healing, that it was as valuable to them as it was to humans, and to willingly give it away to someone above was unheard of. She could not even imagine the fury of her sisters. But as Kira broke through the surface and saw Marino still there, still waiting, still hopeful, she felt at peace with her choice. She would take whatever punishment her sisters saw fit, but she would hold within her the glow of knowing she had saved someone twice over, and another she had never met.

She was not a monster, after all.

Kira held out the shimmering liffen bloom, floppy now that it was out of the water, how she imagined her fins might well look on the shore, and gave Marino a crooked smile.

'Here it is. But you must promise me you will not share it with King Leonel. Or any Solvorans. It is for your sister. It is my gift to you.' Kira laughed a little then, a sharp, short laugh. 'A parting gift.'

'Kira, I will never forget you.' Marino put his hands on her waist, pulling her close to him. She put her nose in the crook of his neck and inhaled, wishing she could just once fall asleep breathing him in.

Then she remembered who she was. She was Kira of the Solvoran Sea. She was no girl to cry over any man. She pressed one last kiss against his neck, where she could smell his blood beneath his skin, and then pulled back. Pulled away from him. She still clutched the liffen bloom in her fist. Kira rolled her shoulders back, held her head high, and again held the liffen bloom out to Marino.

'Marino Pegasi, tell tales of me across the sea. Tell them of the mermaid you met. The one who saved you and your sister.'

Marino, the man who had called to her without words, who had opened her heart, who had shown her a different kind of magic, took her hand and kissed it gently. His lips were warm and soft on her cool skin.

'Kira, I will tell the tale of you so widely and so well that I will make you immortal. You will never be forgotten. Not by me, nor any who I tell of you.'

Kira dropped the liffen bloom into his hand.

'And perhaps, Captain, one day we will meet again, in one sea or another.' She knew they would not, but she knew it would make it easier to leave him, if she pretended she might see him again. And then, without a backwards glance, Kira dived down beneath the waves, leaving Marino with the liffen bloom, and a piece of her heart.

CHAPTER 39
Marino

Marino floated a moment in the sea, grateful that the water was calm.

Kira was gone by choice and Lana taken by fate, but he had the liffen bloom.

He had found the cure.

And he had found his mother. His mother who would know how to brew the potion that would save Celeste.

He still needed to figure out how he was going to leave Solvora, how he would save his crew from the dungeons of the Gilded Palace, and where they would find a ship, but that all seemed possible now that he held the liffen bloom in his hands.

He had found what he had come here for, and so much more.

Terrified that the delicate flower would disintegrate in his hands, or that he would drop it, Marino allowed himself one more moment of respite to catch his breath before he swam fast and hard back to the beach.

Then he wasted no time hurrying across the island, to the furthest point, to the little cottage in the lowlands where his mother lived.

Marino was wary that King Leonel may have sent soldiers to scour the land for him, to punish him for threatening the king, but he saw no one as he hurried through the farmland and marshes leading to the edge of Solvora.

Perhaps he had intimidated the king enough to get what he needed out of him. Perhaps he wouldn't have to fight the king, or anyone, and he could leave with his mother and his crew and the cure.

Leave without Lana.

The thought was a dagger in his heart, but Marino knew he didn't have time to give himself over to grief, he had to get to his mother, had to bring her the liffen bloom while it was still fresh.

Fatigue and grief crashed inside him, and each step was a battle won – he wanted nothing more than to lie down in the sunflower field he was striding through and close his eyes, just for a moment. But he kept going. He had to keep going. He was so close now.

After he had returned home, after he had saved Celeste, then he could let himself rest.

Then he could let himself realise what he had lost, realise that he had been so close to having something that had eluded him for years.

Love. True love.

He would tell Celeste about it, after she had woken, that he wasn't incapable of finding love. That he only needed to sail off the map to find it.

He was almost at the small green cottage now, and as he approached, the wooden door swung open and his mother stood there with her arms out wide.

Seeing his mother before him, her arms open in welcome,

made Marino suddenly feel as if he was a boy of five or six. In his fatigued state, he did not feel as if he was a man or a captain, but a little lost boy.

He staggered towards her, allowing a moment of joy that his mother was alive and she was the key to saving Celeste. But then he saw his mother's gaze shift to his side, and he knew she was looking for Lana.

'Lana,' he choked out. 'Lana slipped into the sea. I saw it happen. I don't understand it. But she's gone. And Kira...' His voice trailed off.

'Kira?' his mother questioned.

'Kira is the mer who helped me. Who saved me. She gave me the liffen bloom. And she's gone now too. I've lost them both.' His voice broke as he spoke the words aloud.

His mother guided him inside her small cottage, her hand on his back. 'Do not blame yourself, Marino. Solvora moves to its own rhythms. The people here, they hear a song, a call to sacrifice for the land and the sea, that we do not. You say you saw Lana slip into the sea – and I believe you. I have seen the people here lay down their lives for reasons I do not understand. But whatever drew her to the sea has nothing to do with you. You have done what you came here to do. You found the cure. You found me. I never thought I would be able to leave Solvora. To return to Eana. I never thought I would see my children again.' She smiled then, dark eyes wrinkling in the corners. 'Seeing you alive and well, knowing all you have achieved, knowing that you have embraced your witch heritage, that you are mastering your gifts – this is a moment I never thought I would have, and I will treasure it.'

Marino took a long breath, grateful for his mother's words. Grateful for her strength and for her wisdom.

'Now let me see this liffen bloom.'

Marino handed the now slightly wilted but still shimmering flower to his mother. She lifted it to her lips and, to Marino's complete surprise, began to sing. It was in a language he did not know, and a melody that seemed strangely familiar, and as the music flowed out of her, the liffen bloom began to open, petals spreading and unfurling, revealing the centre which appeared to be a swirling silver.

Marino was flabbergasted. 'How did you know how to do that?'

'It worked once, long ago. Music and magic are often linked, my Marino. Remember that.'

She crossed the small room to the stove and poured the now liquid centre of the liffen bloom into a pot. 'Marino, there is nothing for you to do now. It must simmer for hours, to turn this into what it needs to be for Celeste. But you found the bloom in time, and we were able to open it while it was still fresh. You have done it, Marino.'

Marino felt his knees nearly buckle underneath him at the relief of knowing that the cure had been truly found. 'Then what?' he asked. 'How long will it last?'

'Once it is prepared, I will bottle it up, and it will remain in your care until we return home.' As she spoke the word 'home' her eyes lit up. Then she gave Marino a gentle smile. 'But now, you should sleep. You look dead on your feet. Sleep while I stir, and when you wake, it will be ready.' She nodded towards the small bed in the corner, covered with a threadbare quilt. 'Sleep, my son.'

Marino nodded gratefully and collapsed on to the bed and for the first time since his childhood, fell asleep under the watchful eye of his mother.

Marino woke to the sound of his mother muttering as she slammed a cupboard shut.

He sat up, rubbing his eyes. His mouth was dry from sleep, and his stomach was rumbling. 'Is everything all right?'

Marino glanced out the window and saw that the light was golden and knew that the sun would be setting soon. He had slept through the whole afternoon. His body still ached, but it was his heart that ached most of all. At least he had the cure, he reminded himself, and that was a salve on everything.

Then his mother spoke. 'It is missing something. The recipe is unfinished. The liffen bloom has simmered for hours, but it is still missing something. I thought perhaps I had something in my stores that I could use, but I know I don't have it.'

Marino sat up, her words pulling him right out of his post-nap sleepy stupor. 'What? But I thought all you needed was the liffen bloom. That is what Lana said, and what you yourself said . . .' His heart began to pound. He couldn't have come so close to fail now.

His mother rubbed her temples. 'It has been a long time since I prepared this particular potion. But I remember what it is supposed to look like, and smell like, and this is not complete. I must have had another ingredient, but I cannot remember now what it was.' She pressed her lips together tightly, and Marino had the distinct impression that his mother was trying not to cry.

Marino stood and crossed the room to put his hands on

his mother's shoulders. It was strange, still, to be taller than her.

'But we have some time to find that, do we not? The liffen bloom had to be found under a full moon, and then boiled down while it was still fresh, we have done that. You did that. You knew the song, Mama.' Saying the word 'Mama' aloud to her, to his mother who he had thought was lost to him and Celeste forever, he felt a hole in his heart heal.

His mother drew a deep, shuddering breath. 'It is a song I would never forget. A song I used to sing to you and Celeste, when you were small. It was the song I sang to myself at sea to keep from going mad, the song I sang when I could barely see with my true eyes because the seeing sickness had made me so weak. It was the song I sang to the sea in desperation. It is the song of hope, and it unlocks the liffen bloom. A song the mer know.'

'Mother, I know it was a long time ago, but do you remember anything else from that day you found the liffen bloom? Anything else you would have included in the potion?'

His mother closed her eyes, and he knew she was casting back in her memory. 'The mer had not stopped me, when I came through the barrier on my small boat. Now I know how rare that is. I was singing, you see, and they recognised the song. But they did not help me more than that. My boat never made it. And I was not washed ashore on a sandy beach. No, my boat crashed against the cliffs, and I had to climb them. I was near feral, like a Gevran snow leopard, scaling the cliffs. But there was something guiding me, there were vines, vines that I could hold on to, vines covered with hundreds of little white and blue flowers.'

Her eyes flew open. 'I used those flowers. Those flowers had saved me once and I thought they would save me again. And I thought it was fitting, that they grew on land and the liffen bloom grew in the sea, and that the balance of it – you know magic seeks balance above all things – the balance of it was what I needed. And I sang to the liffen bloom and I crumbled the petals of those little cliffside flowers and I stole a pot and I made my potion over a fire out under the stars, the stars that I love and the stars that had cursed me and I thought after this I can leave, when I am well I can go home.'

Marino knew the flowers that she spoke of, but he let her continue.

'By this point, I was weak, so weak I could barely stir, barely sing. But I did it. Thinking of you and Celeste gave me strength. And it worked, the potion I brewed. Made of starflowers from sea and from land, to balance the power of the stars in the sky that had caused my sickness. *Remember, magic wants balance.* It has always been this way. And I thought, I've found this cure, and I can bring it back to Eana. That was all I wanted to do.'

Her voice broke. Marino's mother put her hand to her son's face. 'But even if the mer had let me in, they did not let me go. That was too far a breach, breaking a bargain that they never made but were bound by.' She dropped her hand and continued to stir the simmering potion on the small stove. The smell was of sea and faintly metallic, like silver melted down, mixed with the copper tang of blood. 'And once I settled here, in this cottage, I made sure to stay far from King Leonel. I help who I can, if they come to me. And

I grow my own flowers. But I've never seen those flowers, the little star-shaped ones, since the day I came to Solvora. I do not even know if they still grow on the cliffs.'

She tilted her head towards her son. 'Marino, why are you smiling so?'

'Because I have seen those flowers. And I know where to find them.'

CHAPTER 40
Marino

By the time Marino arrived back on Sugar Street, he had never been quite so desperate for a horse. While Solvora was small enough for him to traipse back and forth several times in one day, as he now knew all too well, he was certain he had never taken so many steps before.

But he had to hurry. Sugar Street was strangely quiet, no sign of evening merriment or business, no shops closing up for the night, no anything.

And it was silent. The only sound was the crash of the waves against the cliffs.

A chill ran through Marino as he wondered where the people were, and why it was so quiet. But he did not have time to investigate this, not when his mother was waiting with the liffen bloom on the stove. The sun was still hovering low in the sky, not quite setting below the horizon. Marino calculated that he would be able to find the ria blossoms and get back to his mother before dark. And then he would come up with a plan for what to do next. For how he was going to leave Solvora.

Someone, probably one of the butchers, had managed to close what was left of the bakery's smashed-in front door.

Marino felt a pang of guilt for kicking it down in the first place, but he had been desperate.

He was *still* desperate.

And he was still a fool with hope in his heart. He knocked on the broken door, just in case Lana was in there.

There was no answer. With a heavy sigh, Marino pushed the door open and stepped into the empty bakery.

Perhaps she was there, in her bed, on her balcony – but no. Her room was as empty as it had been that morning when he had been there with Jonah. He wanted to lie in her bed and bury his face in the sheets that he knew would smell of her, he wanted to say a proper goodbye and tell whatever part of her that still lingered here in this room all the things he hadn't been bold enough to say to her face. Tell her he was sorry and how he truly felt about her.

As it was, he felt like he shouldn't linger in her room, for a multitude of reasons, and he went out on to the balcony.

The balcony where he had seen her last alive.

Marino paused a moment, looking down at what she would have seen on her last journey. She would have had to step over the banister, as he did now, to get on to the shallow steps worn into the cliffside.

What had possessed her? What had lured her from her bed and down the steps and into the sea? He listened, trying to hear a song in the wind, but there was only the sound of waves and the occasional squawk of a gull.

So, with a heavy heart, he stepped over the banister as Lana had once done with him, careful not to crush the flowers under his boots, and crouched amid the ria blossoms.

Of course, this would be the missing ingredient.

Of course, Lana would still be guiding him, even though she was no longer there.

Marino carefully plucked a few flowers and then went further along the cliff, wanting to make sure he gathered as many blossoms as his mother might need.

His back was to the sea when he heard it. A buzzing hum like the low thrum of a cello that was growing louder with every minute. When he looked over his shoulder, Marino's jaw dropped.

A wave was rising up out of the sea, rising and rising but not cresting, not yet. It was a wave like Marino had never seen before, not in all the years on his boat. The wave was narrow and tall and, strangest still, rising directly from the small cove down beneath the bakery. All the water around it was still, it was only this wave, and as it grew taller and closer to the cliff, the humming grew louder and more insistent.

Marino realised moments before the wave crashed that he could be swept off the cliff, and so he grabbed on to the railing of the balcony. And then he saw it.

There was a figure lying atop the wave, as if cradled by it.

Long dark hair hung over the side of the wave, and the figure wore a flowing white shift dress. A white nightgown.

It was Lana, he was sure of it.

The wave cradled her gently, carrying her higher and higher until she was level with the balcony. Marino clung on to the railing as the cresting wave came closer. It carefully laid Lana down on the balcony, soaking Marino in the process, and then with one movement the entire wave dropped back into the sea, as if it had never been there at all.

Marino leaped over the railing and kneeled by Lana, his heart in his throat. Was she alive? He put his fingers on her neck, on the delicate skin beneath her jaw, and waited, holding his breath.

There.

There.

There. Her pulse was strong. And then he saw her chest rise and fall as she drew in a breath of air, and her eyes flickered open.

In the golden early evening light, her dark brown eyes looked more gold-tinged than ever, and as she sat up, Marino noticed as if in a dream that her soaking-wet hair had an almost blue sheen.

'Marino?' Lana's voice came out hoarse, and then she coughed, and as she did, seawater spluttered out, dribbling down her chin. 'Marino, what's wrong? Why do you look so upset?'

'You're here. You're here.'

'Of course I'm here.' Lana looked around, confusion dancing across her face. 'Though I'm not quite sure why I'm *here*, specifically.'

'Oh, Lana!' Marino helped her sit up, and ran his hands down her arms, feeling her solid proof of life, of existence, beneath his palms. 'You are here, right? This is real. I'm not dreaming.'

Lana laughed, the sound familiar and beautiful to Marino. 'If I was in a dream, do you think I would know I wasn't real?'

'As long as we're having the same dream, I don't think I care one way or another.' Marino drew Lana closer to him, holding her against his chest. 'You're alive. You're alive.'

Lana laughed again and pulled her head back to look up at him. 'What are you talking about? Of course I'm alive. Although again, I'm not sure why I'm out here, on the balcony . . . in my nightgown.' She looked down at herself and frowned. 'In my mysteriously wet and now embarrassingly sheer nightgown.'

'I hadn't even noticed.' Marino meant it. He'd only been focused on the fact that Lana was alive. A fact that she didn't seem to quite understand was the most important. She seemed dazed but crucially she was alive.

'I don't know if I should be impressed by your honour or offended,' laughed Lana. Then she shivered. 'But I am getting cold. Shall we go inside and warm up?' She offered Marino a shy smile.

'I would like nothing more but, Lana, you don't understand. You shouldn't be here. I saw you walk into the sea. I saw you disappear beneath the waves. You were gone. For nearly a day.'

Lana's smile faded. 'A day?'

'I searched for you. By the stars, I searched for you. I even asked Kira to help, but she said she couldn't hear your heartbeat anywhere in the Solvoran Sea.'

'Kira? Who is Kira?' Lana spoke the mer's name as if it was an enchantment.

'The mer who saved me. The mer who said she would help me find the liffen bloom. And Lana, I have it. But my mother said she needed something else to make the cure for Celeste, she needed the ria blossoms. Your ria blossoms! And now we're so close to having the cure.'

Lana drew back, frowning at him. 'Marino, I am so glad you found the liffen bloom but forgive me for my confusion.

The *mer* helped you? She told you her name? Have you completely lost your senses?'

Marino remembered he'd never told Lana what Kira's name was. Out of respect for Kira, but also to hide how close he had grown to the mer. How much he knew of her.

'Yes. I know her name. And I know her. Lana, I know some mer can't be trusted, but we can trust Kira. She defied her sisters to help me. She even tried to find you . . .' Marino's voice trailed off as he saw Lana's eyes flash.

'When she saw me sink beneath the waves, she did not try to intervene? She simply allowed it? This so-called trustworthy mer?' Lana was brimming with anger.

'Well, she appeared after you had disappeared,' said Marino slowly.

'She was probably the one who lured me into the sea, then!'

'Lana, I know she was not.' Marino knew this in his soul, that Kira may not have helped him save Lana, but she was not the one who had drawn her into the water.

Lana crossed her arms and scowled at Marino. 'She has bewitched you. Even *you* are not immune to the mer's magic. I saw it that night on the beach. When they were trying to draw you into the water. You would have gone with them and you would have drowned that night but I saved you. Kira is not the only one to have saved you. I too have saved you time and time again.'

'I will gladly argue with you about the merits and morals of the mer another time, but for this moment let me focus on the fact that you are alive and safe. And with me.' Marino pushed a strand of her hair, nearly dry now, behind her ears, his eyes catching on how her small pearl earrings glinted in the early evening light. Her earrings reminded him of something, but what was it?

Lana leaned in to his touch. 'Don't get too distracted, Captain.' The longing in her gaze said otherwise. 'And what of the cure? Don't you need to bring the ria blossoms to your mother?'

'Yes. My mother knew she had seen them on the cliffs, when she first arrived long ago, but couldn't remember where on the island they grew. But I knew where to find them, because of you.' Marino tilted her face gently up towards him. 'Lana, again and again you have led me towards what I need, what I am seeking. But I wonder if, perhaps, it is you that I need most of all.'

Lana closed her eyes and brushed her lips against his. Her mouth was still deliciously cold, and she tasted of the sea.

'And what of your mer? Do you need her too?' Lana whispered against his lips.

Marino could not lie to Lana. He pulled back so he could meet her eyes. He would not pretend that he did not have feelings for Kira.

'Lana, when I thought I had lost you, I was mad with grief. And when Kira found me in the sea, found me searching for you, she comforted me.' He sighed heavily. 'I have to be honest with you, Lana. I kissed Kira. I kissed her because I thought you were lost forever but also because . . .' His voice trailed off.

'Because you wanted to,' Lana said flatly. Then she sighed. 'Oh, Marino, I cannot fault you for kissing a mer. Anyone would, given the chance. I am only glad you survived to tell the tale.'

'*Your* survival is the one we should be celebrating,' Marino said. 'But, Lana, I still don't understand. The sea lifted you up, as if it treasured you, and it lay you down so gently. I have never seen such a thing, nor even imagined it. I doubt the sea treats even the mer with such care.'

Lana turned her gaze to the sea, calm below them. 'I suppose I owe it a debt, then.'

'Has this happened before?'

'I . . . I don't know. I've woken up on the balcony before. But I always thought that was because I sleepwalked. Benedita told me I walked in my sleep.'

Marino pressed a kiss to her palm. Her hands were so beautiful, her fingers so long and elegant, and her nails sharper than he remembered. For a moment he had double vision of kissing another palm. He shook his head to shake the memory of kissing Kira's hand away.

'The sea saw fit to give you back. I will not question the choices of the sea.' Marino kissed her hand again. 'But I am going to make sure you don't sleepwalk off the edge of the boat when we sail to Eana.'

Lana's eyes lit up. 'When we sail?'

'I won't lose you again, Lana. When I leave for Eana, I want you to come with me. If that is what you want.'

Lana threw her arms around Marino. 'You know I've longed to leave Solvora. And ever since you walked into my bakery, I have wanted to be near to you. Marino, you say the sea brought me back to you, but before that, the sea brought you to me.'

Marino cocked an eyebrow. 'And who are we to deny the wants and wishes of the sea?'

Lana smiled, and Marino thought it was the most

beautiful thing he'd ever seen. 'I wouldn't dare.'

When he kissed her again, it felt like a gift, like home, it felt like fate. He would have kissed her until the sun had sunk far beneath the horizon, but then he heard the drums.

They shattered the silence that had settled on Solvora. The strange, still silence that Marino had forgotten about in his joy at finding Lana. It was as if the two of them had been in a bubble, floating high above Solvora, and the sound of the drums sent them plummeting back down.

Marino felt the drumming in his teeth, in his bones. And then a great horn blared, echoing all around them.

It sounded like victory.

It sounded like war.

'What is that?' He turned to Lana, who had gone very still, a stricken look upon her face.

'That is the call for battle. Those are the drums of death.'

CHAPTER 41
Lana

Marino and Lana ran hand in hand down the winding streets of Goldwave Mountain.

Lana noted with increasing fear that they saw nobody.

Had she missed a summons for a celebration?

Her mind was still whirling with what had happened to her, how she had ended up in the sea, how the sea had returned her, as Marino claimed it had. And now the streets were empty, and the drums of death were pounding.

Lana felt a draw to the sea like she never had before. She *needed* to get down to the shore. Every beat of the drum echoed the beat of her heart and she heard *danger danger danger*. And she knew in the way she knew how to breathe that the only safe place for her was the sea.

Then she heard a voice in her head. Suddenly and unexpectedly.

COME NOW.

FASTER, HURRY.

It was a chorus of voices and Lana didn't question whose voices they were and where they came from, she simply obeyed the call and hoisted up her nightgown so she could pick up speed.

IT IS ZELLA.
ZELLA ZELLA ZELLA.

The name soared in her mind and she held on to it. Who was *Zella*? Whoever it was, hearing the name felt like the echo of a long-forgotten dream.

She did not tell Marino of the voices. She only urged him to run faster.

And then they reached the beach, the same beach where Marino had been found, and it seemed as if all of Solvora was gathered there. The drummers were on the edge, pounding the drums of death, signalling that it was time for a Solvoran sacrifice. Men and women and children, soldiers and tailors and painters, goldweavers and farmers, and the king himself, standing at the front of it all, his golden-haired soothsayer by his side, and a long hook in his hand. A hook shimmering with sea-gold.

There was a mermaid thrashing at his feet. A silver-haired mer with a glimmering tail that was thrashing on the sand. The sight of a mer out of the sea and on the sand was so unnatural it made Lana feel sick. But not as sick as the sight of King Leonel lowering his glowing golden hook and cutting into the mer's tail. The mer let out a keening cry that made Lana feel as if she herself was dying.

In the shallows of the sea there were a dozen more mer and they were wailing too, and Lana was certain they would call down a storm, but the waves stayed calm and King Leonel was laughing. Laughing as he poked and prodded the beautiful silver-haired mer with his hook.

Lana looked closer at the sea and saw that the twelve mer were all caught in a shimmering gold net, the same gold that coated the king's hook.

'Wail all you like, you wretched creatures. You cannot use your power now. Not while you are in the goldweavers' net. How foolish was I, all these years, to abide by a bargain I did not make. But now I know the true strength of the gold from the sea, that with the help of magic from man, it can be used to bind you abominations.'

'No,' breathed Marino. 'It cannot be. I told the king I would not help him, but it seems he did not need my permission, or my touch, only my nearness.'

'We must save her,' Lana choked out to Marino. 'We must save that mermaid.'

'Hold on to my hand, and do not let go,' said Marino and they charged towards the king and the dying mer. Because Lana knew the mermaid was dying now, she could feel it in her blood.

The mer locked eyes with her and held out a hand and Lana forgot that Marino had said not to let go of him and she dropped his hand and ran to the silver-haired mer. She sank on to her knees, smoothing the mer's silver hair from her forehead and whispering soothing words. She looked up in time to see Marino grabbing the hook from the king and using it to fend off an approaching soldier.

'I should never have trusted you,' said King Leonel. He was shaking now, shaking with rage or fear or both. 'Captain Pegasi.' He spat as he said Marino's title. 'I should have killed you on the spot.'

'But you didn't. And I could say the same to you. Now call off your soldiers, send your people home. Release my crew. And then, maybe then, I will let you live.'

'You have no power over me,' scoffed the king, but Lana could tell he was afraid.

'I have magic, and you do not. I would say that is power over you,' said Marino, as he kicked at another soldier who tried and failed to tackle him.

'So, you side with the mer, do you?' said King Leonel.

The tide was rising, and Lana felt the water against her legs. It was cooling, as if her legs had been sunburnt and she hadn't realised. She still held the silver-haired mer's hand, and while the mer was too weak to speak, she kept her silver eyes locked on to Lana's. She heard Marino's voice as if from far away.

'I do not think it needs to be mer against man. And I won't stand by and let you slaughter the mer here.'

But the king merely laughed. 'I would have helped you, you know. The mer will kill the one you love and then they will kill you. Don't say I didn't warn you.'

Marino let out a shout as Lana felt a dozen hands on her legs, as the mer she had forgotten about, the ones waiting in the shallows pulled her into the waves.

CHAPTER 42
Marino

Marino wasted no time.

The mer were not taking Lana from him. He had not come down here to help them, to save them, only for them to take what was most precious to him. The gold net the mer had been trapped in had loosened, allowing them to escape and drag Lana into the water.

Marino flung himself into the sea, magic tingling in his fingertips.

And then he saw Lana's face.

Her eyes were changing colour. The deep brown flecked with gold had shifted to a violet with shining silver. And her hair was changing from black to blue. As his head spun and his heart beat fast, Marino somehow knew when he looked down what he would see.

Beneath her nightgown, her legs were twining together and purple scales were sealing her legs into one beautiful, powerful tail.

Lana was a mermaid. And not any mermaid.

Lana was Kira.

Kira stared at Marino, blinking in confusion. The other mer moved back, so it was the two of them in the shallow water, Marino up to his knees and Kira looking up at him. The beach was silent.

'Kira?' Marino whispered.

'Who else would it be?' Kira looked at the others. 'Why are we here?'

'Do you not . . . do you not remember?'

Kira cocked her head to the side. 'Do I not remember what?'

'Any of it.'

'I remember you kissing me goodbye. I did not think I would see you again so soon, and certainly not with such an audience.'

Kira spoke with a haughtiness that he associated with her, but now he heard Lana's playfulness there too. He looked at her face, the face he had never seen without a mask but the face he knew so well. Kira had Lana's face, only the eyes were different and the hair . . . but now she wasn't wearing a mask it was so clear, how had he missed it? Even the earrings were the same.

The earrings. The pearl earrings that Lana always wore. That Kira always wore.

And they had gold-backing. Sea-gold backing. Sea-gold that had some power over the mer, that much was clear, and what if . . .

He crouched down so he was next to her. 'Do you trust me?'

'I don't trust men, but I trust you, Marino Pegasi.'

'Good.' He reached out and deftly removed one pearl earring, and then the other.

'Are you robbing me of my jewellery?' said Kira lightly, as she touched her now bare earlobes, and then she gasped.

'I'm not wearing a mask.'
'No.'
'But you can't see me without my mask . . .'
'Kira, I see *all* of you.'

Her eyes swirled, one was gold and one was silver and she tilted her head back in the sea and beneath the setting sun the water was reflecting the sky, a riot of purples and blues shot through with orange, and then Kira sat up again, chest heaving.

'I remember. I remember everything.'

CHAPTER 43
Kiralana

Kiralana felt power surge into her like never before.

Her memories swirled and collided.

A childhood with Benedita, in the bakery, making bread and cakes and feeling loved and safe and trapped.

A childhood in the sea with Zella, Mei and all her mer-sisters, diving deep and swimming fast and feeling loved and safe and trapped.

Never feeling complete.

The days she lost as Lana, days she thought she was sleeping.

No sense of time as Kira, waking in her sea-cave, her sisters always there.

Benedita keeping her far from the castle, far from Leonel. Telling her one day she would fall in love, one day if she was lucky. Whispering to her the importance of finding someone who truly loved her, who loved *all* of her. Kiralana had thought her words the wishes of a woman lonely in her old age, who wanted her surrogate daughter to find the love she had never had.

But it had been so much more than that.

Kiralana reached out to touch Marino's face. 'You loved

me as both Kira and Lana. As mer and human.'

Marino held her hand against his face as he gazed at her in wonder. 'I fell in love with you twice over, Kiralana. I love both sides of you. I love you completely. I love you in your entirety.'

There was a deep rumble in the water, and then an ancient voice rose up out of the sea, echoing all around. It was like being caught in a storm.

The voice was familiar. It was a voice that Kiralana had heard in her dreams all her life. It was the mother of the sea. The sound of her voice seemed to cast a spell on the Solvorans on the beach, even the king, as they all stood in a daze.

'My mer children, you have proven your loyalty to me. And Kiralana, daughter of a mermaid queen and a human king, the love you share with this man with magic of his own has proven to me that the sea and the land can sometimes be joined. After your mother was killed by the one who claimed to love her, I lost belief in humans. I resented my mer children who were both human and sea. I wished that I had never loved the land, that I had never loved a human. I wished I had never brought my mer to life.

And so, I split you, the one destined to be queen of the sea, in two. Your sisters knew, they put your earrings in, the sea-gold blocking your full power, blocking your memories of your other life.'

'Benedita knew too,' breathed Kiralana. She thought of kind Benedita, who had cared for her with such patience. Who had taught her about the sea and about the land too, taught her how to use her hands to bake. Benedita who had raised her.

'Yes, she did. Benedita had worshipped the sea her whole long life. When I needed to find a human to trust, a human who understood the sea, I knew it would be her. She found you in a boat, that much is true, but the night she did I sent one of your sisters to speak to her. To tell her that she must let you sleep on the balcony, so my waves could reach you. And to promise that my currents would return you to her, in safety.' The voice of the sea grew louder. 'And as long as you were in two, the two sides of yourself – the Solvoran and the mer – would always be at odds with each other. And I was happy to leave it like that.'

'Split forever?' asked Kiralana, a strange fury rising inside of her. 'Why would you punish me so?'

'You were not punished. You were protected. To shift between your worlds at will would have made you a threat to the land – you would have been killed as a babe by any king of Solvora, any king of man. So, as a child, it had to be this way. It was a gift for you to learn to live in both worlds, not having to choose. It kept you safe. My waves kept you safe, your sisters, and my devoted disciple, Benedita.'

The sea darkened, even though the sun was high in the sky.

'The young king struck a bargain with my mer – rules for when they could kill each other. But he poisoned the very land I had once loved, Solvora, against me. Tainting it with blood, blood that gave Solvora power. Killing his own people to feed the land itself. The hatred he had for the mer, for me, spread throughout Solvora. And my mer hated Solvora back. They were my soldiers, they proved their loyalty to me and each other.'

The water shifted colour again, this time turning to an

almost glowing turquoise. Kiralana could see flecks of sea-gold sparkling in the waves.

'But I still had a small amount of hope, and you were its form. You, Kiralana, are of both mer and man – and if a human could fall in love with both sides of you equally, truly fall in love, not enchanted, not bewitched, but true love that is stronger than magic and stronger than me, you would become one again, and I would release my hold on the Solvoran mer as well as the Solvorans themselves. But you were the key to it all.'

Kiralana felt dizzy at the implications. What if Marino had never come?

'Did my sisters know I needed to find love?'

'We did not,' said a hoarse voice. It was Zella, who was still bleeding in the waves. 'We only knew you would change. The only warning we had that you would lose your tail was when you grew tired. You would sleep in the sea-cave, and once your tail split into legs, we would dress you in your nightgown, and let the waves lift you up to the balcony on the cliff.'

'It was not me every time,' said the mother of the sea. 'I cannot always be here in Solvoran waters. But my waves know what to do, even if I am not here.'

Zella coughed, and a splatter of silver-tinged blood flew from her lips. Kiralana could hear her sister's heartbeat, it was weak.

She was dying. Zella had taken care of Kiralana all her life, and now Zella was dying.

'Marino,' said Kiralana urgently. 'Heal her, please.'

'I will try, but first I must ask the sea a question.' Marino stood and faced the sea, hands out. 'I have long loved the sea and have spent much of my life on your waters. I want to save this mer, but will my magic harm her? I know it made the sea-gold dangerous to the mer.'

A wave rose up out of the sea and seemed to inspect Marino, the sea foam coming close.

'Good sailor. I recognise you, of course. I know all men and women who dedicate their lives to me. Some I save, some I do not, but you are the humans that keep me from spilling over every shoreline and sinking every ship.' A spray of water appeared to caress Marino's face. 'Your magic is only harmful to the mer if you want it to be. Magic is not inherently good or evil, nor on the side of one or the other. It seeks balance. The sea-gold is magic in the sea, but once it is taken out of the sea, it loses those properties. When it comes into contact with magic in men – your magic – it awakens again, and your magic calls in response. Strengthening it. But magic, like all things, seeks balance. And so, it drains the magic of the mer when it comes into contact with them. I do not like it, but gold comes from the earth beneath me, sifting up through my waters, and is not entirely in my control. But you are not made of sea-gold. Your magic is your own.'

Marino nodded and then knelt next to Zella. 'Give me your hands.'

Zella glowered at him but did as he asked. Kiralana watched as Marino closed his eyes and calmness seemed to radiate from him. For a moment, she even thought she saw him glow. And then she gasped. Zella's wounds were glowing and stitching themselves back together with an invisible thread, and her sister took a breath and another, and when she smiled, Kiralana knew she had been healed.

Healed by Marino.

'I suppose I approve of you,' said Zella, her voice still hoarse but stronger now.

Marino laughed. 'And I suppose I forgive you for trying to drown me.'

Zella gave him a wicked grin. 'Can't promise I won't do it again.' Her expression grew serious. 'Mother of the sea, what now?'

'Now you are free.'

'And what of the Solvorans?' said Marino.

'I do not have power of them on land, but they too are now free to leave.' The voice echoed all around, and the Solvorans on the shore, still dazed and in a thrall, seemed to wake upon her words, and began to cheer.

'And the king? The king who killed his own people?' asked Kiralana. Her voice was sharp, she felt more Kira than Lana. 'The king who would have cut the mer to pieces, given the chance?'

'You are the true queen of both the sea and Solvora,' said the mother of the sea. 'As is your right. You decide what to do with the king who took the throne that belonged to you. I will not stay. I have other waters to be in. But I am always with you, Kiralana, daughter of the sea.'

A wave rose higher and higher, like a great wall, and then disappeared back into the ocean and all was still.

Until pandemonium broke out on the shore.

Kiralana saw King Leonel scrambling to get off the beach, to get away from the sea, get away from her. Talia was running after him.

'Stop him!' Kiralana's voice rang out.

The Solvoran guards, the guards who had served the king

but had seen how he sacrificed his own, grabbed him by the arms and carried him down to the water. To Kiralana.

She felt power within her to move the waves. And so, she summoned one and let it lift her up, so she looked down upon the king, and down upon the Solvorans, whom she did not hate nor blame. It was Leonel who had stoked their fear into hate, Leonel who had taken the power of Solvora for himself.

King Leonel met her eyes. 'I tried to be a good king. I swear it.'

'Did you know of me? Of my existence?'

'I did not know you lived. I saw my uncle throw you into the sea as a baby, and was sure you had drowned. But if you had come back, I would have killed you to keep my crown.'

'So, should I kill you now? To keep *my* crown?'

Leonel hung his head. 'I owe Solvora a sacrifice. I give myself gladly to the land and to the sea. I give myself to Solvora.'

As he spoke, the sand beneath him began to shake, the land responding to his offer. A swirling sandstorm lifted up around him, and when it fell, only his crown remained.

'All hail Queen Kiralana!' cried a familiar voice. It was Florence, wiping tears from her eyes as she cheered for her friend. For her queen. The rest of the crowd took up the chant, and Kiralana smiled at them before speaking.

'Solvorans. You have too long lived under a controlling king. I do not know what it means to rule. But I know what it is to want to be free. I trust you to govern yourselves. To choose a ruler, in my absence. I long to swim far and free. But I will come back with every changing season. To see that Solvora is thriving. To make sure of it. I am mer, but

I am also Solvoran. And Solvora is as much a part of me as the sea.' Then she turned to the mer gathered in the water below her. Her sisters. 'And you are free now to swim where you like. The whole world over.'

'We will always come back to Solvora,' said Zella. 'It is our home, after all. But we will wreck Solvoran ships and sing down storms no more.'

'It is a good start,' said Kiralana. Then she heard a sob and saw that Talia had come to the shore on her hands and knees.

'Forgive me,' Talia choked out. 'I was taught to hate and hide my mer blood. And I used my gift to hunt my own. I betrayed the mer.'

'You are no mer,' hissed Zella. 'You, I would happily drown.'

Talia lifted up a tear-stained face. 'What will you do with me, Queen Kiralana?'

Kiralana felt the eyes of her people on her, both mer and Solvoran. She sighed. 'I will let you live, Talia. But use your powers for good. You can help rebuild Solvora.'

Talia burst into tears. 'I will, I swear it, I will.'

'Do not make me regret it,' warned Kiralana. 'Now please, go and open the dungeons. You yourself can apologise to those you unfairly imprisoned.'

Talia swallowed. 'Of course, Your Majesty.' She slipped away through the crowd, and Kiralana hoped she had done the right thing as a merciful queen.

Then she looked for the one she most longed to see. Longed to touch. Marino was still in the sea, waiting for her.

As the wave lowered her into the water, brought her back down to him, she put her arms around his shoulders, and he wrapped his own arms around her waist, so they were eye to eye, her tail pressed against his legs. He was holding her up, even if she didn't need him to. Even if she could use a wave to lift her up, she liked that it was Marino who was supporting her. Marino by her side, now and for the rest of their days. Marino, who loved her completely.

'Captain.'

'Kiralana.' A smile twitched at his lips.

'Will you travel the seas with me? Will we adventure together?'

'I would go anywhere for you, my Kiralana. I would find you and love you no matter where you were. There is no ocean that could keep us apart, no magic that could make me forget you. I love all of you.'

When he kissed her, it felt like a promise; it felt like fate.

CHAPTER 44
Marino

Emelia, Dooley and George were pale and weak from their time in the Solvoran dungeons, but they were alive. Alive and in remarkably good cheer.

'You never thought to look for us in the dungeons of that giant gold castle?' said Dooley, nudging Marino with his shoulder. 'That would have been the first place I searched!'

'Oi. Captain wasn't searching for us. He was searching for the cure. And found a mermaid along the way,' Emelia teased.

'The last I saw of you three was when you rowed off without me, remember?' said Marino, shaking his head. 'As far as I knew, you'd rowed to safety!'

'Ah, keep telling yourself that, then,' said Dooley, with a good-natured laugh. 'We rowed our way right into the dungeons.'

It was Marino who had unwittingly saved his small crew from being drowned by the mer. Zella had told Marino that the potent scent of his magic-filled blood in the water had been all the mer could smell. A magic so unlike their own, one that drew Kiralana to him, and one that charged the sea-gold. Even after he had washed up on shore, his scent had been all over his ship, drawing the mer to it, making them overlook the three humans in the little rowboat. And Talia had told the truth about what had happened once they had crashed on the beach. She had not sensed any magic in them, but still advised King Leonel to keep them alive just in case they were useful. And once Marino appeared, desperate, she knew that the King could use them to his advantage when the time was right.

'Don't worry, Captain, we never gave up hope,' added George, as he hammered a wooden plank. 'As long as they didn't kill us, we knew we'd get out eventually. And it wasn't too terrible, once you got used to the rats and the dark.'

'Speak for yourself. I had to smell both of you.' Emelia wrinkled her nose and they all laughed. 'And I never want to play knuckle-fish ever again.'

'Knuckle-fish?' Marino asked.

'I made it up myself, I did,' said Dooley, beaming with pride. 'We didn't have any cards, you see. So, we had to come up with our own entertainment.'

'Being stuck in a dungeon isn't too different from being stuck out at sea, now that I think about it,' said George.

'I'm going to choose to not take that personally,' said Marino. Kiralana laughed and handed him a nail. She could shift at will now, from mer to human, and did so often depending on circumstances.

Currently they were on the beach mending a boat. Not just any boat. Mending Marino's boat. Kiralana had used her sea-gift to drag up what was left of the *Siren's Secret* from the seabed, along with help from her mersisters. And now they were mending it and preparing to set sail. For Eana. For home.

It did not take long to return to Anadawn.

Marino had thought he could summon a swift wind using his tempest magic, but with Kiralana on board, the waves did her bidding, and they fairly flew across the ocean.

She shifted from mer to human and back again, and as Marino had promised, he loved both sides of her equally. They spent hours together in the captain's cabin, and in the sea itself, learning everything about each other.

And when it was not just the two of them, they spent time with the crew on board and Kiralana's sisters in the waves. They met other mer too, mer who recognised Kiralana for the queen of the sea that she was.

Of course, Marino and Kiralana were often with his mother, sitting on deck underneath the stars and trading tales. She told them stories of her time on Solvora, and stories of Marino as a child. And in return Marino told her all about Celeste, the daughter she longed to see, as well as stories of his sailing adventures, and of everything that had happened in Eana since she had left.

And then, almost exactly one month after Marino had set sail for a cure off the map, they were home. Back in Eana. In Anadawn.

They wasted no time climbing the tower where Celeste lay under the watchful, worried gaze of Rose and Thea. Anika still paced the floor, and Marino wondered if she'd ever stopped. Rose did not question who either woman with Marino was, simply stepping aside as he guided his mother to Celeste's bedside. His father, Hector, let out a stifled cry of shock and joy at the sight of his long-lost wife.

But Dove Salome Pegasi only had eyes for her daughter. She knelt beside her and with trembling fingers, she spoon-fed Celeste the cure she so desperately needed, the cure that she herself had sought so long ago. And so, her face was the first one Celeste saw when her eyes fluttered open.

Celeste later told Marino that she thought she was dreaming, thought she was dead, and it was only when Marino told her of his journey, that she knew her mother had truly returned home. That her brother had saved her.

That he had found *all* the love that she had foreseen.

And now Celeste, Dove Salome, Kiralana and Marino were in the Anadawn kitchens together, baking bread before the *Siren's Secret*'s next voyage. Queens Rose and Wren were delighted with the fact that Marnio had brought home not only the cure, but a mermaid queen. With Kiralana and the seas on their side, Eana would surely be the most prosperous and protected that it had ever been. Plus, Anadawn now had the best baked goods in the entire kingdom.

Marino watched as the three women most important to him, the women whom he would and had gone to the ends of the world for, laughed together and then looked over to him, waiting for him to join them. Marino grinned, because he knew that he had found everything he had ever wanted. And then his grin widened as he realised the adventures of Captain Marino Pegasi were far from over. They were just beginning.

Acknowledgements

Acknowledgements ahoy! We made it! Thank you for coming along with me and Marino on a new adventure – I hope you enjoyed the journey. If you've been here since *Twin Crowns*, thank you for sticking around and trusting me with a new direction. If this is your first time reading a book set in the Twin Crowns world, thank you for diving in.

Writing this book felt like going on my own quest to find hidden treasure. I had a map to guide me (my outline and some familiar characters) but I was nervous to venture into waters unknown. When I discovered the heart of this story, when Kira and Lana came to life on the page, when Marino fell for them both while trying to save his sister – that was when the treasure chest opened, revealing exactly the book I wanted this to be. I hope reading it feels like finding treasure too.

I never could have written this book without the support of an amazing crew. My first thanks goes to my *Twin Crowns* co-captain, and real life sister-in-law, Catherine Doyle. Cat, creating *Twin Crowns* with you was truly a dream come true, and I'm so happy that we have been able to expand the world with the spin-off books. Thank you for trusting me with our characters, and for giving Marino his signature outfit back in *Cursed Crowns*. He finally found his mermaid! And I can't wait for readers to go feral for your spin-off, *King of Beasts*.

Thank you to my agent – the incomparable Claire Wilson, who deftly steers the ship of my author career no matter how wild the weather may get, and always leads me to safe harbour. Claire, thank you for everything — may we continue to find treasure everywhere we go! At RCW I'd also like to thank Safae El-Ouahabi who helps keep my career shipshape, and Sam Coates, my foreign rights agent, who makes sure my books are read across every ocean.

To my incredible editors at Farshore – Lindsey Heaven and Sarah Levison, thank you for sharing my vision for this book and for continuing to believe in me as an author. Thank you for your insight, enthusiasm, and excellent editorial input – it is a gift to work with you both. Long may we sail on the romanta-sea!

And to the rest of the team at the good ship Electric Monkey – I am so lucky to have so many brilliant people working on my books. Thank you to Sarah Sleath, who is always on board for my bananas event ideas. And thank you to Emily Sommerfeld, who is a wonderful new addition to the *Captain of Fates* crew. I'd also like to thank Olivia Carson, Hannah Penny, Brogan Furey, Rory Codd and Cally Poplak for their support.

Thank you to Susila Baybars for a fantastic copyedit and figuring out mermaid logistics and timeline issues. I am very grateful! And to eagle-eyed Nicki Marshall for making the finished book shine like gold.

Thank you to the King of Design, Ryan Hammond, and the amazing artist Grace Zhu for such a stunning cover. It is so dreamy and beautiful and just perfect. Grace, I'm such a fan of your art – and it is an honour to have a cover illustrated by you! Ryan, this is the seventh (!) cover you have designed for me, and each time you knock it out of the park. Thank you as well to Tomislav Tomic for the beautiful map of Solvora.

I am so grateful to all the retailers and bookshops for their support for my books. Special thanks to Waterstones for the spectacular special editions, with extra appreciation to LJ Ireton at Waterstones Finchley Road and Rhiannon Tripp at Waterstones High Street Kensington. I'd also like to thank Sanchita at Muswell Hill Children's Books.

I am overwhelmed with gratitude for my readers. Thank you for reading, thank you for cosplaying, thank you for commissioning art, thank you for coming to the events. Thank you for being the reason I can keep writing stories. I am so grateful for the community we have created together. I would like to especially thank Abi, Alice, Angelina, Diana, Divya, Elle, Emily, Emma, Gemma, Gigi, Greta, Hannah, Joanna, Katrina, Kellie, Menna, Sam, Saz, Sarah B, Stacey, Victoria, and Zhi Ling for everything they've done to support my books in the UK. I also have to thank Emelie in Germany, as well as Rosa and Steph in the US, for all the gorgeous art and cosplay.

To my author friends who keep me afloat – Cat, Anna, Kate, Kiran, Tom, Abi, KWoo, Samantha, Krystal, Alwyn, Holly, and Rosh. To my publishing gang who keep me sane and make me laugh: Paul, Rosi, Nina, Kat, Bea, Lizz, Simon, and Stephie. Special thanks to Anna James for all the chats about the colour of mermaid tails and the many Captain jokes, and for being the person that I invest in an immersive magic show with (RIP Rhythm & Ruse). To my friends who have been here since my first book and still cheer me on: Jeni, Dyna, Courtney, Jessica, Chloe, Fay, and Janou. I love you all and am so lucky to have you all in my life.

To my far-flung family – the Webber/Tsang/Hopper/Doyle crew all over the world. Thank you for all the support and love. Thank you to my sister Jane, and my brother Jack, who are always there for me. It isn't an accident that I keep returning to the theme of siblings and importance of family in my books.

And to Kevin, who shares this book's dedication with our daughters. I love you more than words can say. Thank you for making me believe in true love, and for the life we have.

Finally, to my daughters – Evie and Mira. You two are magic made real and inspire me more than anyone. I hope you always know how loved you are.

*Read on for a sneak peek of the next
unmissable new standalone novel
from the world of Twin Crowns*

KING ❄OF BEASTS

Written by
CATHERINE DOYLE

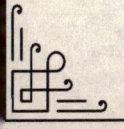

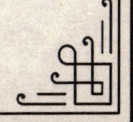

CHAPTER 1

Alarik

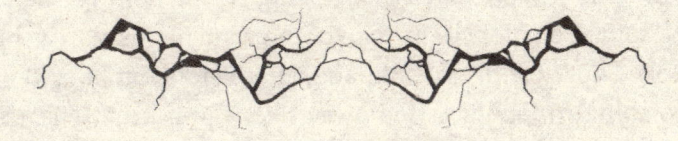

Deep in the icy heart of the kingdom of Gevra, where a towering palace of glass and stone speared up from an ancient mountainside, a young king awoke, restless from his slumber. Though the air swirled with the beginnings of a blizzard and the ground glittered with new frost, Alarik Felsing went barefoot to his balcony.

He scowled up at the night sky. The full moon was far too bright, its determined silvered shards slipping through the gap in his drapes and jostling him from sleep. *Again*. At least that's what he told himself as he stood alone at the balustrade, cursing the stars. It was better than entertaining the alternative – that those awful nightmares, blood-soaked visions of battles long past and ones yet to come, were becoming more frequent. That the king of Gevra, ruler of the fiercest kingdom on the northern continent, was anxious.

And he didn't know why.

Attuned to the shift in his mood, the king's wolves stirred from their place at the end of his bed and followed him outside. Nova, the eldest of the two and black as a starless night, paced the length of the balustrade, guarding his master. Luna, soft and silver as moonlight, came to sit by Alarik, her bushy tail settling across his feet to warm them.

Scratching the sweet spot behind Luna's ears, Alarik huffed a frustrated sigh, watching his breath cloud in the air. Though his chest was as bare as his feet, the cold didn't bother him. Winter was a constant gnawing presence here. He sought comfort in the bite of the wind on his skin as he looked out over his moonlit kingdom. Before him, a spill of frostbitten mountains fell away like waves in an endless grey ocean, reaching towards the curling woodsmoke and flickering lamplight of faraway towns, and beyond them, the meandering fjords and vast stillness of the Sunless Sea.

Gevra was beautiful in its bleakness, but it was not for the faint of heart.

Nor was its king.

A north gust blew, bringing a nighthawk with it. The bird swooped low over the mountains, catching moonlight on its wings. Nova stilled, raising his snout as if to scent it. A low growl rumbled in his throat, echoing the rumble of unease inside Alarik. As the bird drew closer, he noted the metallic glint of its feathers and realized his mistake. Its wings were the colour of steel, longer and slimmer than that of a nighthawk. Its large beak possessed the same shine and was curved at the end, as sharp and foreboding as any man-made blade.

It was not a Gevran bird at all. Rather, a silvertip, a hunting eagle from Vask, one of only two kingdoms that shared a border with Gevra. The same kingdom whose spies had been caught trekking through the Blackspire Mountains barely a week ago. A pair of plain-clothed men who claimed they had got lost on a hike, only to surrender a litany of weapons between them when searched, as well as a partially drawn map of the northern mines of Gevra.

And now this – a silvertip, hundreds of miles south of its territory, circling the palace of the king.

Frost kissed Alarik's forearms as he leaned across the balustrade, his gaze glued to the bird. It was on the hunt, scouring the snowcapped Fovarr mountains that clustered around Grinstad. It floated on a slip of wind, wings barely beating as it watched the terrain. Minutes passed, the midnight moon glowing brighter as though it was watching, too.

At a flash of movement from below, the silvertip shot down like an arrow, spearing the snow and disappearing entirely. Alarik sucked in a breath, holding it until the bird emerged with a shriek of triumph. The sound raked down the king's spine. There was a hare in the bird's talons, neck snapped, its white fur mottled with blood. Alarik watched the eagle as it came to perch high on the mountainside. In one fluid movement, it threw its head back and swallowed its prey whole.

A shudder rippled through the king. Sensing his master's discomfort, Nova's hackles rose. Even Luna, such a gentle creature, surrendered a low growl. Ordinarily, Alarik wouldn't have glanced twice at a bird feeding itself in the night, but he couldn't stomach the sight of a predator of Vask trawling his mountains, gorging on Gevran spoils.

He peeled his lips back, wishing he was as skilled with a bow as he was with his sword. He would have shot that bird out of the sky and sent its carcass back to Queen Regna as a warning.

Keep your predators out of my kingdom.

And yet, as he turned from the mountains, Alarik's unease gave way to a cool prickle of fear. He thought of the rapacious queen of Vask, steel-eyed and ever clawing too close to that northern border they shared, and had the sudden creeping sense that if he were to send her that message, it would already be too late.

This time, when he climbed back into bed, Alarik's wolves curled up on either side of him, as though they had the same disquieting feeling.

❄

After breakfast the following morning, Alarik stalked through Grinstad Palace like an ice bear on the hunt. His bad mood swirled around him, turning the air as bitter as the three cups of coffee he had just downed. Servants lowered their gaze as he passed, some slinking into the alcoves to avoid his ire. They knew their king well enough to steer clear of him in foul humours. And in good ones. Not that there had been many of those lately.

Captain Astrid Vine, head of the royal guard and Alarik's second in command, was waiting for him at the top of the stairwell on the first floor. At six foot, Vine was almost as tall as the king himself, her body a study of hard lines and lithe muscles honed from years of training. She had warm brown skin and keen dark eyes, her cropped black hair better revealing her strong cheekbones and squared jaw. She was wearing her military uniform, a pristine frock coat of midnight blue and silver, black trousers and sturdy boots made for sparring. And winning.

She looked the king over as he stomped up the stairs, her frown pressing a dent between her slender brows. 'You look like hell.'

Alarik offered her his most fearsome scowl. Vine was one of only a handful of people he allowed to speak to him in such a manner. He might have taken her sword for that kind of comment once, but she had proven herself an invaluable soldier and strategist over the last year, and a worthy replacement for her predecessor, Captain Tor Iversen. Tor had left Grinstad over a year ago, following his heart south to the kingdom of Eana, where he had fallen in love with one of its witch queens, Wren Greenrock, a woman Alarik had once thought to seek for himself. A stirring if fleeting notion, which had swept in alongside an ancient curse that had bound Wren and Alarik together, leading them to combine their armies and fight a war against the ancient witch who had cast it.

A war that had decimated his army.

Following a punishing battle on the west coast of Eana, Queen Wren and her sister, Queen Rose, had emerged victorious, though the losses on all sides had been many. The war had cost Alarik a third of his own soldiers and as many beasts. It had cost him his second-in-command and prized wrangler, too. For Tor Iversen had been the only soldier at Grinstad who could train the king's beasts for battle, controlling them in their droves with little more than a whistle. That was the way of the wrangler – a rare and mercurial ability that, for centuries, had led the Gevran army to victory in one vicious battle after another.

A year on, Alarik was still rebuilding his army, intent on maintaining his reputation as the fearless king in the north, a dauntless ruler who would destroy anyone who dared to threaten his kingdom. Captain Astrid Vine, an ambitious, battle-honed soldier, who had risen through the ranks of his own surviving army, was helping him do that.

So, he let her needle him every once in a while.

'I have no need of your frank assessment today, Vine,' he said, a bite in his voice.

Her brows lifted. 'Then you are already aware of the dark circles under your eyes.'

'Take care not to miss the warning flashing inside them,' he said, pointedly. 'I have not slept well.'

She pressed her curving lips together, drawing her arms behind her back as they walked along the upper glass corridor, which provided ample views of the courtyard below. Ordinarily, Alarik looked down on the stone arena within with simmering fondness – the place where he had spent countless hours sparring with soldiers and beasts alike, first as a young boy eager to please his father, the late King Soren, and then as a young king, eager to prove himself to his soldiers. To his beasts.

This morning, the arena was a far cry from the bravery and skill that often graced it. A group of quivering soldiers were attempting to corral a snow tiger and two leopards – a mere fraction of the regiment Alarik had been replenishing all year, and yet the twelve soldiers chosen to train them were all cowering against the walls.

Not a damn wrangler among them.

'Give them time, Majesty,' said Captain Vine, as though reading his thoughts.

He curled his lip. 'The one on the end is openly weeping.'

'No, he's— Oh, *Garvin*.' She muttered a curse. 'He

promised me he was ready.'

'Let's see how ready he is when that tiger makes a toothpick of him.'

'That's not funny.'

'No,' muttered Alarik, folding his arms as he looked down at his trembling soldiers, at the beasts snapping and growling like they owned the arena. Owned the palace. 'This is far from funny.'

Vine chewed on her lip, her silence a reluctant agreement.

'I watched a Vaskan eagle hunt in my mountains last night,' said Alarik, after a moment.

Vine stiffened. 'If Regna's birds are here, her falconers cannot be far behind.'

Alarik frowned. His thoughts exactly. Word had clearly spread of the war in Eana, and the losses the king's army had sustained. 'She thinks I'm weak.'

Outside, a soldier screamed as the tiger began to circle him. He turned and scrabbled up the arena wall, losing his left boot and longsword in the process. Alarik swallowed a growl of annoyance.

'We *are* weak,' said Vine.

He glared sidelong at her. 'That is not what I want to hear from my war captain.'

'Our soldiers are well-trained,' Vine went on, tempering her criticism. 'But they are still fewer than they were last year. And as for the beasts . . . without regular training, the older ones have gone half wild. And the new ones are not trained at all. If we took them to war, they would likely devour as many of our own soldiers as our opposition.'

'Contain your optimism, Vine.'

The kingdom of Gevra was long known for the might of

its war beasts, just as it was for the strength and skill of its soldiers. The combination of both was why the northern kingdom hadn't lost a war in over eight hundred years. Alarik did not intend to start losing now, but he could not deny the sorry state of his army as another soldier's scream rang out. A young leopard had pounced, pinning him with a large, snowy paw. It took five flailing soldiers to beat the beast back, and not one of them seemed to realize the creature was simply playing.

Alarik pinched the bridge of his nose. 'We have to do better than this.'

Vine gripped her sword, a frown tugging at her jaw. 'I'm no wrangler, Majesty. I have tried with the beasts these past months, but it takes a certain skill. A certain type of soldier . . .' She trailed off, the rest of her sentence hanging unsaid between them.

A type of soldier they no longer had. Not since the departure of Captain Tor Iversen. Yes, what Alarik needed now – and sorely – was a true wrangler. Someone who possessed that crucial inborn connection that allowed them to read the shift in a beast's mood, to cajole and coax them, to train them. Wrangling was the closest thing to magic that existed in Gevra, but Captain Iversen's talent, while exceedingly rare, was not entirely unheard of. At least not on the small rock of an island, Carrig, where he hailed from. A blot of grey in the middle of the Sunless Sea, as cold and unforgiving as the scythe of mountains that surrounded Grinstad Palace. Perhaps even more so. And yet the king hoped that Carrig might offer them a solution to their worsening problem. 'It's time to find a wrangler, Vine.'

She stepped back from the window. 'As far as I'm aware, Tor Iversen is the only soldier capable of wrangling your beasts.'

'I don't want a soldier.' He had plenty of those. 'And anyway, Tor is long gone.' The words were crisp, final. Alarik would not drag his former captain – and more importantly his oldest friend – away from the woman he loved, and the peace he had found in her kingdom, only to return to the blood-soaked battles of his past. No, Captain Vine had missed his meaning entirely. 'Send word to Carrig,' he clarified. 'Get me one of Tor's sisters.'

Vine blinked away her surprise. 'Which one?'

A pertinent question. Alarik was aware that Tor had three sisters; he'd even met one of them – the eldest – briefly, many years ago at Grinstad, but he did not know the name of the other two. He did not especially care about their names, only that he knew they shared their brother's gift for wrangling.

Outside, a mewling rasp echoed through the courtyard. Alarik turned from the sound of a soldier's answering shriek. Those infernal cowards would sooner hand his country to Regna on a silver platter than face down a bear cub.

'I don't care which sister,' he said, storming off.

TWIN CROWNS

CATHERINE DOYLE & KATHERINE WEBBER

'Twin Crowns cast a spell on me. I was thoroughly bewitched by this marvellous book' – SARAH J MAAS

ONE THRONE. TWO PRINCESSES.

CURSED CROWNS

CATHERINE DOYLE & KATHERINE WEBBER

SISTERS UNITED. A KINGDOM DIVIDED.

BURNING CROWNS

CATHERINE DOYLE & KATHERINE WEBBER

KILL ONE TWIN. SAVE ANOTHER.

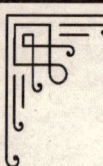

Photo credit: Olivia McDermott

KATHERINE WEBBER is a bestselling and award-winning author of children's and young adult books. Since 2017, she has published over twenty books across multiple genres for readers of all ages, and has been translated in more than a dozen languages. Her recent Young Adult novels include the internationally bestselling Twin Crowns trilogy, co-written with Catherine Doyle, as well as *The Revelry* and *Only Love Can Break Your Heart*. In addition to her YA novels, Katherine also writes younger fiction as Katie Tsang in collaboration with her husband Kevin. She met Kevin whilst studying at the Chinese University of Hong Kong. Together they have penned a number of bestselling children's series, from the Sam Wu is Not Afraid books, to Space Blasters, the Dragon Realm saga and most recently, the Dragon Force trilogy. Katherine was born and raised in Southern California and currently lives in London with Kevin and their two young daughters.